THE APPLE TREE

Also by Elvi Rhodes

Opal
Doctor Rose
Ruth Appleby
The Golden Girls
Madeleine
The House of Bonneau
Summer Promise and Other Stories
Cara's Land
The Rainbow through the Rain
The Bright One
The Mountain
Portrait of Chloe
Spring Music
Midsummer Meeting
The Birthday Party
Mulberry Lane
A Blessing in Disguise

THE APPLE TREE

ELVI RHODES

BANTAM PRESS

LONDON · NEW YORK · TORONTO · SYDNEY · AUCKLAND

TRANSWORLD PUBLISHERS
61–63 Uxbridge Road, London W5 5SA
a division of The Random House Group Ltd

RANDOM HOUSE AUSTRALIA (PTY) LTD
20 Alfred Street, Milsons Point, Sydney,
New South Wales 2061, Australia

RANDOM HOUSE NEW ZEALAND LTD
18 Poland Road, Glenfield, Auckland 10, New Zealand

RANDOM HOUSE SOUTH AFRICA (PTY) LTD
Endulini, 5a Jubilee Road, Parktown 2193, South Africa

Published 2004 by Bantam Press
a division of Transworld Publishers

A catalogue record for this book is available from the British Library.
ISBN 0593 052617

Typeset in 11/13pt Plantin by
Kestrel Data, Exeter, Devon.

Printed in Great Britain by
Mackays of Chatham plc, Chatham, Kent.

1 3 5 7 9 10 8 6 4 2

Papers used by Transworld Publishers are natural, recyclable products made
from wood grown in sustainable forests. The manufacturing processes
conform to the environmental regulations of the country of origin.

This book is for Olwen Homes,
in gratitude for many years of
enduring friendship

Acknowledgements

I thank the following:

My son, Stephen, who discusses everything with me, and gives me great encouragement.

Martin Morgan, who found time in his busy life as a parish priest to make the long journey with me back to the Yorkshire Dales, and helped me with my research.

Mary Irvine, friend and agent, for her never-failing enthusiasm.

Steve Pratt, retired policeman, for helping me with various matters of police procedure.

Shirley Hall, secretary and friend, who never loses patience with me even when my laptop goes wrong and I expect her to put it right.

The landscape of the beautiful Yorkshire Dales is real and unchanging even when I change the names. The events and characters exist only in my imagination.

FRANCES

ONE

Frances turned in at the gateway – there was no longer a gate, just the posts where it had once hung – and drove across the flagstoned yard, pulling up at the gabled porch that sheltered the front door of the house. The yard itself sloped upwards from the low stone wall which divided it from the lane in front of the house. From the level where the river ran along the floor of the U-shaped valley, scoured out by glaciers eighty thousand years ago, everything sloped upwards in Cordale, and continued to do so with varying gradients until whoever climbed them sooner or later, and almost certainly out of breath, reached the highest tops of the fells.

From there, if one turned away from the long, wide vista of Cordale, though it narrowed and closed in towards the north, and turned one's back on the view of green terraced slopes, on the long limestone escarpment to the east, the scattered villages, the hillsides dotted with ewes, which seemingly wandered at will at unlikely heights and into awkward places, and from the flat meadows on the floor of the valley where both sheep and cattle grazed, if, standing on the highest ridge of Cor Fell, one made a rightabout turn, then spread out to the west was Tendale. It was the same kind of landscape, yet subtly different, since no two dales in North Yorkshire are alike, especially to those who belong there. It is not correct to say Tendale spreads out. Tendale is

11

closed in, steeper. It has no settlement large enough to be called a village, only two small hamlets, one of which, surprisingly, has both a church and a pub. The meadows bordering its river are narrow, there are more frequent outcrops of rock, and the river Ten runs faster and deeper, more often darting underground than does the Cor.

But all this is essentially sheep, not cattle, country: sheep for wool, sheep for meat, ewes' milk for the cheese for which they have been famous for longer than the memory of even the oldest inhabitant can possibly stretch back. The months of the year, the lives of the inhabitants, follow the rhythm of the lives of the sheep.

What is common, however, to both Cordale and Tendale – and to the dales that join up with them – are the dry-stone walls which run from the valley straight up the hillsides, crisscrossed at random angles by yet more walls of the same pale limestone, making strangely shaped fields all over the slopes; walls which shine like gold and silver when the sun comes out. There is more than one theory as to why and for how long the walls have been there. What is for sure is that bits of them are constantly in need of repair and those who know how to do it are these days few and far between. Meanwhile, the sheep get through the holes, and stray.

Frances switched off the engine, got out of the car, then paused, looking up at the house, savouring the moment. There it was, Beck Farm, stone-built and solid, all hers (except for a modest mortgage with the Shepton Building Society). It had stood for nearly two hundred years and there was no visible sign that it would not still be standing two hundred years hence. Viewed from the front it was nothing special: a plain, symmetrical Dales house, no frills. A long frontage, two windows to the left of the front door, one to the right. Four windows above – one was over the front door – exactly in line and exactly the same size as the lower ones. And then on the right of the original house an extension, one window downstairs, one up, and in line with the rest of the house so that the whole building was balanced. The extension had been built a long time ago and of the same local stone, which had weathered almost to match the original. The windows were not so small that one couldn't see who – friend or foe – was approaching, but were not over-large, because of the need to keep the cold out in the winter.

It was exactly the kind of house, Frances had thought when she set eyes on it for the first time, that she used to draw as a small child, except that hers had had diamond-lattice windows, which were to her, then, the height of desirability, and roses and hollyhocks in full bloom round the door.

Everything was quiet, so still that she could hear the sound of the beck, from which the house took its name, as it rushed down the east side of the building before it went under the road on its way to join the river. From her handbag she took out a massive key – quite separate from the enormous bunch of assorted keys the estate agent had given her – then walked through the porch, inserted the key into the lock of the heavy-looking front door, and turned it. The action was as smooth as silk. A turn of the knob, a slight push, and the door swung open. Stepping into the hall, she bent down to pick up two square white envelopes from the floor. No catalogues, no offers of new window frames, bargain-price painting and decorating, no take-away menus. Was it possible that junk mail had not reached Cordale? She opened the envelopes: both contained cards from friends in Brighton, wishing her well.

Brighton seemed so far away, already a foreign country which eventually she would perhaps remember with some affection but had no plans to visit again, yet it was no more than twenty-four hours since she had left it behind. She had waited until the removal men had packed the last of her furniture into the van, which had called first for her mother's things, and she had waved them off down the road. Then she and her mother had at once got into the car and she'd driven away – on her part, without a backward glance. Her mother had been all but silent, hardly speaking at all until the M23 and the M25 had been left behind and they'd stopped at a service station on the M1 to fill up with petrol.

'I think we should have something to eat here,' Frances had suggested. 'It's a fair way to the next one.'

They'd looked at the menu board, from which Madge had chosen fish and chips.

'You find a table,' Frances said. 'I'll see to the tray.'

'Haddock and chips, bread and butter and a pot of tea,' Madge said a few minutes later, tucking in, 'and I feel I'm up north already. I dare say this will be a decent pot of tea as well.'

Thirty years of living in the south had never totally eradicated Madge Fraser's West Riding accent, but now with her nose pointing due north it was already strengthening, the vowels spreading out and flattening as if she was getting herself ready for what was coming.

'We're still a long way off, Mother,' Frances warned. 'Well over two hundred miles to go. We're hardly in the Midlands yet.'

'We're going in the right direction,' Madge had said. 'That's what counts. From here on it's straight up.'

I hope I'm going in the right direction, Frances had thought as, fed and watered, they drove on again. I hope it's right for both of us. It suddenly all seemed so final; that last locking of the door, taking the keys around to a neighbour, as arranged. And am I right, she'd asked herself – though it was really too late to ask – to be bringing my mother all this way? Letting her, encouraging her, in her seventies, to sell up, leave her home and start again? Or am I being incredibly selfish?

She'd put the question before, out loud. 'You could look at it this way,' her mother had said: 'you could say I'm returning home, going back where I came from. Well, not Cordale, of course. When your dad and me went up there at bank-holiday weekends and so on – on our bicycles, we went, before you came on the scene – I never thought I'd end up living there. I never thought I'd live anywhere outside the West Riding. And look where I got to!'

When the shipping firm Tom Fraser had worked for since leaving school closed down in the fifties – it had never quite recovered from its wartime losses – and he was left with a moderate pay-off but no job, he had reached the biggest decision of his life, possibly the only decision of any consequence he had ever made (and as it turned out, ever would). 'Why don't we . . .' he'd said to Madge – it was towards the end of a particularly cold winter with a prolonged fuel crisis – 'Why don't we sell the house and take a little business down south? I'm bloody sick of Bradford.'

Madge had been so flabbergasted by his boldness that it had never occurred to her to argue. Before the end of the year they had bought a small café and baker's shop, sight unseen, in one of the less fashionable small towns in Surrey. The fact that the only qualifications they had between them for running such a business were that Tom fancied himself as a man who would get on well with the customers – and he was not wrong about that – and Madge had always been a dab hand at cooking and baking did not deter them. To the surprise of everyone, especially the friends they left behind in Bradford (for even those who had served in the war as far afield as the jungles of Burma still thought Surrey was on a par with Outer Mongolia), Tom and Madge succeeded.

Seven-year-old Frances was not asked for her opinion on the move. If she'd had the spirit she was to acquire as she grew older she'd have been dragged kicking and screaming from Bradford. As it was, she tagged along, comforted on the journey by the sight and sound of Beauty the budgerigar in her cage and Korky the cat in his basket, both of whom would have been confined to the guard's van had not an animal-loving attendant turned a blind eye.

The train journey was one of the few things Frances still remembered of the north. There'd been so much going on in the south; new things to learn, new friends to make, even a new way of speaking. Unlike her mother, thirty years of Surrey, followed by Sussex, had wiped away almost every trace of Yorkshire from her voice. She took to saying 'barth' and 'larst' and 'arfter' like a duck to water.

Now, standing in the hall, Frances took a few seconds to glance around. Only twice before had she been in the house, and each time with Mr Walter Birkett, scion of Birkett, Birkett & Lance, the estate agents, but she had carried in her mind what she had seen then, and here it was, very much as she remembered it: the oak staircase rising from quite close to the front door; to the left, the door to the sitting-room; and, further down the hall, doors to the other ground-floor rooms, which she would put to her own uses. The large kitchen and a smaller scullery, together with two walk-in pantries, were at the back of the house, and, behind them, the back door led to the yard with its various outbuildings: stable, cowshed, henhouse, dairy – for this *had* been a working farm, though not for some years now.

She went into the sitting-room, put the two greetings cards down on one of the deep windowsills – all the windowsills in the house were deep because of the thickness of the walls – and allowed herself to sit there briefly, looking at the view. The narrow road, not much more than a lane really, sloped away from the front of the house and then when it made a left bend was temporarily lost to view behind the stone walls and a bank of trees. There were not many trees in the dale, so beyond these few the village was visible. Grey stone houses, with shallow-pitched sandstone-tiled roofs and squat chimneys sitting on the roofs at the gable ends, huddled together, and rising up from somewhere in the middle of them was the square tower of the church. The whole village seemed protected by the height and steepness of the hill behind it, thought Frances. Kilby was ten minutes' walk going away from Beck Farm but at least fifteen minutes coming back because of the gradient.

In the end she made herself turn away from the view. She had no business to be mooning about here, it was self-indulgent to have made this visit, but it was one small thing she wanted to do on her own, in advance of the bustle she knew the rest of the day – more likely, the whole of several days – would bring. She wanted to walk round all the rooms in the house, to get the feel of them again, perhaps decide where some of the larger pieces of furniture would go, after which she would hurry back to Shepton – it was a thirty-minute drive – to pick up her mother, whom she'd left at the Heifer, where they'd spent last night after the long journey north. ('What exactly is a heifer?' Madge had asked. 'I was never quite sure. I know all the names of the joints in the butcher's shop – you couldn't fault me on those – but not the animals.') I was a bit mean this morning, Frances thought, feeling guilty. I almost sneaked away. Her mother had been understanding, though, and said it was quite all right, she'd

16

amuse herself looking round the town while waiting for Frances to return. The plan was that they would lunch in Shepton, then check out of the Heifer before going to the house to await the arrival of the furniture van, due some time in the afternoon.

At the top of the stairs – the stairs were one of the things she'd liked at first sight; solid oak, polished by years of wear, and to cover them with carpet would be an insult – an L-shaped landing led to four double bedrooms and two smaller ones, one of them hardly more than a boxroom, though it might have looked more roomy had it not been cluttered with everything that the firm who had cleared the house after the owner's death had thought not worth taking.

'Mr Thornton died sudden, poor man,' Walter Birkett had informed her when he'd brought her to see the house. 'It was very unexpected. The house was a bit of an untidy mess when we first took it on, but Alice cleaned it through before she left.'

'Left?' Frances had said. She'd heard about Alice, who had worked for Ben Thornton, but not that she had left. She had looked forward to Alice giving her a hand with the myriad things that would have to be done. 'Why did she leave?'

Walter Birkett had then told her that Mr Thornton had willed Alice a sum of money. 'Not a lot, and, as I told you, everything else, including the proceeds from the sale of the house, went to charity. He had no family. But it was enough to take Alice off on a long holiday to visit her sister and brother-in-law in Australia. If you ask me,' he'd said, 'I doubt she'll return.'

Frances looked briefly now at the contents of the small room – a couple of chairs, two tea chests filled to the brim, a table piled high, a chest of drawers, various boxes, an old TV (probably black-and-white) and an even older radio – then she shut the door firmly and left it. That sorting out would have to wait until the very last. There were far too many other and more important things to do.

Farmhouses in the days when Beck Farm was built had clearly catered for large families, she thought as she went into one room after another. The double bedrooms were spacious: two of them, she judged, large enough to take a single bed in addition to a double. They could be let as family rooms. Each double room

17

had a large, floor-to-ceiling cupboard and a wash basin with hot and cold water, which, by its design, she judged had been installed when the house had begun to be used as a bed-and-breakfast place rather than as a farmhouse. Water was not laid on to the two smaller rooms but there was a spacious bathroom and an extra lavatory at the far end of the landing.

But all this will have to change, Frances thought. She had done her homework and she knew that a B&B that didn't have showers, lavatories and basins en suite would get nowhere. It would cost a pretty penny but it would have to be done, among many other things, and she had budgeted for it. For now, she looked at the rooms with an eye to what furniture she and her mother had between them would fit in best, what she should tell the removal men to do this afternoon. In any case it would probably all have to be changed around before she started taking guests, which, if she got her advertising right, would be next Easter.

Back on the landing she took another look out of the window at the back of the house. It gave onto the walled garden, which appeared unkempt and neglected. Its only redeeming feature was the apple tree, large and venerable. When she had first viewed the house the apples, green, tinged with red, were on the tree; now they were mostly lying on the ground, bruised, decaying, part eaten, presumably by birds. She had asked Mr Birkett then what kind of apples they were but he hadn't been sure. 'I think Bramleys,' he'd said. 'Normally they don't like the frost – it kills the blossom – but I suppose the tree's protected by the wall. This could be a nice garden if someone looked after it.'

'I'm no gardener,' Frances had admitted, 'but of course I'll clear it up.' Fleetingly, she saw the garden as an area where she might serve teas in the summer.

Now she went back downstairs and walked around there. She loved the sitting-room; long, with two windows to the front, it was light and airy. She wouldn't like giving this up to guests but she supposed she would have to. It was the largest room on the ground floor and would become the breakfast room. But never mind, she consoled herself, we'll have it to ourselves right through the winters. She couldn't imagine many people choosing to spend winter weekends in Cordale.

18

The two windows facing out to the other side of the front door belonged to two smaller rooms, the larger of which, in the extension, also had a window to the side, in the gable end. Perhaps that could be her mother's, and the smaller one hers. Or vice versa, since her own might also have to double as an office. Perhaps, she thought, she might so arrange her mother's that when the house was, all being well, full in the summer season it could function as a bed-sitting-room. They had agreed that whenever possible they would each have their own bolt hole, but that in the tourist season they must be flexible, squeeze in wherever. Once they had settled in, she would also have to give a lot of thought to the various outbuildings at the back of the house. She was sure that something could be made of them but that would need more money.

But now, she thought, pleasant though it was to dream and to plan, she must return to Shepton. They'd arranged to have an early lunch and be back at Beck Farm by two o'clock.

TWO

Madge was already waiting when Frances arrived back at the Heifer; she was sitting in the lounge, clasping her large patent-leather handbag while at the same time reading a copy of the *Dalesman*.

'You should put an advertisement in this,' she greeted Frances. 'I mean, when you're ready for visitors. It's got lots of ads for B&Bs, and hotels of course.'

'I will,' Frances promised. 'Sorry I'm a bit late. Shall we eat, or would you like a glass of sherry first?'

'Not in the middle of the day,' Madge said. Her voice hovered on the edge of disapproval. 'Perhaps this evening before we have our supper. But if *you* want one now . . .'

'You know it's not my tipple, Mother. Anyway, I'm driving,' Frances reminded her. 'Let's go in.'

The dining-room was already busy. They seated themselves at a small table in the corner. Madge picked up the menu and studied it carefully.

'Did you do any shopping in the town?' Frances asked.

Madge shook her head. 'Not what you'd call shopping. I bought a few postcards and some stamps. Just in case they didn't have any in Kilby.'

Frances laughed. 'Mother, it's not the back of beyond. They do actually have a post office, *and* a village store.'

20

'I wasn't to know, was I?' Madge protested mildly. 'I wanted to be on the safe side. I've got friends and neighbours who'll be waiting for a line from me – waiting to hear I've arrived safely.'

Most of them had thought she was mad, and hadn't hesitated to say so. 'At your time of life!' was the most frequently used expression. 'Are you sure you're doing the right thing?' and 'What if it doesn't work out?' were among several others. Well, it had to work out, didn't it? She'd have to make sure it did. There was no going back. She was seventy-two, she'd sold her home and put most of the money – quite willingly – into the bed-and-breakfast venture, and packed her bags. But what alternative had there been? Frances had been set on leaving Sussex, and who could blame her? She hadn't had the best of times there over the last few years. And why would I want to stay behind in Brighton with Frances two-hundred-and-fifty miles away? Madge asked herself. 'What's the point,' she'd said to the critics, 'with only me and Frances left in the family, of us living at opposite ends of England?' It didn't make sense. But that didn't take away the trepidation that sometimes came over her when she wakened in the night. 'Did you have to go so far?' she'd tentatively asked her daughter.

Frances had been certain about that. 'It's not just the distance,' she'd pointed out. 'Where else would we go? Yorkshire is, after all, where we connect with, if anywhere. I've thought it out and reckon I could make a living there. You know I wouldn't be happy leaving you behind.'

'I just don't want—' Madge had begun, but was interrupted.

'Don't give me all that "don't want to be a burden" stuff,' Frances had said. 'We've done all that! I've told you, and I mean it, I want you with me. Apart from wanting you, you'll be a help to me – and I don't just mean financially.'

It was the realization that Frances needed me that in the end made me decide, Madge thought now. Wasn't it the best thing in the world to be needed, especially when you were old, and particularly by someone younger? And your own flesh and blood. Not that she spoke her thoughts out loud. Neither she nor Frances said that sort of thing.

'Right,' she said, putting down the menu. 'I'll have the

steak-and-kidney pudding, followed by the apple tart. We can't be sure when we'll get the next proper meal.'

Frances sighed. 'There's a pub in Kilby, Mother, and they do serve food. I've only seen it from the outside, when I came to view the house, but it looked OK,' Frances assured her. 'We won't starve. And tomorrow we can shop in the village.'

'If you say so, love,' Madge said. 'How long will it take us to get there?'

'Not long. But I wouldn't like the removal van to arrive before we did,' Frances said.

When they'd eaten, Frances said, 'I'll get the bags down and pay the bill. You wait for me in reception.'

'Shall I give you a hand?' Madge asked.

Frances shook her head. 'I can manage.' They had brought only overnight bags to the hotel. Everything else was in the removal van.

Madge watched her daughter as she left the dining-room. She was so tall and slender, her dark hair, now tied back, so thick and glossy. She moved gracefully, but then she got that as well as her looks from her father. Six foot three, he'd been, and he'd never put on an ounce of spare flesh from the day she'd met him until the day he died. Handsome too. She didn't know what he'd seen in a little roly-poly like herself; five foot nothing and as plump as a robin. 'What I saw,' he'd said, paying her a rare compliment, 'was your lovely skin, the way your eyes screwed up when you laughed, and how you enjoyed things. Will that do for you?'

It had had to. He'd not been one for repeating such things, but what he'd said had set her up for a long time. When she looked in the mirror, often dissatisfied, she still remembered it with pleasure.

She left the table, and moved into reception just as Frances was coming down the stairs, carrying the overnight cases.

'There!' Frances said. 'All done. Off we go!'

There was no sign of the removal van when they arrived at Beck Farm, which pleased Madge. 'I'd like a chance to get my bearings before they arrive. I'm keen to see where I'm going to sleep, for one thing.' She was out of the car now, gazing up at the house, giving it a quick appraisal. 'I must say, it looks quite big.' It was difficult to know whether she considered that good or bad.

'It's the right size for what we want,' Frances said. 'Though I admit the two of us will be rattling round in it until the guests start coming. But we'll have plenty to do before then.'

'Well, what are we waiting for?' Madge demanded. 'Let's go in. Let's be seeing it.'

Frances unlocked the door and they stepped into the hall. 'I'll show you which room I thought you might like to have for your bedroom, though if it's not what you want there's a choice. You must just say . . .'

'Oh, you'll not find me too fussy,' Madge assured her. 'You know me, love. And I don't need anything big. Just enough to take my bedroom furniture, which I've had since I was married and wouldn't want to part with. And near to the bathroom, for when I have to get up in the night. That's all I'm asking.'

For the moment, Frances thought. But, to be fair, her mother wasn't a demanding woman, except from time to time and almost without knowing it. And it will be my duty to see that my mother settles happily. I owe her that, at the very least, she reminded herself. 'So do you want to go straight to it, or do you want to look around the rest of the house first?' she asked.

'Oh, let's do things properly,' Madge said. 'Start at the bottom and, when we've done that, go upstairs. That way I'll know where I fit in.'

They did exactly that, though not including the outhouses: those could wait. 'You might also be able to have your own sitting-room downstairs – at least, when the house isn't full,' Frances said. 'Somewhere you can be on your own if you want to.'

Madge nodded briefly. She wasn't too sure that she wanted to be on her own. It was one of the things she'd most disliked after Tom died. She liked to look up and see someone there, someone sitting opposite, even if there was no conversation going on. Talk didn't matter. Tom had always had his head in a book anyway. Just the odd word, or a glance, and then at the end of the evening a hot drink and going up to bed together. Well, those times were gone, they wouldn't come again, but she hoped she wasn't going

23

to live too separately from her daughter, not in a place where she knew no-one. Following Frances around from room to room, and then up the stairs to the bedrooms, she said nothing of this.

'I reckoned this might suit you as your bedroom,' Frances said, opening a door from the landing. 'It's right next to the bathroom – though that won't matter when we get the loos and showers in—'

'I'm not gone on showers,' Madge interrupted. 'I like a bath. You can't have nice soak in a shower. But of course the lavatory will be handy.'

'Come and look at the view,' Frances said, crossing to the window. 'This being the back of the house, you can see right up the dale. 'It's a stunning view.'

Madge joined her, and they stood together, looking out. The large meadow closest to the house was on level ground, and though the summer was over and autumn well set in, the short grass was still bright green, and even now was being cropped closer by black-faced sheep. The confines of the meadow were marked by dry-stone walls, and beyond them further meadows sloped up the sides of the fell. To the left of the view the land dropped gently down towards the road that ran along the floor of the valley, and beyond that more fields climbed up again on the other side of the dale. And in almost every field there were sheep.

'It's beautiful,' Madge said. 'Your dad would have loved it. It's views like this we used to come up to the Dales for all those years ago. Don't you remember?'

'I can't say I do – at least, not much,' Frances admitted. 'The near meadows on this side of the road once belonged to Beck Farm. The owner sold them off to the neighbouring farmer. He just kept the house, which the neighbour didn't want in any case.'

'Why on earth did he do that?' Madge asked.

'I'm not sure,' Frances said. 'I don't know much about him, except that he died, and this house came on the market. I was told he'd run it before that for a while as a bed-and-breakfast. I don't know how well.'

'What about his family? Didn't they want it – I mean either the farm or the B&B?'

24

'It seems he didn't have any family,' Frances said. 'As I told you at the time, it was an executors' sale. Everything was to be sold and the proceeds were to go to charities. That's why I got the house more cheaply than I might have done. That's all I know.'

'It's just that I'm interested in people,' Madge said.

Frances smiled. 'You mean you're nosy! Well, I dare say as soon as we get to know one or two people in the village we'll be told everything – if there's anything to tell, that is. Shall we look at the rest of the rooms? I don't think the removal van can be much longer. I hope not, or we'll be emptying it in the dark.'

Five minutes later, looking out of the window of the room on the opposite side of the landing that she had mentally marked out as hers, Frances saw the removal van being driven slowly up the main street of the village and then following the road round to the left towards Beck Farm. She ran down the stairs, calling out to her mother, 'They're here!' Madge had gone downstairs to explore the kitchen cupboards, to see if by any chance there was as much as a pan left behind in which she could boil water to make some tea. She had taken the precaution of buying a packet of tea and a pint of milk in Shepton, unsure that her daughter would think of such things. Now she rushed to join Frances, who was opening the front door.

'Not before time,' Madge said as the van slowed to a halt. 'I only hope they'll know where the kettle is. I'm dying for a cup of tea, and I dare say they are.'

'The first thing they'll see when they open the van', Frances said patiently, 'is a packing case containing the kettle, tea, milk, sugar and mugs – as well as a loaf of bread, butter, and some boiled ham and tomatoes.' She had asked them to pack it last so that it would be handy. 'Don't worry, we always do,' the foreman had said. 'We can't start work till we've had our cup of tea.'

'You're very organized,' Madge told her.

'It's not the first time I've moved house, is it?' Frances called out as she walked down the path to meet the men.

It certainly isn't, Madge thought. Her daughter had left home for good when she'd first gone to university. No-one had said it would be for good at the time, but Tom had said it was all you

25

could expect, she had to fly the nest. Well, she'd flown in several directions since then, to at least three different places even while she was at university, and before she'd finally moved in with Malcolm in her last year there. 'It's all right, Mother,' she'd said. 'Don't look so disapproving. We're going to be married as soon as we've got our degrees over with. We don't have the time right now.'

Madge remembered what she'd replied. 'In my day we got married first. Your dad and me courted seven years.'

'Good for you!' Frances had said. 'If that's what you wanted. I certainly wouldn't.'

It hadn't been what they'd wanted, Madge thought, remembering how most of that time she'd longed, body and soul, to be married; and so had Tom, but it wasn't possible. She'd met Tom, ten years older than she was, at a dance when he was home on embarkation leave from the army. She was sixteen and her mother had thought she was too young to go to a dance, but Madge had defied her. 'And thank goodness you did,' Tom had said, 'or you and me would never have met and you'd have been snapped up by someone else.' But all she'd known of him from then until the end of the war was in the slim, blue air letters she received spasmodically from somewhere in the Far East. He wasn't allowed to say where, just that it was hot and damp and there were more and bigger insects than she'd have thought possible, and they had an old gramophone on which he constantly played the record she'd given him as a not very convenient parting present. They'd married as soon as Tom was demobbed, though from the ending of the war in the Far East to the day when he walked up the path to her parents' house in his newly acquired civilian suit seemed the longest period of her life so far. They were blissfully happy together, but several years went by before she became pregnant. No doctor – and she and Tom had consulted several – could say why this was. It appeared it was just bad luck. But when at last she did become pregnant, and Frances was born – a healthy seven-pound baby – then that made up for everything.

So she'd bitten her tongue and said nothing more to Frances on the subject of her living with Malcolm. Looking back on it now, and given the chance with Tom, she'd have done the same. And she'd quite liked Malcolm. Tom hadn't, but she'd reckoned that was because he was taking his lovely daughter away. Since then, both with Malcolm and later on without him, Frances had made several more moves, some willingly, some forced upon her. 'But this time is the last,' she'd said when she'd found Beck Farm. 'This time it's for good.'

As Frances had predicted, the removal men brought in the chest with the kettle and its accompaniments first.

'Did you have a good journey?' Frances asked them.

'Tolerable,' the foreman answered. 'We did an overnight stop, as we'd said we would, but today we got held up in Harrogate, or we'd have been earlier. I think there was some sort of show on.'

'If you'll carry this chest into the kitchen I'll get on with the tea. You must be ready for it,' Madge said.

'Always ready for a cuppa,' the foreman said. He signalled to his young assistant, who picked up the case as if it weighed no more than two ounces, and followed Madge into the kitchen.

It was amazing, Frances thought, how rapidly, once they'd made a start, the men emptied the van of its contents, far more quickly than she could decide where everything should go. 'The important thing', she instructed them, 'is that we get the beds, my mother's and mine, and the bags with the bedding in, into their respective rooms. Everything else we can sort out as and when.'

One of the things she *had* learned, thanks to her previous moves, was that you made up the beds while you were still reasonably fresh so that you could fall into them when you became – inevitably – exhausted beyond measure. She'd learned a great many things since she'd first moved into Malcolm's cramped little furnished flat, in Whiteladies Road near to the university in Bristol. They'd been so happy there. It hadn't mattered that it was tiny, the bed was too narrow – it was no barrier to their lovemaking – nor that there were noisy students on the floor below. They were students themselves, living for the moment. It was when they'd graduated and, soon after that, married that they'd made the big move.

When this came it could hardly have been more different.

They had moved to Sussex, where Malcolm's parents owned and ran a successful prep school. Both Malcolm and Frances, it was planned, would teach at the school – she English and Malcolm mathematics – until eventually, several years ahead, it would all become his. In the meantime Malcolm's parents bought their son a house, not far from the school gates, since he had no wish to live in the school with his new bride.

We were happy there, Frances had thought many times since, but everything had changed two years later when Malcolm's parents, a week into their summer holiday, were killed when their car ran off a mountain road in Spain. At the start of the autumn term Malcolm found himself Head of the school, and Frances the Headmaster's young wife, both of them inexperienced in these new roles. Nevertheless, barring a few hiccups, it had gone reasonably well for another couple of years – or so Frances thought, until the evening Malcolm informed her that he'd had enough of it, he wasn't cut out to run a school, it had been his parents' idea, not his, and he was putting it on the market as a going concern. Moreover, he told her, getting it all over in the same breath, he was sorry but he no longer loved her – 'Well, not as I once did' – because he had fallen in love with the French mistress and they were going to start a new life in France. 'Bergerac,' he said. 'It's in the south-west.' 'I know where Bergerac is!' was all Frances could say at the time.

He would be quite fair with her, he pointed out reasonably. The school business would sell at a good price and she'd have half of it, as she would have of the house nearby, which they still lived in. He would like to put that on the market at the same time as the school; it would be an added attraction. He wanted a quick sale because he and Michelle were anxious to make the move to Bergerac. He was truly sorry about all this but he felt sure she would understand. They had married too young, that was the top and bottom of it. Didn't she agree?

She didn't; nor had she understood. None of it made sense to her. She loved him and she'd thought he loved her. She'd thought things were rubbing along well enough but now she found herself in a state of almost blind obedience to his wishes, too numb to fight. She moved out, found a flat and a temporary job in a state school, both in Brighton, where her parents now lived. The flat and the job were the first of the several moves that followed, largely because she couldn't settle, and they were all in the Brighton area. She had this feeling of wanting to be* somewhere near her parents, though no way would she have gone to live with them. As time went by she had made some friends through work, had a few temporary relationships – discovering along the way that most men were married anyway, and, though that was no bar to them, it was to her. She would have liked to have settled down with someone but it never happened.

And now here she was, thirty-nine years old, in a place of which she knew next to nothing; all her worldly goods were being carried in and strewed around a house to which, if she added up the hours she had spent in it, she was almost a total stranger; and she was about to embark on a business of which she knew nothing at all. Moreover, she had dragged her elderly mother – who had been living a contented life in Brighton, surrounded by friends – into all this with her. For a brief moment, standing there in the hall, she was terrified for both of them. How could she have done this? She must be out of her mind.

The moment was interrupted by the two removal men carrying in a dresser she had known in her mother's kitchen since she was a small child. It had always contained jars of dried fruit – currants, raisins – from which as a child she had sometimes been allowed to help herself. Somehow the sight of it, with its long association, its familiar shabbiness, calmed her down. Not everything was strange. All right, it was a new life, but she had brought something of her old life with her. And, she thought, looking at the dresser, so had her mother. They would be OK.

The men put the dresser down. 'This is a solid piece and no mistake,' the foreman said. 'They don't make them like this these days. Where do you want it to go?'

'In the kitchen,' Frances said. 'I'll show you.'

Madge was already in the kitchen, unpacking a box of pans and dishes. She smiled broadly when she saw the dresser being carried in. 'That's more like it,' she said. 'Now I can put this stuff where it belongs. Make it seem a bit more like home.'

'We'll be through in half an hour,' the foreman said. 'Mostly bits and pieces now.'

'I'll make you another cup of tea while you're finishing off,' Madge said, 'and I've found the toaster, so I could do you some toast.'

'A quick cup of tea but we'll not bother with anything to eat,' the foreman said. 'I'd like to get as far down the road as possible before the light goes. We'll have a meal on the motorway. It'll be the early hours before we're home, but my wife's used to that. And the lad here doesn't have a wife, so he's no-one to answer to.'

When they had left, having been handsomely tipped by Frances – he would never know what it had meant to her the way they'd brought in the dresser exactly when they did – she and her mother waved them off, then went back into the house. And now, Frances thought, though it was in a state of disarray that would no doubt take weeks to sort out, she felt, closing the door, as if she was in her own home.

'How do *you* feel?' she asked her mother.

'Grand,' Madge said. 'A bit tired – well, quite a lot tired, to be honest – but grand.'

'Then I suggest we get our bedrooms ready – I'll give you a hand with yours – then we go down to the pub for a meal, and back here to bed. An early night. Everything else can wait until tomorrow.'

The Shorn Lamb came as something of a surprise to Frances. At least, the inside did. For a start, though the rough plastered walls, the low, beamed ceiling yellowed by tobacco smoke, the unevenness of the floor, and the huge inglenook fireplace all spoke with one voice of past centuries, the pub was, overall, of the moment, alive, and busy. An array of every kind of bottled drink under the sun filled the shelves behind the bar, there were comfortable stools, chairs, carefully arranged lighting, curtains at the window. There were one or two men standing around the bar who looked and sounded as if they might be locals; and two or three of the tables were occupied by diners. It clearly attracted people, even in late September. Frances knew it took visitors: she had checked that in the guidebook.

She seated her mother at a table, then went to the bar. Two men, talking together, moved aside to give her space.

'I'd like a medium-dry sherry and a gin-and-tonic,' she said. 'And have you a dinner menu I could see?'

'Certainly,' the barman said. 'Here you are. And the specials are written up on the board. Not many specials, because it's a weekday evening, but I'm sure you'll find something to your liking.'

And a friendly welcome too, Frances thought, and that worked favourably with her own plans. When she started taking guests she had no intention of offering evening meals and to have a good place to send them was certainly a bonus. On the other hand, possibly the Shorn Lamb was the place where people would choose to stay rather than in a guesthouse. It was lively, it was welcoming.

'I'm sure we shall,' she replied, glancing at the menu.

The barman poured the drinks and put them in front of her. 'Are you visiting, then?' he asked.

'No,' Frances said. 'As a matter of fact I've come to live here. I moved in this very day, with my mother.' She indicated her mother and the barman smiled in Madge's direction. 'I've bought Beck Farm,' Frances said.

'Oh! Well now, that would be where the removal van was heading for,' he said. 'We heard it had been sold, and to a lady. We also heard she was going to run it as a bed-and-breakfast. Is that a fact?'

'It is,' Frances confirmed. 'Who told you?'

'Now, that I don't rightly remember,' the barman said. 'But you won't be here long before you'll learn that news flies around the dale like a bird on the wing. Anyway, my name's Bernard Grayson, and I'm the landlord here . . .'

'Oh, I thought . . .'

'You thought I was the barman? Well, I am when it's Jim Kettle's night off. I like to keep my hand in.'

'Thank you. I'm Frances Hamilton. Actually, I don't intend to start up in business before the spring. There's a lot to do in the house to get it as I want it.'

'That doesn't surprise me at all,' the landlord said. 'Ben

Thornton's heart wasn't in it. But if you take to it, it could be a nice little set-up. And I dare say I might be able to put a bit of business your way from time to time. I often get more enquiries than I can cater for, especially in the summer.'

'That would be wonderful,' Frances said. 'Thank you very much. And perhaps you can tell me where I can get some help.'

'What sort of help would that be?' Bernard Grayson asked.

'All sorts,' Frances said. 'I intend to have showers and loos put in all the bedrooms, make alterations in the kitchen, and so on. Then everything needs a coat of paint. I can do some of that but I can't do it all.'

'You want a jack-of-all-trades, I take it?'

Frances nodded. 'I certainly do. And then I need a woman to help me in the house – cleaning, sorting things out and so on.'

'Well, that bit's my wife's department,' Bernard Grayson said. 'She'd be able to tell you but she's not here right now; she's over visiting her sister in Settle. She'll be back late. I'll tell you what: why don't Joyce and me take a walk up to Beck Farm tomorrow? We can sort it out – tell you who's best for what, and I dare say put you in the way of a few things you need to know.'

'That would be great, Mr Grayson,' Frances said.

'Call me Bernard, love,' he said. 'Everyone else does. We'll come in the afternoon. It's our quietest time. And now I'll carry your drinks across for you and you can introduce me to your mother.'

THREE

At half-past three in the afternoon Frances was on her knees in the bedroom, unpacking yet another suitcase. Odds and ends of clothing, this one contained. Tops, winter sweaters, scarves, an embroidered waistcoat which at the time she'd bought it she'd reckoned was the utmost in style but hadn't now been worn for many a year. She'd been surprised when it came to packing her clothes to realize how many she had. Most of them, though not necessarily worn out or even shabby, went back a way and she should have been sensible enough to get rid of those she would almost certainly never wear again instead of bringing them all the way up here. Oh well, she supposed they had jumble sales in Cordale.

She had started to sort them into three piles: one lot to get rid of, one to keep, and the third, already the largest pile, to decide about later. It was like living parts of her past again. Mostly she could remember where she'd bought the garment, sometimes how much she'd paid, and on which occasion she'd worn it, and, if the occasion had been a special one, whether it had turned out happy or otherwise. Anything that brought back less than happy memories, she decided, she would put in the 'get rid of' pile. And that went double for the pale pink, silver-beaded top which she now took out of the case, unfolded, and held up in front of her. Worn only once, it had been bought it especially for a staff outing, all the teachers going off with their partners for an evening meal together to celebrate someone's birthday. She'd been pleased by the purchase then, though she'd paid far more than she'd intended to. It was so pretty, and obviously it became her, because she'd received several compliments about it. But that had turned out to be the dinner after which Malcolm had informed her, almost as soon as they were back home – they were standing in the bedroom, she was still wearing that top – that everything was over between them. He'd outlined all his plans – Michelle, Bergerac – everything cut and dried; no basis for discussion. So definitely the 'get rid of' pile! Why hadn't she cut it into ribbons the very next day? Or thrown it in the dustbin? Why in the world had she brought it here? It had all happened a few years ago now; there'd been other men, other events. She hoped that whoever in the end bought it from some jumble sale would have better luck than she had had with it.

Her mother, calling from downstairs, interrupted her thoughts. 'They're here! They're walking up the lane.'

Frances rose from her knees and went to look out of the window. Bernard Grayson was wearing a tweed suit and a cloth cap – every inch a countryman, he looked. Mrs Grayson wore a blue coat, sensible shoes, and a scarf tied round her head. Bernard was taller and bulkier than he'd seemed in the pub, and his wife was not much shorter than he was. Her right arm was linked through his and in her left she carried a shallow basket. As they climbed the slope, as close to each other as if they were both carved from one piece of wood, they leaned forward into the wind, which was blowing quite strongly from the north.

'I'll be right down,' Frances called out.

'I'll put the kettle on,' her mother shouted back. There was no occasion in her mother's life that couldn't be improved by putting the kettle on.

Frances screwed the pink top into a ball and threw it to the far side of the room. Then she ran down the stairs and was at the open door to greet the Graysons as they reached the house.

'This is my wife, Joyce,' Bernard said as they stepped into the hall.

Madge appeared from the kitchen.

34

'And this is my mother, Madge Fraser,' Frances said.

Madge held out her hand to Bernard's wife. 'Pleased to meet you, Mrs Grayson,' she said.

'Oh, Joyce, please!' Bernard's wife said. She had a strong voice with a north-country accent. Her face was round and plump and her shiny pink cheeks glowed with health.

'Come into what I think I have to call the front sitting-room,' Frances said. 'I'm afraid it's not all that warm, though. I haven't sorted out the heating yet – in fact, I don't quite know how it works – but luckily we did bring an electric fire with us. Perhaps you might like to keep your coat on for a bit, Joyce?'

'I will for the moment,' Joyce Grayson agreed. 'But we're used to the cold here. It doesn't bother us too much, not until we get to the winter. Then it's a different matter. What you learn then is to keep all the doors closed.'

'Excuse me,' Madge said. 'The kettle will be boiling. I'll go and make the tea. That'll warm us up.'

'I've brought a few fruit scones I made this morning,' Joyce said, handing over the basket to Madge. 'I reckoned you'd not have had time for baking.'

'That's kind,' Frances said. 'Do come and sit down.'

Bernard took the armchair by the fireplace; Joyce sat opposite him. 'Well then,' Bernard said. 'What sort of a night did you have, your first at Beck Farm?'

'Not bad,' Frances said. 'We were tired. We went to bed as soon as we got back from the Shorn Lamb.' She wasn't going to tell him, or anyone else, and that included her mother, how long into the night she'd lain awake, asking herself if she was stark raving mad, and not finding the answer. In the end she'd fallen asleep from sheer exhaustion.

'It was a bit windy,' Joyce said.

'We're used to that,' Frances told her. 'It's frequently windy in Brighton. Sea breezes!'

'I think of Brighton as being bright and sunny,' Joyce said. 'That's the way it usually is on the telly. And, of course, crowded with people, always something happening. It looks lovely.'

'Oh, it is,' Frances agreed.

Madge came in with the tea, poured it, handed cups round,

offered the scones, joined in the small talk – until Bernard said, 'Well, ladies, we've got to sort out what's to be done. Where shall we make a start?'

'Actually,' Frances said, 'I've begun to make a list, but not in any order. One of the first things I'd like to do is get all the furniture in the rooms where it's likely to belong. I tried to do so as the men were moving it in but they tended to put things in the nearest available space. They were anxious to get away and I couldn't blame them. It's a long journey back. The thing is, I still don't know where everything is, not by a long chalk. So if you know someone who could come and give me a hand with moving things . . .'

Bernard looked at his wife. 'Do you think Jim?' he asked.

She nodded agreement. 'Absolutely.'

'Jim Kettle's the barman,' Bernard said – 'the one you'd have seen last night except it was his night off. He doesn't work quite full-time for me, at least not out of season, and he's always ready to earn a bit extra. He has four bairns.'

'And he's as strong as a horse,' Joyce put in. 'Just the person to move furniture.'

'Well, if you think he'd do it . . .' Frances said.

'Oh, I'm sure he would,' Bernard said, confidently. 'I'll have a word with him this evening, see if he can be round tomorrow.'

'That would be wonderful,' Frances said.

'And now what were the other things you wanted to know about?' Bernard asked. 'Shall we take a look around? You can point things out as we go on.'

'Certainly,' Frances agreed. 'I expect you know the layout of the house already?'

Bernard shook his head. 'Oh, no. Not a bit of it. Beck Farm wasn't a house you got invited to, at least not by Ben. Ben Thornton was never a hospitable man. The only way you ever got your foot under his table was if you paid for it, if you were a bed-and-breakfast guest.' He turned to his wife. 'Am I right, Joyce?'

'To an extent,' Joyce said. 'But that wasn't true of Moira.' She turned to Frances. 'Moira was my best friend. I was here often before she died, but not since.'

36

'It seems strange for a man who wasn't hospitably inclined to run a B&B business,' Frances said.

'He didn't,' Joyce said. 'It was Moira who started it up and ran it. Ben ran the farm.'

'And I wouldn't say his heart was in that, either,' Bernard added. 'Not that he hadn't been in farming all his life, but it would never have been his first choice. You see, the farm belonged to his father, and his grandfather before him, and Ben was his father's only child so he inherited it. He would have liked to have been an artist. A painter, sculptor – a woodcarver. He always had a lump of wood to hand, whittling away with a penknife, carving it into something or other.'

'It was a lucky day for Ben when he married Moira,' Joyce observed. 'A real lucky day. She was a farmer's daughter, from over near York, so she took to being a farmer's wife like a duck to water. She knew what she was doing. She took a hand in everything here. Helped with the lambing, kept poultry, made cheese – lovely cheese. She was well known for it. Took the farm produce and sold it in the markets round about. Chickens, eggs, cream, curd tarts. Lovely apple chutneys and the like. All that as well as keeping the house spotless.'

'So why did she start a B&B?' Frances asked. 'She must have had her hands full.'

'Indeed she did,' Joyce agreed. 'But Moira could always take on something else. All the same, I don't think she'd have done it if Ben had been more of a success with the farm.'

'Now, we must be fair to Ben,' Bernard interrupted. 'Farming was in a bad way at that time. It often is, but there'd been two bad harvests, the prices for lambs at the market fell so low it was hardly worth while rearing them. There was a lot of foreign meat coming into the country. So Ben, who'd never had his heart in it, was struggling and when Joseph Clark offered to buy most of his land and stock . . .'

'Joseph Clark?' Frances queried.

'His land marched with Ben's,' Bernard said. 'Does so with yours now, what little bit you've got left.'

'You mean that narrow strip beyond the garden?' Frances asked.

'That's right,' Bernard said. 'Moira wanted a little bit of land to continue to keep a few hens. She'd done so all her life. Joseph had come into money from somewhere or other and he reckoned farming would be on the upturn if you waited long enough. I don't know what he offered for the land but, whatever it was, Ben couldn't resist it, especially as Joseph didn't want the house with it. That was when Ben and Moira decided to take in visitors as a proper business. There was scope for that. We've always had visitors coming to Cordale.'

'Of course, the work fell on Moira,' Joyce put in. 'But she'd lost the farm work so she reckoned she could cope. She did it very well too. She was friendly as well as hardworking. She needed to be.'

You're not exactly fond of Ben, Frances thought, and wondered why.

'We'd best make a move at looking round the house,' Bernard said. 'Helps to see everything in daylight. Where shall we start?'

'I think upstairs,' Frances said. 'That's where there's most to be done. Structural things, I mean. You might be able to advise me on that, or tell me who I can go to.'

'I'll clear away the tea things,' Madge said. 'I'll leave you to it.'

'Shall I give you a hand, Madge?' Joyce offered.

'Oh no,' Madge said. 'It won't take me more than a minute. You go on up.'

The three of them went into each bedroom in turn. Frances explained the alterations she wanted. 'Mainly to make every room on this floor en suite,' she said. 'When that's done I can think about the furnishings, and what extra furniture I need.'

'You're quite right,' Bernard agreed. 'First things first. Their own facilities is what people expect these days, and why shouldn't they? We made all our bedrooms en suite at the Lamb two or three years ago. It's surprising what a small space you can fit such things into. Not much more than a corner of the room is enough. But of course you've got to have the expert to do it. You can't let an amateur loose on such things as drains.'

'Which is where I'm hoping you can help me,' Frances said. 'Can you recommend who I can go to? Preferably someone local, of course. Perhaps whoever did the Shorn Lamb?'

Bernard shook his head. 'The Brewery saw to that,' he said. 'They brought in their own experts.' He turned to his wife. 'What about Alec Spence?'

'I don't think you could beat Alec,' Joyce said, 'if he has the time, of course. He'd do a good job and he wouldn't cheat you on the money. But he's always busy. You wouldn't get it done tomorrow.'

'I suppose none of it's red-hot urgent,' Frances admitted. 'But I do want everything spick-and-span in time to open up next spring. So where can I get in touch with him? Does he live in the dale?'

'He lives right here in Kilby,' Bernard said. 'He has one of the little cottages in the row by the church. But his business place is in Shepton. You'd have to go there to choose things.'

'Oh, that's easy enough,' Frances said. 'I reckon I'll be making quite a few trips to Shepton over the next few months.'

'I'll tell you what,' Bernard said: 'he comes into the Lamb most evenings, so if you were to be coming down – say, this evening or tomorrow – I could introduce you and you could tell him what you have in mind.'

'We'll do that,' Frances said.

'Right, then,' Bernard said. 'Now, have we seen everything up here? If so, we'll go downstairs and look at the rest, and then me and Joyce will have to be getting back.'

'You've seen everything except the small room at the end of the corridor,' Frances said. 'It's not big enough for an en suite bedroom. I expect to make something of it in the end, but for the moment it's filled with junk that was left behind, nothing to do with me. I've closed the door on it for the time being.'

'Then we'll leave it closed for now, shall we?' Bernard said.

Back downstairs they went into every room, and then outside to view the outbuildings at the back.

Bernard looked them over with a critical eye. 'They're sound enough on the outside,' he remarked, 'but not much cop inside, are they?'

'You're right,' Frances agreed, picking her way through bits of – to her – unidentifiable machinery, buckets, rakes, oil cans, piles of wood. 'It's all an awful mess, isn't it?'

'It wouldn't have been like this in Moira's time,' Joyce said.

'But, as you say,' Frances said to Bernard, 'the walls seem sound and the roofs could be worse. I reckon there's potential here. They could make extra living – which means letting – space. But not to be dealt with just yet, perhaps not for some time. It would take money.'

'And not only that, you'd have to get permission,' Bernard pointed out. 'You can't just do whatever takes your fancy to your buildings. We're in the National Park area. They have strict rules. And rightly so.'

'Of course,' Frances agreed. 'Well, there's no rush.'

'That's right,' Bernard said. 'But I think this is where me and Joyce have to rush, if you'll excuse us. Things to do and all that. We'll see you in the Lamb this evening, then?'

'I look forward to it,' Frances answered. 'And thank you for your help.'

'And perhaps I'll have a minute then to tell you things about the village,' Joyce said. 'What you can get in the shop, what you can't. When the butcher's van calls and all that.'

Frances and her mother stood in the doorway, watching the couple as they walked, again arm in arm, down the hill. How fortunate they were to have each other, they fitted so well together, Frances thought, with a rare pang of envy, as the Graysons turned the corner and were lost to sight.

Though it was not yet evening, the colour had gone from the day. Grey clouds hid the sun and there was a chill in the air. 'Too cold to stand here,' Madge said, turning back into the house. 'Very nice people, weren't they – especially considering you'll be rivals in business once you get going.'

Frances laughed as she followed her in. 'Oh, I don't think so, Mother. There are people who'll always prefer an inn; more going on.'

'And also those who'd rather have something quieter,' Madge said. 'And cheaper.'

'Perhaps. What I'm sure Bernard will do – in fact, he said as much yesterday evening, didn't he? – is recommend Beck Farm to the people he doesn't have room for,' Frances said. 'It should all work out quite nicely once we get to that stage.'

'Seems to me Ben Thornton wasn't a popular man,' Madge said, changing the subject. 'Did you get that impression when you were dealing with the estate agent? You didn't say anything.'

'Not at all,' Frances admitted. 'He said very little about him. I think I assumed that he didn't know much about the owner and wasn't particularly interested. It was just another sale.'

'More interested in his commission, I suppose,' Madge said.

'It was mostly Joyce Grayson who didn't have much good to say about Ben Thornton, wasn't it?' Frances reminded her mother. 'Bernard made allowances. But from what she said herself, Joyce was a special friend of Moira. Anyway, I must go and do a bit more unpacking. Shall we aim to go down to the Shorn Lamb about seven-thirty?'

Madge nodded. 'Suits me. And for now I'll get back to sorting the kitchen cupboards.'

It was decidedly cool, though not yet dark, when, later than they'd intended, the two of them set off down the hill towards the village. Madge gave a shiver. 'I shall have to unpack my winter coat,' she said. 'This jacket just isn't warm enough. It's much colder here than in Brighton, isn't it?'

'Of course it is,' Frances said. 'It's a good deal further north. On the other hand, it will stay light longer here in the summer.' She didn't want to think about where she'd come from, only where she was going. She had made a pact with herself not to look back on the life she'd lived in the south, not even to make comparisons with the weather. Every day now was a new one and she hoped her mother wasn't going to harp on the past, though being the age she was it was a lot to expect. 'Anyway,' she said, 'you've lived half your life up here. You should be used to it.' She was aware that her tone was sharpish, more than her mother deserved.

'It was a long while ago,' Madge said mildly. 'I've got used to soft southern ways.' In the context of what they'd been saying it would have been natural, and she would have liked, to mention the beautiful sunsets they'd frequently enjoyed in Brighton, the whole of the western sky lit up in flame, turning the sea red, but she bit her lip against the words. She'd noted and she understood

Frances's tone of voice. It was easy to guess what was in her daughter's mind, though Frances didn't always appreciate, Madge thought, how much the true meaning of some of the things she said *was* understood. They weren't really talking about the weather right now. They were talking about all the complications of leaving things behind and going forward. Frances wanted it to be as if the last few years of her life had never happened – but you couldn't do that, they left their mark.

It was warm and welcoming in the Shorn Lamb, busier than the previous night, more people standing at the bar, more chattering going on and there was a background of not-too-intrusive music.

Bernard, standing talking at the bar, saw them as soon as they came through the door and broke off his conversation to greet them. 'Hello there! I was wondering if you'd changed your mind,' he said. 'Drinks on the house as it's your first real visit. What would you like?'

'Thank you,' Madge said. 'I usually like a sherry.'

'And you had a G & T last night,' he said to Frances. 'Is that your usual?'

'Please.'

They followed him to the bar.

'Meet Jim Kettle,' Bernard said. 'I've told him about your plans. He'll be glad to help. I'll leave you to make the arrangements.'

Frances was surprised at the sight of Jim Kettle; not that she'd had any fixed idea in her mind of what he'd be like, but she realized she'd expected him to be large, burly, muscular, visibly suitable for heaving barrels of beer and cases of spirits about. Instead he was small, thin, balding and what hair he had was wispy and grey.

Bernard caught her expression of surprise – she couldn't quite conceal it. 'Don't worry,' he said with a grin that also included Jim Kettle and was returned by him. 'As Joyce told you this afternoon, he's as strong as a horse. He could pick me up with one hand.'

'Would you like me to demonstrate that, Mrs Hamilton?' Jim offered.

'Well, *I* wouldn't,' Bernard said. 'Not in my bar. I'm sure she'll take it on my say-so.'

'I will,' Frances said. 'When would you be able to come to give me a hand, Jim? The sooner the better for me.'

'I could give you a couple of hours tomorrow morning,' Jim Kettle said. 'Say, from eight o'clock, if that's not too early.'

'Not a bit,' Frances said.

'Then we'll see how it goes from there,' he said – and went off to serve a customer.

'You'll find he's all right,' Bernard promised.

'I'm sure he will be,' Frances said. 'And what about Mr Spence? It was Mr Spence, the builder you suggested, wasn't it?'

'That's right. Alec Spence. Well, he hasn't been in yet and he usually comes early. Perhaps he's away, but he didn't say anything.' He gave Frances the feeling that in Kilby everyone knew what everyone was about, that unexplained absences were unusual. 'I'll ask around, get a message through to ask him to call on you. Now, have a look at the menu. I hope you're hungry.'

'Starving,' Frances admitted. 'What about you, Mother?'

'I'm pretty hungry,' Madge said. 'And it's always nice saying what you'll have and somebody else cooking it.'

'Right,' Bernard said. 'Well, choose your table and I'll be back with you in a few minutes to take your order and Joyce will cook it. She's in the kitchen at the moment. Week nights out of season we do it between us. At weekends, and every night in the season, we have help.'

When he came back from the kitchen he said, 'Joyce hasn't forgotten that she promised to put you in the way of things. She says perhaps you'd like to go through and have a word with her when you've finished.'

'Thank you. That would be great,' Frances said.

FOUR

They were finishing their apple pie when Bernard approached them. 'I shall pay for this,' Madge was saying. 'Light though it is, pastry at this time of night lies heavy on the stomach.'

'Then why didn't you choose something else?' Frances asked. 'There was plenty on the menu.'

'Because I like apple pie,' Madge answered. 'I always have.'

'Joyce says, when you've done would you like to go through to the kitchen for your coffee,' Bernard interrupted. 'Everybody's been served but she can't leave yet, just in case.'

'We'd be glad to,' Frances said. 'And we have finished. If I could have the bill . . .'

'I'll see you get it before you leave,' Bernard promised. 'So if you'd like to come with me . . .'

The kitchen was large, warm, untidy. The top of the big Aga was crowded with pans and every other surface was covered with plates, cutlery, dishes. Joyce, looking rosier than ever, cleared a space on the central table and brought up chairs.

'Coffee for both of you?' she asked.

'Would it be a lot of trouble', Madge said, 'if I were to ask for a cup of tea? If it is, please don't bother, but coffee at night keeps me awake.'

'It's no trouble at all,' Joyce said. 'In fact, I shall have tea too.'

She turned to Frances. 'But the coffee's made, so the choice is yours.'

'Coffee, please,' Frances said. 'What a lovely big kitchen!'

'It is,' Joyce agreed. 'You're seeing it at its worst, though. I'm not a tidy worker.'

'I could give you a hand,' Madge offered quickly. Frances could tell she was dying to get in and restore some order.

'Oh no, that's all right,' Joyce said. 'I shall put the food away and stack the dishwasher before I go to bed, and the rest can wait until Rosie comes in the morning. She knows what to expect when I'm doing the cooking.'

'Rosie?' Madge believed that if you wanted to know, then you had to ask.

'She helps generally, wherever she's needed. In the rooms, in here, in the bar. She has two children, Dawn and Darren, so she comes as soon as she's seen them off to school. She's glad of the work – her husband doesn't earn much.'

'And what does he do?' Madge asked.

'Any work he can get on the farms, mostly unskilled,' Joyce said.

'I could do with a Rosie, or I will when I've got things a bit straighter,' Frances chipped in. She could tell her mother was going to demand the whole history of Rosie's family if she wasn't stopped.

'When you're ready,' Joyce said, pouring the tea, 'I'll give it some thought. Is your coffee all right? Would either of you like a biscuit?'

'Not after that lovely meal,' Frances said. 'I couldn't eat another thing.'

'What about you, Madge? I've got some shortbread I made this morning,' Joyce offered.

'Well, now, I never could resist shortbread,' Madge said happily.

The conversation flowed easily. Frances learned that the butcher's van came to Kilby on Tuesdays and Fridays, in the morning, and the baker's on Wednesdays. 'I'll ask them both to go up to Beck Farm,' Joyce said. The village shop and post office – known as Eileen's, though the original Eileen had long

45

gone to the post office in the sky – sold bread too, but only sliced loaves. 'I have a bread machine,' Joyce said, 'and if you haven't I recommend one.'

'I used to bake all my own bread; flatcakes, currant tea-cakes and everything,' Madge said. 'But you get out of the way of it.'

There was a school in the village and the little ones stayed for their dinners, Joyce said, but when they got older they had to bus to Shepton and some of the children, from the more remote dales or farms, were weekly boarders there. 'So you couldn't say we see many children around in the village,' she said, 'except the tiny ones with their mothers.'

'Are there many young people in Kilby?' Frances asked.

'Not really,' Joyce said. 'They move away when they get married. People who've been born and bred here, lived here all their lives, now they can't afford to stay. The price of houses is too high. A lot of homes, you see, are bought by people from places like Leeds, Bradford and so on; people who can afford them. They're just used at weekends or for holidays. It's a great shame, but that's the way it is.'

There was a pause. Did this mean the village didn't like newcomers, Frances wondered. She hadn't felt that so far, but it was early days.

'I was hoping', she said, changing the subject, 'to meet Mr Spence, but apparently he hasn't been in this evening.'

'No. Bernard said not,' Joyce answered. 'It's unusual. Anyway, I'm sure you'll catch up with him. It might be he's gone to see his children. A birthday or something.'

'Oh! Are they away at school?' Frances asked.

'No, not at school. Well, yes and no. They are at school, in Leeds. They don't live here with Alec, except sometimes they come up in the school holidays. He's divorced. The children live with their mother. She married again.'

'I see,' Frances said. 'Well, I expect I'll catch up with him sooner or later.'

'Oh, sooner, I'd think,' Joyce assured her. 'He's never away for long. And I don't even know that he is away. Perhaps something came up.'

Bernard came in. 'Everything all right?' he enquired.

'Fine,' Joyce said. 'We were just talking about Alec Spence. I was wondering if he might have gone to see the kids – a birthday or something.'

'Could be. Anyway,' Bernard said to Frances, 'as soon as I set eyes on him I'll give him your phone number. And now, I'm not rushing you, but when you two ladies are ready to go I'll run you up to the house. I know it's not far, but it's a hill and it's a cold night. It's not all that busy in the bar at the moment. Nothing Jim can't deal with. But there's no rush.'

'There was just one thing I'd like to discuss with you,' Frances said. 'Both of you. I'd be grateful for your opinion.'

'For what it's worth you'll get it,' Bernard said. 'What's it about, then?'

'I wondered . . .' Frances said, 'I was toying with the idea of changing the name of the house. I mean from Beck Farm to something like Beck House, or maybe Beckside House. What do you think?'

Bernard raised his eyebrows in surprise and shook his head in dissent at the same time. 'It's always been Beck Farm,' he said. 'It's never been anything else from the day it was built, and that's going on two hundred years ago now.'

'That's right,' Joyce agreed. 'You might decide to change it, but everyone in Kilby would still call it Beck Farm; everyone in the dale who knows it would.'

'Why would you want to change it?' Bernard asked.

'Partly because it isn't a farm, not any longer, so maybe the name gives a wrong impression, but perhaps more because from what I hear – not that I've spoken to many people about it – Beck Farm doesn't seem to have a good reputation as a bed-and-breakfast place. What I hear is how it was run down, how it tailed off . . .'

'It wasn't like that when Moira ran it,' Joyce interrupted. 'It was a very nice place to stay. You couldn't have found better.'

'Oh, I'm sure it was,' Frances said, 'but that was a while ago, wasn't it? You see, I'll need to advertise and "Beck Farm" isn't going to appeal to anyone who's experienced it in the last year or two; nor is anyone who's heard of it as Beck Farm going to

47

recommend it. And not everyone wants a farm atmosphere. I thought with a new name, and a nice new photograph, it might be a fresh start.'

'Well, I get your point,' Bernard said. 'And I have to admit it did go off after Moira stopped running it. All the same, you'd never get people around here to use another name.'

'But I'm not looking to people in Cordale to be my customers,' Frances pointed out. 'I'm looking to a wider area. That's what I intend to do. And Beck House, or Beckside House, isn't all that much of a change, is it?'

'There's not a great appetite for change hereabouts,' Bernard persisted.

'But you're right, Frances, it isn't something completely different,' Joyce conceded, though still reluctantly. 'What people don't like is when someone from the city buys a cottage that's always been known as Number Five Church Row and puts up a fancy board saying "The Haven". Somebody did that in Kilby once, but everybody, even the postman, went on calling it Number Five. Still do!' She smiled. 'I quite like "Beckside House". If you're set on changing.'

'Yes, Beckside House would be my choice – if I decided to do it,' Frances said.

And it's my bet you will, Joyce thought. She was a bit of a goer, this lady – though pleasantly so. And nothing wrong with that. To run a successful business, you had to make it pay.

'I'd have to put up a new board, or how would anyone find me? Anyway,' Frances said, 'I'll give it some thought and bear in mind what you say. And now I'd like to take you up on your kind offer, Bernard, to give us a lift home. I think my mother's looking tired. It's been a long day.'

'I'm perfectly all right,' Madge said. She was dog-tired but she hated people saying she looked it.

'The car's right outside; won't take us more than a few minutes,' Bernard said. 'And I'll stop off and take a look at your heating. If this cold snap continues you're going to be needing it.' He turned to his wife. 'I'll not be long, love. Back before closing time.'

As they walked back through the bar, Jim Kettle called

out to them. 'Goodnight, Mrs Hamilton, Mrs Fraser. See you tomorrow.'

'What a friendly man,' Madge said as they got into the car. 'It feels nice to be called by your name in a strange place.'

'Jim's all right,' Bernard said. 'And now they'll all be asking him who you are and where you come from!'

My mother's right, Frances thought. It was pleasant – as if they were no longer quite strangers. And when they went into the house, though she couldn't immediately and automatically put her hand on the light switch, when she did so, and the hall was flooded with light, there was the strongest feeling she had yet had that this was home.

The following morning, on the dot of eight o'clock, Frances opened the door to Jim Kettle. She took him through to the kitchen, where Madge was still at the breakfast table.

'You're nice and prompt,' Madge said with approval. 'Would you like a cup of tea before you make a start?'

'Thank you, Mrs Fraser. I had one last thing before I left home. I'll not bother now.' He turned to Frances. 'So if you'll show me where you want me to begin, I'll make a start. As soon as it's convenient to you, of course.'

'It's convenient right now,' Frances assured him. 'I've finished my breakfast, and it's a two-person job anyway; me to decide where things go, you to put them there. And of course I'll give a hand with anything that's too heavy for one person to move. I'm quite strong. Shall we make a start in the hall?'

'If you need me,' Madge said, 'you know where I am. I've got a few things to do in here.'

'As you can see,' Frances said to Jim as he followed her into the hall, 'it's all a bit cluttered here. I think the removal men got to the stage where they dumped everything in the nearest space.'

'Not to worry,' Jim said cheerfully. 'You just say where you want everything to go and I'll put it there. We'll soon get a bit of order into things.'

'Good!' Frances said. 'Now, these four chairs should be six chairs, though I've no idea where the other two can be. When we find them, all six should go in the dining-room, which is that room there.' She pointed across the hall. 'The table is already in there, but we might have to move it around.'

'Right,' Jim said. He picked up a chair in each hand as if they weighed no more than two bags of toffees. 'I'll put these four in place, then I'll look for the other two.'

'They could even be upstairs,' Frances said. 'Just go anywhere you like.'

The telephone rang in the kitchen. Seconds later Madge appeared in the hall. 'It's for you, love,' she said. 'A man. He asked for you. It's not Bernard: I would have recognized his voice.'

Frances followed her mother into the kitchen and picked up the phone. 'Frances Hamilton.'

'Alec Spence. Bernard Grayson asked me to ring you.'

The voice at the other end was not what Frances had expected – though why in the world would I know what to expect, she chided herself. It was deep and clear, the voice of someone who might be a good singer; a northern voice, but only slightly accented. All this, she thought, from just a few words. How silly I am!

'Thank you for ringing so promptly,' she said. 'Did Bernard tell you what it was about?'

'More or less,' Alec Spence said. 'Not in any detail. So what can I do for you?'

'I suspect quite a lot,' Frances said. 'You'll have to come to the house to see exactly what.'

'Of course,' he said. 'When would suit you? I can't come this morning, I have an appointment in Shepton. I expect Bernard told you my business is there. Would this afternoon suit you? Say, about five o'clock?'

'That would be fine,' Frances said. 'See you then.'

'Alec Spence will be here this afternoon,' she said to her mother. 'He sounded quite nice.'

Madge was happily ensconced in the kitchen, deep in the task of unpacking all that belonged in the old dresser, and the kitchen crockery which would go into the wall cupboards. She insisted on washing every pot and pan, though Frances knew for certain that they had all been as clean as a whistle before they'd been packed. 'Do you need to wash them again?' she asked.

'Oh yes,' Madge said firmly. 'We don't know who used these packing cases before us, do we? Better safe than sorry.'

'OK, if you say so,' Frances said. She could foresee from the way her mother was immersing herself in the job that she was going to be queen of the kitchen. And that was fine, since she herself had no aspirations in that direction.

'If you're all right here I'll go and sort out things with Jim Kettle,' she said.

She worked with Jim for the rest of the morning, she deciding, as best she could for the moment, where things should go, and he putting them into place. Only occasionally did he call on her for help with something awkward. Joyce was right. This pint-sized man was uncommonly strong. By half-past eleven, which was the time he said he must leave to get down to the Shorn Lamb, things were beginning to look more shipshape. 'Though there's still a lot to do,' she said to Jim, 'so you will be able to help me for a few days yet, I hope?'

'I'll be glad to,' Jim said. 'Where would you like me to put these two tea chests?'

'My best china is in those,' Frances said. 'If you'd take them into the dining-room, then I can unpack them. The sideboard is one of the things the removal men did put in its right place, so if you'd leave the chests somewhere near it . . . Do you want a hand?'

'No, thanks, I can manage. I'll just do that, then I'll be off. I'll see you at half-eight in the morning – unless, of course, you're coming down to the Lamb for a meal tonight?'

'We might,' Frances said. 'It depends on what we can concoct from what's here in the house – and how much energy we have left.'

She saw him to the door, then stood there a few minutes as he walked swiftly down the hill. What a likeable man he was. He had a quietly contented look about him, as if he was happily married, loving his wife and enjoying his children. She hoped that was so.

It was a pleasant day. The autumn sun picked out the ancient stone church tower, which she had not realized was visible from her own door, and lit the remaining leaves on the few trees. One

51

good storm, one gale-force wind, and the leaves would go, leaving bare branches. Still and all, she had always liked trees in winter: she liked the architecture of them, from the trunks to the smallest twigs – a beauty hidden in summer. There was very little wind today, not enough to dislodge a single leaf, she thought. It would be a good day for a walk if only she had the time. As it was, she turned back into the house, closed the door behind her and went into the dining-room, where she knelt down and started to unpack the two tea chests.

They contained the dinnerware she and Malcolm had been given as wedding presents, mostly by members of the Hamilton family. Wedgwood. Gleaming white bone china with a crimson and gold border. It was beautiful, of course, there was no denying that, but it would never have been her choice. It was the choice of Malcolm's mother. She herself would have preferred something lighter, more modern, and indeed less expensive – something she would not have been in terror of dropping and breaking every time they used it. Not that they had used it often. It was dinnerware made to accompany a long marriage and hand down to one's children. Her marriage had been short, and had encompassed no children, only a swift, early miscarriage in the first year of it. Every piece of china in the set had outlived their marriage. The truth was, and it came to her suddenly as she put the pieces carefully away, that she hated it. She would like to throw it against the wall. Or, she thought when the fierce rage had passed over almost as soon as it had begun, I could be sensible and sell it. It would pay for at least one bathroom. As it was, she put every single piece in the sideboard – it took up a lot of room – and closed the door on it.

Her mother came in from the kitchen. 'Shall we have beans on toast for lunch? Would that be all right, love?' she asked.

'Fine,' Frances agreed. 'I'm more than ready to break off.'

'I was thinking,' Frances said later as they were sitting at the table, 'I was thinking I could sell the Wedgwood.'

Her mother could hardly have been more shocked had she said 'I'm thinking of selling my body'.

'Selling the Wedgwood?' she cried. 'Frances, you can't sell the Wedgwood!'

52

'Actually, I can,' replied Frances – and felt a certain lightness as she said the words. 'It's mine. I never use it. I didn't want it in the first place. It would probably pay for two bathrooms.'

'Frances, you can't sell the Wedgwood to pay for bathrooms!' Madge was genuinely perturbed. 'If you're short of money I could let you have a bit more. You made me keep more than I'll ever need.'

'Mother, you are a sweetie,' Frances said. 'And it's not that I'm desperate for the money. It's such a waste keeping dinner plates when I could put them to better use.'

'But it's so beautiful,' Madge said. 'And such lovely quality.'

'I know. But I have no love for it,' Frances said. Should I have given it to Malcolm when he went off with Michelle? she asked herself. She could cheerfully have thrown it at him, plate by plate, meat dish, gravy boat and two tureens. 'Anyway, I haven't decided. I don't have time to think about it right now.'

After lunch Madge said, 'I think I'll go and have my little nap. I've missed it the last day or two and I always feel better for it. Just to lose myself for a little while.'

'You do that,' Frances said. 'I was thinking earlier I'd like to go for a walk. It's such a lovely day.'

'Then you do that, love,' Madge said. 'A break will do us both good. We've worked very hard. Where will you go?'

'I'm not sure,' Frances said. 'Perhaps I'll walk up the side of the beck, see where it leads me.'

'Be back before Mr Spence arrives,' Madge cautioned.

A gate at the bottom of the garden led onto the path that ran uphill alongside the beck. Walking through the overgrown garden Frances thought, not for the first time, that she must do something about it. Shrubs and bushes, a few scabby pink roses among the thorns on some of them, ran riot, each one tangled with its neighbours. Apples still lay on the ground where they had fallen from the tree. She was surprised to see, as she approached the gate, a few bronze chrysanthemums in bloom – and badly in need of staking – next to a mass of untidy Michaelmas daisies. When she came back, she decided, she would cut some of them to take into the house. Who in the past had made this garden? she wondered. Who had had time to spare from farming? It didn't sound like something Ben Thornton, from what she had heard of him, would do – and when would the hardworking Moira have had a moment? But whoever had made it in the first place, plainly nothing had been done here for quite some time. It would also, she reckoned, be another stretch of time before she had the leisure to garden. Fortunately, being at the back of the house, its neglect wouldn't show, just as long as she dealt with it before the first visitors came.

The path beside the beck was well marked and negotiable, the grass short. Possibly sheep wandered here? It climbed more steeply as she went on, the beck, brown and peaty, rushing by on her right, hurling itself over stones, as if desperate to join the river and be swept, eventually, out to sea. Wasn't that the end and the ambition of all becks and streams and rivers? The steepness of the fell meant that she had to press on without really seeing the view ahead, so when at one point she stopped to straighten up and to take her breath she was surprised to find that she was already halfway up the hill. She looked back towards the village. It seemed so compact, so all of a piece, clustered round the church. She picked out the Shorn Lamb and noted two black-and-white collies waiting outside the door. A woman in the High Street pushed a small child in a buggy and a man was cutting the grass in the churchyard. Possibly the vicar?

Turning her back on Kilby she decided to walk further up the hill. The beck was narrower here; she reckoned she must be near its beginning. There was a stone escarpment ahead and she wondered if that might be its source. Even at this height there were sheep around, if only a few. She looked at her watch, checking to see if she had time to carry on, and was surprised to see that it was after four o'clock. Alec Spence was due at five and she had a few things to do before he arrived. The escarpment, and the top of the fell beyond it, would have to wait for another day. If the weather held, she would endeavour before long to give herself a day off, pack a picnic, and climb to the very top.

It was quicker coming down. In parts she had deliberately to slow her steps because of the steepness. She was back in the house before half-past four and found her mother in the kitchen, making a pot of tea.

'Did you have a good walk?' Madge asked.

'Lovely,' Frances said. 'Did you have a good sleep?'

'You know me, love,' Madge said patiently. 'You know I never sleep well, never have. But I closed my eyes for a while.'

'I've decided on the new name for the house,' Frances said. 'Definitely Beckside House. It's perfect.'

FIVE

A little after five o'clock Frances, looking out of the window, saw a silver Mercedes coupé being driven up the hill and, as she watched, taking the turn towards Beck Farm – though no longer to be thought of as that, she reminded herself, but as Beckside House. A silver Mercedes? Surely not? But, as once having made the turn from the road the lane petered out a few yards past the house, where else could it be going? And indeed it came to a smooth halt immediately outside her front door. It had to be Mr Spence. But *why not?* she chided herself. Why the surprise? Why should she have expected – if she had thought about it at all – something in the nature of a Ford that had seen better days, or an estate car piled up in the back with the mishmash of a builder's trade?

She watched the driver alight from the car, unfolding himself because of his height, and then pulled herself together to go to the door, which she reached exactly as he rang the bell. Her mother, who must surely have been watching from another room, was no more than a few yards behind her as she opened it.

He certainly was tall. About six-foot-three, she guessed. He would have to stoop to step into the house, but he was also so slender that it would take at least two of him, standing side by side, to fill the width of the doorway. His black hair, cut short, grew well back from his high forehead – in another year or so it would be described as receding – and his brown eyes were set deep beneath straight, thick eyebrows as dark as his hair. With his perfectly oval face, his olive skin and the blue five o'clock shadow round his chin and upper lip, he looked as though he had arrived on the doorstep from some Mediterranean country. Italy perhaps, Frances thought, if it weren't for his height. But when he spoke it was the same pleasant voice she had heard on the telephone.

'Alec Spence,' he said. 'And you must be Mrs Hamilton?'

'I am,' Frances said. 'Please come in. This is my mother, Mrs Fraser. It's good of you to come so quickly.'

'Bernard said you wanted to make an early start,' Alec Spence said.

'Come through to the kitchen,' Frances said. 'It's the only really habitable room in the house, as yet. And it's not so much that I'm in a hurry to have the building done as that I need to know what's possible and what it will cost.'

'Would you like a cup of tea, Mr Spence?' Madge interrupted.

'Thank you. Yes, I would,' he answered.

'Then it would make more sense if I took you round the house and told you the plans I have in mind while my mother's making the tea,' Frances suggested. 'Shall we do that?'

He nodded. 'Sure.'

'Most of the alterations I want to make are upstairs,' Frances said as they left the kitchen. 'There are a few things on the ground floor, and quite a number out at the back, but I think those will mostly have to wait.'

As she walked around the bedrooms with him she told him what she envisaged, and he listened. She had expected him to come out with several reasons why what she had in mind wasn't possible – the walls wouldn't stand it, the floor wasn't strong enough, the drains couldn't cope, whoever had built the house had got it wrong in the first place – but there was none of that. He listened, and for the most part he nodded agreement. 'Though I have one or two suggestions I'll put to you when we get down to it,' he said. 'There's very little you'll need permission for, and there's no change of use, which can sometimes be a bit tricky, because it's been a bed-and-breakfast before. It'll be different when it comes to doing something with the outbuildings – depending on what you have in mind, of course – but we'll meet that when we come to it.'

'Perhaps you know the house,' Frances said. 'Have you done any work here before?'

'Nothing at all,' he said. 'Though there are certainly things that should have been done. I can see it's been neglected.'

'Did you know Ben Thornton?' asked Frances.

'I did. I suppose I've always known him but not well. I lived away from Kilby for a while. According to my mother he wasn't an easy man to know, especially towards the end. She said he was becoming a bit of a recluse.'

'Did you know his wife?' she asked.

'I knew his first wife, Moira – or, I should say, my mother did. I didn't know the second one well. I heard she was very different. Years younger. She didn't come from around here. And then, as I said, I lived away from Cordale for a while and it was mostly then that she was here. I met her once when I was over to visit my mother. We went in the Lamb and she was there with her husband . . .'

Madge's voice floated up the stairs. 'The tea's ready. Don't let it get cold.'

'We'll be down in a minute,' Frances called back.

Back in the kitchen, as they drank the tea Alec said, 'I'll send a man to measure up, tomorrow if that suits you, and then I think your next step is to come to my place in Shepton and see what's on offer. Style, colour, that sort of thing.'

'Yes, I'd like to do that,' Frances said. 'I don't want anything over the top but I do want things to look nice.'

'Sure,' Alec said. 'And when it comes to tiles, fittings and so on, white is nearly always cheaper – and, what's more, it never goes out of fashion. Colours come and go. What about next week, then? That would give me time to do some drawings for you.'

'That would be fine by me,' Frances agreed.

'Then I'll give you a ring and we'll fix it. Or maybe I'll see you in the Lamb, if you happen to be there.'

'We might well be,' Frances said. 'It seems a good place to get to know people, which I want to do. You live in Kilby, don't you?'

'I do now,' he said. 'I came back to live here after my mother died. She left her cottage to me. As I'd been born and brought up in it I decided I'd rather live there than sell it. It's plenty big enough for one person. And as a place to live I prefer Kilby to Shepton. It's quieter. And it's far enough away from my business, but not too far.'

He jumped to his feet. 'Right, well, I'll be off.' He turned to Madge. 'Thank you for the tea, Mrs Fraser.'

Frances watched him drive off in his silver Mercedes. In fact, she conceded, on better acquaintance he had turned out to be a man well suited to drive an expensive car. There was something about him, though at the moment she couldn't define what. He seemed in charge. He had an air of confidence, of success, about him. She wondered what had gone wrong with *his* marriage. It must have been something serious to cause him to be parted from his children.

'He seems a very nice young man,' Madge said when Frances went back into the kitchen.

Her mother's idea of young was different from her own. 'I'd think he's about my age,' said Frances. 'Perhaps a year or two older.'

'Yes,' Madge repeated, 'a nice young man. And very successful, wouldn't you say?'

'Oh yes, I'd agree with that,' Frances replied. 'And he had some good ideas.'

The following afternoon the doorbell rang while Frances was on the top of a stepladder, taking down the sitting-room curtains. She had reached the last of the windows in this room and the curtains from the others lay on the floor, waiting to be dealt with by her mother. These and the curtains in all the other rooms, as well as sundry rugs and carpets that had mostly seen better days, had been left in place by the executors, who considered them to be of no use to anyone except possibly the new owner of Beck Farm.

'I don't like any of them,' Frances had said of the curtains. 'I shall replace them as soon as I can find what I want.'

'Well, in the meantime they've absolutely got to be washed,' Madge declared. 'They're filthy.' She wrinkled her nose in disgust. 'How anyone could live with them . . . but, then, men don't notice these things, do they? Your father, bless his heart, never did, though he was the cleanest of men himself. Never a day without his shower.'

But she couldn't wash curtains, she'd pointed out, until the washing machine was plumbed in, and this very morning it had been.

'Damn!' Frances said. 'Who in the world can *this* be?' But her mother had already gone to find out, so Frances remained where she was, hoping it was no-one she need see. And yet, she thought, struggling with a recalcitrant hook that had somehow embedded itself in the material, shouldn't I be glad people are ringing at my door, even if uninvited? Wouldn't it be worse if everyone bypassed me?

She was still at the top of the stepladder when her mother returned, accompanied by a man.

'It's the vicar,' Madge announced.

He didn't look like a vicar, Frances thought, but then they often didn't. In the neighbourhood where she'd lived in Brighton the vicar was more often to be seen in shorts and a sweatshirt than in a cassock and clerical collar. This one wore blue jeans and a black roll-neck sweater. He had untidy red hair and a freckled skin. She judged he was his thirties and immediately found herself wondering what, at that age, he was doing in a country living. She would have expected someone more venerable, on the edge of retirement perhaps, though she hoped she didn't show her surprise as she came down the steps and shook hands with him.

'Clive Moorby,' he said. 'I heard you'd moved in. I thought I'd come by to welcome you.'

'That was kind,' Frances said. 'Do sit down.'

'Thank you. Just for a minute,' he said, seating himself on the edge of the nearest easy chair, and Frances also sat, although she hoped, not unkindly, that he wouldn't stay long.

60

'Would you like a cup of tea?' asked Madge, inevitably, and with a show of eagerness Frances didn't at the moment appreciate. She was far too busy to break off and drink tea, even though it *was* nice of him to call. In any case he was probably offered tea wherever he went and was quite sick of it.

'Thank you, I won't,' he said politely. 'I just popped in for a minute or two.'

There was a longish pause. Frances wondered why someone who seemed so shy should have chosen to be a priest. She cast around for something to say but in the end he beat her to it.

'I'm pleased to see someone living in the house,' he said. 'I'm sure everyone is. It's a nice house, isn't it? Not that I know it well.'

'You didn't know the previous owner, Mr Thornton?' Frances asked.

'Not really,' the vicar said. 'I met him once or twice. I haven't been here long, you see. He seemed rather a sad man, I thought, but perhaps that was because he was ill and I didn't know it. He died not long after I came here. I buried him.'

'So you wouldn't have known his second wife, then?' It was Madge who asked the question.

'I didn't know he had a second wife,' the vicar said. 'No-one mentioned her. There was no-one at his funeral except the villagers. I always find it rather sad when there's no family present.'

Why is so little known, or said, about Ben Thornton's second wife? Frances wondered fleetingly.

'Well, I must be going,' he said. 'I have to pick up the children from school. They'll be out soon and I like to be there.'

'That's nice,' Madge said. 'How old are they?'

'Six,' he told her. 'Twins. A boy and a girl.'

'How lovely!' Madge said.

What she really wanted to know – Frances could read her like a book – was why his wife wasn't picking up the children. It was, after all, a wife's job.

As if he too could read her mind he said, 'Laura's a teacher. She teaches maths at the comprehensive in Lofton. She's lucky if

61

she gets home before six o'clock any day. So I'll be off. Anyway, I can see you're both busy.'

Frances saw him to the door, her mother hovering near. 'Thank you for calling, Mr . . .' Frances said.

'Clive,' he said. 'People usually call me Clive. It was a pleasure. If there's anything I can do, just let me know. I'm actually quite a handyman.' He fished in his pocket. 'I brought you the church magazine,' he said. 'You might find bits of it interesting. Am I . . .' He hesitated. 'Am I likely to see you in church?'

Frances shook her head. 'Probably not. You might see my mother from time to time.'

He turned to Madge. 'You'd be very welcome. There's quite a lot goes on,' he said.

He walked off vigorously along the lane, turning to wave when he reached the corner.

'Well, it seems to be our day for people calling,' Madge said. 'First the plumber, then the vicar. Who next, I wonder? You know things go in threes.'

'*You* know,' Frances said. Her mother was full of folklore like that. Break two of anything on the same day, for instance, and you must then prevent a third breakage of something precious by snapping a match in half.

'It's true,' Madge said. 'I've noticed it time and time again in my life.'

'If you say so,' Frances said. 'Anyway, while we're waiting for the next mishap I'll get this curtain down.'

'Well, before you do that I'd like you to go outside with me and help to shake the ones we've taken down. They're full of muck and dust; they'll clog up the washing machine if we don't.'

'OK,' Frances agreed.

They were shaking the second curtain when the phone rang. My mother was right, Frances thought, they were full of muck and dust. 'Wasn't that the phone?' asked Madge.

'Yes,' Frances said. 'But I can't leave in the middle of shaking this, can I?'

The phone stopped.

'There, you see,' Madge said: 'I was right. You pooh-poohed me, but I was right.'

'What are you talking about?' Frances asked.

'Things going in threes. Two visitors ringing the doorbell, and now the telephone.'

'And does that count as a visitor?'

'Of course it does,' said Madge. 'It was someone wanting to get into the house, wasn't it? A visitor by phone.'

'OK, Mother, you win,' Frances said, laughing.

She folded the curtain and went back to the house. On the doorstep she turned round. 'What if it was a wrong number?' she said. 'Does that count?'

'Oh *you*!' Madge said. 'Don't you believe in anything?'

Do I? Frances asked herself as she climbed back up the stepladder and resumed the struggle with the hook. Do I? Surely I must? She had felt awkward and sad when she'd given the vicar such a blunt refusal when he asked her about going to church – and with no explanation. If there was an explanation it lay in the fact that she had thrown out so much over the last few years. The less baggage you carried, the more easily you moved forward. She knew, in her heart, that somewhere in that thinking there was a flaw, but didn't want to explore it. It would be a sad person, though, who believed in nothing, no-one. But in fact she did: she believed in herself. She believed that what she wanted she must go after. She must set her own goals, and reach them by her own efforts. To rely upon anyone else, to be too deeply involved with another, didn't work. She'd tried it and it wasn't for her. Self-reliance was the key: 'master of my fate . . . captain of my soul', that sort of thing. For a minute the bleakness of the words, written by the poet in his self-confessed dark night, was something she understood. She had been there. But she no longer was, she reminded herself. He had defied the bleakness, and so would she.

At that point the hook, for no reason that she could see – she had simply persisted in making random movements against the cloth – slid out of the curtain and was there in her hand. She gave a cry of delight. 'Whoopee!' It seemed an affirmation that she could do whatever she made up her mind to do.

Her mother, coming into the room, said, 'What's the whoopee for?'

'Just a small triumph,' Frances said. 'I won the battle of the hook.'

'Good,' Madge said. 'I've got the first batch of curtains in the machine. But there's going to be a heck of a lot of ironing to do before we can hang them all, and the windows will have to be cleaned first. I don't think the panes have been touched for months, let alone the woodwork.' The words came out in a rush. She moved to the nearest chair and sat down heavily.

Frances gave her a sharp look. Something was wrong. It was not so much the words her mother had used, it was the unusual note of fatigue in her voice, as if her strength had left her. What she had just said was the kind of thing she might normally say, but usually it would be with the cheerful note in her voice of someone who would rise to whatever challenged her, and win, no question. Now she sounded defeated.

'Are you all right, Mother?' asked Frances. 'You sound tired.' Looking at her more carefully she saw that her mother was much too pale and there was a darkness around her eyes.

'I am a bit,' Madge confessed. 'It's nothing, it'll pass. It's just . . . well, there's a lot to do, isn't there?'

'There is,' Frances agreed. 'But we don't have to do it all in one day.' She understood her mother's feelings: she wanted to get everything spick-and-span, everything normal and fit to live in, with no delay. It was what she was used to in her own home, in fact, but then that was small and compact, not at all like this. 'Nor do you have to do quite so much,' she added. 'Really, you mustn't. For a start, why don't I get someone in to do the windows, not to mention some of the other jobs? Joyce said she'd try to think of someone who could help.'

'I'll be all right,' Madge said. 'No need to fuss. It was just something came over me. I'm quite capable of doing these things, you know.'

'Yes, I do know,' Frances said. 'But it's been hard going for us lately. You've been doing far too much and I shouldn't have let you. Anyway, you're not to do one more thing today, and that's an order. I shall move your own armchair into the kitchen where it's warm, and you're to sit and do nothing except watch television. Then if you feel like it later we can go down to the Shorn Lamb for a meal, not bother to cook here.'

Madge submitted willingly to having her chair moved into the kitchen and, with the television switched on, sat down with a deep sigh of satisfaction at the comfort of it. 'That's lovely,' she said.

This in itself disquieted Frances. It was so utterly unlike her mother. She was the one who always kept going when everyone else had flagged.

'Will you mind', Madge said after a while, 'if I don't go down to the Lamb? I think I'd sooner stay in.'

'Of course I don't mind,' Frances assured her. 'You can do whatever you like. I'll make us a light supper – might you fancy an omelette? – and you can have an early night.'

'Lovely,' Madge said. 'But you could go down to the pub. After supper, at any rate. It would make a change for you.'

'And leave you on your own?'

'That wouldn't bother me at all,' Madge said. 'Don't forget I've lived on my own for years now. You get used to it. Even if you were nervous at first – and I was – you get over it.'

'Well, we'll see,' Frances said. She might, she thought, make a quick visit to the Lamb to ask Joyce about getting some help rather more quickly than she'd planned to. Or she could phone her. She'd see how it went, how her mother was, though she was already looking more rested.

The washing machine switched itself off. She took the curtains out, then put in the second dirty pair. 'Will it drive you mad to have this on while you're sitting here?' she asked. 'They could wait until the morning.'

'It won't bother me,' Madge said. 'The noise will be drowned by the television.'

'One of the things I mean to do sooner rather than later', Frances said, 'is to get all these appliances, plus the freezer, out of the kitchen and into one of the outhouses. There's electricity there, so it shouldn't be difficult. Just a question of checking that everything's in working order. And now it's my turn to make *you* a cup of tea. Or what about a glass of sherry? It might perk you up a bit.'

'As a matter of fact,' Madge said, 'I think I will. It's after five o'clock so I suppose it's not too early.'

Frances smiled. 'Of course it isn't. There are no rules.' She took the sherry bottle from the dresser cupboard, poured a generous glass and handed it to her mother.

'Aren't you going to join me?' Madge asked.

'Not right now,' Frances said.

'If it's a nice day tomorrow you could hang the curtains on the line,' Madge said. 'I'm sorry I missed *Countdown*. I used to watch it every day but I haven't seen it for the last week or two. That Carol's really clever with figures. Your dad was like that. He never used a calculator. Did it all in his head. I'll watch *Neighbours*. I haven't seen that for some time.'

'You do that,' Frances said. She was practised in following her mother's digressions of talk.

Madge continued to chatter quietly as if there was nothing in the world wrong with her and, Frances observed, the colour was coming back into her cheeks, both things no doubt helped by the sherry. What would I do if my mother were to be ill? Frances asked herself. I must look after her better. When she herself had been a small child and her mother had fallen ill – which, thankfully, was seldom – she had always been terrified that she might die. Of course she'd got rid of that fear as she left childhood behind. But I must keep an eye on her, she thought now.

'I've one or two things to do,' she said. 'But you're to stay right where you are.'

'Don't do too much, love,' Madge advised. 'You know what I've always said about housework: it doesn't need salt on it to keep it. If you leave it today it'll still be waiting for you tomorrow.'

'You're a fine one to talk,' Frances said. 'When did you ever leave anything undone? But I won't be long. I'll be down to watch the seven o'clock news on Channel Four, and after that we'll have an early supper.'

'I hope you're not going to take down the curtains in my bedroom,' Madge said. 'I don't want to treat the village to a striptease.'

★   ★   ★

When she came back into the kitchen, just before seven, her mother had fallen into a sleep, her head lolling sideways, her glasses slipped down her nose, her mouth slightly open. In sleep she looked old, older than she really was, Frances thought. Seventy-two was no great age these days. She looked smaller, too, more vulnerable. I've brought her all this way, Frances chided herself uneasily – and did she really want to come? She had never actually said, one way or another, not in so many words. But I must cherish her, she told herself.

Moving quietly, she set about laying the table and preparing the meal. A can of good minestrone soup between them, and then an omelette.

She waited until the soup was ready to serve, then she tapped her mother lightly on the hand. 'Supper's ready, love,' she said gently. She supposed she could have left her alone, but she might have slept until bedtime and then had a wakeful night.

Madge came to with a start, her eyes suddenly wide open, startled, as if she didn't know where she was. 'What? Where . . . ?'

'It's OK,' Frances said. 'You've had a nice little nap and now supper's ready.'

Afterwards, Madge said, 'Are you going to go down to the Shorn Lamb? I'll be perfectly all right, you know.'

'I'm sure you would be,' Frances said. 'But I'm not going. I'm quite tired. Shall we both have an early night? And then I thought tomorrow morning we might go down to the village and do a bit of shopping. We're running out of a few things. And it would be nice to have some fresh bread. I'll take the car so we needn't carry everything back up the hill.'

'I'd like that,' Madge said. 'And I'll buy a few more postcards and some stamps.'

SIX

It was later than Frances had intended when she and her mother arrived at the village shop. She had taken advantage of the perfect day, crisp and dry, with a breeze, to hang out the curtains and she devoutly hoped it wouldn't rain. She was not familiar enough with the area to be able to take one look at the sky, or the direction of the wind, or the way the sheep were behaving in the fields or the birds were flying through the air, and from that forecast the weather. That, she hoped, would come. 'Do you remember, Mother,' she said, as they got into the car, 'how in Brighton we used to look at the sea to forecast the weather? Not only at how rough or smooth it was, but at the colour. Dull grey, menacing pewter, calm blue, or that exquisite turquoise which meant windy weather was on the way.'

'Of course I do,' Madge said. 'It's not that long ago, is it? Only a couple of weeks.'

'True,' Frances said, though already Brighton and Sussex seemed another world, some place known in the past with which she now had only the most tenuous connections. She had, she hoped, buried all the emotions which had ever bound her to that world.

'But I don't need any signs and portents to tell me it's nippy here today,' Madge said. 'I'll have to get my winter coat out even if it is only just October. It's nice and bright, though. I'll say that much for it.'

The shop was modest enough from the outside, with a window on either side of the central doorway (over which a narrow board said 'DORA LAYCOCK, PROP.). No attempt at window displays had been made. Cardboard models and cut-outs from various manufacturers of soap powders, hairsprays, medicines and confectionery were placed cheek by jowl, wherever there was space. In fact the lack of design hardly mattered, because much of the window was obscured by notices of meetings and events happening not only in Kilby but everywhere in the Cordale area – Women's Institute, British Legion, Horticultural Society, jumble sales, concerts, evening classes – with a large section in the right-hand window taken up by postcards offering services or secondhand ('as new', 'hardly used') items for sale. An armchair, a violin, puppies, a riding hat, and boots, size 5, CDs and videos, a single bed, piano lessons, a bedroom carpet.

Madge read them with interest while Frances went to find a place to park the car. 'You could furnish a house from this lot,' she said when her daughter returned.

The inside of the shop came as a surprise. For a start, it was much larger than might have been expected, because, clearly, a room behind the shop had been incorporated so that instead of a shop counter with a smiling Dora Laycock, proprietor, behind it wearing a white apron, it was all self-service: shelves chock-a-block with cans, bottles and packets, a greengrocery section, a large fridge with dairy produce and a wide selection of ice-creams and yoghurts, and at the end of the circuit, near to the door, a proper checkout. It was Kilby's answer to Sainsbury's, Frances thought, except that there were no shopping trolleys. Two trolleys would never be able to pass each other in the narrow aisles. It was not easy, as she quickly discovered, for two customers each with a wire basket to do so. There would have to be a lot of give-and-take, a constant murmur of 'excuse me, please' and 'would you mind?' to make it here.

Dora Laycock, her comfortably plump body encased in a pristine pink-and-white checked overall, her dark hair tied back in a ponytail, was standing at the checkout, attending to a customer. This hadn't, however, prevented her noticing Frances and Madge as they came in and breaking off for a second to say 'Good morning, ladies.' One up on Sainsbury's.

Between them, Frances and her mother found everything on their list with the exception of garlic bulbs. When Dora Laycock noticed them searching the greengrocery section, and her customer having left, she joined them. 'Can I help?' she said. 'Is there something you can't find?'

'Garlic,' Frances said. 'But perhaps it's here and I can't see it.'

'No, you're right, it's not,' Dora Laycock said. 'I'm sorry about that. I've sold out. I think everyone must be making stews and casseroles because it's turned cold. It *will* be here this afternoon, that's for sure. And in the meantime if it would help I could let you have some of mine. Perhaps not a whole bulb, but certainly a few cloves. So are you new to Kilby?'

'Yes,' Frances said. 'We've moved into Beck Farm. I'm Frances Hamilton and this is my mother, Madge Fraser.'

'Ah! I thought you must be,' Dora Laycock said. 'Word gets around.' She didn't say that a detailed description had been given to her two days ago, since when she had been awaiting their visit. 'Well, you're very welcome. And I hear you're going to set it up as a bed-and-breakfast again. That's nice, I must say. It was a good one once, in Moira's time. Quite successful. So I wish you luck.'

'Thank you,' Frances replied. 'And I can see I won't have to go into town to buy my supplies. You seem to have everything.'

'I do try,' Dora Laycock said. 'And of course if there was anything you wanted that I didn't have I could always get it for you. Anyway, I'll leave you in peace to finish your shopping. Take a good look around.'

They continued to do so, Frances popping things into their baskets until they were almost too heavy to carry.

'I reckon Kilby could withstand a siege,' she said. 'Especially if they managed to trap the butcher here at the start. They seem to have most other things.'

'Oh, but they do have a sort of siege from time to time,' Madge said knowledgeably. 'I can remember just after the war,

70

in that dreadful winter – it was before you were born, of course – several of the villages round here were cut off because of the snow. I expect Kilby was one of them. They had to drop food by plane. And the dairy farms couldn't get the milk away, though they had to go on milking the poor cows.'

'That's cheerful,' Frances said. 'Perhaps we should keep emergency supplies in the house?' But she was laughing.

'It was no laughing matter,' Madge said sharply. 'And yes, we probably should do that. After all, the winter's not far off. You never know.'

They had reached the checkout and were unloading the baskets when the shop door opened, letting in a blast of cold air and the vicar.

'Good morning, Mrs Fraser, Mrs Hamilton,' he said. 'Nice to see you. He nodded to Dora Laycock. 'Good morning, Dora. Everything all right?'

'Yes, thank you, Clive,' she said. 'Did you want much? I'm sure these two ladies would let you go in front of them if you're in a hurry.'

'No need,' he said. 'I'm OK.'

Frances went on unloading while Madge stood aside, chatting to the vicar. He seemed easier to talk to, less shy, than when he'd called at the house.

'I thought,' she said when they had exhausted the weather, 'I thought I might come to church on Sunday.' She was surprised to hear herself saying it. She didn't quite know *why* she was saying it. It just tripped off her lips. Out of the corner of her eye she saw Frances give her a telling look and hoped the vicar hadn't noticed. 'What time's the service?'

'It's at ten-thirty,' the vicar said. 'A parish Eucharist. A family service. I would prefer to have it earlier – people tend to watch the clock to get back to make Sunday lunch – but St Luke's is the main church around here and a number of people come in to Kilby from other parts of the dale, so I must allow for their journey time. And I've three other churches, so I have to juggle the times a bit. You would really be most welcome.'

'Thank you. It sounds just the right time to me,' Madge said. 'So, weather permitting, I'll be there.'

'Good,' the vicar said. 'And there's coffee in the hall afterwards. I hope you'll be able to stay for that, meet a few people.'

Frances completed her purchases, paid the bill, and joined them. If she had heard the conversation, she gave no immediate sign of it.

'These bags are heavy, Mother,' she said. 'Would you like to sit and wait here while I fetch the car?'

'Look, I only want two things,' the vicar interrupted. 'If you could just wait a minute I'll carry the bags to the car for you. No problem. Where are you parked?'

'By the Shorn Lamb,' Frances said. 'That would be very kind of you. I'd no intention of buying so much.'

He disappeared down an aisle, Dora Laycock with him. Frances and her mother sat on the two chairs by the door, and waited.

'What made you say you'd go to church?' Frances asked. 'You didn't have to do that, just because he's the vicar.'

'I know I didn't.'

The mixture of defence and defiance in Madge's voice was not lost on Frances. 'Well, I know you used to, but it's a long time ago,' she said. 'You didn't go much in Brighton.'

'I just decided I would,' Madge said. 'I thought I'd give it a try. New place, new lifestyle, what's wrong with new habits? Besides, he's such a nice young man. I feel a bit sorry for him. And I might meet a few people – I expect you heard him mention coffee after the service. I also read that church magazine he brought. He was right, there is a lot going on.'

'Suit yourself,' Frances said.

It might not be such a bad idea, she thought. It might be good for her mother to meet a few other people, especially those nearer her own age, start a social life of her own.

The nice young man came from the back of the shop to the checkout, followed by Dora Laycock. She dealt with his purchases, handed him a plastic bag and said, 'Goodbye, Clive. Give my best to Laura.'

He came to join Frances and Madge. 'Give me your bags,' he said. 'No, I can manage them all quite easily.' He handled them as if they were filled with cotton wool and set off at a brisk pace down the slope towards the Shorn Lamb.

When he had put all the shopping in the boot of Frances's car, 'There you are,' he said. 'Now, is there anything else I can help you with? What's the next item on your agenda?'

'We'd thought we'd call in at the Shorn Lamb for a drink and a sandwich lunch,' Frances said.

That's news to me, Madge thought. They hadn't discussed any such thing. All the same, it was a welcome idea.

'Would you like to join us?' she was surprised to hear her daughter saying. Why had Frances said it? Perhaps because she'd been offhand with her about the church, though the vicar wasn't to know that – or perhaps it was a thank-you for carrying the bags.

'I would like to, very much,' he said. 'Laura and I enjoy popping into the Shorn Lamb when we can. When we're lucky enough to have a baby-sitter we like to have a meal here. But I can't at the moment. Some other time, perhaps?'

'Sure,' Frances said.

'I'll be off, then,' he said – and shot away down the High Street.

It wasn't at all busy in the Lamb. Bernard was behind the bar and at one table a trio of walkers in shorts and heavy boots sat drinking beer. Apart from a couple of locals, that was all.

'You're quiet,' Frances said. 'Mother and I have been doing a bit of shopping in the village. We thought we'd pop in for a snack. Do you do food at lunchtime?'

'We do and we don't,' Bernard said. 'In the summer we have a lunch menu every day but at this time of the year there's less call for it. We'll always do something like ham and eggs, if asked. Something we can do on the spot, if we get walkers dropping in. After the end of October we don't do evening meals, except on Saturday nights. November is when me and Joyce take our holiday.'

'Oh!' Frances said. 'Where do you go?'

'Somewhere warm and sunny,' Bernard said. 'Majorca. Tenerife. We both like Tenerife.'

'So who looks after the Shorn Lamb?' Frances asked.

'Jim Kettle does that. We only go for a week. Anyway, you'd

like a bit of lunch, would you? I'll have a word with Joyce, see what's on offer. She's in the kitchen.'

As if summoned by thought, Joyce came into the bar. 'Hello. Nice to see you both,' she said.

'We were food shopping,' Frances explained. 'I must say, I was impressed by the village store.'

Joyce nodded. 'Oh yes. Dora keeps a good stock. I buy as much as I can there.'

'So shall we,' Madge put in.

'Frances was asking about lunch,' Bernard said. 'What can we offer?'

'Just a snack or a sandwich would be fine,' Frances said.

'As it happens,' Joyce said, 'I've made a batch of lasagnes. Individual-portion sizes. I could heat a couple of those if that takes your fancy.'

'Great,' Frances said. 'Does that suit you, Mother?'

'Down to the ground,' Madge said.

'Then I'll pop them in the oven right away,' Joyce said.

When she'd left the bar Bernard said, 'My wife's lasagnes are the best you'll get anywhere. They sell like hot cakes.'

'Why does everyone say "like hot cakes"?' Frances wondered out loud.

'I've no idea,' Bernard said.

'Frances has to know the why and the wherefore of everything,' Madge said apologetically. 'Always did, from the minute she could talk.'

'No harm in that,' Bernard said. 'What would you ladies like to drink?'

While Bernard was pouring the drinks Joyce returned from the kitchen. 'Won't be too long,' she said.

'There's no hurry,' Frances told her. 'Anyway, I wanted a word with you. I'm really anxious to get someone to help in the house. There's so much to do; every bit of paintwork needs washing – and lots of other things. We haven't finished unpacking yet. It's all hard work and my mother's getting rather tired.'

'I'm perfectly all right,' Madge protested.

'I know you are, love,' Frances said. 'But you're working too hard.'

74

'Well, I might have the answer,' Joyce said. 'I was going to give you a ring if you didn't come in this evening. I spoke to Rosie and she said her sister, Violet, will be glad to help out. She has two small children at school, so she'd come during school hours. The only thing is, she also has a baby, Daisy, and she'd have to bring her along. She's four months old and according to both her mother and her auntie Rosie she's as good as gold. What would you think about that?'

Frances felt uncertain: she wasn't into babies – she had sometimes wondered if she had any maternal instincts at all. And if she had had, would it have been better for her marriage? But before she could voice the faintest doubt her mother chipped in.

'That would be lovely, wouldn't it, Frances? No bother at all.'

Well, Frances thought, if my mother would concentrate a bit on the baby and stop heaving furniture around and scrubbing floors, that would be no bad thing. 'That sounds OK,' she said.

'What are the other children's names?' Madge asked.

'Heather and Hyacinth,' said Joyce.

'All flower names?' Madge said. 'Why is that?'

'It started with Rosie's father,' Joyce replied. 'Then Violet kept up the tradition. Rosie and Violet have two other sisters . . .'

'And they are named . . . ?' Frances asked.

'Pansy and Lilac. Their dad – that's to say, the granddad of Heather, Hyacinth and Daisy – is the president of the Cordale Horticultural Society.'

'What a good thing none of them had boys,' Madge said. 'All I can think of in that line is Sweet William.'

Two days later Frances went to Shepton to keep her appointment with Alec Spence. She hadn't realized it was market day there, and the town car park, though sizeable, was packed: not a space anywhere. In the end she gave up and drove off to find Alec Spence's showroom, which he had told her was near the top of the High Street, close to the church. There was no missing the church. Where the High Street divided, branching both left and right, the church stood square on raised land looking down over the town, as it had for hundreds of years, from what was possibly the most prominent position in Shepton. And as Alec Spence had promised, she found his shop not far away. There was no space to park in front of it but she risked leaving her car where it was and rushed into the showroom.

'I'm stuck,' she said. 'Right outside – and illegally. I just can't find anywhere to park.'

'I'm sorry,' Alec said. 'I should have warned you it was market day. I've got a space round the back. I'll come and direct you.' He turned to an assistant. 'Back in five minutes,' he said.

He guided her round to the back of the building, where a cobbled space was reserved for local traders. His silver Mercedes was already there. They got out of the car and went into the building by the back door. 'That was stupid of me,' he said. 'Having my own space I just forget what a horror it is parking in Shepton. It's bad any day but there are sheep sales today. That brings extra traffic – heavy stuff.'

'It certainly seemed very busy as I drove up the High Street,' Frances said. 'I didn't notice any of that when I stayed overnight with my mother, but of course the hotel had its own parking.'

'Where did you stay when you were in Shepton before?' Alec asked.

'At the Heifer,' Frances said. It was no more than a dozen yards from his showroom.

'I know it well,' he said, 'though I've never stayed there.'

He took her into his office and asked his secretary to bring coffee.

'My man brought the measurements of your rooms,' he said. 'Did he do everything you wanted him to do?'

'Oh yes, Mr Spence,' Frances said. 'He was most helpful. And very quick.'

'Alec,' he said. 'We are, after all, near neighbours. Yes, he's a good chap, Denis. He's been with me a long time. Anyway, I've done a few drawings. If you don't like them, if you'd prefer something different, then there are alternatives, though not in every room. It depends on the shape of the space.'

He spread out the drawings on a table and between them they scrutinized them.

'If you would be happy to have a shower cubicle in most places, rather than a bath with a shower over it, that would help.

76

You can fit a shower in quite a small space – like here, for instance.' He pointed it out to her. 'And the loo and basin can go next to it, simplifying the plumbing, which is always a good thing.'

'Yes, that's fine in some cases,' Frances agreed. 'But I would like one or two bedrooms with bath. There'll always be people like my mother who prefer baths. She wouldn't give you two-pence for a shower. So we'll find a compromise, I think, don't you?'

It didn't take long to sort it out between them. There were after all, Alec pointed out, limits to what could be done.

'Right, then,' he said. 'If you're happy about that, shall we go and look at some fittings and tiles, that sort of thing?'

'That's the bit I'm happier with,' Frances confessed. 'I'm not good at seeing where things will fit and where they won't. I read an article in the newspaper the other day which said that men are usually spatially gifted and women aren't. That's why women can't reverse cars well!'

Alec laughed. 'And did that annoy you?'

'It annoys me that I don't have the gift,' Frances said, 'but I had to agree with it. I hate reversing my car.'

'But women are better on colour,' Alec said. 'I'm not sure that men see the finer shades of colour differences. So shall we put that to the test?'

'We can,' Frances said, 'but bearing in mind that you advised me to choose white . . .'

'You don't have to take my advice,' Alec said, 'though it might be as well to take it on the actual fixtures and fittings.'

She was surprised by the range of the stock in his showroom. Most of the things she'd seen in the glossy magazines she'd been studying over the last weeks were here in some form or another, though her choice was limited by considerations of money as well as space. 'I'm trying not to think what I'd like in my own ideal bathroom,' she said as they went around.

'Save that for a later date,' Alec said. 'Remember you're running a business.'

In the end she settled on white for the basics, but added a few small coloured tiles as accents and to make for variety.

'Would you like to take some samples home with you?' Alec asked.

'That would be nice to show my mother,' she said. 'I would have brought her with me but she was rather tired so I persuaded her to have a rest.'

'I'll tell you what I'll do,' Alec said. 'I know now what you have in mind, so I'll make up a box of sample tiles for your mother to see, and I'll take photocopies of some of the drawings for her. I'll bring them round to you later this week.'

'That would be wonderful,' Frances said.

Alec looked at his watch. 'And now I'd like to give you lunch before you go back,' he said. 'We could go to the Heifer. They do a decent lunch.'

'How nice of you,' Frances said. 'Thank you.'

The Heifer was packed, though a table was soon found for Alec, who was clearly a regular customer. While they were waiting to be served he said, 'Shall we discuss timing, Frances? When do you hope to open up?'

'Definitely by next Easter,' Frances answered. 'I want everything ready a week before Easter. I'm sorry I won't be able to do anything about the outhouses by then. I wish I could. There's so much potential for letting them. If I made them self-contained I'm sure I could get two units, possibly three. But of course it will need planning permission and I don't know how long that will take – or even if I *would* get it . . . or could afford it just yet.'

'Oh, I think you'd get permission,' Alec said. 'You'd have to keep to rules and regulations but I reckon the Powers That Be are quite keen to do anything to improve the economy in the Dales. Tourism is the thing. It brings employment, and it brings visitors who spend money. We need visitors. Farming's such an up-and-down thing and the young aren't going into it as they once did.'

'I'll have to see,' Frances said. 'It would be interesting to know what it would cost.'

'Well, I'm not a builder,' Alec said, 'but I do know a bit about conversions. I could look at it with you and if you decided you wanted to go further I'm sure I could recommend a builder.'

'That would be great, as long as you know I can't commit myself, not just yet,' Frances said.

'OK,' Alec said. 'You'd set the pace. And speaking of pace, if you want bookings for next Easter you'll have to get your advertising in the right places by Christmas at the latest. I'm sure you've thought of that.'

'Of course I will,' Frances said. 'I have a good idea where I'll place the ads. I've been looking into that and I'll need a good photograph of the house – which reminds me, I'm going to change the name.'

'Change the name?' He looked surprised.

'Oh, not vastly,' Frances said. 'I'm going to call it Beckside House.'

'Well, if you must change it, then that's quite good,' Alec said.

'So I will need a new house sign. Where would I get one done? I want something good.'

'As it happens, I do know a chap in Tendale,' Alec said. 'Malachi Flint, an old shepherd. He does things in wood. I'm sure he'd do a good job. Lives in Kirkholme – it's a hamlet in Tendale. Do you know Tendale?'

'No,' Frances admitted. 'I know of it, of course. I know where it is, but I've never been there even though it's only over the hill from Cordale.'

'Then that's something to be remedied,' Alec said. 'It's beautiful, though very different from Cordale. And, of course, the drive over the top is spectacular. In fact . . .'

She looked at him while waiting for him to continue. He was not only attractive – that alone, she thought, wouldn't have interested her: good-looking men were too often aware of it – he was not overly charming, setting out to impress her. She could also recognize that when she met with it. He was . . . well, *real*. The sort of man who, if one knew him better, might become a friend.

'In fact,' he continued, 'I could take you there, if you like. I could introduce you to Tendale and to Malachi at the same time.'

'I'd like that very much,' Frances said quickly.

'It would have to be a Sunday,' Alec said. 'Would that be all right?'

'Absolutely,' Frances said.

'So shall we make it next Sunday?' he suggested.

They finished the meal and he took her back to her car.

'Thank you, Alec,' she said. 'You've been most helpful. I'm looking forward to it all happening. And I look forward to Sunday.'

'So do I,' he said. 'I'll let you have written details of everything, and all the costings, one evening this week.' He saw her into her car, closed the driver's door and guided her out into the heavy stream of traffic.

SEVEN

True to his promise, Alec Spence turned up at Beckside House at seven in the evening, bringing with him a folder full of drawings and a box of sample tiles.

'This is exciting,' Madge said. 'And very kind of you. Frances told me what she'd seen and what you'd discussed, but it's nice to set eyes on things, isn't it? I'm sorry I wasn't quite up to coming into Shepton.'

'So Frances told me. I hope you're feeling better,' Alec said.

'Oh yes,' Madge assured him. 'I'm as fit as a fiddle again. And I hear you're going to take Frances to see a man about making a new sign for the house.'

'That's right,' Alec said. He turned to Frances. 'If I pick you up about ten-thirty, would that be all right?'

'Fine,' Frances said.

'I'm sorry I shan't be able to come,' Madge said. 'I'm going to church. I promised the vicar and I wouldn't want to let him down. A promise is a promise, isn't it?'

'That's true,' Alec agreed. 'But perhaps some other time.'

'Would you like a drink?' she offered.

Alec shook his head. 'It's kind of you, Mrs Fraser, but I mustn't stay. I've brought a load of work home with me. There's never enough time in the day to keep up with the paperwork.'

'You shouldn't make a habit of taking work home,' Madge

reproved him. 'Burning the candle at both ends isn't a good idea. I used to tell my husband that – not that he took any notice. And you can call me Madge.'

'I'd be interested to go through the drawings with you, Alec,' Frances interrupted. 'Standing in the rooms where it's going to happen would make it seem more real. Do you have the time for that?'

'Of course,' he said.

He followed her upstairs, where they went from room to room. Everything in the plans, all his suggestions, made good sense to her and when he gave her the final cost, though it was a little over her budget, it was well within her reach.

'I'm so pleased,' she said. 'And I'm truly grateful.'

'It was a pleasure,' Alec said. 'And when the work starts I promise to keep a close eye on it.'

'Good,' Frances said. 'Do you really not have time for a drink, or a cup of coffee?''

'I really don't,' he said. 'But I look forward to Sunday.'

'He's a nice young man,' Madge said when he'd left. 'Did you say he was divorced?'

'I did,' Frances said. 'And before you ask, Mother, I've no idea why. We didn't discuss it. Why would we? He has two children who live with his ex in Leeds. She married again.'

'Oh yes. I remember now. It's sad, isn't it? But there's a lot of it about.' Madge spoke as if it was some sort of virus.

The following morning, at a quarter to nine, Violet turned up, pushing a pram in which baby Daisy was so cocooned that little remained visible of her except her small nose, and her eyes, which were closed in sleep.

'Oh, isn't she sweet,' Madge cooed. She never said so, nor would she ever, but it was one of life's disappointments that her only child didn't have babies, didn't seem to mind that she hadn't, and time was racing by. In her heart she had looked forward to an old age in which there were children running around, never mind if they were noisy. She would have been able to do things for them. Knit, read stories, make gingerbread men. Take them to the park and push them on the swings. All the things she'd enjoyed doing for Frances when she was little, but being a child didn't last long, did it, and Frances had grown up quickly.

'Do come in,' Frances said to Violet. 'Will it be all right to leave Daisy in her pram in the hall while you and I go into the kitchen and talk about what there is to do?'

Violet was rather like her name: slender, pretty in a delicate-looking sort of way, not very tall. Frances wondered if Violet's sisters, Pansy, Rosie and Lilac, resembled the flowers they were named after. And what about the two siblings of this little one in the pram? Heather and Hyacinth. Heather sounded a bit prickly, Hyacinth stately. People sometimes did grow into their names.

'She'll be fine,' Violet said. 'She usually sleeps a couple of hours at this time of day.'

'Don't worry. I'll keep an eye on her,' Madge offered.

Frances took Violet into the kitchen and they sat at the table while Frances outlined what Violet's duties would be. 'Though at the moment,' she warned her, 'it's a case of turning your hand to whatever needs doing next. There's plenty to do before we can even start on a routine.'

'I'll do whatever you say, Mrs Hamilton,' Violet said agreeably. She had a soft voice, which somehow also fitted well with her name. 'Just tell me and I'll get on with it. Of course, I won't be able to come every morning. I have to take Daisy to the Baby Clinic once a week while she's so young – that's in Dr Fortune's house on a Thursday morning. Then there's school holidays, but I might be able to juggle jobs with Rosie, or perhaps bring the children here with me. They're very good.'

'Well, we'll see,' Frances said. She wasn't at all sure about that. 'We'll meet it when we come to it. So to begin with, four mornings a week, two hours a time. And I'll pay you whatever the going rate is here. You must tell me that.'

'It's usually four pounds an hour,' Violet said, somewhat apologetically. 'That's what Mrs Grayson pays Rosie at the Lamb.'

'That's OK,' Frances said. In Brighton it had been five pounds or more – and in cash. 'Do you want to make a start now? I'll go round with you, show you what there is to do and we can decide what's best to begin with.'

'I might as well,' Violet said.

She took off her coat, revealing a pale mauve overall that made her look even more like her namesake.

While Violet cleaned the paintwork in the downstairs rooms – to her mind it hadn't been touched for a *very* long time – Daisy did as had been promised, and slept, at least for the first hour and a half, at the end of which she gave a few little whimpers and then broke into a full-blooded cry. Violet climbed down from the steps – she was cleaning the tops of the window frames – and went to her daughter, but Madge was in the hall before her, jiggling the pram. 'Poor little lamb, I expect she's hungry,' she said.

'I don't think so,' Violet said. 'She's not due to be fed for another hour or so.' She opened a plastic box that was lying at the foot of the pram and took out a dummy, which she offered to the baby. Daisy seized on it eagerly and began to suck.

'Well, that did the trick, didn't it?' Madge said to Violet. 'Now, when I was younger, dummies were frowned on. They said they caused buckteeth.'

'Times change, don't they?' Violet said politely. 'And they call them "pacifiers" nowadays.'

'It's a nicer name,' Madge said. 'And whatever it's called it seems to work.'

While they watched, Daisy gradually stopped sucking, the pacifier fell from her mouth and she was asleep again.

'I'll get back to work,' Violet said.

'You do that, love,' Madge said. 'I'll just stay here for a minute or two, see she's all right.' In her heart she would have preferred it if Daisy had refused to be pacified and she had been called upon to pick her up and nurse her.

Sunday came, and at quarter-past ten Madge set off for church. It was quite a time since she'd been to church – though she never missed Christmas Day and Easter Day – so she was looking forward to a new yet familiar experience. Churches, vicars and even congregations did, after all, differ from one another. She expected she would know the service, and perhaps, this being a

84

village, they would stick to the old hymns. She hoped so.

Madge walked at an even pace, listening to the church bell now ringing, and when she arrived at the door a friendly man smiled at her and, in answer to her question, said yes, she could sit anywhere she liked. 'No seats are reserved in St Luke's,' he assured her. She chose a pew halfway down, not so far forward as to be conspicuous, not so far back that she couldn't hear if the vicar chose to mumble. He didn't when he was out and about, but you never knew what it would be like when vicars started using holy words. Some of them had special voices for that. She knelt down and said some prayers, including one for Frances, who had given up church when her hypocrite of a husband, who had been a regular churchgoer, had gone off with the other woman. She knew she should also have prayed for him but she could never bring herself to do it.

On the dot of half-past ten the Mercedes drew up outside the house, Frances picked up her handbag and was at the door by the time Alec had got out of the car.

'You're very prompt,' she said.

'I'm afraid so,' Alec said. 'It's a habit with me. Not everyone likes it.'

'But I do,' Frances said.

He held the car door open while she got into the front seat. 'It's a beautiful morning,' he said as they drove off. 'We'll be able to see the countryside at its best. There could just as well have been a mist or rain at this time of the year. I thought we'd go by way of Kingsdale to Kirkholme. It's the quickest route and it's beautiful, but it's not the most spectacular. We'll save that one for the way back.'

'This is pretty good,' Frances said as they drove on. 'Did you let Mr Flint know we were coming?'

'Actually, I didn't,' Alec said. 'But it'll be all right. He's sure to be around.'

'He might be in church,' Frances suggested.

Alec laughed. 'I doubt that. He quarrelled with the vicar. He boasts about it. Something to do with a sheep, but I can't remember the ins and outs.'

'Not with Clive Moorby?' asked Frances.

'Oh no,' Alec said. 'Clive's not been here long. It was before his time. Malachi is a bit crotchety anyway. I get on with him, and you'll be all right. He likes a pretty woman.'

In less than half an hour after leaving Kilby they were walking up the path to Malachi Flint's cottage. Alec knocked hard on the door – 'He's a bit deaf,' he explained – and several minutes later (Frances was beginning to think he wasn't at home) it was opened a few inches and an elderly man peered out at them.

'Come on, Malachi! Open up!' Alec said briskly. 'I've brought a beautiful young lady to see you.'

'In that case, and seeing it's you, you can come in,' Malachi said.

He was a small man, made smaller by the fact that he was bent. He had a shock of untidy white hair, white whiskers yellowed at the edges, and he was, Frances thought, decidedly rough-looking. But there was nothing rough about his voice: it was as smooth and soft as velvet, as if, living in a quiet place, he had never had to raise it to make himself heard.

'I'm allus glad to welcome a pretty lady,' he added. 'And what's thi' name, love?'

'Frances Hamilton. And you must be Mr Flint,' Frances said.

'Tha can call me Malachi,' he said. 'Frances. It's a nice name. I had a cow once, name of Frances. A Friesian, she was. They're good milkers, but I don't keep cows now.' He turned to Alec. 'And what might thee be after, Alec Spence?' he demanded. 'Not that I'm not pleased to see thee, but tha's usually after summat.'

'True,' Alec agreed. 'But this time it's Frances who's after your services. She's moved into Beck Farm and it's going to be a bed-and-breakfast again, so she needs a new house sign.'

'Only now it's to be "Beckside House",' Frances said.

'Beckside House?' Malachi looked shocked. 'But it's been Beck Farm ever since it were built! They'll not recognize – what did tha call it? – Beckside House.'

'They will if you do a lovely new sign for it,' Frances told him. 'Anyway, it doesn't have any name at all on it at present.'

'Nor does it need one,' Malachi said. 'Everybody knows it's

Beck Farm. Allus has been. I've known it all my life. I knew Ben Thornton. My father knew his father.'

'But that's marvellous,' Frances said. 'I'm delighted to meet someone who knew the people who lived in the house before I did. Perhaps another time you would tell me something about them.'

'Oh, I could do that right enough,' Malachi said. 'But let me tell thee if Ben had wanted a sign for the house he could have made it hisself. I'm not bad when it comes to wood, but Ben was better. Allus whittling away at summat, he was.'

'But you will do it for me, won't you?' Frances pleaded. 'I promise you, I'm really going to look after the house. Ask Alec.'

Alec nodded. 'It's true. It'll be brought back to life.' In fact, he agreed with Malachi about Frances's plan to change the name, but she had her reasons and it was, after all, her house.

Malachi sighed. Then he was silent.

He's going to refuse, Frances thought.

'Very well!' he said at last. 'I don't hold wi' it, but a pretty woman allus could twist me round her little finger. And it happens I've got a piece of seasoned oak that'll be just the thing. I'll show it to thee afore tha goes and tha can write down the fancy new name tha's after. I'll see what I can make of it.'

Moving slowly, grumbling, though without malice, about people wanting to change things – 'Why can't they leave things be?' he demanded – he took Frances and Alec round to the shed at the back of the house and picked out the piece of wood he had in mind.

'If tha must change what's allus been a perfectly good name,' he said, 'then this is the piece for it. I've been wondering what I'd use it for. But don't expect it in a hurry. I don't do things in a hurry.'

'I promise I won't rush you,' Frances said.

'As long as it's in place before next Easter,' Alec added.

'I'll see what I can do,' Malachi said. 'But I make no promises, mind.'

'He'll do it,' Alec said as they left. 'Don't worry.'

★   ★   ★

He drove north towards the head of the dale. It could hardly have been more different from Cordale, Frances thought, from which it was separated only by the steep fell to the east, and from the neighbouring dale to the west, the name of which she didn't yet know, by another precipitous fell, the two hills between them closing in on Tendale as if deliberately keeping it secret from the rest of North Yorkshire. The river, at no point very wide, and its banks at one point shallow, at another deeper, rushed turbulently over stones and boulders along the floor of the narrow valley, crossed in two places by narrow, insecure-looking bridges.

'We're heading towards the source of the river Ten,' Alec told her. 'About a mile or so from here. You'll see it looks not much more than a small brook at that point. It's amazing how, once it leaves Tendale, it widens out so much. It's as if it's been set free.'

Close to the point of the source of the river the road veered away from it, taking a decided turn to the right, and although they had been climbing steadily since leaving Kirkholme, now the ascent was suddenly much steeper. There were not many signs of human habitation on the way, no more than a few houses and farm buildings huddled together here and there, or sometimes standing solitary in unlikely places, but sheep were everywhere, in the small flat areas at the valley bottom and up on the fellsides. The car continued to climb until, without warning, almost as if they might tip over it, they were at the summit.

Frances cried out in amazement at the breadth and distance of the scene suddenly revealed in front of them. 'I don't believe it! It's another world,' she gasped.

Alec had turned the nose of the car again to the right, and now he pulled in to the inside edge of the road and turned off the engine. 'Let's get out and take a proper look,' he said.

He took her arm and they walked to the outside edge of the high road. 'I'm keeping a tight hold on you,' he said, 'because the wind can be gusty up here and if you weren't aware of it you could literally be blown down into the valley.'

'You are so right,' Frances said as they stood close together looking at the view. There was no more than a yard or two between where they stood on the short-cropped and slippery

88

grass and where the land descended, not so much sloping as plunging, into the valley. She was glad of his supporting arm.

Nearer the bottom of the steep descent the gradient eased and the valley broadened out, stretching for a distance before it started to climb again on the opposite side, but more gently, one slope leading to another with terraces in between until at the crest it reached a height similar – though not quite as high – to the one on which they stood. And beyond that could be glimpsed other slopes in the far distance, ranging all the way until the land met with a sky so blue and cloudless that it might have been high summer.

It was like a huge painting, irregular patches of yellow ochre and sepia blending in over the canvas with the many shades of green, and the few scattered farm dwellings and isolated barns no more than brush strokes against the rest. There were few trees other than a large group of conifers, newly planted and intruding on the scene.

'It's wonderful,' Frances said. 'I had no idea . . .'

'Few have,' Alec said. 'I've never seen many people here, and certainly never a crowd.'

They stood there for a while, looking, not speaking, until Frances gave an involuntary shiver.

'You're cold,' Alec said. 'I'm sorry. It *is* chilly here. It's so high. I think, but I could be wrong, that this is the highest motor road in Yorkshire, possibly one of the highest in the country. But we'll move on before you freeze.'

The descent was precipitous and winding until finally it reached the northern end of Cordale and civilization and they were on the road to Kilby. 'It's all so different,' Frances said. 'I couldn't have believed it if I hadn't seen it with my own eyes.'

Approaching Kilby, Alec turned left and soon drew up in front of Beck Farm. 'That was truly wonderful,' Frances said. 'Thank you very much. Will you come in and have something to eat? My mother will be cooking lunch and I'm sure there'll be enough for three.'

She was sorry, in a way, that they'd done so little talking. The scenery had taken over. Nothing could compete with it. It took away the power of speech. She'd learned little more about him than she'd already known, nothing personal to him except for his deep and obvious love of the part of the world in which he lived. It was not that she'd had the intention of prying into his life, not at all, no more than she was about to tell him her history. It was just that she would have liked to get to know him better. On the other hand, their silences had been comfortable, more so than constant conversation might have been with someone else.

'Thank you, I won't,' Alec said. 'I have quite a lot of work to get through this afternoon. But some other time. I'm glad you enjoyed it. I certainly did. And when Malachi lets us know the sign is ready I'll take you over again. Or perhaps . . .' He was hesitant. 'Perhaps I could take you somewhere else? You don't know this part of the world. There's lots I could show you. If you want to, if you have the time.'

'I'd like that,' Frances said.

Madge, who had happened to be standing by the window when Alec drew up, was disappointed that he didn't come into the house. She had quite taken to him. 'But I'm glad you had a nice time, love,' she said when Frances had described it all as well as she could.

'I could never describe that view, though,' Frances said. 'I'll have to take you to see it. But how did you get on? How was church?'

'Lovely,' Madge said. 'I enjoyed it. I knew the hymns – though they sang one of them to the wrong tune, which made it sound strange. Clive preached a good sermon, quite short, and I went in to coffee afterwards. Laura introduced me to several people and they were all friendly.'

'Laura?' Frances queried.

'The vicar's wife. She's so neighbourly. You'd like her. Anyway, lunch is nearly ready. I just have to make the mint sauce. I must say, I feel a bit uncomfortable at the thought of eating lamb when I see all those cuddly white ones every which way we turn. We shall have to eat pork more often. You don't see pigs running around as much, do you? And anyway, they're not as pretty.'

During lunch Frances said, 'I've decided I'm going to have a change of occupation this coming week, now that we've got Violet helping in the house.'

90

'Oh yes? What's that, then?' Madge enquired.

'I'm going to spend a few hours working on the garden, while the weather holds. If I want it decent for when we open next Easter I'll have to make a start on it. You can't do a garden in a day, can you? And at the moment it's like a jungle.'

'Well, I can't say I'll help you with that, because my back won't let me,' Madge said. 'And in any case I might be needed to look after baby Daisy.'

'Of course,' Frances said. 'But I'll make a start tomorrow. By the way, did I tell you that Malachi Flint knew Ben Thornton? And their fathers knew each other. When I have time I'm going to visit him again, see what he can tell me.'

'Why do you want to know?' Madge asked.

'Only because I'm curious about who lived in the house before we did,' Frances said.

It was the weather that put paid to Frances's gardening plans, not only on Monday, but for most of the week. It rained incessantly from Monday morning to Thursday afternoon. 'How *could* it!' Frances said crossly on Wednesday afternoon as she looked out at the leaden sky. 'When I think how beautiful it was at the top of Tendale on Sunday morning, how could it do this?'

'That's the English weather for you,' Madge said amiably. 'You can't ever rely on it. But never mind, love, we've got on very well with the work in the house.'

That was true. Violet was proving a tower of strength, able and willing, ready for anything, and baby Daisy was no trouble at all. Quite the reverse. In her waking moments she was a source of delight to Madge, who from time to time had been allowed to hold her and had also been initiated into the wonder of disposable nappies. 'Marvellous,' she said. 'What a pity they came too late for when Frances was a baby.'

On one evening they went down to eat at the Shorn Lamb, which made a change of company for both of them. It was amazing how many locals dropped into the Shorn Lamb and they were all friendly towards the two women.

Then, towards midday on Thursday, the rain stopped and a watery sun came out. 'Now I *shall* do something in the garden,'

Frances said, 'even if everything is soaking wet.' And as soon as lunch was over she was out there, secateurs, shears, rake and fork to hand. Where do I start? she thought, surveying it. In the end she simply went hard at it, cutting down, tearing out, clearing beds, with no particular strategy in mind. Everything was an overgrown mess. Ben Thornton must have neglected it totally in the last year or two. The apple tree looked sorry for itself. It probably needed pruning but she wasn't expert enough to judge that. She would have to seek advice.

It was on Friday morning that she discovered, propped against a wall behind a thicket of brambles that scratched her hands until they bled, the block of wood. It was not much of a find. Maybe a foot across and about eight inches high, it had a name carved into it. 'Lottie'. Obviously it was a memorial to a well-loved dog, which might well be buried right beneath where she was raking. The notion worried her, but she thought it unlikely to be the only dog buried in the garden, or in the small piece of field that still belonged to the house. No doubt every previous owner of the house had had dogs and possibly this one had been Ben Thornton's favourite. Why is everything I learn about Ben Thornton so sad? she asked herself. In the end she leaned the block of wood against the wall and went into the house. She had done enough for one day. Her back was aching.

She told her mother about her find. 'Do you think we should have a dog?' she asked her. 'Would you like one?'

'I'm not sure,' Madge said. 'We've never had one. As you know, your father wasn't fond of dogs. But it might be a good idea.' One could get quite fond of a dog, she thought. 'It would be protection, wouldn't it?'

'We'll think about it,' Frances said.

On Saturday evening they again went down to the Shorn Lamb for supper. 'We've earned it,' Frances said. 'We've both worked hard all week.'

'Oh, you don't need to sell it to me,' Madge said. 'I enjoy going there – for the good company as well as the meal.'

They arrived later than usual. The bar was busy. Some people were strangers, visitors who were obviously taking advantage of a fine Saturday after a nasty week, but there were also several familiar faces. Dora and Henry Laycock from the shop, and – it gave Frances a warm feeling of pleasure – Alec Spence, who immediately joined Frances and her mother as they sat at a table close to the bar. Jim Kettle was serving drinks and Bernard was hovering, as was Joyce. And then, within minutes of Frances and her mother arriving, Clive Moorby and his wife came in.

'Hello!' Bernard greeted them. 'Special occasion, is it?'

'Not really,' Clive said. 'Well, it's a special occasion for Laura and me to be out in the evening together, but it's not a birthday or anything. Laura's mother is visiting for a few days so she encouraged us to have an evening out.'

What a lovely group of friends, Madge thought.

The talk, going round in circles from kind mothers-in-law to the football results, the weather, the price of petrol, *EastEnders*, somehow drifted on to dogs. 'We were vaguely wondering whether we'd get a dog,' Frances said.

There was immediate advice on which breed would be suitable. 'Go for a Yorkshire terrier,' Jim Kettle said. 'They're unbeatable. Brave as a lion, full of character, and a nice size for you two ladies to handle.'

Henry Laycock shook his head. 'Now I', he said, 'would recommend a labrador. A black labrador. Lovely temperament, labradors have – and they're big enough to see off any intruders.'

'A Yorkshire terrier would deal double quick with an intruder,' Jim Kettle said. 'Small they might be, but fierce when it's necessary.'

'What breed of a dog was Lottie?' Frances asked. Without waiting for the answer, she explained about the block of wood she had found in the garden. 'There's just the name Lottie carved on it,' she said. 'I realized it must have been Ben Thornton's dog.'

Talking away, she hadn't noticed the silence fall. When she broke off, the only sound in the room was from the strangers sitting away from the bar. Everyone nearby was listening intently, more than the subject demanded. The atmosphere had changed and she didn't understand why.

Bernard broke into it. 'Lottie was Ben Thornton's wife,' he said.

93

'She was his *second* wife!' Joyce said sharply. 'Moira was his first wife. *Moira* was the love of his life, not . . .' She spat out the name. 'Not Lottie.'

'Joyce!' Bernard frowned at his wife. 'This isn't the time, or the place . . .'

'I'm sorry,' Frances interrupted. 'Have I said something wrong?'

'Of course you haven't,' Bernard said. 'It's just that, well, there are different opinions.'

'I'm talking about facts, not opinions.' Joyce's voice was thick with hate, her face flushed, her eyes bright with anger. 'She left him nothing. Not even the memories of Moira. Once Lottie was on the scene, Moira was banished. She took everything from him and then when it suited her she left him.'

'I'm sorry . . .' Frances began.

Joyce ignored her. 'And don't think I'm sorry for Ben Thornton,' she said bitterly. 'He deserved all he got. What did he want with that common little floozy? How *could* he put her in Moira's place? She was . . .' The words all but choked her. 'She was the best friend I ever had. She was . . .' The tears streamed down her face now. 'I hope she rots in hell,' she screamed. And then she turned and ran out of the bar, back to the kitchen. Bernard went after her.

'I'm sorry,' Frances repeated. 'I didn't mean . . . I don't know what . . .'

'. . . If you like the flashy type.' A woman Frances didn't know was the speaker. 'Handsome is as handsome does – and a good woman she was not.'

'Ben never said another word about it,' Jim Kettle said. 'Not a word. But he was never the same man again. Went into a shell, you might say. Anyway, he more or less stopped coming to the Lamb. And in the end . . .'

Bernard came back into the bar. 'I'm sorry about that, everyone,' he said. 'You must excuse my wife. It's a subject she gets very upset about. And now I reckon it's drinks all round, and we'll change the conversation. This is a public house, we're not here to stir up trouble – especially old trouble.'

LOTTIE

EIGHT

There was a sharp wind blowing down the dale from the north, penetrating even the thickest overcoats of those who stood around the grave in St Luke's churchyard. A good number, for Moira Thornton had been a popular woman in Kilby as well as in the whole of Cordale, and even beyond. She'd been well known in the markets, too. Shepton, Hawes, Leyburn. The produce she brought there was always of the best quality. Apple pies of her own baking. Apple chutney that was like no-one else's and for which she never gave away the recipe; her butter and cheese were sought after, though in the last year or two – since Ben had given up the sheep, had sold them and most of his land to Joseph Clark, his neighbour – she had ceased making the cheese. A pity, customers still said, remembering that Beck Farm cheese had been especially tasty, with a sweetness and sharpness of its own. Though it was made from ewes' milk it was never quite like the other Dales cheeses. She had brought the recipe, and possibly the method, when she had come as a bride from her father's farm in York. She and Ben had had two days' honeymoon in Whitby – it was all Ben could spare from the farm – before he'd brought her back to Kilby.

That had been thirty years ago. They had married young. But not too young for either of them, Ben thought, now standing on the very edge of the grave, looking down on the blackness that had come into his life – not suddenly, it had come gradually since the start of her illness eighteen months ago, darkening slowly at first, then faster and faster. Now he could see no glimmer of light ahead.

The undertaker picked up a handful of soil from the edge of the newly dug grave and scattered it into the black hole. Ben heard it smack on the coffin like a short, sharp hailstorm.

'Earth to earth, ashes to ashes, dust to dust,' the Reverend Saul Denham said, '. . . in sure and certain hope of the Resurrection . . .'

Ben had sure and certain hope of nothing, nothing at all; not now, nor any longer. His hope had been in Moira.

The vicar finished. Ben picked up a handful of earth and dropped it into the grave and a second later Joyce Grayson gently threw in a single rose, and then drew back, sobbing, and went into her husband's arms. Moira and Joyce had been the greatest of friends since the day they'd met, with that special bond some women seemed to have for each other. Like sisters, really. He'd never had that sort of closeness with a man. No David-and-Jonathan stuff. He was not without friends, but that sort of intimacy was unknown to him.

They moved slowly, in twos and threes, from the graveside to the church hall, where places had been set at two large trestle tables, heaped with food. Ham, ox tongue, slices of turkey breast left from Christmas; stand pies, pickles, salads, trifles, apple pies, Christmas cake, Wensleydale cheese. It was a lavish spread, deemed worthy of the departed. In any case it would have been shameful to have done any less and it was amazing how grief – in its various degrees, according to the familiarity with Moira – sharpened the appetites and loosened the tongues. Ben could eat nothing. He didn't even want the ample tot of whisky Joseph Clark pressed on him.

'Get it down you,' Joseph said. 'It'll keep the cold out.' As well, he thought, as letting out some of the grief. Ben Thornton was far too contained. It was not healthy. But then, he was that sort of man, and his nature had intensified during his wife's illness.

By now everyone else was chattering nineteen to the dozen and mostly, at least to begin with, about Moira. The praise was fitting – she deserved it, if ever a woman did – but inevitably the talk veered round, as it usually did, to sheep – the ewes in lamb, the prices at market, the cost of vets' bills – and then to the weather: the prospects for the month ahead, for the winter in Cordale would be a very long one, there was no doubt about that. It always was. The snow was already on the ground and there would be far more to come. January and February were the worst months.

Ben sipped at the whisky, then, surprisingly, drank down the rest in one gulp, which was unlike him, for he was no great drinker. It was more the action of a man swallowing a draught of medicine, instantly bitter to the taste but guaranteed to do good.

Joseph took the glass from him, refilled it and handed it back. 'Get yourself on the outside of that, and then have something to eat.'

'I'm not hungry,' Ben protested, accepting the fresh glass of whisky as if the first one had given him a taste for it.

'Nevertheless, you're going to eat,' Joseph said. He took Ben's empty plate and heaped it with tasty bits, like a mother tempting a finicky child. 'Now, get that down you,' he ordered. 'It's what Moira would have wanted. She always kept a good table, Moira did.'

There were murmurs of assent all round.

'She certainly did. And she made the best gingerbread I've ever tasted,' the vicar's wife said.

Apart from Ben, the only person not applying herself to the food with serious but evident enjoyment was Joyce Grayson. How could they do it? she asked herself. The thought of it choked her. But no-one tried to tempt her to eat. She was not, after all, the chief mourner. And Bernard, who might have noticed and done so, was, by some mischance, at the other end of the table.

It wasn't just her cooking, Ben thought, she was good at everything, though never in a showy way. She was quiet, un-assuming, but with her own authority and confidence. And then he pulled himself up. The word which hit him was 'was'. *Was*, he thought, not *is*. Not any longer, and never will be. It was over. It was just him.

Unlike Moira, he had never deeply grieved that they hadn't had children. She had longed, all the time, to be a mother but he had never yearned to be a father. That had always been something he could take or leave. If it happened, it happened. But Moira had shed tears over it as the monthly cycles went by without any variation, until it was all too late anyway. Perhaps that was why, when they'd still had the sheep, she'd been so wonderful with the newborn lambs, especially when they weren't thriving; she'd bring them into the house, keep them warm by the oven, get food into them. It was as if she'd been attending one of her own babies.

But now, he thought, if we'd had a son, he'd have been here for me. Or perhaps a daughter, who would have her mother's round, rosy face and her dark hair, which had never gone entirely grey, even at the end. As it was . . .

He looked round the table and wished they would all go home. He wished he could go home – but to what?

Alice leaned across, touched him briefly on the hand, and spoke to him. 'Are you all right, Mr Thornton?'

Alice had worked for them since he had given up farming and they'd set up the bed-and-breakfast at Beck Farm, where his father and his grandfather had lived before him. They would both turn in their respective graves at the knowledge that he had given up the farm. He was aware of that, but he had never wanted to farm and they hadn't listened to him. Farming was in their blood, but they hadn't passed it on to him. He had wanted to be a sculptor – either in wood or stone, it didn't matter which – but an artist of any sort was foreign to the Thornton family. Another race. He had not exactly been a shining light in the bed-and-breakfast business either, but he had done his best. Moira had carried that as if to the manner born. And in the tourist season, which was any time from Easter to mid-September, Alice had been her right hand.

And she had been much more than that through Moira's illness. How would he have managed without her? Joyce Grayson, though she'd been there for part of every day in the last few weeks, couldn't take on what Alice had; she had her own job to do in the Shorn Lamb.

He nodded at Alice. 'I'm all right,' he lied.

'Would you like to be leaving?' she asked him.

'I would,' Ben admitted. 'But we'll have to wait for the tributes. It would look rude otherwise.'

'Well, the minute they're over,' Alice said, 'we'll slip away. I'll go with you, see you settled in.'

The tributes were full, lengthy and sincere. It didn't surprise him. As soon as they ended, people began to move their chairs, chatting again as if it was just an ordinary day. Without a word to anyone, he and Alice left.

She had been at Beck Farm earlier that day, plying people with warming drinks before the cortège left the house to go to the church. It had been Moira's last wish – she had spoken of it with such common sense – that her coffin should be in the house, not in some small room in the funeral director's premises, and that those who were attending should gather there and walk together down to the church. It was the old-fashioned way and it was what she wanted.

Alice had seen to it that the heating had been left on for Ben to come back to, and the fire in the kitchen banked up so that on their return it would need no more than a poke to coax it into a welcoming blaze. She had also left on the top of the stove a pan of vegetable soup, which would only need re-heating.

'There's a fresh loaf and two currant teacakes in the bread bin,' she told Ben now. 'You'll find cheese and eggs, and bacon, in the larder. I'll be here in the morning to bring you anything else you need. And I'll do the washing.'

'Thank you, Alice,' Ben said. 'You've been very kind to me. I'll not forget it.'

'Nonsense,' she said gruffly. 'And think on, you've got to eat. You've got to look after yourself.'

'For what?' he asked himself when she'd left.

Nevertheless, he drank some soup, though without tasting it, then switched off the lights and went upstairs to bed.

Hours later, still lying awake in the dark, he realized it was the worst thing he could have done. The bed seemed so wide. They had slept in it since they were married and it was hollowed in the middle. He lay down deliberately on his own side, where he had always slept, but there was no way he could stay there. Gravity, after a few minutes, rolled him into the middle. But Moira was not there.

Looking back, Ben never knew how he had come through that winter, and in truth he didn't remember all that much about it. It was colder and darker than anything he'd ever known. The wind was keener, the ice was thicker, the snow was deeper and lay on the ground longer, except in Kilby High Street, where it was hard-packed and flattened, and precariously slippery.

Ben was kept going by Alice, who came to Beck Farm most days, tidied the house and prepared food for him. Sometimes he ate it, sometimes he didn't. It depended on his mood. Joseph Clark visited him, and occasionally persuaded him to go down to the Shorn Lamb, where they met friends. Joyce Grayson was always solicitous of him. She, he thought, was the one who came nearest to knowing what he felt. But 'nearest' was still a long way off.

'You'll feel better when spring comes,' Joseph said, as did several other friends.

'You'll feel back to normal, Mr Thornton, when we start getting the visitors again,' Alice assured him.

He would have to.

Spring came. The days grew gradually longer. After the winter's snow and the spring rains the grass was emerald green and the beck ran down the side of the house in full spate. The birds were busy, mating and nesting. Everywhere there were signs of renewed life. In another month – lambing came late in the northern Dales – the fields would be dotted white with the ewes and their new lambs, and loud with their bleating. All this, but he felt no better. He was empty.

The sharp, agonizing pain that had gripped him earlier was, to an extent, dulled. There was no longer the daily distress of watching, helplessly, Moira's suffering. That was over. He was not one for visiting her grave, even though it was close by. He knew he never would be. He couldn't think of her as being there. But on the one occasion when he did go he found the grave bright with a vase of daffodils and realized that Joyce Grayson must have left them there. Who else? He knew he should have felt ashamed of himself, but in fact he felt nothing. The future stretched before him, grey and lifeless.

When each day's work was done he went to bed, though not to sleep. He had almost stopped visiting the Shorn Lamb and it was Joseph, together with Harry Foster, who farmed higher up Cordale, who called in on him one evening and persuaded him to go down to the Lamb with them. He had been at the point, there being nothing else to do, of going to bed and he was reluctant to go out, but the two men would not take no for an answer.

'It will do you good,' Joseph said.

'You'll have to snap out of yourself,' Harry Foster added. 'You can't go on like this.'

There speaks a man, Ben thought, who doesn't know what he's talking about. Nevertheless he went with them.

It was when they were on their second pint that Joseph brought up the subject of the trip. 'The Agricultural Exhibition's in Manchester this year,' he said. 'It was Harrogate's turn last year. It's in a week's time. We thought we could fit it in before the lambing starts, leaving our wives in charge.' It was not the most tactful way of reminding him of his position, but he meant no harm.

'Two nights in a decent hotel,' Harry continued. 'Treat ourselves to a bit of the high life. So how about you taking a break, Ben, and coming with us?'

'Oh no, I couldn't,' Ben said quickly. He'd been once or twice to the exhibition in former years, but not since he'd given up farming. It no longer had any practical purpose and it wasn't the kind of thing he'd do for pleasure.

'*Why* couldn't you?' asked Joseph. 'Give me one good reason. It would make a change, do you good. We'd have a nice time, a few drinks, a few laughs.' He reckoned Ben Thornton was sorely in need of a good laugh or two, and as far as drinks went he'd like to take him out and get him really sozzled. It was time now he came to terms with his mourning, stepped back into real life.

'So come on, why couldn't you?' he repeated. 'Give me one good reason.'

In the end, Ben was persuaded. He had no real enthusiasm for it, he simply gave in.

'A good idea,' Alice said when he told her. 'It'll take you out of yourself.' It would also give her time to get the house properly ready for the visitors. She reckoned she'd be far better on her own than with Ben mooning around, remembering all the times he'd done it with Moira.

So Joseph had booked them in at the Carlton, one of the hotels recommended by the exhibition organizers. Joseph and Harry would share a room; he would have a single room to himself. They set off soon after breakfast on a bright Monday morning, Harry driving them in his Volvo estate – which he'd cleared of its usual farming impedimenta and cleaned inside and out – Joseph sitting in the front with Harry, Ben on his own in the back, which was the way he preferred it. Harry and Joseph were like two boys let out of school, but he wasn't in the mood for singing and telling slightly dirty jokes. He wondered, hunched in the back of the car, looking out of the window as they crossed the Pennines, why he had agreed to come, since he wasn't going to enjoy it. He'd been too easily swayed. Given the chance he would, at that moment, have turned back, but it was too late, he would have to make the best of it.

He concentrated on the landscape. Though as the crow flew it wasn't all that far from Cordale, it was different. The hills were less steep, less green; the nature of the stone was different – dark millstone grit instead of limestone – and driving, as they eventually did, through the suburbs of Manchester towards the centre of the city was something he didn't enjoy. Large cities were not to his taste. He had once been to London by coach to a cup final and had been relieved afterwards to be back in Kilby.

He would have preferred this trip if it had been Harrogate's year for the exhibition rather than Manchester's. He quite liked Harrogate. He and Moira had enjoyed visits there from time to time, especially in the summer. Looking in the posh shop windows in Parliament Street, that was what she had liked. Tea in Betty's Café as well, and a stroll in the Valley Gardens. They had done that last summer before her illness had become too much for her to venture out of the dale.

The Carlton Hotel looked resplendent from the front: a great deal of glass and chrome, wide steps up to an imposing entrance and everywhere brightly lit, even though it was not yet the middle of the day. More posh than he had expected. They registered, and were advised to leave their car in the hotel garage for the duration, since parking was difficult in the city. The conference hall was not far away and there were plenty of taxis.

His room was adequate though not nearly as glitzy as the public rooms. It was small, and the only window overlooked a stair well, but what did he need with a view or a large room? There was a bed, a bedside light, a chest of drawers – and a trouser press, which he was sure he would never use, probably wouldn't know how to. He had hardly unpacked his few belongings when the telephone rang.

'Everything all right?' Joseph said. His and Harry's room was on the same floor but a distance away.

'Fine.'

'Then we'll meet you in the ground-floor bar in fifteen minutes,' Joseph said. 'We passed it on the way in.'

'OK,' Ben said. He wouldn't hurry. There was nothing else to do in the bedroom except read through the leather-covered information folder, but he didn't want a drinking session in the bar so early in the day. He could have coffee, of course, but that wouldn't go down well with the other two. He picked up the folder and began to study it. The hotel – he hadn't realized this – was one of a prestigious chain of which even he had heard. There was very little it didn't offer for the comfort and pleasure of its clients. Conference rooms, beauty parlour, barber shop, heated swimming pool in the basement, restaurant. There was also, within its pages, a leaflet about the exhibition, which he read. Having done with that, he then left his room in search of the ground-floor bar and his friends.

Charlotte Harper stood in her designated place at the front of the stand, Portman's Agricultural Supplies, handing out leaflets, but more important than the leaflets, and what caused people to slow down long enough to take one, was her wide smile. Her pretty red lips curved upwards at the corners, her white even teeth gleamed, her bright blue eyes creased into fine lines at the corners and her perfect nose wrinkled ever so slightly as if she found the handing out of leaflets the greatest fun. All that – not to mention her shoulder-length mane of rich brown hair, her generous and shapely bosom beneath its tight top, and her legs, which seemed to go on for ever, from the hem of her short skirt to the narrow feet in her high-heeled silver shoes – had the desired effect on the passers-by, which was not only to take a leaflet but to pause, linger and look at the goods, check a few prices, then gradually move back to her to ask a question or two.

The warm-up was what she was there for. It didn't matter that she couldn't answer the questions; what she knew about farming equipment and foodstuffs could have been engraved on the small silver medallion she wore on a chain round her neck. She would just about recognize a tractor if it hit her in the middle of the road. No, she wasn't there for that. She was there to look beautiful, to entice, to tempt the public – which, given the nature of the exhibition, was largely male – with exhibits totally untempting. That done, Kenneth or Les would move in with the gen and, it was to be hoped, take down the order. After which Charlotte would polish up her smile and start again.

She was not alone in her job. At the opposite end of the stand stood Dulcie, more or less Charlotte's clone, except that Dulcie's equally bouncy hair was a deep auburn and her outfit was green and cream. She was almost, but not quite, as pretty as Charlotte. She was equally tall and shapely but her smile revealed dental work that was not of the same high standard. Charlotte's mother, recognizing early on her daughter's potential in a world where good looks could be the passport to fame and fortune, had from the very first, from the moment those little white pearls had pushed their way through the pink baby gums, spared no expense when it came to her daughter's teeth. Charlotte was also, throughout her childhood, given dancing lessons – ballet and tap – which taught her the value of deportment. One never knew, Mrs Harper told herself, where all this might lead. It could be well worth the investment.

It was not yet lunchtime but there was a lull, not many customers about. In fact, it being only the first day of the exhibition and not everyone having arrived, there had been quite a few lulls. Dulcie drifted over to speak to Charlotte, a move normally frowned upon, but Ken had gone off somewhere and Les was seizing the opportunity to chat up Karen, who was the third girl in the trio but who, since she was fractionally less pretty than Charlotte and Dulcie (and had less shapely and shorter legs), normally did her stint behind the counter.

'Lottie,' Dulcie said, 'I'm starving hungry. Can you take over while I go and get a buttered bun? Also, if I don't go to the loo I'll burst.'

'OK, if you clear it with Les,' Charlotte agreed. 'If he can tear himself away from Karen, that is. But don't take for ever. And get one for me.' They were not allowed to eat on the stand, not so much as a Smartie. It was common. To be addicted to chewing-gum was to risk being banned from the whole exhibition circuit, but they would find ways to eat the buns.

You also got jobs in the better exhibitions if you spoke well. Speech was another area where Mrs Harper had come up trumps. Her daughter's Midlands accent had been carefully, and again not without cost, replaced from the age of seven and she now seldom slipped back into it. Certainly never on the job. Dulcie's speech, however, had remained much the same since she had uttered her first Lambeth vowels.

Dulcie had a word with Les, then went off in search of food. Since, for the moment, there were no customers in sight Charlotte leaned against the counter, easing her back. She would have liked to have taken her shoes off. No use thinking in those terms, though. She was there until half-past seven each evening, and on Wednesday up to four o'clock.

It had been a boring exhibition so far, and looked likely to continue that way. She preferred a fashion one, or even Home Interiors, though the Motor Show was her first favourite. The punters there were usually well-heeled and stylish. The Boat Show wasn't bad, but there was no joy in accepting an offer of a boat trip, since she could get seasick in a rowing boat on the park lake. An agricultural exhibition, especially in the north, was pretty low in appeal. Full of farmers in flat caps. Though, as her mother had pointed out, in spite of appearances and the fact that they usually cried the poor tale, farmers were often quite rich. And, she had added, a farmhouse could be a very desirable residence.

Still, she wasn't in this job only to catch a husband, was she? She was in it because it had variety, offered the chance to travel to places she'd never set eyes on if she worked in a shop or an office; she got to wear nice clothes as well and her hairdo came on expenses. Also you never knew who you *might* meet. You never knew who was just round the corner and would come along in the next ten minutes. Some exhibitions brought foreigners. You could well end up living in New York or Paris, though not from this one, and she'd have to get a move on to get anywhere. She was twenty-nine, only a few months off thirty, and really at the top age for this kind of lark unless you were something of an expert in what was being sold. She didn't look her age, but what about when she was older?

She missed her wonderfully supportive mother, who had died suddenly a year ago. Oh, how she missed her! Especially when the exhibitions ended and she didn't have her, with her outstretched arms and warm welcome, to go home to. She had no idea where her father was. He had skipped years ago. It was because of this, and partly as a tribute to her mother, that she had decided, after her own short marriage ended in divorce, to go back to her maiden name.

NINE

By two o'clock in the afternoon Lottie, Dulcie and Karen, and also the two men, were back on the stand. As well as various eating places for the general public there was a self-service restaurant set aside for exhibitors, and here they had lunched in relays. There was also a considerably more upmarket bar and dining-room with waiter service, tablecloths and napkins, which was reserved for company VIPs and any guests of theirs who might possibly be the source of large orders. But this was holy ground, not available to Lottie and co., not even to Ken and Les, who were employees of Portman's, unless either of them had a rare invitation from someone on high in the company.

Mr Harold Portman, the managing director, was visiting today and he was even now, with a guest, taking advantage of the dining-room. He had been most gracious before lunch, speaking to each of the girls in turn, asking them how they were and if they had ever worked in agricultural supplies, which they hadn't. 'Well, never mind,' he'd said in a kindly fashion, 'you all look lovely and I'm sure you'll do well' – while at the same time making a mental note that someone should get onto the agency who'd supplied them and suggest that they might at least send someone who would know a tractor from a trowel.

It was deadly quiet at the moment. Lottie looked at her watch.

Twelve minutes past two. She risked walking over to Dulcie for a little chat.

'Where are they all?' Dulcie asked.

'Stuffing their faces,' Lottie replied.

'My feet are killing me already,' Dulcie said. 'Not to mention my back. It's these heels.'

'I know. But we can't wear flats on this job, can we?' Lottie pointed out. 'It would spoil the effect.'

'Well, I'm going to sit down,' Dulcie said. Stools were supplied, but their use was not encouraged. In any case they were high ones, which didn't help one's back the least bit, but sitting on a high stool looked more elegant, especially when it came to one's legs.

'Hold on a minute,' Lottie said. 'I think we might have customers.'

Three men were strolling together down the aisle towards the stand. As they reached it they slowed down.

'I'd better make a move,' Lottie said. 'I'll take one and send the other two on to you.'

She was back in her place as they drew level with her, her mouth widening into a lovely smile, giving them the full benefit of her beautiful teeth while at the same time taking stock of them. Two of the three looked to be typical farmers – or at least what she thought farmers looked like, since she didn't actually know any. They were tweedy, broad-shouldered, stocky men, with fresh complexions. Probably in their early fifties, they appeared affable and friendly as they returned her smile. The third man was different. He might have been a few years older than the others. Certainly he was three inches or so taller, and thin to the point of emaciation, so that his dark suit hung on him. He had a much more serious look, not unpleasant, but there was no affability about him. Lottie liked placing people at first glance – it was an occupation that helped to make the dull patches of the job more interesting – but she couldn't place this one.

'Good afternoon, gentlemen,' she said in her well-modulated voice, pitched low as she had been taught. 'I hope you're enjoying the exhibition.'

'Thank you,' one of the jolly-looking ones said. 'We've not

seen much yet; we've not been here that long. And there's not a lot going on at the moment, is there?'

'It's a quiet time, early after lunch,' Lottie conceded.

'But it's brightened up considerably in the last minute or so,' the other one said. He was not exactly leering at her: he was one of those men – she had met them before – whose immediate response to a pretty woman was to flirt with her. She didn't mind. It meant nothing to her. And even if she had minded she wouldn't have shown it. It was part of the job, after all. She gave him a little smile, all to himself.

'Now, Joseph,' the other man said. 'Come off it! Don't embarrass the young lady.'

'Now, would I do a thing like that, Harry?' Joseph asked.

The third man said nothing. He stood there, not awkwardly, but not joining in the repartee. Lottie looked at him directly and for a brief moment their eyes met, then he looked away. He had rather fine blue-grey eyes but there was no warmth in them. Nor was there hostility. She just didn't register with him and she wondered why. It was not a reaction she met with often and she felt herself slightly challenged to do something about it, but, before she could decide what, Dulcie came across and joined them. It was the usual procedure. If you had a group of potential customers and the other girl had none, then she moved in, or vice versa, and you shared them between you, thus making it less likely that some of them would escape.

'Hello,' Dulcie said. 'Can I help?'

'Thank you, Dulcie,' Lottie said. 'I think these two gentlemen would like a leaflet.' She made it quite clear which two gentlemen she meant. She would deal with Mr Gloom herself.

'Dulcie, is it?' Joseph said. 'That's a pretty name.' He was not at all disconcerted at being turned over to someone else; in any case, he was particularly partial to redheads. 'And what's your friend's name?'

'Charlotte,' Dulcie said. 'But we call her Lottie.'

'Lottie. That's nice, too,' Harry said.

By some manoeuvre or other of which they were not quite aware, though Lottie was, Dulcie enticed the two men to her side of the stand, leaving Lottie with the third one. On second thoughts, however, she was no longer sure she wanted that. He looked a real streak of misery. Perhaps, she thought, he was rich. He didn't appear to be, but then the rich didn't always.

'Let me give you a leaflet,' Lottie said pleasantly. 'Or if you're interested in anything special . . . what kind of a farmer are you? I mean, do you have sheep, or cattle, or do you grow things?'

'I'm not a farmer,' Ben said, speaking for the first time.

'Oh, I'm sorry. I thought . . . I mean as you were here . . .'

'I *was* a farmer. I sold my farm,' Ben said.

'And your friends?' Lottie queried. 'Are they farmers?'

He nodded. 'Both of them.'

'I see,' Lottie said. She didn't really. She was even less sure that she should have bothered to take him on, especially as Portman's probably wasn't going to get a sausage out of him. 'So where do they farm?' she persisted. 'And do you all come from the same area?'

'The North Yorkshire Dales,' Ben said. 'Cordale.' It was clear to him that it was no more familiar to her than was the North Pole. She probably came from London.

'I don't know the Yorkshire Dales,' Lottie admitted. 'In fact, Manchester is the furthest north I've ever been.'

'Manchester is nothing like the Yorkshire Dales,' Ben said.

'I suppose not. Is it cold up there?'

'It can be.'

They were both running out of things to say. Lottie glanced along the aisle, hoping for another prospective customer to whom she could turn her attention without appearing rude to this man she was getting nowhere with, but though there were far more people about than there had been earlier they all seemed intent on something else. Then, after another pause, it was Ben himself who broke the spell.

'I'd best be joining my mates,' he said. 'Thank you. I'm sorry I can't be a customer.'

'That's all right,' Lottie said.

'Good afternoon, then.'

'Good afternoon to you,' she said.

He gave her a nod and moved away to join Joseph and Harry who were at the point of being handed over by Dulcie to Ken.

112

Dulcie, when she returned, made a swift trip across to Lottie. 'They live in a place named Cordale,' she said. 'It sounds like the back of beyond to me, but they must be worth a bob or two. They're staying at the Carlton.'

Lottie raised her eyebrows. 'Is that so?' she said.

Some hours later – it was after eight in the evening – the three men were sitting in the Carlton's ground-floor bar, halfway through their second drink. They had expected by now to be in the hotel restaurant, but it was unusually busy and they had been advised they would have to wait a little while for a table.

'We could find somewhere else,' Harry suggested. 'There's no shortage of restaurants in Manchester.'

'Oh, let's not bother,' Joseph said. 'It's raining cats and dogs out there. We're not starving, are we? We had a good lunch; we can wait a bit.'

'I suppose you're right,' Harry said. 'And it's comfortable here.' He turned to Ben. 'What do you say, Ben?'

'I'm all right,' Ben answered. 'I'd as soon stay here. We can have a meal and then an early night.'

'Oh no, we can't,' Joseph protested. 'Not a bit of it! We didn't come to Manchester to have early nights. We can have those in Cordale. We'll have our dinner here and then we'll find out where we can go on to something afterwards. A night club, or a casino. And now, while we're waiting, what about another drink?'

'Go on, then,' Harry said.

Ben said nothing.

Joseph was about to raise his hand to summon the waiter, when in at the door walked Lottie, Dulcie and Karen, dressed to the nines.

'Wow!' Joseph said. 'Just look what the wind's blown in. That's a bit of luck and no mistake.' He stood up, waving his hand so that there was no way they could miss him. Not that they would have anyway. 'Bumping into' the three men was exactly what they had hoped for. Nothing heavy, nothing wrong, just a bit of fun – that was what they'd said to each other before, on the dot, they'd left the exhibition, rushed back to the small

113

hotel where Portman's were putting them up, changed into their gladrags and, because of the rain, hailed a taxi to take them to the Carlton. They might just as easily have spent the evening with Ken and Les had it not been made fairly clear to them that the two men had other fish to fry.

'Come and join us, ladies,' Joseph called out.

The ladies did so.

'Surprise, surprise!' Harry said as they sorted out where they would sit.

'Isn't it just!' Dulcie said, taking the seat beside him. 'Who would have thought it?'

'Who indeed?' Joseph said. 'So now what would you three lovely ladies like to drink?'

Lottie, who found herself sitting beside Ben, asked for a dry Martini, Dulcie and Karen chose gin-and-tonics. The three men, who had been drinking beer, switched to Scotch.

'Have you eaten?' Joseph asked.

'Oh no,' Dulcie answered, helping herself liberally to nuts and crisps. 'Not since lunchtime, actually.'

There had been no time to eat. They'd debated, in fact, whether they might be too late. It had been a relief to see the men sitting there.

'Well, then, perhaps you'd join us,' Joseph said. 'We've been waiting for a table. Lucky for us we have or we'd have missed you.'

'Oh, what a lovely idea!' 'How kind!' 'Thank you very much,' the girls said, more or less in unison.

When the waiter came to take the order for the drinks Harry said, 'We're waiting for a table for three. Will you make that for six?'

'Certainly, sir.' The waiter was impassive. It was not an unfamiliar situation. And they would tip well because they would be showing off in front of the women. The women looked all right; brightly dressed, with big hair and loads of make-up, but not the sort who might have come in from the street. They were a cut above that. In any case, such clientele was discouraged at the Carlton. It wasn't that sort of place. 'You might have to wait a bit,' he added, 'but I'll see what I can do.'

114

'Good man,' Joseph said.

Drinks were brought, and fresh supplies of nibbles, but it was almost half an hour before a table became free. It didn't matter. Dulcie and Karen had second drinks, though not Lottie, who made her Martini last. Conversation flowed, tossed from one to another, but none of it to and from Ben. He was not unamiable but he had little to say. Lottie found him difficult, though, curiously, it didn't either annoy or irritate her that he sat there so silently. The others were cheerful and talkative, obviously out for a good time, and he wouldn't – or more likely couldn't, she thought – join in. She wished she could understand why, or do something about it. Then, when the waiter came to say their table would be ready in not more than five minutes, and Ben excused himself to go to the cloakroom, she plucked up courage to mention him to the other men.

'Your friend doesn't seem very happy,' she said. 'He's not enjoying himself. Is there something wrong?'

The men looked at each other.

'Well, yes,' Joseph said. 'The fact of the matter is, his wife died. It's not that recent, it's several months ago now, and you'd think he'd have got over it to a certain extent, but he doesn't seem to.'

'That's why we brought him with us,' Harry said. 'To try to cheer him up.'

'Poor man,' Lottie said. 'But that was nice of you. Was he very happily married?'

'Oh yes,' Harry said. 'She was a lovely woman, his wife. Everybody liked her.'

'Let's hope in time he'll find someone as good as Moira was,' Joseph said. 'He's a man who ought to be married. He doesn't seem to function well on his own.'

'And he could well afford to take on someone else,' Harry put in. 'He'd be a catch for any woman. Ben's not without a penny or two, not by any means.'

'He told me he'd sold his farm,' Lottie said.

'That's right,' Joseph said. 'His heart was never in it. It was a fair-sized farm – eight hundred acres – and he got a good price for it. And I can vouch for that because I bought it, I wanted to increase mine. He could drive a hard bargain, Ben could. Of course, this was well before his wife died. He didn't sell the house with it but I didn't want that, I wanted the land.'

'A lovely big house,' Harry said. 'After they'd sold the farm his wife ran it as a bed-and-breakfast business, very successfully too. Ben reckons he's keeping that on, but I don't know whether he will.'

'He doesn't need to,' Joseph said. 'He can live very well without it. In fact . . .'

He didn't finish the sentence. Ben was on his way back to the table, with the waiter only a stride behind him.

'Your table's ready now, gentlemen,' the waiter said. 'I'm sorry you've had to wait.'

'That's quite all right,' Joseph said. 'It's been very pleasant. Very pleasant indeed.'

His words were not quite slurred, Lottie thought, he was just a bit tipsy. It was nothing Dulcie couldn't handle, and Dulcie seemed to have chosen to attach herself to Joseph, as Karen, even now, was doing with Harry, as they all followed the waiter to the table. It left her with Ben, which she didn't mind that much. She felt truly sorry for him and decided there and then that she would do whatever she could to cheer him up, at least for the short space of an evening. She gave him an extra-special smile as he took the seat beside her. One corner of his mouth turned up fractionally in response.

The meal was good, exceptionally so, and they all did justice to it, and to the wine that accompanied it. Ben, Lottie noticed, did less justice to the food than the rest of them but every bit as much to the wine. But what did it matter, especially if it made him feel better? He spoke only occasionally and he needed a great deal of encouragement even to do that. The others were well away, talking with ever-higher raised voices, laughing immediately at everything and nothing. Dulcie, in fact, was making a bit of an exhibition of herself with Joseph, but then, as Lottie knew because their paths had crossed more than once, Dulcie never could hold her drink.

As the evening went on, Lottie felt as if she was at a party where everyone else was having great fun while she was sitting alone in a corner. It was a long time since she had experienced that – not since she was a shy teenager at a dance – but that was what it was like now, sitting next to Ben. Trying to have a conversation with him was like swimming in treacle or wading through porridge. She could, of course, join in the merriment of the others, but this would be to abandon him, which she didn't want to do. She remembered all too clearly what it had been like when her mother had died. Unhappiness cut you off. She took a deep breath and decided to have another stab at getting him to talk. She tried to think what might possibly interest him but nothing much came to mind. How could it? They lived such different lives.

'Tell me what the Yorkshire Dales are like,' she said in the end. Surely if she asked questions about where he lived he would have to answer them? 'People say they're marvellous, but what do *you* think?'

There was a long pause before he replied. It was as if he was searching for words. For a moment she thought that he wasn't going to answer at all. When at last he did it surprised her. His voice was quite different. It was strong, totally sure. She did wonder if it was the wine speaking, but if it was it didn't matter. It was a relief to hear him utter more than a monosyllable.

'The Yorkshire Dales', he said, emphatically, stating a truth that for him was not to be denied, 'are the best thing God ever made. They are the finest of his handiwork. And Cordale is the Queen of them.'

His raised voice cut across all other conversation at the table. He had not risen to his feet, or thumped the table, but the effect was every bit as powerful as if he had, and in the sudden, surprised silence that followed all eyes were on him. He was not abashed, not in the least. He looked from one face to another, challenging them to disagree with him. No-one did.

Joseph was the first to break the silence. 'Well said, Ben. Well said.'

'I quite agree,' Harry added. 'But I'd say Swaledale comes a good second to Cordale.'

'That's as may be,' Ben said firmly. 'It's a matter of opinion. But Cordale is first.'

The waiter came to serve the coffee and the conversation took another turn.

'The night's young,' Joseph said. 'What are we going to do next? Let's go on somewhere.' He looked round the table. 'What do you say?'

'Great,' Dulcie said.

'Super,' Karen agreed.

Only Ben demurred very quietly, as if he'd put all his strength into his earlier outburst. 'I'm not sure I—'

'Oh, come on, Ben,' Harry said. 'Don't be silly!'

Lottie was not sure whether she wanted Ben to come or not. If he didn't, she'd be the odd one out – the rest were well away – but if he did, it would fall to her to entertain him, she had no doubt of that. On the other hand she *was* still sorry for him and she'd been quite impressed by his outburst about the Dales, but most of all she didn't fancy being the odd one out. It wasn't something she was used to. In the end it was that which swung her. She put her hand on his arm. 'Please, Ben. I'd like you to come.' If all else failed she would ask him questions about Cordale.

When the waiter brought the bill Joseph asked him about night clubs in the area. 'You're spoilt for choice, sir,' the waiter said. 'There are several round here. Our clients seem to like the Night Owl – or Lamptons. They're both nearby.'

'So which would you recommend?' Joseph persisted.

'People do say the music at the Night Owl is good,' the waiter said. He himself had never been to either – or to any other night club, for that matter. All he wanted at the end of the evening was to get home to bed.

They decided on the Night Owl because Dulcie liked the name. It was no more than ten minutes away, the waiter said, and the rain had stopped, so they went on foot, each girl with her – by now – chosen escort. Not that mine is exactly chosen, Lottie thought. It was unusual for her, she thought as, none too steadily on the part of the men and of Dulcie, they walked the narrow pavements, she and Ben bringing up the rear, not to have the pick of the bunch in this sort of circumstance. She wasn't at all sure how that had come about. But never mind.

118

A wave of heat hit them as they went into the Night Owl. The club was larger than Lottie had expected, but crowded, so that the only place they could find to sit together was at the back of the room; nor was it easy to find their way to it, pushing between the too-close tables, since the whole interior was dim to the point of dark. The clientele, as far as she could make out, was verging on middle-aged and some had passed it. A plump attractive black woman was singing 'Let's Fall in Love' and on a minuscule dance floor close to the band several couples were shuffling around, since shuffling was all there was room for. In no time at all, once they had downed their first drinks, Joseph and Dulcie, Harry and Karen had joined them.

'I'm sorry,' Ben apologized. 'I was never much of a dancer.'

'That's all right,' Lottie assured him. 'I don't really want to dance.'

It was a black lie. Dancing was one of the things she liked most in the world, always had. She could dance into the early hours of the morning and never feel the least bit tired, but how could she say that to him? Dulcie had complained that their table wasn't closer to the band and the dance floor, but as it turned out, Lottie thought, that was a good thing. If it had been, since she and Ben would somehow have to carry on a conversation, they would have had to yell at each other. She doubted he was capable of yelling.

'Would you like another drink?' Ben asked.

'That would be nice,' Lottie said.

He called the waiter and ordered for both of them. He had switched to Scotch and Lottie, since the first one had been very pleasant, opted for another champagne cocktail.

'So tell me,' she said, taking a large gulp of the drink, 'what are the Yorkshire Dales actually like? I know you said they were the best place on earth and all that, but what are they *like*? I mean, what makes you say that?'

It was her hope that having put a direct question to him he would actually have to talk to her. She doubted, having witnessed his short but passionate words on the subject when they were at the table, that he had nothing in his mind to say; but rather it was there, and he simply had difficulty in expressing

119

it. She had to get him talking. She simply could not continue to sit here in near silence, especially as all the time she was itching to dance.

He was silent for what seemed a never-ending moment, then he made a slow start. 'To begin with,' he said, 'they're all different. Every one of them from the others. People who don't know any better lump them all together, but except that every dale has its hills and its valley, they're not alike. You could set me down, unconscious, in any one of them and when I came to – well, I might not know exactly where I was but I'd be likely to know where I wasn't.'

'How do you mean?' Lottie asked.

Ben paused, searching for the words. 'Well,' he said, 'if I woke up in Tendale, for instance, I'd know it wasn't Cordale. It would be too narrow, the fells too close in, with not much in the way of meadows because there's not enough flat land. But if I woke up in Cordale and you told me it was Littondale I'd say you were lying.'

'Why?' Lottie asked.

'The fells are high in Littondale, but they're closer than in Cordale, and the river Skirfare seems further down from the land – it has deeper banks, I mean, and sometimes it's dark and hidden. It seems narrower, more turbulent, than the river Cor.'

Her strategy was working, Lottie thought. Clearly, he would never be a fast talker, he thought before he spoke, but in the end he wasn't short of words to describe what he knew. And then she wondered if she was being patronizing, questioning him like this, putting him through his paces as if he were a backward child. She hoped not. In fact, what he said interested her, and that was strange in itself because she was no countrywoman, never had been. The urban life was hers – she liked towns and cities with perhaps the sea a pleasant extra – but he made the country come to life.

'Why do you especially like Cordale?' she asked. 'You said it was the Queen of the Dales. Why is that?'

'I suppose because I was born there,' he said. 'And my father and grandfather before me. I've never lived anywhere else. I suppose that has something to do with it.'

'Did you never want to live anywhere else?' Lottie asked. 'When you were a young man, didn't you ever want to leave?'

'Why would I?' Ben said. 'What has anywhere else got to offer that Cordale hasn't? Except I'd like to have gone to art school, but that wasn't on the cards. If you're the only son left and your dad's the farmer, then you have to carry it on.'

'Only son left?' Lottie queried.

'I had a brother,' Ben said. 'He was three years older. He was killed in an accident in his teens. He would have been the one to take on the farm. He loved it, it was in his blood, and that would have made me free.'

'Why art school?' she asked. 'Did you want to be a painter?' The thought surprised her.

'Not a painter,' Ben said. 'A sculptor. In stone, or in wood. That's what I wanted to do. I thought . . .'

What he had thought she wasn't to know, because at that moment the others came back from the dance floor. Flushed, laughing, talkative, they sat down at the table.

'That was good,' Joseph said. 'You're a very good dancer, Dulcie, love.'

But not as good as I am, given the chance, thought Lottie.

'Drinks all round,' Harry said. 'What's everyone having?'

'I shouldn't, really,' Lottie said. 'We had a drink while you were dancing.'

'Nevertheless,' Harry said, 'you're going to. And so are you, Ben.'

They were no more than halfway through their next round of drinks when the band struck up a tango.

'Oh!' Dulcie cried. 'Oh, come on, Joseph, we must do this. Excuse us, everyone.' They were up and away, followed almost immediately by Karen and Harry. Lottie stared after them in amazement. How could they do that? Then she realized Ben had seen her anger.

'I'm sorry,' she said.

'It's not your fault,' he said. 'It's me. I'm the one. But if I tried to tango with you we'd both be even more sorry. I think when I was born they left out the rhythm.'

'It doesn't matter,' Lottie said. 'It doesn't matter at all.' She now felt worse for him than she did for herself. 'In any case, there isn't room to tango properly on that tiny floor and I don't want to dance. I'm a bit tired,' she lied again.

'Would you like to leave?' Ben asked gently.

'Could we? If I say yes, does that sound rude?'

'Not a bit,' he said. 'I could get a taxi and take you to your hotel, then I'll go back to the Carlton.'

'Right,' Lottie said. 'Then let's go. They can work out where and why for themselves.' She would give those two so-called friends a piece of her mind in the morning. Selfish cows!

Within minutes they had left and within a few more minutes they were at the door of Lottie's hotel. Ben got out of the cab and asked the driver to wait while he saw her to the door.

'Thank you,' Lottie said. 'I did enjoy myself, really I did. I liked hearing about the Dales.'

Ben nodded. 'You should see them for yourself,' he said. 'They're better than I could ever describe.'

She stood on tiptoe and gave him a swift kiss on the cheek. 'Goodnight!' she said, then turned quickly and went into her hotel.

TEN

Lottie stood in front of the reception desk and waited as patiently as she could while the man behind the desk conducted a long phone conversation that sounded completely personal. 'Well,' he said at last, 'I suppose I'll have to go. See you later.' He rang off, and looked resentfully in Lottie's direction, without speaking.

'Could I have my key, please?' she asked. 'Room thirty-seven.'

He unhooked it from the board and handed it to her.

'My friends will be in later,' she said. 'Will you have another key for them?'

He shook his head. 'You'll have to let them in,' he said, pleased with the power behind his refusal.

Room thirty-seven was on the third floor. There was no lift. The flights of stairs grew narrower, and the stair carpet shabbier, the higher she climbed. The room she entered was what the Dawson Hotel described as a family room, which meant that it had three beds: twin beds pushed together and a third, a narrow single, close by. There were two upright chairs, a double wardrobe and a small dressing table. Nothing matched, not even the covers on the beds. The dressing table had a small, spotty mirror, over which the three of them, earlier in the evening when getting ready to go out, had fought for their turn. But thank goodness there was a shower. It had been fashioned from a cupboard and was claustrophobic, but at least the hot water worked. There was also a kettle, a tray with cups and saucers, tea and coffee bags, powdered milk and three biscuits. If the Dawson Hotel was Portman's idea of a suitable place for its temporary exhibition staff to stay, she thought, then they were cheapskates. She'd bet Mr Portman wasn't sleeping in a room like this. His immaculate bed would have been turned down by the chamber-maid and a bedtime chocolate left on the pillow.

She hung her coat in the wardrobe – they had shared the inadequate supply of coathangers strictly equally between them, three each – and then filled the kettle. She would get undressed, make a cup of tea and drink it in bed, taking a chance by leaving the door unlocked. She wasn't going to stay awake for the others. Heaven knew what time they would turn up or what state they'd be in. She was a trifle dizzy herself, but not too bad, so perhaps it was true that champagne didn't give you a hangover? Ten minutes later she was sitting up in bed, sipping her tea and nibbling at a digestive biscuit. Then she turned out the light and lay down in the dark, pleased, at least, that as the room was so high up no light from a street lamp would shine in through the skimpy curtains. The mattress was lumpy and she tried to arrange herself around the lumps. In the end, unsuccessful, she decided it wouldn't matter; she was tired out and she would sleep in spite of them.

It had been a funny old evening, or it had been for her. For the other two it was most likely par for the course, as hers would have been if she hadn't been saddled with Ben. She doubted he had enjoyed it and she questioned in her mind whether his friends had been right to drag him on this trip. Was it what she would have wanted if she had been in his position? She didn't know, but there was a point at which you had to start living again; she'd learned that after her mother had died. But could anyone else recognize that point for you? Anyway, he was all right, she thought, sliding down further under the bedclothes and pulling the sheet up to her chin. He was quite a nice old boy, really. A gentleman. And obviously – or not obviously, because he wasn't ostentatious – from what the others had said about him when he'd been out of the room, he was well off. A large house, a business, money in the bank. It all helped. He'd said she should visit Cordale. It hadn't been an invitation, just one of those things people come out with, but supposing he were to ask her? Would she go? Her thoughts went round and round until tiredness, or perhaps champagne cocktails, overcame her and she fell asleep without answering herself.

In his comfortable, deep-mattressed bed in his luxurious hotel bedroom Ben Thornton lay awake, wide-eyed in the darkness. He knew he had not made a success of the evening; he should have tried harder. She was a very nice young woman and she'd been stuck with him. He was sure he had bored her. On the other hand, and it was a small comfort, she'd seemed interested when he talked about Cordale. Cordale was where he belonged and probably he should have stayed. He should have been firm and not have taken up Joseph's invitation. Turning over in the bed, pummelling his pillow, telling himself there was no way he should be uncomfortable in this good bed, he pondered whether he would ask Lottie – he said her name to himself – if she'd like to visit there. Perhaps on his own ground he could make up to her for this not too successful evening. And what would Moira think? But it would be nothing more than a friendly gesture, a thank-you. Lottie would simply be a guest at Beck Farm, along with other guests who would almost certainly be there. Moira would have understood.

Lottie was sitting beside Mr Portman in his brand-new gleaming Ferrari, which he was driving dexterously at great speed with one hand while the other rested lightly on her thigh. On her lap she had a large, open box of handmade chocolate truffles and there was a small tray in front of her on which stood, firm as a rock and quite unaffected by the high speed of the car – the speedometer showed a hundred miles per hour – a glass of champagne. She didn't know the road but she knew he was taking her to Yorkshire and that from there they would fly to Paris. She was just about to take a sip of the champagne, when Dulcie and Karen, giggling, possibly singing – she wasn't sure – stumbled into the room, switched on the light, banged into her bed and wakened her.

'Are you asleep?' Dulcie asked.

'I *was*,' Lottie said. 'Did you have to come in like a herd of elephants?'

'*Sooo* sorry,' Dulcie apologized.

'The trouble is, and I'm sorry to say this,' Karen said haltingly, 'I think we're both a teensy bit tight. Just a teensy bit.'

'You are both as drunk as skunks,' Lottie said. 'So now can we have the light out and get some sleep. We have to work in the morning. And I wouldn't like to have either of your heads then.'

'We've had a smashing time,' Dulcie said.

'Do me a favour and don't tell me about it,' said Lottie, yawning.

It took an age before the two of them stopped messing about, doing this and that, and climbed into bed, but that done they fell asleep quickly. Within moments, though, they began snoring rhythmically and in two different keys. Lottie, furious, lay awake for a long time.

She was, nevertheless, the first to wake up next morning. Dulcie and Karen lay there in deep sleep, only the tops of their heads, one red, one blonde, showing above the bedcovers. She wondered if they would notice if an eight-wheel truck were to drive through the room. Oh well, no matter! She would have been in the same state if the evening had turned out as well for her as it had for them, but now the bonus was that she would get first turn in the shower.

They were still asleep when she emerged from the shower. She dressed and put on her make-up without attempting to waken them. That done, she made tea, drank a cup herself, then stood by the beds, shaking each girl gently in turn. 'Come on,' she said. 'Wakey, wakey! I've made a cup of tea.' As they yawned and stretched, and finally sat up, she took their tea to them. 'So how do you both feel this morning?' she asked.

'Fine,' Dulcie answered.

'Great,' Karen said. 'Slept like a log.'

'There is no justice,' Lottie observed.

At breakfast they discussed the previous evening. 'We wondered where you'd gone,' Dulcie said, 'but Joseph said Ben would have taken you here and then gone back to the Carlton. He said Ben wasn't one for the night-life.'

I could confirm that, Lottie thought, but I shan't. 'Oh, we had a pleasant evening,' she said. 'He's a nice man – just a bit quieter than the others.'

'He certainly was,' Karen agreed, helping herself to more toast. 'We just hoped you weren't being bored, didn't we, Dulcie?'

'I wasn't the least bit bored,' Lottie said defensively. She didn't want to be pitied. 'He was an interesting man. He told me quite a bit about himself. We got on very well indeed. In fact . . .' She hesitated, then out it came: 'In fact he's more or less asked me to visit him in the Dales.'

'Well, I never!' Dulcie said. 'Lottie, you are a dark horse. So what did you say? Did you accept?'

'Not exactly,' Lottie said. 'I sort of left it in the air, for the time being at any rate.'

'It's more than happened to either of us,' Karen said.

'It would be,' Lottie said smoothly. 'After all, he's not married, is he? I expect yours both have wives at home. Not to mention that you have boyfriends.'

'Too true,' Karen said. 'But we didn't do anything wrong, not really. It was all a bit of fun. Anyway, the way yours turned out you'll be pleased to hear they've asked if we'd like to go out with them again tonight.'

'Oh, really,' Lottie said. She hadn't bargained for that; she wasn't sure she wanted it and nor was she sure that Ben would. 'I'll see what Ben says,' she told them. 'I don't know that night clubs are his thing. He's more the thoughtful type.'

'Is that how you'd describe him?' Dulcie asked.

'It is,' Lottie said. 'Is there anything wrong with that?'

Dulcie smiled sweetly. 'Not if it's what you fancy.'

'We'd better make a move,' Karen said. 'We don't want to be late. Who knows, Mr Portman might be around again.'

'I wonder what *he* does with his evenings,' Dulcie mused.

At that moment Lottie remembered her dream. Vividly. 'He drives a Ferrari,' she said.

Dulcie stared at her. 'How do you know?'

'I just do,' Lottie said.

When the exhibition opened again at ten o'clock the three of them were back on the stand, bright-eyed and bushy-tailed, hair and make-up immaculate; no sign of a hangover in any one of them. Dulcie and Karen had claimed at breakfast to be tired and have headaches, but no after-effects showed now. Of course, Lottie reminded herself, they were both eight years younger than she was. If she'd had the sort of evening they'd had it would have shown in her face and she'd have felt awful. Twenty-one, she thought gloomily, was different from pushing thirty.

The morning was busy, with far more people stopping at the stand than on the previous day and several of them placing orders. Mr Portman came along at about eleven and was pleased with everything, speaking personally to one or two customers, partly to show the staff how it was done.

'You're doing a good job,' he said to each of the girls in turn. 'Keep it up the rest of the week, won't you. And now, unfortunately, I have to take my leave. Duty calls elsewhere.' He shook hands all round, including Ken and Les, then strode away. I wonder how Lottie knows he drives a Ferrari, Dulcie thought. She must ask her. He didn't look like a Ferrari man. More the dark-blue-Jaguar type.

Half an hour after Mr Portman had left, Joseph, Harry and Ben came along. All three girls were busy, so there was no time to stand and chat, but when Joseph and Harry went to Ken – actually to make purchases, about which Lottie somehow felt pleased – Ben turned back to speak to her. She was busy with a customer so he waited patiently until she was free.

'I expect your friends have told you that there's a suggestion we should repeat last evening's programme, or something similar,' he said. 'I wondered how you felt about it. I don't think it actually suited you, did it?'

'Well . . .' Lottie began. She didn't quite know what to say. The meal had been fine but did she want the Night Owl experience again? Not really.

'I did wonder', Ben said hurriedly before she could answer, 'whether you might like to go out for a meal somewhere. I mean the two of us.' There, he had said it! The idea had come to him at breakfast when the others had mentioned the plan they'd made, but he hadn't been sure enough to say anything. Now, seeing the surprise on Lottie's face, he was even less sure that his idea was a good one. Supposing she refused? Nevertheless, he ploughed on. 'We could go a bit further out, somewhere quieter. I could ask at the hotel, find out where would be best. That's to say, if you'd like to, but please don't hesitate to say—'

Lottie interrupted him. 'I'd like that very much,' she replied. 'It's a lovely idea.'

Ben smiled his relief. He had a nice smile, she thought. He should try it out more often. 'Right,' he said. 'Then I'll sort it out. What sort of food do you like?'

'Anything,' Lottie said. 'Absolutely anything.'

'Shall I pick you up at your hotel at about eight?' Ben asked.

She agreed to that, though she was not keen on him coming to Dawson's. She'd hate him to think that it was the sort of standard she was used to, so she would make it plain that it wasn't her choice. And she'd be down in the entrance before he arrived. The reception area wasn't quite as bad as the rest of it.

A couple walked towards the stand, then hovered.

'I'd better be off,' Ben said. 'Leave you to it.' He went to join Joseph and Harry, giving Dulcie, who was occupied, a polite nod as he passed her.

Later – it was around lunchtime and Karen had already gone for her break – there was a lull and Dulcie came across to speak to Lottie. 'It's all arranged,' she said chirpily. 'Joseph had a word and it's all fixed. We're to be in the Carlton bar as soon after eight as we can make it. He'll book a table for six.'

'How kind of him,' Lottie said, trying not to sound too pleased with herself. 'But I'm awfully sorry, I won't be able to make it.'

'Don't be silly,' Dulcie said. 'Come on, love. You'll enjoy it.'

'No, I mean it,' Lottie said. 'Truly, I can't. I'm going out to dinner with Ben. That's all fixed too. He's taking me into the country somewhere, so I'm not sure what time we'll get back, but I'll come in quietly, try not to waken you.' She smiled sweetly.

Dulcie shrugged. 'If that's what you want . . .'

'It is,' Lottie said. 'I'm looking forward to it.' She was surprised to find that she was speaking the truth.

At the exhibition business fell off as closing time drew near and Ken, when she explained that she had a date, agreed that Lottie could leave a quarter of an hour early. It gave her a head start over Dulcie and Karen, with first turn at the mirror, but even so it would be a scramble to be ready and waiting in the reception area by eight o'clock.

She was wearing one of the two dresses she had packed for such contingencies. It was what she considered to be the more elegant of the two: black, bias-cut and clinging, it was sleeveless and had a low – but not too low, since she judged that wouldn't be to Ben's liking – neckline that showed off the creamy skin of her long slender neck and gave a discreet glimpse – no more – of the upper part of her breasts. All her ensemble was in good taste, including the pearl (artificial) necklace round her neck and the matching drop earrings. She was well aware – it was something else her mother had taught her – how pearls set off a good skin, and a good skin was something she did have, pushing thirty or not. It was not that she was out to impress Ben unduly, nothing like that, but it was no more than polite if a man was taking you out, spending money on you, she thought as she applied a spot more pale-mauve shadow on her eyelids and stroked her lashes with a second coat of mascara, to look one's best.

'I have to say, Lottie,' Dulcie remarked, 'you do look quite good. I'm sure he'll be impressed.'

'I'm not out to impress anyone,' Lottie protested. 'It's not like that at all. It'll be just a nice, friendly evening. No big deal. All the same,' she added, taking a last look at herself in the mirror before leaving, 'I just wish I didn't have to wear this coat. Beige tweed really doesn't go with this dress. It needs something a bit more glamorous.'

Dulcie and Karen stood side by side, looking at her critically.

'You're dead right, it doesn't,' Karen agreed. 'I'll tell you what, I'll do a swap with you. You can borrow mine. It's not exactly an evening thing, but it's black and it's plain and it won't show up so much.'

'Oh, Karen, you are so good,' Lottie said. 'But what about you?'

'Yours will go better with my outfit than it does with yours,' Karen said.

So now here she was, standing in reception, not exactly wearing Karen's coat but draping it over her shoulders so that what showed most was the dress. She stood there a full five minutes before Ben came in at the door. He smiled at her and she wasn't sure that he had even noticed what she was wearing. He himself looked very respectable in a dark suit with a silver-grey tie. He also looked nervous.

'There you are,' he said. 'I'm sorry if I'm late.'

'Oh, you're not,' Lottie said. 'I've only just this second come down.'

'I've got the car at the door,' Ben said. 'It's Joseph's, actually. He said they wouldn't need it this evening – they're going to be in the city. It's better for them to take taxis.'

How kind people are, Lottie thought. Karen's lent me her coat and Joseph's lent Ben his car. 'Where are we going?' she enquired.

'It's called Fountains and it's about ten miles out,' Ben said. 'I hope you'll like it. It was well recommended.' He sounded anxious.

'I'm sure I will,' Lottie said.

It was surprising to Lottie how quickly they were out of the city and through the suburbs. She remarked on it to Ben.

'It's like that with a lot of northern towns,' he said. 'They're closely built, densely populated, and then suddenly you're in the countryside. I hope we can find this place. The man in the hotel said you couldn't miss it but I've heard that tale before.'

Even though the light was fading they did find it easily. It was signposted about a mile before it appeared, which it eventually did in a glow of fountain-shaped, delicate lighting.

Ben parked the car and they went in. It didn't have the feeling of a hotel, more of an old country house that had seen better days but where everything was clean, and shining with years of polishing. It seemed not so much smart as lived-in. There was a large hall, several comfortable-looking leather chairs, people sitting around, a log fire burning in the wide fireplace. Flowers were clustered in large vases, not exquisitely arranged but looking more as if the lady of the house had wandered around the garden, picking something here, something there, whatever happened to be in bloom, and mixed them together without too much precision. They looked happy enough.

There was no formal reception desk but behind a mahogany table a middle-aged lady, who looked as though she had been born in the house and grown up in it, smiled a welcome as they approached her.

'I booked a table,' Ben said. 'Thornton.'

'Ah yes. Good evening.'

'We're a bit early,' Ben said.

'Then, you'll have time for a leisurely drink,' she said. 'Would you like it here, in the hall? Or there's a small sitting-room round to the right. Whichever you prefer. Shall I take your coat, madam?'

Lottie let Karen's coat go with some relief. Though pleased that it wasn't her beige tweed, she knew, even so, she looked better without it. Her little black dress was more suited to this place – not that the place was at all flash or glitzy, it just gave her a feeling that people inhabiting it would always know what to wear, without being overly smart.

'Where would you like to sit?' Ben asked her. 'Here, or in the sitting-room?'

'Oh, here, by the fire,' Lottie said. 'It's lovely, isn't it?'

'I'm glad you like it,' Ben said.

A young woman, neatly dressed but not in uniform, took their orders for drinks and gave them each a menu. A large black labrador ambled around the hall, then came to greet them before stretching itself out in front of the fire.

'I like this place,' Lottie said. 'It's different, isn't it?'

The drinks came, gin-and-tonic for both of them, served in large glasses. Ben studied the menu.

'The food sounds good,' he said. 'Not fancy, but good. What would you like?'

Lottie read her menu. 'As you say, it all sounds great. I think I'll go for the *coq au vin*.'

'Me too,' Ben said.

When the young woman came back he ordered. 'It will be about fifteen minutes, sir,' she said.

'Fine,' Ben said. 'There's no hurry.'

Of course there was no hurry, but there was time to be filled, Lottie thought. What would they talk about? They were little more than strangers and a very long way from the stage where they could sit in companionable silence. But when in doubt, she thought, when every aspect of the weather has been exhausted, ask people a question about themselves, or their job. She wasn't even sure that Ben had a job, as such, nevertheless she plunged in.

'Joseph said you had a guest-house,' she said. 'Do you run that yourself? Do you enjoy it?'

'It's more of a bed-and-breakfast,' Ben said. 'We'll do packed lunches if asked, but we don't do evening meals. It was Moira's thing, really, and she was very good at it, she enjoyed meeting people. I don't mean I didn't help – I did the financial side and several other things – but she was the real organizer.'

'And will you keep it on?' Lottie asked. 'I mean . . .'

'Now that I don't have Moira?' Ben said. 'Yes, or at least I'll try it for this summer. It's actually quite profitable.'

'Then who will help you?' Lottie wanted to know.

'Well, I have Alice,' he said. 'She lives in the village. She used to help Moira and she helps me in the house now. She's quite competent at that, but running it and being what you might call the hostess isn't in her line at all.'

Nor, I reckon, Lottie thought – but did not say – are you cut out for being Mine Host.

'Anyway, I'll give it a go,' Ben said. 'I ought to because we've already got one or two bookings. People do tend to come back again, and these were made when Moira was alive. I've never got around to cancelling them. And there will be others, as well as people turning up casually.'

He fell silent, as if the topic was exhausted, but before Lottie could think of something else to talk about rescue came in the shape of the young woman to tell them that the meal was ready to be served, and they followed her into the dining-room.

The *coq au vin* was particularly appetizing and Ben had chosen a pleasant wine to go with it. That in itself came as a surprise to Lottie, since he didn't come across as a man who would know about such things. He was what she would call unsophisticated. That was the word. He was nice, he was pleasant, but worldly he was not. Perhaps that was because he had been born and brought up in the depths of the country – but no, that couldn't entirely account for it, since neither Joseph nor Harry were the least bit unworldly. They, she felt sure, knew their way around, knew all the ropes.

And then, at a point where they had finished the main course and were waiting for the dessert, Ben seemed suddenly to change a little. He came to life, brightened up. Perhaps it was the wine, Lottie thought. Perhaps it had loosened his tongue or given him courage. Goodness knew she had seen that happen more than a few times in her life. And yet somehow she didn't think it was the alcohol speaking; that wasn't in his manner at all. His voice wasn't louder, he wasn't showering her with fulsome compliments, which in her experience would have been par for the course with most men at this stage. He just seemed a little more confident.

She was not to know that he was screwing up his courage to pay her a host of compliments. He wanted at this very moment to tell her how beautiful she was – she was like some gorgeous, exotic butterfly that had flown into his life from a foreign country – how the softness and depth of her voice moved him, no matter how ordinary were the words she uttered. He was sharply aware of the smooth creaminess of her neck and the glimpse of her breasts against the dark silkiness of her dress. And yes, the wine had helped. He was aware of that. And as he leaned across the table he wanted to say something which would express what he was feeling about her at this minute. Something memorable, extravagant.

Yet even as he opened his mouth to speak, the confidence went out of him. 'We've talked about me all the time,' he said. 'Tell me what you do.' It was all that came out of him and it was not at all what he had intended.

'You've seen what I do,' Lottie said. 'It isn't always farm stuff, but it's much the same whatever's on sale.'

'Oh,' Ben said. 'And do you enjoy it?' This was not the conversation he had envisaged only a few minutes ago.

She pulled a face. 'I don't know that "enjoy" is the word I'd use. I earn a living – of a sort. I get the chance to travel around. And sometimes,' she looked directly at him, her eyes soft, her voice warm, 'sometimes, if I'm lucky, I meet some especially nice people.'

The promise in her voice and his hopes were broken by the arrival of the dessert.

'Ooh!' Lottie said. 'I do like sticky toffee pudding. I'm an absolute pig when it comes to sticky toffee pudding.'

At that moment Ben would have liked to give her the world's supply of sticky toffee pudding. He knew now – he had firmly made up his mind when she had said 'especially nice people' – what he was going to say to her, and he would not fail to do it, but for now she was occupied with the pudding. He would keep it back until they had finished eating.

'Would you like your coffee in the hall, or will you have it at the table?' the waitress asked.

'Oh, in the hall,' Ben said. He turned to Lottie. 'Would you like a brandy?'

'Not really,' she said; 'but a glass of port would be nice.'

He ordered port for her and brandy for himself and they went back into the hall, where, happily, the same armchairs by the fire were free for them. When the drinks came Ben took a swig rather than a sip of his brandy, and spoke. 'Would you like to come for a visit to Cordale? I mean to Beck Farm.'

'Oh, I would. I really would,' Lottie said. It was the invitation she had been waiting for.

ELEVEN

Ben stood on the platform, waiting for the train that would bring Lottie to Shepton. It was due at quarter-past two but it had now gone half-past and there was no sign of it; nor had there been any explanation over the loudspeaker system as to why it was late and when it might arrive. Perhaps delays were now so common that they no longer bothered to give reasons for them, though he did remember – it was some years ago now – an announcement regretting the delay of a train into King's Cross because there was a body on the line. It had sent a frisson of horror through the people, of whom he'd been one, queuing to travel north on that particular train. It had also been an immediate and gripping source of conversation between people standing in line who would otherwise never have considered speaking to one another. But right now, he thought sensibly, it was probably no more than a points failure, or a signal delay. There was nothing to be done about it. Who could do anything about a late train?

He walked along to the news-stand and bought a paper. By now the nationals had sold out, so it had to be the *Dales Chronicle*, but no matter, he would be able to catch up with the local news, such as it was. Births, marriages and deaths, Women's Institute meetings, sheep sales. He found a space on a bench, next to a woman with a cat mewing in a basket, and sat down to read.

He couldn't concentrate. His mind was on Lottie. He was looking forward so much to seeing her but he was, at the same time, apprehensive. There had been some awkward moments in telling one or two people that she was coming, or, more particularly, why. Alice, in the first place. Alice liked to know everything, from thread to needle. She felt she had a right to; they had known each other since they were children, and in the last few months she had been especially good to him. He owed her a lot. All the same, there was no way he was prepared to tell all. However innocent the trip to Manchester had been, and it *had* been, would it sound so in the telling? Kilby was a small place, nothing much of interest happened, and Alice would make the most of it. So in view of Lottie's imminent arrival, he'd given her an edited version of events. No need for more.

'She was working on this stand, selling farm supplies,' he'd said. 'Joseph and Harry were interested – after all, it was why we were there, wasn't it? We got talking. It turned out this lady had never been to the Yorkshire Dales and she'd quite like to do so. "But where would I stay?" she asked. So – I suppose it was natural enough – Joseph said, "Well, Ben here runs a B&B in Cordale." And it went from there.

'That was how it happened,' he'd said. 'Quite by chance. So she's coming on Easter Saturday and she'll stay until Wednesday.'

Nothing had been said of the fact that they'd all gone out to a meal, and most certainly not that he'd spent the following evening with her on his own. Dulcie and Karen hadn't come into the story at all. In any case he wouldn't have mentioned them, because there were Joseph's and Harry's wives to think about. He didn't want to cause trouble there. When he'd first told the two men that Lottie would be coming to stay with him they had laughed immoderately. It was unbelievable, he must be joking. 'Pull the other one!' Harry had said, but in the end, when he'd convinced them that it was true, they'd been alarmed.

'What if Peggy and Beryl meet her – which is more than likely – and they find out? We'll never be allowed out again,' Joseph said. 'My wife's a very jealous woman.'

'It's simple,' Ben had assured them. 'As far as they're

concerned Lottie will be a routine visitor to Beck Farm. I'll put Lottie wise. I'm sure she'll understand. Anyway, as luck would have it I've got four other visitors coming at the same time. They made the booking with Moira when they were here last year and I forgot to cancel it. So don't worry, Lottie will just blend in.'

'I can't see Lottie just blending in,' Harry said with grudging admiration.

'Just be careful, that's all,' Joseph warned.

'I will, I will,' Ben promised. 'And you'd better be likewise.'

'I must say,' Harry said, 'I've known you all my life, Ben Thornton, but I never knew you could be so devious.'

Nor did I, Ben thought with a certain amount of pleasure. Nor did I.

So in speaking to Alice he had blown it all light. That Lottie was young and quite beautiful had not come into it at all. If Alice liked to think that the proposed visitor was middle-aged and plain, well, that was her look-out. With any luck, and knowing him, she wouldn't read anything into it at all. She knew how he had loved Moira and how genuinely he mourned her. 'And since she hasn't got a car and I was likely to be in Shepton,' he'd added, 'I said I'd meet her at the station.'

'If she hasn't got a car, why is she coming to Cordale?' Alice had asked.

'Apparently she's fond of walking,' he'd said, though he couldn't imagine that to be true and he was a bit shocked at the way it had all tripped off his tongue.

By now he had read all the parts of the *Chronicle* that interested him. As a last resort he turned to the Wills and Legacies column, which listed how much local people had left, and to whom. In his parents' time it had been a matter of pride to have left a good sum of money, but now, he thought, everyone being wiser about tax matters, it would simply show inefficiency. He was halfway through the list, no surprises there, when the train was announced. He jumped to his feet and hurried to meet it, leaving the newspaper on the bench, from where it was immediately picked up by the woman with the cat.

Lottie was the last person off the train. For one terrible moment he thought she had changed her mind, wasn't coming, and then she stepped down at the far end of the platform. He felt a surge of pleasure at the sight of her, a slim figure in a dark suit, her hair, almost shoulder-length, curling around her neck. At first she stood there for a few seconds, not seeing him, but when he waved she caught sight of him and they walked towards each other, both of them smiling. It was not possible to shake hands, since she was carrying a suitcase in one hand, a handbag and magazine in the other and a topcoat slung over her arm.

'Let me take your case,' he said. 'How are you? Did you have a good journey?' The suitcase was larger and heavier than he'd expected for a four-night stay. He supposed young women carried more stuff around with them than he would.

'I'm well,' she said. 'And it was a very good journey. I had to change trains at Leeds but that wasn't difficult. How are you?'

'I'm fine,' he said. 'It's good to see you.' It was better than good. He'd been looking forward to it, though still not sure whether he'd done the right thing in inviting her or how it would work out. Well, he still didn't know how it would work out but he felt unusually hopeful.

'The car's in the station car park,' he said. 'It's quite close. Let me take your coat.'

'It's OK,' she said. 'I thought I'd better bring a warm coat in case it was cold up here. I was working in Bournemouth last week; it was quite warm there, for the time of the year, I mean.'

'It would be, down south,' Ben said. 'It's not been too bad here. A bit breezy, on and off.'

Talk about the weather lasted them until they reached the car. Ben put the suitcase and the coat in the boot.

'On second thoughts,' he said, 'would you like to stop in Shepton for a bit before going on to Kilby?'

'What I *would* like', Lottie said, 'is a cup of tea. I didn't have one on the train. Or would you rather get home?'

'A cup of tea would be fine,' Ben said. 'One thing Shepton's not short of is cafés.'

It being Saturday, and Easter weekend, Shepton was busy. There were as many street stalls and almost as many people buying as on a market day. Making their way through the High Street, Lottie seemed really taken by it. 'It's cute,' she said. He had never thought of Shepton as being cute. It was a place he visited mostly for business reasons, a place where on market days Moira for years had brought her produce to sell. And the moment after Lottie had spoken he realized they were passing the very stall Moira had used, though he said nothing about that. In any case, it had been taken over by someone selling household linen.

They crossed the road to a teashop and, busy though it was, managed to get a table.

'This is great,' Lottie said. 'I like what I've seen of Shepton. So many shops, so many stalls!'

'Yes,' Ben said. 'I reckon you can get most things here, though the ladies sometimes like a trip to Leeds or Bradford by way of a change.'

'You can keep Leeds and Bradford,' Lottie said; 'not that I've anything against them – well, I wouldn't have, would I, I don't really know them – but I'm really looking forward to being in the country.'

'I hope you're going to enjoy it,' Ben replied.

Lottie chatted like an excited child through two cups of tea and a cream cake, then Ben said, 'I ought to be back before Alice leaves.' He paid the bill and they walked back to the car park. It was clear to him that Lottie would have liked to linger at some of the stalls, but he had to discourage that. 'I have four guests due,' he explained. 'Alice is holding the fort until I get back, but it's time for her to finish for the day. She goes home before teatime and comes back in the morning to do the breakfasts, and so on.'

'So you have to do the teas yourself?' Lottie asked. Somehow she couldn't imagine it.

'Oh no,' Ben said. 'We don't do teas. Perhaps we ought to. We don't do evening meals, either. I wouldn't consider doing that. We recommend our visitors to go to the Shorn Lamb just down the road. I thought we'd go there ourselves this evening.' He wasn't a hundred per cent comfortable about that, because Joyce would be there, and Joyce could be a bit funny. She'd been so attached to Moira. Still, he'd only be taking a guest from Beck Farm, wouldn't he? Just showing her the ropes.

They were quickly out of the town and into the country. Lottie was delighted with everything, as pleased as a child let loose in a sweet-shop. 'It's so *green*!' she exclaimed. 'The fields and the trees. I've never seen anything so green.'

'You've come at the best time of the year for that,' Ben said. 'It's not all that long since the snow melted. It leaves everything new and fresh. Every year it surprises me, the way it looks when the spring comes. It's my favourite time of the year.'

The road, at first, ran close to the river, which was full and rushing. On the other side there were already new lambs in the lower meadows, keeping close to their dams.

'They're so sweet!' Lottie enthused.

Ben nodded, though it wasn't quite the word he would have used. It was a woman's word, especially a townswoman's, but he agreed with the feeling. The birth of the new lambs, though it brought long hours of work and not a few sleepless nights, was about the only thing he missed since he'd given up farming. When Moira was alive and if it was necessary she could run the house and look after the visitors on her own, leaving him free to turn to and help one or other of the neighbouring farmers. They all gave one another a hand, if required. It would usually be Joseph, because the land he farmed had once been Ben's own and he was familiar with every acre of it. This year, however, he would not be available.

'Will there be lambs in Kilby?' Lottie asked.

'Not just yet,' Ben said. 'It's that bit higher than where we are at the moment. In a few minutes from now you'll see the road starts to climb. The lambs will be a week or two yet in Cordale. Tupping time is later for that reason, so that the lambs will be born later, when it's likely to be a little bit warmer – though of course the weather doesn't always oblige. I've known it snow in late May in Cordale.'

'Tupping time?' Lottie said. 'What's that?'

For a second Ben was amazed that anyone shouldn't know what tupping time was, but then, why should she? he reminded himself. She didn't live in sheep country.

'It's when the farmer lets the rams go to the ewes,' he said. 'A few each day. He knows which have been served, and when, and how long it takes a lamb to come, so he can reckon when they'll be born. And he hopes when they do come it will be warm enough for them to be out in the fields.'

'I see,' Lottie said. 'What a lot there is I don't know about the country! You'll have to teach me.'

And I'd enjoy that, Ben thought. She seemed so pleased by everything.

'What's it like where you live?' he asked.

'Oh, it's all right, I suppose,' Lottie said without enthusiasm. 'I'm not there much. The one good thing about my job is that it takes me round the country quite a bit. But the best times used to be when I went home after I'd finished a job, and my mother would be there. Sometimes we'd have a week or more together before I went off to something else. After she died there wasn't much to go back to. I miss her a lot. She looked after me.'

'I know how you feel,' Ben said.

'We lived in a rented house,' Lottie continued. 'It was too expensive for me after she died, so I moved out. I live in a small flat now.'

'And you never . . .'

'You mean did I ever marry? Well, yes, I did. It didn't work out. My mother always told me it wouldn't. We divorced.'

'I'm sorry,' Ben said.

'Yes,' she said. 'It was pretty awful at the time, but you get over these things. I'm pleased to say I'm footloose and fancy-free now. Is Kilby much further?'

'No,' Ben said. 'Not more than four miles or so. It's on the other side of the river.'

They said very little for the next mile or two. Poor girl, Ben thought, she's had a hard time of it. He wondered for a minute or two what her husband had been like, and then dismissed it from his mind. When they reached the bridge he made a right turn and drove across it. 'That's Kilby,' he said: 'you can see it straight ahead.'

'Oh, it looks lovely,' Lottie cried. 'Really quaint.'

'It's quite old,' Ben said. He hadn't thought of it as quaint. It was just – well, it was Kilby, as it had been all his life and long

142

before that. You didn't question the place where you'd always lived.

There was a large Ford parked outside Beck Farm and as Ben pulled up beside it Alice, who explained that she just happened to have been looking out of the window, opened the house door and came down the path towards them.

'The others have arrived,' she said. 'They had a very good journey and they turned up before time, so just as well I was here. They've gone down to the village.'

Ben got out of the car and went round to help Lottie out. 'This is . . .' he began, then realized he didn't know Lottie's last name – he had never thought to ask it – but she came to the rescue.

'Lottie Harper,' she said, smiling as she held out her hand. 'And you must be Alice. I've been hearing about you. All of it good!' she added quickly.

'That's all right, then,' Alice said. This guest was not at all what she'd expected. Much younger and . . . well . . . a bit flashy, that was what she'd call her. Skirt halfway up her thighs, black patent shoes with high heels. She'd not walk far in those, that was certain. Nevertheless, she took Lottie's case and carried it into the house, Lottie and Ben following behind.

'I'll show you your room,' she said.

Lottie, with a quick, backward glance at Ben, followed Alice up the stairs. Ben was relieved to see it. It meant that Alice was treating Lottie as she would any other guest. Politely, but not effusively.

Alice came down on her own a few minutes later. 'She seemed very appreciative,' she said. 'So I'll be off, then. I'll see you in the morning.'

'Thank you for staying,' Ben said.

He went into the kitchen and filled the kettle, which was where Lottie found him when she came downstairs having unpacked, tidied her hair and renewed her make-up.

'What a lovely house!' she said. 'I like my room. What a wonderful view! What are you doing? Can I help?'

'I was going to make a pot of tea,' Ben said. 'But perhaps you're not ready for another just yet?'

'I'm always ready for a cup of tea,' Lottie assured him.

143

He made the tea, took the fruitcake – which Alice had made – from the tin, and cut two slices. 'Shall we take it into the sitting-room?' he suggested.

'Oh no,' Lottie protested. 'It's nice in here. I like kitchens.'

It was not quite true, and certainly not what the late Mrs Harper would have expected to hear. Afternoon tea was to be taken in the front room, and Lottie seldom had a hand in making it, which was quite reasonable because she worked hard all week at these wonderful exhibitions where she was such a success and she was entitled to a little spoiling when she came home.

When they had finished their tea, Lottie showed willing by putting the cups and plates in the dishwasher, then she said, 'Would you like to show me around the house – if that isn't being cheeky? I love looking at houses. I suppose it comes from not having one of my own.'

'Of course,' Ben said, 'you're welcome. Not that there's anything grand.'

He showed her everything, though when they came to the two rooms occupied by the other guests he did no more than open the door and let her peek inside. He took her into the garden that ran at the side of the house. 'It's a bit of a mess,' he said. 'The garden was my wife's job – not that she had much time to spare – so it's been neglected this last year. I keep meaning to get down to it.'

'I like the apple tree,' Lottie said. 'That looks healthy enough.' It was just beginning to break into blossom.

'Moira set great store by the apple tree,' Ben said. 'It always fruits well. Never fails.'

'I love gardening,' Lottie told him, not quite truthfully. Or I know I would if ever I had the chance, she told herself. 'What a pity I won't be here long enough to give you a hand with it.'

He showed her the outbuildings, where they had kept the animals before he'd given up farming. 'Though Moira continued to keep chickens, and a goat,' he said.

'How wonderful,' Lottie said. 'Who would live in a town if they could live in the country? I really think I must be a country girl at heart.' She laughed happily.

144

Having done the tour, they were in the sitting-room when the other guests returned. Ben introduced everyone.

'Mr and Mrs Davis, Mr and Mrs Weatherfield – Miss Harper.' The last name came awkwardly to him.

'Oh, please!' Lottie said. 'Lottie!'

'Likewise, Cynthia and Mervyn,' Mrs Davis said.

'And Angela and Bruce,' Mrs Weatherfield added.

Small exchanges followed. The Davises and the Weatherfields had been here last year and nothing would have prevented them coming back; Lottie had been last week in Bournemouth, and the week before that in Brighton. If they gathered that she was some sort of model it was not quite her fault, it was the impression they gained from her appearance.

'We popped into the Shorn Lamb and booked a table for this evening,' Cynthia said. 'It was nice to see Bernard again. Joyce wasn't around. Are you eating there?'

'We are,' Ben said. 'Though I haven't booked. Perhaps I should have as it's Saturday night and Easter weekend. Anyway, I expect they'll fit us in.'

It was, in fact, impossible when Ben and Lottie arrived at the Shorn Lamb to give them a table to themselves. The place was crowded. 'The only thing is to sit with your other guests,' Bernard said. 'I could fit in two more chairs there.' It was not what Ben had envisaged, but no-one else, including Lottie, seemed to mind. She was as happy as a sandboy and so were the others. And in a way, Ben thought, it was easier, at least for this first occasion, than if he was with Lottie on his own. It would keep the conversation going, and there would be nothing there for anyone to question.

'Ben's got another guest apart from the Davises and the Weatherfields,' Bernard reported to Joyce when he went into the kitchen. 'She's a real bobby-dazzler, this one!' Joyce, busy with the cooking, didn't take in what he said. Even if she had, it would hardly have registered with her. It was the kind of thing men did say and Bernard was no different from the rest. It was not until the meal was well under way – they were mostly finishing their main course, the cold puddings were ready to be served and the hot ones plated and in the hot cupboard – that she took a break and did what was usual for her at this stage. She wiped the steam off the glass panel in the kitchen door and looked out into the restaurant. She always enjoyed this minute, seeing all the customers happy with the food she'd cooked. Her eyes darted round the room before coming to rest on Ben's table in the far corner. And there was Ben, smiling happily at this young woman and she looking back at him as if she could eat him. And yes, Bernard was right, she *was* a bobby-dazzler! She looked exactly the kind of woman, Joyce thought, you couldn't trust as far as you could throw her.

'So who is this floozie Ben Thornton's with?' she asked Bernard.

'She's not a floozie. I never said that,' Bernard corrected her. 'She's just a guest at Beck Farm. She seems a very pleasant young woman from what I can tell, serving her.'

Joyce snorted. 'You men are all alike,' she said. 'You can't see beyond a pretty face and a shapely figure.'

'Of which she has both,' Bernard said, teasing her.

'She's not Ben's usual style of guest,' Joyce pointed out.

'Now, with that I have to agree,' Bernard said. 'Anyway, I'd better serve these ice-creams before they melt on the plates.' With practised ease he picked up more plates than any one person could have been expected to carry at one time, and left the kitchen. She watched through the glass panel as he took them to Ben Thornton's table and bent over the so far unnamed guest, smiling excessively as he placed the ice-cream sundae on the table in front of her. Men were such idiots when it came to pretty girls, she thought – though, of course, she would trust Bernard to the ends of the earth. It was all show with him. But Ben Thornton wasn't like most men when it came to women; he was the quiet, reserved type. He'd probably drunk too much wine – they'd ordered a second bottle – but even that wasn't like him.

'It's been a lovely evening,' Lottie said as they all walked back to Beck Farm together. 'I didn't realize there was so much fun in the country.'

'But of course there is,' Angela Weatherfield said. 'Simple fun, but it's all there if you want it.'

'And if you know where to look,' her husband said.

'We're going to walk tomorrow,' Cynthia Davis said. 'You're welcome to join us if you'd like to. Nothing too strenuous for the first day. We're a bit out of practice.'

'Climb the fell this side,' her husband said, 'drop down into Freshdale, walk a mile or two along the valley . . .'

'Stop for a spot of lunch before we tackle the slope back to the top, walk along the ridge for a couple of miles, then drop down into Cordale again,' Angela said. 'It's lovely walking along the tops. The fells are quite high between here and Freshdale. You can see for miles. Will you come with us?'

'Thank you,' Lottie said. 'I think I won't, if you don't mind. I've had a busy week, so I thought I'd have a lazy day tomorrow – explore the village and so on.' And spend some time with Ben, she reckoned, though they had clearly assumed that she was here on her own, a fellow guest, not someone personally invited by Ben.

Their assumption was borne out the following morning when she went down to breakfast and found that Alice, who had turned up for duty well before Lottie had even got out of bed, had laid a small, one-person table for her in the dining-room. The only sign of the others was a table at which breakfast had obviously been eaten.

'Mr Thornton's nipped down to the village,' Alice explained. 'One or two things we needed. He does like a proper breakfast. Would you like one? Bacon, eggs, mushrooms, tomato, fried bread?'

Lottie, whose breakfasts never varied from a small dish of cereal and a half-slice of toast, usually on the hop, heard herself saying, 'Yes, please. Why not? And coffee, please. Where are the others?'

'Oh, they've gone off walking,' Alice said. 'They never waste a minute when they're here. They're nice people. The late Mrs Thornton was very fond of them, as they were of her. But then, she was a lovely lady. This was a happy home.'

'Mr Thornton must miss her,' Lottie said.

'Oh, terribly,' Alice agreed. 'Terribly. We all do.'

She left the room and some minutes later returned with Lottie's breakfast.

'That looks lovely,' Lottie said.

'Well, set to and enjoy it,' Alice said. 'Mrs Thornton always liked to see everyone enjoy their breakfast.'

Lottie ate it all, not only because she was physically hungry, which at this hour of the day was unusual for her, but from some feeling – she couldn't quite define it – that she must do so. Perhaps eating a hearty breakfast was what a countrywoman did? She was disappointed that Ben hadn't been there to greet her. She wished he had waited, so that they could have gone down to the village together.

She had finished her breakfast but was still sitting at the table, wondering what she might do next, when Ben returned, carrying two large plastic bags.

'Oh, there you are,' she said pleasantly. 'If I'd known you were going to the village I'd have been down earlier, I'd have gone with you.' Her smile robbed the words of their faint note of disapproval.

'I thought you might need a bit of a lie-in,' Ben said. 'I mean, after travelling yesterday. I hope you slept well.' He thought how bright and lovely she looked. 'I always go down to the village early. I suppose you could say I stick to a routine. I'm a bit set in my ways.'

'Well, we must do something about that,' Lottie joked. 'At least while I'm here.'

TWELVE

Walking down to the village, Lottie was still slightly disappointed that Ben had elected to follow his own pursuits this morning. 'Running repairs' was how he'd described them. And no, there was no way she could help, thank you all the same. A dripping tap; a window in the Weatherfields' room that refused to close and was letting in a draught; a fuse in the back scullery; a couple of letters to answer. 'Always something when you have a business like this,' he'd said. 'Will you be all right for an hour or two?' What could she have done but agree? 'In that case I'll walk down to the village,' she'd said, trying not to sound piqued. She had hoped and expected that she would have had all of his time in her short visit, that he would go with her to the village, guide her around, perhaps introduce her to people. Now it seemed it wasn't to be like that, at least not this morning. Perhaps he had sensed her disappointment, because as she was setting off he said, 'I thought we could go out for a drive this afternoon. Would you like that?' 'Very much,' she'd said.

It was a bright day, cool but sunny, with a breeze, and the air was as clear and crisp as if it had been newly made that morning for the benefit of the inhabitants of Kilby. Spending most of her time in towns where the air often felt second-hand, as if it had been inhaled and breathed out again by several hundred people, she was not used to this feeling of freshness. It came as a pleasant surprise and in spite of her disappointment her spirits lifted. She was surprised also by the number of people out and about in Kilby. Was this because it was Easter Sunday? It seemed early in the day for tourists.

And having reached the village, she asked herself, what was there to do? What did she want to do? Well, for one thing, if there was a shop open she supposed she could buy some picture postcards – a few to keep for herself and one to send to Dulcie. Whenever she'd been away from home, on the job, she'd been used to sending a card to her mother almost every day, but Dulcie was now the only person who might possibly expect to hear from her. Her job was not one that led to a wide circle of friends. Acquaintances, yes, but it was too spread out, too here-today-and-gone-tomorrow to make friends. She might have sent a card to Karen, especially as she had been one of the party in Manchester, but that had been the only time she'd met her and she had no idea of her address. Sometimes she wondered why she had no friends from her schooldays, and the answer was that she had always spent most of her time with her mother. As everyone used to say, they were more like sisters than mother and daughter.

There *was* a shop open. In fact, although Kilby didn't boast many shops, they all, except the butchers, seemed to be open. She opted for the village store since, peering in the window, it seemed to sell most things. There were certainly cards and as it was also a post office there would be stamps. She went in. Among the cards on the rack was a nice one of the Shorn Lamb – she'd enjoyed yesterday evening, she hoped they'd go again – a view of the main street and the war memorial, and two of the church, one inside, one outside. She bought all four, and a block of milk chocolate. 'Could I have a stamp?' she asked the woman behind the counter.

'Usually you could,' the woman answered. 'But today being Sunday, the post office is closed, as it will be tomorrow, that being a bank holiday.' She spoke as if the post office was a separate building instead of a small area behind a metal grill at the back of the shop. Oh well, Lottie thought, I'll find some-where to have a cup of coffee and I'll write Dulcie's card. Perhaps Ben will have a stamp.

She walked down the length of the main street, paused to look in the window of a gift shop, then continued and found a small café, the Honey Pot, which advertised coffees, teas and lunches. It appeared to be full, but as she entered two people left a table in the window, which suited her down to the ground. She would watch life, or whatever passed for life in Kilby on a Sunday morning, while drinking her coffee and eating her scone. Perhaps, she thought, since the place was so busy, someone might come in and ask to share her table. There was a spare chair. It would be someone to talk to. But no-one did, and eventually, to pass a little more time, she called the waitress and ordered a second cup of coffee.

She could probably have had coffee in the Shorn Lamb, she thought. It had not looked particularly open when she'd passed it earlier, but most pubs served coffee nowadays. She might even have found one or two familiar faces there from the previous night – certainly Bernard's. He'd seemed quite friendly; she was sure he would have had a word with her. She might well have found out a little bit more about Ben – small things, no doubt, but she'd have liked to have heard them. She wanted to know more about him than the few facts she'd already gathered, which had been mostly from Joseph and Harry. That's what I should have done, she thought: I should have made straight for the Shorn Lamb in the first place. But it was too late now; she couldn't go around the village from coffee to coffee.

She dragged out drinking her second cup as long as she could, and then left. What now, other than go back to Beck Farm? With any luck, by this time Ben would have finished his chores. As she walked past the Shorn Lamb the door was open and she could see people in the bar, but – and it was unlike her – she lacked the courage to go in and join them. At the top of the road, on a spur of slightly higher ground, the church, squat and square-towered, stood in several acres of grassed graveyard. Deciding that she might as well take a look at it, she went through the lychgate and walked up the path, but, nearing the church door, which stood half open, she heard the sound of the organ. It was being played with all stops out, loud and triumphant, as befitted the Easter Day hymn, which she recognized. 'Jesus Christ is risen today,

151

Alleluia'. Years ago she had sung it in Sunday school. The congregation was going at it full pelt, and then it came to an end with the last 'alleluia', the organ died away and for some seconds there was complete silence.

She moved away from the door – she didn't wish to be caught up in the congregation – deciding that what she could do now was look round the churchyard. That would pass some time. It was definitely not one of her usual occupations but it looked so fresh and green, the grass so well cut, with the edges neatly trimmed and the midday sun lighting up the gravestones, that it seemed almost cheerful. She moved around at random, in no particular direction, reading the inscriptions, and then, a minute or two later, and to her surprise though not entirely to her pleasure – she wouldn't have chosen it – she found herself standing in front of Moira Thornton's grave. It was marked by a simple, new-looking stone that had not yet had time to weather. The only adornment was the words carved into it, MOIRA THORN-TON, BELOVED WIFE OF BEN THORNTON, AGED 47, and the dates of her birth and death, and underneath: FULL OF GRACE AND TRUTH. There were fresh spring flowers – daffodils, with paper-white narcissi and purple irises – in a metal vase in front of the headstone. Had Ben placed them there? Was he still mourning her? He had said next to nothing about Moira except that since she died Alice had helped in the house and with the guests. If Joseph and Harry hadn't told her otherwise, she might have thought that his wife's death had happened years ago instead of only months.

Nevertheless, even though she would not have chosen to be where she was, she felt uncomfortable about rushing away: it would somehow have felt bad-mannered. And then, while she was still lingering there, a woman, probably one of the church congregation, she thought, came and stood beside her. She was middle-aged, plain and plump, but decently dressed, as became the special day.

At first neither of them spoke, and then when Lottie was about to move the woman said, 'Did you know Moira?'

'No. No, I didn't,' Lottie replied. 'I'm a visitor to Kilby. I was just looking round. Did you know her?'

'Oh yes,' the woman said. 'I remember her coming to the village as a bride. She wasn't local, she came from York, but she very soon was one of us. She really was a lovely lady. It's true what it says there: she *was* full of truth and grace. Everyone loved her. She's very much missed.'

'Someone's left beautiful flowers,' Lottie said.

'That would be her best friend, Joyce,' the woman said. 'She does it regularly, week in, week out.'

'How nice,' Lottie said. 'I thought it might have been her husband.'

'Oh no,' the woman said. 'He was broken-hearted, of course, and I reckon maybe he can't bear to visit the grave. It takes some people like that, doesn't it? We're all different. So I'd never say Ben didn't miss her. He was devoted to her when she was ill. Did everything for her. Where did you say you were staying?'

'I didn't,' Lottie said. 'Actually, I'm staying at Beck Farm. Just for the Easter holiday.'

'Well, there's a coincidence,' the woman said. 'Then you know Ben Thornton?'

'I've met him, naturally,' Lottie said. 'I wouldn't say I knew him well.'

'A sad man,' the woman said. 'And lost on his own, I would think. Most men need a wife, don't they? They're helpless creatures without us. So let's hope he eventually finds someone, poor fellow – though she'd have to be a bit special to take Moira's place.'

She certainly would, Lottie thought as she walked slowly back to Beck Farm. Or for her own sake she'd have to be totally different. It didn't sound as though anyone could equal Moira on her own ground. Whoever spoke of her said something good. It might of course be a case of 'speak no ill of the dead', but it didn't come over like that, not from anyone. Joseph and Harry had both praised Moira highly, as had Alice – though that was to be expected – and the Weatherfields. and the Davises.

On reaching the house, she rang the bell and Ben came to the door. When she stepped into the hall she was met by the smell of cooking. She sniffed the air appreciatively. 'Something smells good,' she said.

'It's a shepherd's pie,' Ben said. 'I thought we'd have an early lunch. It'll give us more time for a drive out. I hope you like shepherd's pie?'

'Oh, I do,' Lottie said truthfully. 'I didn't know you could cook.'

'I can't,' Ben admitted. 'Well, not much. Eggs and bacon, that sort of thing. Alice made this, left it just to be heated up in the oven. I did some carrots and peas. Alice is very good like that.'

In the early days, in fact throughout this past long, dark winter, he'd made very few meals, simply boiling himself an egg if he felt like it, or eating bread and cheese. It had been people like Alice and Joyce and one or two other friends from the village who'd kept him going, though most of the time he hadn't cared about being kept going. This was not only because of his bereavement, it was also because he was so physically tired, so drained, after the long months of nursing. And, it being out of season, there had been no visitors to Beck Farm to push him into any activity that could possibly be avoided. But he'd felt better these last few weeks; he felt he'd turned the corner, especially since his trip to Manchester. Joseph and Harry had proved good friends. And now, of course, the weather was better, the days were brighter and gradually getting longer, and with the return of the visitors like the Davises and the Weatherfields – though he would certainly have put them off if he'd realized in time that they'd been booked in – there was a bit of life in the house. He didn't know what had possessed him to invite Lottie, or where he'd found the courage, but he was glad he'd done so.

'It'll be ready to serve in about fifteen minutes,' he said.

'Can I do anything to help?' Lottie offered. 'Can I lay the table?'

'It's all done,' Ben said. 'I wonder . . .' He hesitated.

'Yes?'

'We might have a glass of sherry while we're waiting,' he said tentatively. 'I know there's a bottle in the cupboard. Moira used to like a glass of sherry from time to time.'

'That would be lovely,' Lottie said. 'I enjoy a glass of sherry

154

before a meal.' She wasn't sure whether she wanted to encourage him to talk about Moira or not. She would take it as it came.

He poured the sherry and handed her a glass.

'I came across your wife's grave in the churchyard,' she said. 'Naturally I wasn't looking for it, I was just taking a walk. Another lady joined me. She said she knew Moira – is it all right for me to call her Moira?'

'Of course it is,' Ben said. 'She'd have been the first to say so. She didn't stand on ceremony.'

'I don't know the other lady's name,' Lottie said. 'I think she'd known Moira quite a long time. She seemed to think a lot of her.'

Ben nodded. 'It could have been almost anyone. Everyone did. Not just in Kilby, either; she was very well liked in the markets.'

'I suppose you don't have time to do any of that now?' Lottie asked. 'I mean the markets.'

'It's not so much time as inclination,' Ben said. 'It was never my thing. It was usually the sphere of the farmers' wives and Moira was especially good at it. All I do now is keep a few chickens, just for the house, and the guests' breakfasts in the summer months. If there's a surplus of eggs the village shop sells them for me. Can I refill your glass? The pie should be ready but it can wait a minute or two.'

'No, I'm fine, thank you,' Lottie said.

They ate at one of the tables in the guests' dining-room. Lottie praised the shepherd's pie, which was exceptionally good.

'Are you a good cook?' Ben asked her. 'Do you like cooking?'

'I don't suppose I am,' Lottie said. 'I mean a good cook. I did it when I was married, but that wasn't for long. When I went back to live with my mother she did all the cooking. She was great at it. I suppose I could learn. My mother said if you could read a recipe book you could cook, but I think you'd have to have a bit of a flair for it.'

Silence fell between them. They seemed to have said all there was to be said about cooking.

When lunch was over Ben said, 'I'll stack the plates in the dishwasher, then I'm ready for off if you are.'

'I am,' Lottie said.

'I think you should take your topcoat,' Ben suggested. 'We might want to leave the car to take a bit of a walk. It could turn chilly.'

'Very well,' Lottie agreed. 'And in that case some lower heels. Give me a few minutes.'

She hated flat shoes. They did one's legs no favours. She had expected just to tour around the countryside in Ben's car and perhaps stop for tea somewhere. She should have realized that country pursuits would inevitably include walking. She gave a passing thought, with no envy at all, to how the Davises and the Weatherfields were faring, what dizzy heights they were scaling.

Once behind the wheel of a car Ben seemed to change. Showing her the countryside he so obviously loved, his own country, he lost his diffidence and his shyness and talked freely. They travelled the length of Cordale, then crossed into Swaledale; they drove up hill and down dale, through small and larger villages, and at one point Ben parked the car and they walked by the side of the river. Ben knew something about everything; every tree, every shrub; he could name every bird and he spotted them so quickly. 'Look, there's a lapwing,' he said. 'See the way it twists as it flies upwards? And you can recognize it by the crest of feathers on the back of its head.' He knew what prehistoric climatic changes had shaped the fells the way they were; he knew what the inhabitants worked at – which was mostly farming – or had worked at in days gone by. 'There was a lot of lead mining round these parts,' he said. 'It was here in Roman times and before. It ceased not all that long ago.' What 'not all that long ago' meant, Lottie didn't know. He spoke of centuries as if they were no more than decades.

'But I'm sure you know all that,' he apologized. 'You must excuse me. I get carried away!'

'I didn't know,' Lottie said. 'Really, I know so little about this part of the world. It's so beautiful, isn't it? As well as interesting. I had no idea.'

'Oh, it is,' Ben agreed. 'I'd never want to live anywhere else. Never. I suppose it's whatever you've been used to, and I was born here. I couldn't settle in a town. A few hours in Shepton, when necessary, is quite enough for me, thank you. I don't suppose you'd be happy in the country? I suppose you belong in the town?'

Would I be happy in the country? Lottie wondered. She didn't know. Today the country was perfect, it couldn't be faulted, but it was a fine day in spring and common sense told her that it wouldn't always be like this. And did she belong in the town? For some time now, she supposed since her mother had died, she wasn't sure where she belonged, where her home was. It certainly wasn't the dingy little flat she'd go back to on Wednesday. She felt no affinity with Luton.

'I'm not sure that I do,' she said. 'Now, if it was a little town like Shepton . . .'

'I'd have liked to have taken you to Ripon,' Ben said. 'There's a nice town. And we could have gone to Fountains Abbey, but there isn't time. I have to be back before the others arrive. I should have had the sense to give them a key so they could let themselves in, but I didn't.' He looked at his watch. 'All the same,' he said, 'I think we could stop for some tea in Leyburn. That's a nice little town.'

To Lottie's eyes it was more like a large – and very pleasant – village. 'But it has a cinema,' Ben protested when she said so. 'True, you have to figure out when it might be open, and the films won't be all that recent, but it *is* a cinema!'

When they'd had tea he drove back to Kilby as fast as the road would allow him, passing everything he could, and faster, Lottie thought, glancing at the speedometer, than he should. Only when they were held up by a small herd of cows being taken home for milking did he slow down. And in that situation he showed infinite patience. Clearly, she thought, as the car crawled behind at walking pace, he preferred cows to other road users. Once the leading cow had guided the rest of the herd through a gateway, which was clearly a daily routine, Ben put his foot down again, and kept it down until they arrived in Kilby. To Lottie it seemed out of character, but then, what did she know of Ben's character? she asked herself. Very little.

At Beck Farm they found the Weatherfields and the Davises

sitting on the low wall in front of the house. They looked tired and slightly dishevelled. Ben leapt out of the car and hurried towards them.

'I'm terribly sorry,' he said. 'I should have given you a key. Have you been waiting long?'

'About fifteen minutes,' Bruce Weatherfield said.

'But it really doesn't matter,' his wife said quickly. 'It's not raining.'

'All the same,' Ben said, 'I shall give you a key the minute we get into the house. I want you to be able to come and go as you please.'

'Well, yes,' Mervyn Davis pointed out. 'Otherwise you're going to have to wait in for us, aren't you?' He sounded annoyed.

'Anyway, never mind,' Cynthia said. 'You're here now. And we've had a lovely day. That's what matters, isn't it?'

Ben hurried ahead to unlock the door, while Lottie walked behind with the others. She was interested to see that everyone, as a matter of course, took off their walking shoes or boots and left them in the porch. Was this a country habit? It wouldn't have occurred to her to do so, but now she followed suit. Once in the house Ben made for the kitchen and the other men went upstairs. The women lingered, stocking-footed, in the hall.

'You should have come with us; you'd have loved it,' Cynthia said to Lottie. 'I always say there's nothing like getting out on the hilltops.'

'I had a pleasant day too,' Lottie said. She put Cynthia down as a woman who would organize everyone into playing a game of tennis, or a nice swim – something healthy. 'We had a walk by the river.'

'So Ben is a friend of yours?' Cynthia asked. 'I didn't realize that. I thought you were just a casual visitor, though I did wonder how you'd come to decide on Kilby.'

And if you didn't know you'd make it your business to find out, Lottie thought. 'I met Ben in a business capacity,' she said. That sounded quite good for something thought of on the spur of the moment. And in a way it was true.

'So did you know Moira?' Cynthia persisted. There was nothing unkind in her probing. She simply wanted to know.

'No. I'm sorry to say I didn't,' Lottie answered. 'She'd already died.'

'So sad,' Cynthia said. 'They were such a happy couple, though in the last year life was hard for them.'

Angela Weatherfield joined in the conversation. 'I think he should get married again. Anyone can see he's lonely. I think you feel it more when you've had to do a lot for someone – I mean in an illness. It must leave a void afterwards.'

'True,' Cynthia agreed. 'But where would you find someone to fill it? Where would Ben find someone like Moira?'

Angela nodded agreement.

But if the two of you were to stay here long enough, Lottie thought, between you you'd get him married off. For his own good, of course. And did he want to get married again? It had never come into any conversation with him or about him. If he did he wouldn't find it easy, by which she didn't mean the state of marriage – she reckoned he would be a good husband – but the preliminaries; everything that led up to it, including the actual asking. He was such a shy man. Not weak, not flabby, far from it. Simply shy. Strong and shy. It was an attractive combination.

She followed the other women upstairs and went into her room. The first thing she did there was to put on her high-heeled shoes. She felt more herself, more in charge, wearing the right shoes. Looking in the mirror, her mind still on Ben, she wondered whether, all those years ago, he had proposed to Moira or she to him?

The rest of the holiday flew by. They had supper again at the Shorn Lamb and it seemed natural, after the previous evening, that the six of them should sit at the same table. It was during the meal, when Mervyn wondered what they might do the next day, that Ben said he had thought of taking Lottie to see Ripon, and then on to Fountains Abbey.

'Why don't we all go?' Cynthia said at once. 'It would make a nice party. It's years since we've been to Fountains. In any case, I don't feel like another long walk tomorrow.'

'Me neither,' Angela said. 'What a good idea!'

Ben raised no objections. How could he? Lottie thought. It was he who had mentioned the idea and in any case he was too polite to refuse his four guests. All the same, she was disappointed, not at where he proposed to go but because she had looked forward to some time alone with Ben, time to get to know him. She did so wish that Ben had kept quiet. The only small comfort was that she would be travelling with him, in his car, while the others went in theirs.

In the event the day turned out well. The weather continued fine, which everyone agreed was a near miracle. She liked Ripon; and Fountains Abbey, though it was as crowded as Ben had predicted it would be, was magical. Ben knew everything there was to know about it, every bit of its history from the time it was built, and he was good at telling it. He made the past come alive. It was interesting that when he had something to impart which was not in the least personal he was not shy at all. The story poured out of him. Indeed, Lottie observed that from time to time other people, strangers, stood within earshot to listen to what he was saying.

'You know such a lot about it,' Angela said, full of admiration.

He smiled. 'I should. I've been coming here since I was a schoolboy.'

Afterwards, Mervyn suggested that they should move on to Harrogate. 'Especially as Lottie has never been there,' he added.

'No, I haven't,' Lottie confirmed. She had once almost landed a job at an exhibition there – health foods, alternative medicines, that sort of thing – but it had fallen through. She saw no reason to mention it.

Back in Kilby in the evening it seemed natural to eat at the Shorn Lamb again and once more to share a table. By the time the meal was over and they had walked back to Beck Farm she was dropping with sleep, as was everyone else. So it was off to bed.

'We're leaving tomorrow morning,' Cynthia said as they said their goodnights. 'But what a lovely break it's been. We must all meet up again.'

It had been good, Lottie thought before she fell asleep, but she was pleased at the thought of having Ben to herself the next day.

THIRTEEN

Tuesday, once the Weatherfields and the Davises had left, with many promises to return the following year, flew by. Ben made non-committal replies to their intentions. He might or he might not be taking visitors next year. He didn't know what he would be doing. His life felt rudderless; he hardly knew in which direction to steer. Today was the only reality.

'I thought I might show you a bit more of the Dales,' he said to Lottie when they had waved the others off. 'Do you think you'd like that, or is there something you'd rather do?'

'I'd love it,' Lottie assured him. 'Anything you like to suggest. There's so much I don't know.' And will I ever have the chance to find out? she wondered. Who was to know? If Ben did, he had so far dropped no hint.

They went, via Hawes, to Tendale. She liked Hawes. It seemed lively. 'It's a nice village,' she said.

'Oh dear,' Ben said, smiling at her. 'Don't ever let the locals hear you calling it a village. It's a market town and, as they would tell you, very important.'

'Sorry,' Lottie said. 'You see how ignorant I am.'

From Hawes they drove up the steep hill and across the top into Tendale. It was magnificent, of course. The scenery was splendid, but Tendale was not to her taste. It was too closed in, the hills too high, and once the two small hamlets were left behind there was hardly a house to be seen. She would not like to live here, she found it claustrophobic even on this sunny day with the clouds high, but she said nothing of this to Ben, since it was clear from the few observations he made that he loved it. She felt more at ease when they had left its confinement behind and reached Wharfedale. Here the villages were larger and there were more houses, more trees, and people to be seen. It was civilized. She enjoyed being driven, all the more because, the roads being for the most part narrow and winding, Ben drove less furiously than he had yesterday.

He pulled in to the side of the road by a high rock, which rose totally vertically until it reached a large and ominous-looking overhang that jutted out close to the top. To Lottie it seemed there was no reason for it to be there, so suddenly, so incongruous, but Ben said it was the result of a glacier rushing down the valley thousands of years ago. He spoke as if it had happened last week. To Lottie it seemed impossible that it could ever be climbed, except by a fly, and yet three men, hung about with ropes, were trying to scale it.

'I can't believe it!' she said.

'They do it all the time, different climbers,' Ben said. 'Any time of the year, but particularly from now until the autumn. Every holiday, every weekend, people have a go at climbing Kilnsey Crag.'

'Have you ever done it?' she asked him.

His answer was decisive. 'Not me! I'm no climber, never was. I like my feet on the ground.'

It figured, she thought, as they drove off again. She sensed he was a feet-on-the-ground person, not given to wild ideas or flights of fancy. But you would always know where you were with him. He would be reliable but there wouldn't be many surprises. But did she want surprises? Most of hers had not been particularly pleasant. Hey, what did it matter whether she liked surprises, or feet on the ground? She was only here for the weekend and today was the last day. Tomorrow she would be back in Luton; she might never set eyes on Ben again. She was a little sorry, but not devastatingly so. So why not make the most of what was left?

A little later they drew up outside a white-painted inn. 'I thought we might have lunch here,' Ben said. 'I haven't been for some years but it always used to be good. Moira and I would come here if we had something to celebrate, like a birthday, I mean.'

She wished he hadn't brought Moira into the conversation but it was probably inevitable, and, to be fair, he didn't continue in the same vein.

Sitting at the table they looked across the road to meadows filled with ewes and very small lambs, which Ben explained were earlier here than in the region they had passed through, because the land lay lower and was a little warmer. 'It will be like this in Cordale in a week or more,' he said. In the distance, at the far side of the meadows, a line of trees showed where the river ran. 'I may not have climbed the Crag,' Ben said, 'but I've fished in that stretch of river more times than I could count. It's chock-full of fish.'

'Are you a good fisherman?' Lottie asked.

'I was,' Ben said. 'I don't do much of it now. No real reason why. Would you like to walk down to the river?' he asked. 'There's a narrow lane runs down the side of the meadow. But only if you'd like to. It might be a bit muddy.'

'That's all right,' Lottie said. 'I'm wearing my flat shoes.' She had learned in one short weekend how little use her high heels were in this part of the world. Would I like a life where I hardly ever wore heels? she asked herself. And then pulled herself up for day-dreaming. She wasn't being offered it; it wasn't likely that she would be.

They drove back to Kilby by what seemed to her a circular route, taking in a small town – or was it a village? It had a variety of shops – named Grassington. She had never heard of it but clearly a great many people had. The narrow, hilly High Street was so crowded there was hardly room to move. 'Which is why I left the car in the car park,' Ben said. 'I thought you might like to see the shops.'

She bought picture postcards, again one to send to Dulcie and a couple for herself as reminders in case she might never be here again. In the same shop she bought a pound box of home-made

163

vanilla fudge, which she would eat, back in her flat in Luton, to console and remind herself of the weekend.

It was early evening when they reached Kilby. 'How would it be if we ate at home?' Ben asked. 'Alice left some chops in the fridge and I could do some vegetables.' He didn't fancy going to the Shorn Lamb now that the others had left. Too many locals asking themselves what Ben Thornton was doing accompanied by a young attractive woman. Not that it had anything to do with anyone else, but Kilby was a gossipy place. Not unkindly, of course. Just gossipy. It was interesting, he thought, that Joseph and Harry had kept well away from the Shorn Lamb during the last few days. It being the holiday period, they might well have been there with their wives.

'But if you'd rather go out . . .' he said to Lottie.

'Not at all,' she said. 'I'm very happy to stay in. It'll be relaxing. It's been a lovely day, hasn't it?'

He brought out the remains of the sherry and they each had a drink before Ben cooked the lamb chops – and it was a strange, slightly uncomfortable feeling eating them after having watched the small lambs in the fields – new potatoes and frozen peas. With the meal they drank a bottle of red wine, which after the sherry, and all the day's fresh air, made Lottie sleepy. Ben was quite competent, she thought. He'd made a good meal for the two of them. But then he would have had to cook lots of meals when Moira had needed to be looked after, wouldn't he? Alice couldn't have been there every minute of the day.

They watched television for a while and then, she couldn't help it, she wasn't able to stifle a yawn.

'You're tired,' Ben said quickly. 'I'm sorry.'

'It's more that I'm sleepy,' she said. 'All the fresh air – and the wine. I'm not really used to either.'

'And you have an early start in the morning,' Ben said. 'Don't feel you must stay up if you really want to go to bed.' He didn't want her to go. He wanted to prolong the visit in any way he could, but it wouldn't be fair.

'You're so kind,' Lottie said. 'But if you don't mind, I think I will. It's been a wonderful weekend, Ben. You're so lucky to live in a lovely place like this. I don't think I've ever been anywhere

164

so good.' She was surprised to hear herself saying the words. Given the choice, a weekend in the depths of the country would have been at the bottom of her list. She liked bright lights and cities. She liked the seaside – Brighton was her idea of a fun place. She liked cinemas and theatres and dancing. She enjoyed being in a crowd. And here she was, saying how much she was enjoying this place, which now, at ten-thirty at night, was pitch-dark and as silent as the grave.

'I'll go up, then,' she said.

'Are you sure you wouldn't like a warm drink, or a hot-water bottle?' Ben asked. 'It's no trouble.'

'I'm fine,' she said. 'Goodnight, Ben.'

'Goodnight, then,' he said. 'Sleep well.' It was good, he thought, to have someone to say 'goodnight' to.

For a while, Lottie lay awake in bed. Would I *really* like to live here? she asked herself. It had been a lovely weekend; good weather, wonderful scenery, and she'd been happy with Ben, he was kind. But what about when the weather was cold and wet or, heaven forbid, Cordale lay under deep snow? But before she could answer herself she was asleep.

Ben did all the night-time chores he had had to get used to doing himself, the ones he used to share with Moira when she was well enough: washed the coffee cups and glasses, put the cat out, set the guard around the fire – it would die down quite soon – and locked the doors. He had grown to hate this last hour of every day. It was the loneliest of all.

Next morning he was up and about early. It was the habit of a lifetime and he couldn't break it, any more than he could give up the habit of a proper breakfast: bacon, eggs, fried bread, and porridge in the winter. It was something Moira had always insisted on and which he was now quite competent at cooking for himself on the days when Alice didn't come in, the days when there were no guests – which was most days in the year.

It was the smell of frying bacon that wakened Lottie. A quick bowl of cornflakes or Shreddies was her usual breakfast, all she ever wanted, but surprisingly this unfamiliar aroma, wafting up the stairs, was tempting. It went with the place. Not stopping to shower or dress, she put on her dressing gown and went down-stairs. Ben, hearing her and turning round from the Aga, seeing her standing in the doorway, thought how lovely she looked. Not tidy. Her hair was tousled and it fell down over her face, which was devoid of make-up. She looked as he imagined a child just wakened from sleep would. The thought that in an hour's time she would be leaving, and he didn't know when, if ever, he would see her again, swept over him. 'Don't go,' he wanted to say. 'Please stay.' He stood there, staring at her.

'Good morning,' Lottie said. 'Do I smell bacon burning?'

He came back to earth and pulled the pan off the heat. 'Sorry,' he said. 'It's only just caught a bit on the edge.'

'That's all right by me,' Lottie assured him. 'I like it a bit burnt.'

She had caught the expression on his face when he'd seen her standing in the doorway. It was a look she'd detected before on men's faces, the kind of look that undressed her, except that it wasn't like that with Ben. He was different, not the kind of man she was used to. For a moment she felt she was in the wrong: she shouldn't have come downstairs in her flimsy dressing gown with her feet bare. It was too intimate. If there had been any wrong intention in her doing so she would have felt cheap, but there hadn't been. She had acted without thinking, almost as if she had been in her own home.

Pulling her dressing gown tight around her, she went and sat at the table. 'I slept like a log,' she said. 'Shall I pour myself a cup of tea?'

'I'll do it,' Ben said. 'Or would you prefer coffee?'

Lottie shook her head. 'No. It's tea for me in the morning, always.'

'And for me,' Ben said. 'Are you ready to eat? How do you like your egg?'

'As it comes,' she said. 'And then I must go and pack – not that that will take me long.'

She enjoyed her breakfast. 'At home I'd never dream of eating like this at this time of day,' she said to Ben.

'Oh, but you should,' he told her. 'It's important.'

When she had eaten the last scrap, completely cleared her

166

plate, she said, 'Well, then, I'll go and pack.' She didn't want to leave, not only this warm kitchen, but the whole house, Kilby itself. At least not just yet. But she had to, she had an exhibition to go to in Croydon, starting tomorrow morning. She couldn't get out of it, nor could she afford to. She climbed the stairs, then stopped to look out of the landing window, which over-looked the garden and then away up the dale. The garden was badly in need of attention but its untidy appearance was improved by the apple tree, which was now almost in flower. How nice it would be, she thought, when it was a bit further advanced and the weather was warmer, to lie out underneath it.

An hour or so later it was time for Ben to drive her to Shepton to catch the train. It was a near-silent drive. She didn't know what to talk about and clearly nor did Ben, so they fell back on the weather, what time the train left, when would it reach Luton, and how early she would leave for Croydon the next day. 'I suppose you enjoy visiting all these different places?' Ben suggested. 'It must make for variety.'

'Not really,' Lottie told him. 'The inside of one exhibition hall – which is mostly what I see – is very much like any other. And the food's always the same.'

She selected a couple of magazines from the bookstall. Ben paid for them and they went onto the platform to wait for the train, which had already been signalled, to arrive. I don't want to go, Lottie thought. I wish she weren't going, Ben thought. Neither of them said anything.

The train came and Ben helped Lottie in with her suitcase. She remained at the door of the carriage, he on the platform, while various things were loaded onto the rear of the train. It was not until the final door was slammed shut that Ben found his voice and his courage.

'Please come again, Lottie,' he called out. The train was moving away now and he repeated his words, shouting at the top of his voice, not certain she had heard him. 'Please come again.'

'I will. Oh, I will,' she called out, waving her hand, nodding her head vigorously. She wasn't certain that he heard her words, but by the swift smile on his face she thought he had got the message.

'I'll telephone,' Ben shouted, but he was too far away now for

167

her to hear that. She was, however, quite certain he had invited her, there was no mistake about it, just as she was totally sure she would accept. She stood there until he was out of sight, then she found her seat and sat down.

Lottie came out of the station at Luton and joined a short queue for taxis. She couldn't really afford a taxi – also there was a bus waiting that would take her almost to her door – but it was raining hard and in any case she was suddenly in the mood for taxis. The weekend, she reminded herself, except for her train fare, hadn't cost her a single penny. Ben had been most generous. He had treated her like a lady and had asked nothing in return, which was not her usual experience of men.

At the front door of the house, in which she rented a furnished flat on the top floor, she paid the driver, giving him a rather good tip, and let herself in. As usual, there were two or three small children playing on the stairs. Since they had no intention of giving way, she manoeuvred herself round them and climbed the two flights to her room. Her door opened immediately onto the living room. She put down her suitcase and picked up two envelopes from the mat. One was the monthly rent bill from her landlord, or, rather, a reminder because she should have paid it before she'd gone away; the other was a begging letter from a charity she had never heard of. It would be nice if from time to time she were actually to receive some personal mail that wasn't chasing money. Perhaps Dulcie might write, she thought. She had after all sent her two postcards from Cordale.

Standing there, she took a quick glance round the room. As far as she could see, everything was normal and, moreover, she hated it as much as ever. She hated its beige carpet, its brown and orange three-piece suite, which had seen better days, its oak-framed mirror on the wall above the fireplace, the television in the corner, the heavy green velvet curtain against the windows. Nothing matched, nothing went with anything else. Only the jazzy cushions on the sofa, which she had taken from her mother's home before it was sold up, welcomed her. This was a place that should be her refuge, a place to which she returned with pleasure at the end of the day, and it was nothing of the sort. She threw the charity's mailshot in the waste-paper bin and the rent bill on the table. She must pay that tomorrow or old Soames would be paying her a visit. Then she picked up her case and went into the bedroom, which was just large enough to take the single bed, a narrow wardrobe, an old chest of drawers and an upright chair. Coming back to this was all so different from going home to the warmth and comfort of her mother's house and she wished she could have afforded to keep that on. The bottom line was, and she knew it, that in this place she was never anything but lonely.

Lottie left her suitcase on the bed – she would unpack it later – went into the small kitchen, which was partitioned off from the living-room, and immediately contrasted it in her mind with the size and warmth of Ben's kitchen at Beck Farm, with its Aga and its large, square table. She toasted a slice of bread and opened a tin of baked beans, made a cup of instant coffee and took the tray into the living-room, where she switched on the TV. Thank heaven for television, she thought – though not right at the moment, since it was teatime and there were children's programmes on all channels. Nevertheless, she left it on. The voices were company.

When she had eaten she decided she would telephone Dulcie; she had the number in her diary. She let the phone ring at the other end for a long time, but there was no reply. In the end she gave up. She was fairly sure that Dulcie didn't have an exhibition this week; on the other hand, she had once worked in an office and when there were no exhibitions going she could usually get herself a job as a temp, which was probably the case now. Lottie would try again later.

If my mother had let me be trained to do office work, she thought, or manage a shop, I'd have something to fall back on. But no, her mother's ambition had been for Lottie to present herself as bright, attractive, well-dressed, and that she should marry a man of means and be happy ever after. It hadn't worked out like that, had it? OK, she was attractive and she tried to dress well, but not the rest. Here she was, about to be thirty and living in this dump. No friends, because no-one had ever been quite good enough for her mother.

169

The news came on the TV. It was full of doom and gloom, but she kept it on, only half listening.

Ben stood on the platform for several seconds after the train, taking Lottie away, had left. He had heard her reply to his invitation, or not so much heard her words as understood her actions – the smile on her face, her nodding head. His spirit, which had been at rock bottom as he watched her begin to go out of his life, had risen with the suddenness of the river Cor after heavy rain, or like Moira's bread dough when the yeast started to work. He walked purposefully back to the car park, certain of what he would do next. He would not linger in Shepton for any reason, he would drive straight home, and there he would immediately write a letter to Lottie – she had insisted on leaving her address in the visitors' book – and post it this very day. He would repeat the invitation he had shouted at the departing train, and he would set a date. He would do all this while the courage was still in him.

Taking short cuts, he drove quickly. When he reached home Alice was there, cleaning through the house, changing the beds after the visitors. She was in the mood to talk but he cut her short and went into the small room that served as an office, and sat down to write. There were things he would like to have written – just how much her visit had meant to him – which he'd only fully realized at the moment when the train left the station. In the end he thanked her for coming, said how much he'd enjoyed it all and that he was pleased she was agreeable to coming again. 'Would you like to come over the Whitsun weekend?' he asked. 'The weather should be good then. Write and let me know.'

It seemed, reading it through, a stiff little note, not at all the way he felt, but he had never been much good at expressing his feelings, either in speech or on paper. The only time he was able to do this was when he was woodcarving. He always felt a sense of freedom then.

He addressed and stamped the envelope and took it at once to the post office. He could have given it to Alice to post but he wanted to see it go in the box himself.

170

FOURTEEN

Ben stood on the platform. The train was overdue. He looked at his watch again. Ten minutes late and no reason given why. But no matter how long he had to wait he would not move from this spot lest when she arrived she wouldn't find him there, as he'd promised he would be.

In the five-and-a-half weeks she had been away he had missed her every single day. In a way it had been – though this was an exaggeration – like the first few months after Moira's death. He had truly and grievously missed Moira, but he had gradually come to terms with the fact that he would not see her again, at least not in this life, and he was by no means sure about the afterlife. There were too many unanswered questions there. But Lottie he had known he would see again. The time and place had been fixed. Friday afternoon at ten past three on Shepton station. They had kept in touch, he by letter, she by telephone. He was better with a pen in his hand than he was at speaking; she had proved not much good at writing but fluent on the phone.

The train came in, leisurely, as if it was not the least bit late. Doors opened and people stepped out, but there was no sign of Lottie. Where was she? Had she changed her mind? Had she decided not to come – and if so, why? His spirits plummeted. Now, at this moment, he realized how very much he wanted to see her again.

And then he saw her. She was stepping out of a compartment in the very last carriage. She spotted him at the same time as he saw her and with some difficulty – she was impeded by a handbag and a magazine in one hand while with the other she was guiding a wheeled case – she waved to him. He waved back and set off at a brisk walk to meet her. He would have liked to run, like a small boy, but he didn't find it easy to show his feelings.

'How are you?' he said formally, taking the case from her. 'You look well.' He wanted to tell her that she looked beautiful, her skin glowing, her eyes shining. A sight for sore eyes. And he had her to himself for the best part of five days. Today was the Friday before the May bank-holiday weekend, which he still thought of as Whitsun, and she wouldn't return until Tuesday afternoon.

'I'm fine,' she said. 'You look suntanned.'

'I've been working outside a lot,' Ben said. 'I've been helping Joseph Clark with the lambing. I don't think you saw Joseph last time you were in Kilby. His land marches with mine – it used to be mine. He's a man short at the moment and we all muck in, help out when it comes to lambing.'

He stopped speaking, realizing that they were standing still and that almost everyone else had left the platform.

'Would you like to go straight back to Kilby,' he asked, 'or would you rather stop off in Shepton?'

Lottie had no hesitation. 'It would be nice if we could have a cup of tea where we went before. Can we do that? Have you got time?'

'Of course we can,' Ben said. 'And my time is yours while you're here. Well, almost. I have two visitors – two men – booked in for Saturday and Sunday nights – just bed and breakfast – but they won't be much trouble.'

'Will Alice be there?' Lottie asked.

'Oh, yes,' Ben said. 'She'll see to the breakfasts and do the bedrooms.'

They went back to the same café in the High Street. Ben ordered tea and toasted teacakes. As they ate and drank he looked across the table at Lottie and thought how right it seemed that she should be sitting there. The weeks of her absence faded away as if they had never been – and yet that absence had been productive. The fact of just missing her had, in its way, been the cause of drawing her closer to him. He hoped it was the same for her.

'"How like a winter hath thine absence been from me",' he said.

'What?' She looked startled.

'Shakespeare,' he said. 'Sorry! I don't often go around quoting Shakespeare. I suppose I learnt it at school and it suddenly seemed to fit.'

'Oh, I see,' Lottie said. 'Well, actually it's rather nice.'

'What do you want to do while you're here?' he asked. 'Just say. Anything you like.'

'Whatever *you* choose,' she said. 'I don't have anything special in mind.' That was not quite true. She would like to spend some time in Shepton, though not today, having a really good look round the shops. There were some interesting ones in Shepton. But probably that wasn't to Ben's taste, so she would leave it for now. 'But I'd like to go to the Shorn Lamb, of course,' she said. 'I enjoyed that.'

'And so you shall,' Ben promised. And this time he would take her openly, as a friend, not as a bed-and-breakfast guest. He would be proud to do that, let folks think what they might. 'We'll start by going there for supper this evening. Would you like that?'

'Very much,' Lottie said.

'Then I'll ring and reserve a table,' Ben said. 'It's the start of a holiday weekend so they're bound to be busy.'

'Why would Ben Thornton be booking a table for two?' Joyce Grayson said to her husband as she put down the receiver. 'He didn't say who he was bringing and I wasn't quick enough to ask him. Who do you think?'

'How do I know?' Bernard replied. 'And does he have to tell you? I suppose he can bring a friend if he wants to.' But Joyce was right, it *was* strange, because Ben didn't have many friends: he was too shy, he kept himself to himself. He was liked and respected in the village, of course. He was one of them, one of their own, but he wouldn't be taking any of the villagers out to supper, would he?

'There we go,' Ben said to Lottie. 'Half-past seven. I dare say Joyce was dying to ask who I was bringing but I didn't tell her. I thought I'd let it be a surprise.' In fact, he had told no-one that Lottie would be coming to Kilby. He had hardly dared to do so in case it didn't happen.

And I don't suppose it'll be a pleasant surprise, Lottie thought. But she didn't care, and she said nothing to Ben. If the Joyce Graysons of this world didn't like it – and she was pretty certain Joyce didn't – then they'd have to put up with it.

At half-past six she went up to her room to change, see to her make-up and do her hair, and at twenty past seven she came down again looking – or so Ben thought as he stood in the hall and watched her descend the stairs – a vision of loveliness. She was wearing a cream skirt, mid-calf length and clinging to her slender figure – she could have told Ben that that was because it was bias-cut, had he wanted to know – and a silky top of the same shade with an amber neck scarf, which had the smallest amount of glitter in it, tied around her throat. Amber-and-silver earrings, which had been her mother's, dangled from her ears. She wore no other jewellery, not even a ring. Her nails were painted a pale, pinky amber, matched by her lipstick. Her shoes were cream, and high-heeled. Her rich brown hair had been skilfully highlighted with fine amber streaks by Luton's very best hairdresser two days before. Most of these details went unobserved by Ben. He saw only the total ensemble and was enchanted by it. He could hardly wait to show her off in the Shorn Lamb. He himself was dressed in his best suit.

There were already several customers in the bar when Ben and Lottie entered. Bernard and Jim Kettle were behind the bar, which was their place on a busy evening, and so was Joyce. It was not her place, she should have been in the kitchen, but she was curious to see who Ben's friend might be. It was possibly the look – a mixture of fury and horror – on Joyce's face when she saw Lottie on Ben's arm that made some of the customers around the bar turn their heads to see what could have caused it. Ben Thornton all dressed up was an unusual sight, but as for the lady

174

– well, words failed them! A low whistle escaped one of them and was quickly cut short by Bernard's murderous look. Joyce turned on her heel and marched back to the kitchen. Bernard gave a slight glance to her departing back, then turned to meet the newcomers.

'Well,' he said, smiling, 'how nice to see you, Lottie, and what a surprise. I must say, Ben has kept quiet about this, the sly fox! So how are you?'

'I'm very well,' Lottie said. 'It's nice to see you too.' She had seen Joyce make her swift exit but no way was she going to let that, or anything else, upset her. She was here for a pleasant evening.

'What's it to be to drink?' Bernard asked. 'On the house, to welcome you.'

By the time he had served the drinks, other people round the bar were speaking to Ben and he was introducing Lottie, whom some of them remembered from the Easter weekend. Bernard took the opportunity to go to the kitchen. There would be some calming down to do there.

'I won't serve her,' Joyce stormed the second he entered. 'Don't ask me to serve her.'

'I'm not asking you to serve her,' Bernard said. 'I'll do that myself, and with pleasure. She's a very nice lady. What you *will* do is serve up on the plate, and with your usual skill, whatever she chooses to order.'

'She comes in here,' Joyce shouted, 'hanging onto his arm, dressed like a tart.'

'I thought she was particularly nicely dressed,' Bernard said smoothly.

'You would!' she retorted. 'You men are all alike. Even Ben Thornton. I'd have thought he'd have had more sense. As well as more respect. Moira's not been—'

'That's enough, Joyce!' Bernard's voice was sharp. 'You have no sense of proportion where Moira's concerned. What about Ben? Has he to spend the rest of his life without a friend because his wife has died? We all loved Moira – you don't have the monopoly on that – but Ben has to go on living. And that's enough on the subject. We both have work to do. And remember, this is a public house. We don't refuse to serve people, ever, not without a very good reason. And that's a decision *I* make!'

He marched out of the kitchen, put the smile back on his face and went into the bar, where he showed Ben and Lottie to the table he had reserved for them and brought them a menu. 'The lamb is good,' he advised.

'Then that's what I'll have,' Lottie said. 'Living on my own I don't often have a roast.'

'The same goes for me, so I'll have the same,' Ben said. 'In fact,' he said to Lottie, 'I come down here once or twice a week. There's no joy in cooking for one.'

Lottie nodded agreement.

It was a pleasant evening. Bernard was assiduous in his attention. He knew Lottie had seen Joyce's reaction when they'd walked in and he wanted to make up for it. Ben, he thought, hadn't been aware. All his attention had been on Lottie. But in any case Lottie was a pleasant young woman in addition to being the most attractive creature he had seen in his bar since her last visit at Easter. He didn't know how Ben had done it. He was a nice man, a very nice man, and totally genuine, but he was no oil painting; nor would he have described him as having a sparkling personality. It was funny where love struck – and he thought it was love, certainly on Ben's side. He was like a new man. About Lottie he wasn't as sure, but then he hardly knew her. In any event these were thoughts he would keep strictly to himself. Not a word of them would he breathe to Joyce.

The meal was enjoyable, as was the bottle of red wine, which they almost, but not quite, finished between them. 'You'll have me tight!' Lottie protested (though not too seriously) as Ben topped up her glass for the third time. It was almost closing time when they left; outside, the sky was cloudless and star-filled, the air not too cold: a fine night.

'Do you know the stars?' Ben asked.

'Not the least bit,' Lottie admitted. 'But you could teach me.'

'It would take a long time,' Ben said. 'My dad taught me and I've been learning ever since.' But why shouldn't I? he thought. He lifted his head and pointed forward and upwards. 'That's the North Star,' he said. 'The Pole Star. Once you can identify that, which isn't difficult, you can start to learn the rest from where they are in relationship to it.'

At first she couldn't find the North Star, so he stood behind her, his hands on her shoulders. 'Now look higher,' he said, and put a hand on the back of her head to tilt it backwards. 'Now do you see it?' he asked.

'Yes! Yes, I do,' Lottie said. 'It's beautiful, isn't it?'

They stood there for a few minutes while he pointed out other constellations to her, then she gave a little shiver and he said, 'I mustn't let you get cold,' and he took her arm and they walked back to Beck Farm.

When Lottie came down next morning it was again to the smell of bacon cooking. Alice was already there but there was no sign of Ben.

'He's feeding the hens,' Alice said. 'He'll not be long. He knows I've put the bacon on. Are you going to have a proper breakfast or are you going to pick at a bit of toast like most young women seem to do?'

'Not me! I mean no, I'm not one for picking at toast,' Lottie said. 'I'd like whatever's on offer. It smells good.'

Ben came in.

'I'm sorry if I've kept you waiting,' Lottie said at once.

'You haven't,' Ben said. 'I always like to do a few odd jobs before breakfast. It comes from being brought up on a farm. You get up early and you see to the animals before everything else, though all I have now is a few hens. Did you sleep well? Were you comfortable?'

'I was very comfortable *and* I slept well, much later than I intended. It must be the country air.' In fact, when she didn't have to get up early to go to work, she enjoyed staying in bed a bit longer, especially if she'd been out late the night before.

Alice brought in the breakfast plates. It was a beautiful day out there, she said. She'd been up two or three hours. She reckoned it was the best part of the day.

'Well, there's no timetable while you're here,' Ben assured Lottie. 'I'm at your disposal. It's all up to you. We can do whatever you choose.'

After breakfast they went briefly into the garden. 'It's a pity you've missed the apple blossom,' Ben said. 'You should have been here a week ago. It was a picture.'

'What sort of apples are they?' Lottie asked.

'I don't really know,' Ben admitted. 'My dad planted the tree. It's a good many years ago, but apple trees can live a long time. I never heard them given a name, they were just always there. I know they're cookers. Moira used to make good use of the crop. She made chutneys and pies to sell on her market stall, and what she couldn't use straight away she stored. There were always enough to last well through the winter. Of course she couldn't do that in the last year. She was too ill. I picked what I could and gave most of them away.'

He fell silent for a moment.

'It sounds admirable,' Lottie said. 'I don't think I'd be much good at that sort of thing. I'm afraid I'm not very domesticated.' She gave a little deprecatory laugh. The truth was, she was not domesticated at all. Her mother had seen to that. She had not envisaged her daughter's future as one in which domesticity played a great part.

'We all have different talents,' Ben said gently. 'I was never as good a farmer as my dad, or his father before him. Anyway, what would you like to do for the rest of the day? Would you like to spend it around the house, or would you like to go out somewhere?'

Lottie hesitated, but not for long, only long enough not to sound impolite about staying in the house and the village. 'It would be nice to go for a drive around,' she said. 'It's such beautiful country, isn't it?' All the same, she hoped that the drive would include a town or two. 'Harrogate would be nice,' she ventured.

'If that's what you'd like,' Ben said. 'Though it's sure to be very busy this weekend.'

'Busy' was what she would enjoy. 'I don't mind,' she said. 'If it's all right by you, of course.'

'It's fine by me,' Ben said. Just to be with her, to watch her enjoying herself, was enough for him. When she was really enjoying herself she was like a child. It showed in her smile and in the brightness of her eyes.

As it turned out, it was a most pleasant day. The weather stayed fine, without a cloud in the sky. As promised, the two visitors turned up early, by car, having come only from Halifax, eager to deposit their suitcases and abandon the car to put in a long day's walking over the fells. Ben gave them a key so that they could let themselves in whenever they returned. 'We might well be out,' he explained. 'And if you're looking for an evening meal you could do a lot worse than the Shorn Lamb, in the village.'

As he had forecast, when he and Lottie reached Harrogate it was busy, but that didn't matter to Lottie – indeed, it was an added attraction: such fashionable people. They lunched in Betty's café and afterwards they walked down the hill and meandered round the antique shops. Lottie spotted in one of the windows a small enamelled brooch with green leaves and delicate pink flowers on a silver base, which Ben insisted on buying for her.

'It's lovely,' she said. 'But I didn't mean you to treat me to it. I was simply admiring it. I like pretty things.'

'And why not?' Ben said. 'Anyway, it was a pleasure. So what shall we do next? Would you like to go for a walk in the Valley Gardens?'

'Certainly,' Lottie said. 'Whatever you say.'

I could get used to living here, she thought, even though it wouldn't be every day in Harrogate with Ben buying her presents. It was a lovely part of the world. It was – she searched for the right word – it was *satisfying*. Yes, that was it, satisfying. And secure. And she was growing fonder of Ben by the hour, though she knew, of course, that she would never be madly, passionately in love with him. She had had that with her husband, and where had it landed her? But Ben hadn't asked her, hadn't even hinted at such a thing, and she was going back to Luton on Tuesday. There was no telling when she would see him again.

As they walked through the gardens, the warm air scented by the late spring flowers, small insects flying in mini-clouds

179

through the air, Ben's hand lightly under her elbow guiding her along the path, she allowed herself to daydream. She would be a good wife; she would be prepared to help him in every way. She would play her part in the business, though of course no way would she take Alice's job from her. No, she would be the hostess. Well-dressed and smiling she would welcome everyone, be nice to them so that they would come back again and again. In fact, she would be an asset.

She was standing in the doorway of Beck Farm, waving off a group of grateful visitors. 'It's been wonderful,' they were saying. 'We'll certainly recommend it to all our friends.' 'Come again,' she was saying. It was as they were replying 'We most certainly will. You'll not keep us away,' that Ben's voice sounded in her ear, over the top of the others.

'I thought we might have a change from the Shorn Lamb this evening,' he was saying. 'We could have a meal on the way back. We could go via Wharfedale. There are one or two very nice places for food there. What do you think?'

'I think that would be great,' Lottie said.

He took her to a hotel where the restaurant, and the strip of garden in front of it, faced onto the river, which, being wide at this point, was more tranquil, not so fast flowing. It was a remarkably warm evening for the time of the year so they sat in the garden, sipping their drinks, while they waited for a table to be free in the restaurant. Dusk fell. The lights in the trees and shrubs at the edge of the garden were switched on, and reflected in the water, shimmering slightly in its slow movement. A late blackbird sang its last song of the day.

Lottie wondered for a moment whether Ben had been used to bringing Moira here – and then put the thought from her. 'This is magic,' she said.

Ben nodded agreement. For him the whole day had been magic. He had not been himself at all. He had been in another world from his everyday one and all he could compare it with were the occasions, much rarer in the last year than they used to be, when he was involved in a piece of carving. Time always seemed to stand still then, which was what he wanted it to do now. Experience told him that it never did for long, that at some point real time intervened and the carving had to be put away, and so would this weekend all too soon be over. What would he do with himself when Lottie left on Tuesday afternoon?

His thoughts were interrupted by a waiter, coming to tell them that their table was now ready. They followed him into the restaurant.

'This is lovely, too,' Lottie said. 'I was just beginning to get a little bit chilly.'

Her thoughts had been running along the same lines as Ben's. What's it going to be like when I'm back in Luton? Or back on the job, because she had another exhibition lined up. She was not looking forward to either prospect, but for now she would put them out of her mind. She would live in the moment.

They lingered over the meal, each of them trying to make it last, until they were the last people in the room and the waiter brought them the bill without being asked. Ben, who might normally have checked every item, scarcely glanced at it; instead he simply put his credit card beside it on the table.

'It's been a wonderful day,' Lottie said as they left. 'I hope you've enjoyed it as much as I have.'

'I certainly have,' Ben said. 'And whatever we decide to do tomorrow I'm sure it will be another wonderful day.' And after that we will have one more full day together, he thought as he started the car. This time he did not drive fast, he crawled along the country roads, trying to make the journey last. His head was full of things he wanted to say, but could not bring himself to utter. And then, summoning his courage, he decided he would say them. Taking his eyes off the road for a moment he turned to look at Lottie. She was fast asleep, her head thrown back, her mouth slightly open.

She slept on until they reached Beck Farm, only wakening when he stopped the car and switched off the engine.

'Oh, did I drop off? I'm sorry. I'm dead tired, but pleasantly so. It must be the wine.'

Perhaps it was the wine with me, Ben thought, though he didn't believe that. Whatever it was, the moment had gone.

★   ★   ★

The weekend flew by. The weather stayed fine. On Sunday they explored Cordale, taking the car, but leaving it at different points so that they could take closer looks on foot. Ben showed her the places he enjoyed with his friends when he was a boy, pointing out the school he had attended, the spot on the river where they had fished, and a mile or so beyond that a calm stretch below and beyond a waterfall where they had bathed.

'It sounds a wonderful place to be a child,' Lottie said.

'It was,' Ben agreed. 'Of course it wasn't all play. I had to help on the farm after school, not to mention for most of the holidays. But then we all did, old and young alike, men, women and children, especially in the summer. We'd go on until we could hardly see a hand in front of our faces, getting the hay in and suchlike. In fact we were allowed time off school to help with the harvest.'

'It sounds totally different from my childhood,' Lottie said. 'I've always lived in a town. The nearest thing we had to a wide open space was the park, and there it usually said "Please keep off the grass".'

'I'd hate that,' Ben said.

But I didn't hate it, Lottie thought. It was what I was used to. And when she got a bit older there'd been the cinema and the shops, and dances.

On the Monday they went again to the Shorn Lamb. It was packed out. Joyce, busy in the kitchen, didn't put in an appearance. Joseph and Harry were there with their wives, and when Ben introduced them neither they nor Lottie showed the slightest sign that they had met before. She understood why. Bernard was rushed off his feet in the bar but when they were at their table he managed to have a few pleasant words with them. 'So you'll be off tomorrow, then?' he said to Lottie. 'It's a pity you couldn't stay longer but I hope you'll come again.' She was doing Ben a power of good. He was a different man.

She and Ben were silent as they walked back to Beck Farm. It was as if neither of them had any words left to say, though Ben knew exactly what he wanted to say, and couldn't get the words out. They sat up late, drinking brandy. In the end it was Lottie

182

who said, 'I'm afraid I'll have to go to bed, Ben. I'm falling asleep. It's the fresh air.'

He saw her upstairs and left her at her bedroom door, then went to his own room. It was a long time before he fell asleep.

On Tuesday, before Alice went home, she prepared their lunch: cold meat and a salad, followed by an apple pie. Lottie wondered if the apples had been gathered and stored by Moira in her last few months, and if Ben was reminded of her when he ate the pie. He seemed unusually thoughtful.

It was a quiet drive to Shepton, a struggle on Lottie's part to keep the conversation going. Ben had said nothing about when she might come again, which disappointed her. They arrived on the platform less than ten minutes before the train was due. And it was then, as they stood there side by side – there was nowhere to sit, every bench was filled – her case on the ground beside Ben's feet, that he found his voice. The words came out in a rush.

'Lottie, will you marry me?'

She looked at him in astonishment.

'Please,' he said. 'Please say you will. I love you, Lottie.'

She looked up at him, her eyes shining – and wide with surprise. 'Oh, Ben, I will. I will.'

He took her in his arms and kissed her. She was surprised at the strength of him.

The train came in.

'I'll telephone you,' he said.

FIFTEEN

Ben stood on the platform, his eyes fixed on the retreating train that was taking Lottie away from him. At first it moved slowly, with Lottie leaning out of the window, waving to him, and he to her. And then it gathered speed until Lottie was no longer visible and the train itself was a vanishing dot on the horizon – and then nothing. He would have liked to have jumped on the train and gone with her; all his instincts had urged him to do that. As it was, he stood quite still, continuing to look at the space that had swallowed her up, as though the strength of his longing to have her here beside him could somehow bring her back. He might have continued to stand there had not a porter, driving a cart piled with luggage along the platform, tooted his horn at him, warning him to get out of the way.

He began the walk back to the car park. He had no desire to linger in Shepton. He wanted to be back home, close to a telephone, on the off-chance that Lottie would ring him when she had to change trains, though common sense told him she wouldn't have the time to do that. In any case, he had said he would phone her – those had been his last words to her – and it would be quite some time before she would be back in her own flat. Common sense, at the moment, was not much comfort. He wanted magic. He wanted her voice to come to him from out of nowhere; he wanted a bird to land at his feet with a message from her in its beak. He wanted all these people who passed by him, hurrying between the station and the car park, to know that Lottie had said she would marry him. He wanted to share his delirious happiness.

Less than a hundred yards from the exit to the station he passed a pub, the Railway Inn. He walked past it and then, on a sudden impulse, turned back and went in. He *had* to celebrate or he would burst. He walked up to the bar. There were three or four men standing there – perhaps more, he didn't count them.

'A Scotch-and-soda,' he said to the barman. 'And the same for you, or whatever you'd like.' He looked down the bar at the other men. 'Drinks all round,' he said. 'Whatever these gentlemen fancy. I'm celebrating!'

The barman served everyone quickly. Surprised thanks rained on Ben.

'A win on the horses, then?' one of the men asked.

Ben shook his head. 'Much better than that.'

'Then, what *are* we celebrating?' another man asked. 'What shall we drink to?' In his own mind he had decided it must be a first grandchild. Men did go a bit overboard for that. He had himself.

'I'm engaged to be married,' Ben said. The note of pride in his voice brought congratulations all round. If there was surprise he didn't even notice it.

'And what's the lucky lady called?' one of them asked.

'Lottie,' Ben said. 'Lottie.' It gave him so much pleasure to say her name.

'Do you have a photograph?' someone asked.

'I haven't,' Ben said. 'Not with me.' The fact was, he didn't have one at all. 'I wish I had. She's very beautiful,' he added.

'Then we'll raise our glasses to the beautiful Lottie,' the barman said.

Ben drank his Scotch quickly. 'Thank you,' he said. 'Thank you all. And now, if you'll excuse me, I'll be off. I have to get home. A phone call, you understand.'

'There goes a happy man,' the barman said when Ben had gone.

★   ★   ★

185

Back at Beck Farm Ben waited impatiently for the time to pass. Eventually, the three hours he had calculated it would take Lottie to reach her home went by. He picked up the telephone and dialled. There was no reply. Why was there no reply? he asked himself. Was she there, and not answering? Had she changed her mind? But surely not? She'd looked every bit as happy as he'd felt. Why would she change her mind? Had there been an accident? Don't be silly, he admonished himself. Everyone knows how rare railway accidents are. No, he was being neurotic. And just possibly, in his haste, he had dialled the wrong number. He redialled, taking great care to get it right. He could hear the phone ringing at the other end. No reply.

Why hadn't he proposed to her last night, while she was still here? He had known he wanted to; he'd been just too nervous to put it into words and he'd not been sure how she would react. But if he had done it then, and if she'd accepted as quickly as she had today, they'd have had the pleasure of luxuriating in it, of sitting side by side and planning everything. But thank God he'd found his courage today, even though it had been at the very last minute. Now, he would steel himself to wait another fifteen minutes and then he'd ring again.

Lottie had thought she'd heard a telephone ringing as she came through the front door of the building, but she couldn't be sure it was her phone. Whatever, it was silent again before she was three steps into the hall. She had had a frustrating journey. There had been several slow-downs, said to be due to works on the line, and just north of Luton a very long wait for which no reason was given, not even an apology as they'd left the train. On the other hand she'd had plenty to think about. The whole of the journey had been taken up by her swirling thoughts of Ben's proposal and of what it would mean to her. It was not so much that he *had* proposed to her as the timing of it. The evening before, she had almost expected it. They had had a wonderful day, she had sensed that they were very close, there had been opportunities in plenty, but in the end nothing had happened and she had gone to bed deciding that it had been wishful thinking on her part. And this morning, on the journey from Beck Farm to Shepton

186

neither of them had said much at all. And then, almost too late, it had happened. But it *had* happened. He had said 'Will you marry me?' and she had said 'Yes', so why wasn't he ringing her?

She'd meant it when she'd said 'Yes'. She'd thought about it most of the time since then. It would be a new kind of life in a new place, all the old things cast off. Everything about it would be ideal. All right, she'd reminded herself, Ben wasn't in the first flush of youth, but that didn't matter, did it? She'd experienced a young husband. It hadn't worked. Ben would be kind to her, he would take care of her. What was the saying? 'Better be an old man's darling than a young man's slave.' Yes, all in all she was sure they'd make a great success of it. Of course, she thought, she wouldn't be like Moira, it wasn't in her, but she would bring other things to the marriage. So why didn't he ring?

She went into the kitchen and put the kettle on, making sure she left the door open so as not to miss the call when it came. Not that there was any likelihood she would miss it. The flat was so ridiculously small that it was possible to hear a pin drop in the next room.

She was pouring the boiling water onto the teabag in the mug when the phone rang. Was it her imagination or was it louder, more insistent, than usual? She rushed to answer it.

'Lottie!' It was Ben. He sounded anxious.

'Ben!'

'Are you all right?' he asked quickly. 'I rang three times. I wondered what had happened to you.'

'I'm fine,' Lottie said. 'The train was late. Are *you* all right?'

'More than all right,' Ben said. 'Couldn't be better – unless you tell me it isn't true and I'm dreaming. I *did* ask you to marry me, and you *did* say yes, didn't you? I'm not dreaming?'

'Of course you're not, silly!' Lottie assured him. 'I mean, you're not dreaming. But if you want to ask me again . . . I mean, if you want to make sure . . . ?'

He knew she was teasing but he took her up on it. 'Lottie, I love you,' he said. 'Will you marry me?'

'Oh Ben,' Lottie said, 'of course I will.'

'So when?' Ben asked. 'The sooner, the better.'

'I agree,' Lottie said. 'But you must give me a bit of time to make arrangements.'

'What arrangements?' Ben queried. 'It seems simple to me.'

'That's because you're a man,' Lottie said. 'It's different for a woman. I'll have lots of things to think about. What to wear, for a start. Whether I'll have a bridesmaid, and if so, who. I want it to be the most wonderful wedding. I'm sure you do too.'

'Naturally,' Ben said. 'And it will be. Whatever you wear, whether you have no bridesmaids or a dozen.' In his mind it was being married to her that counted, not so much the wedding. But she was a woman, wasn't she, she had different ideas. 'But we don't want a fuss, do we?' he said. There had been little time as yet to give it any thought, but a quiet ceremony in Shepton Register Office would seem to be the thing. And he would not want to announce his plans – not even his engagement to Lottie – in Kilby beforehand. He knew it would not be popular with everyone; it would cause dissension. No, he thought, they would marry quietly and he would bring her back as his bride. And in time, probably quite a short time, they would all learn to love her.

'Not a *big* fuss,' Lottie agreed. 'But it is something special.'

She knew it couldn't be a big affair. It would have to be in a register office – with perhaps a blessing in church afterwards. And it wouldn't be appropriate to wear white. Nor did she really know enough women to have a bevy of bridesmaids even if she had wanted them, or for that matter even people to invite as guests. She had never had a large circle of friends. She hadn't needed them, she had had her mother. But perhaps one bridesmaid? Dulcie would be fine. And then she remembered – in all this excitement she had forgotten for the minute – that in ten days' time she and Dulcie had a contract to do a three-month tour of exhibitions in different towns. She didn't really want to break the contract, because she needed the money for clothes, shoes and the like, and especially for her wedding dress. She didn't know what style it would be but she wanted it to be ultra smart, and it would almost certainly be very expensive. She wanted people in Kilby to see that she was worthy of Ben, an asset to him.

She told Ben about the contract. 'I can't let them down,' she said nobly. 'And in any case I *would* like Dulcie for my brides-maid. She'd probably expect it.' And then she had another thought. 'Don't you have guests booked in during the summer? You wouldn't want to let *them* down, would you? And you couldn't leave Alice to cope with them on her own.'

Ben's sigh came over the telephone. 'Oh dear! You're right, of course.'

'So shall we say the end of September?' Lottie suggested.

'I suppose so,' Ben agreed reluctantly. 'I don't have any bookings for October.' It was not how he wanted it but, apart from not wishing to let anyone down, he could do with the money from the guests. Especially – the thought warmed him – since he would soon have a wife to keep. He was aware that Lottie would cost more than Moira ever had. Not that he cared. He'd give her the world if it was his to give.

'Right, then,' he said. 'The end of September it is, my love. But I can't wait until then to see you again.'

'Of course not. We'll sort something out,' Lottie promised. 'I might be able to get away for the odd day at a weekend, especially if there's an exhibition not too far away. Leeds, or maybe Harrogate.' No suggestion was made that Lottie might visit Kilby for the odd day. They both knew, though each of them kept the thought secret from the other, that her appearance in Kilby at this stage would not be a good idea.

'Promise me you'll try to do that,' Ben said. 'Three months is a long time.'

'It will soon pass,' Lottie said.

Ben contradicted her. 'It will crawl, I know it will.'

At the back of his mind there was also the thought that throughout that time she would be at the exhibitions, and such places abounded with men, almost all of them younger and smarter than he. Men who were away from the restraints of home and had evenings to fill in. Wasn't that precisely how he had met her? He chided himself for his untrusting thoughts but he could not quite banish them. 'Promise you'll ring me every day we're apart. Give me a number so that I can phone you, and an address where I can write to you.'

189

'Of course I will,' Lottie promised. 'Don't worry, Ben!' It was, though, quite nice to have someone worry about her. Her mind raced on. 'So is it OK if I ask Dulcie to be my bridesmaid?' she asked. 'I'd quite like to have a bridesmaid.'

'If that's what you want, then of course you must,' Ben agreed.

It was decided, while they were still on the telephone, that Ben would go to the register office in Shepton and make arrangements for the wedding, that Lottie and Dulcie would travel there on the day before the ceremony and stay overnight at the Heifer; that after the wedding had taken place the next morning, the three of them would go back to the Heifer for lunch. After that, Ben and Lottie would leave for a two-night honeymoon in the Lake District. Ben could not go for longer because of the difficulty of explaining, in Kilby, the reason why. He would find it hard to explain even two nights away. Everyone in Kilby knew what everyone else was up to but his wish was to present a fait accompli. It was for this reason that he had decided against having a best man. He wanted the wedding, he told Lottie, to be a secret between the two of them – and Dulcie, of course – which Lottie found a very romantic notion.

She would rather have a honeymoon in Blackpool or, better still, London – somewhere livelier than the Lake District – but Ben promised that at some time in the next few months they would have a proper honeymoon and she should choose where it was to be. She also felt slightly guilty at the thought of swanning off and leaving Dulcie to her own devices in Shepton so soon after the wedding, but she could make amends by inviting Dulcie to visit them at Beck Farm for a week or so once they were settled in. Perhaps at Christmas, Lottie suggested.

By now they had been on the phone for more than an hour. 'I must let you go, love,' Ben said. 'But I'll ring you tomorrow. Six in the evening. You will be in, won't you?'

'Of course I will,' Lottie said. 'Where else would I be?'

'I shall phone you at six o'clock every evening while we're apart,' Ben said. 'What about when you're working? You must let me know where to get you.'

'I'll ring you then,' Lottie promised. 'It will be easier. I can't say exactly where I'll be.'

That was what Ben feared, though he wouldn't say so. He'd be glad when he had her to himself.

When she had put down the phone, Lottie's first thought – well, not quite the first: that was a tremendous feeling of pleasure and satisfaction, of excited anticipation about what was to come – was that she was hungry. It must be hours since she had eaten. She would scramble a couple of eggs and make a pot of tea, and when she had eaten she would phone Dulcie. She longed to give her all the news; she really did hope Dulcie would agree to be her bridesmaid. They could choose their outfits together, perhaps go up to London for that. She wanted something quite stunning. And if Dulcie was strapped for cash and couldn't afford much, then she'd help her out. She was in a mood to help the entire world.

In the end she couldn't wait. She dialled Dulcie's number and her call was answered immediately. Dulcie must have been sitting right beside the phone. Lottie poured out her news.

'You dark horse!' Dulcie said. 'Though in a way I'm not totally surprised. He obviously took to you from the first.' To her mind Ben was rather dull; nice enough, well-mannered and all that, but dull. She wasn't quite sure what Lottie saw in him, except perhaps security – and he probably wasn't short of money. 'Good for you!' she said. 'I must say, he sounds besotted with you. I'd say you're onto a good thing there.'

It was not quite what Lottie wanted to hear. The bit about Ben being besotted was all right – she thought that was true, and it was a nice feeling – but not the remark about her being onto a good thing. That sounded as if she was a gold-digger, which was *not* true. She was very, very fond of Ben and she would be a good wife to him. For a moment she felt quite cast down, but then, she told herself, it was the kind of thing Dulcie would say. She almost wished she hadn't invited her to be her bridesmaid.

'And of course I'll be your bridesmaid,' Dulcie went on. 'I'd just love it! What are we going to wear?'

'I haven't had time to think yet,' Lottie said. 'But something really nice. Not too bridal, but smart. We'll go together to look.'

'Super,' Dulcie said. 'And sorry, love, but I have to ring off now. I've got a date. Tell you all about it next time we speak – perhaps tomorrow, eh?'

It all went according to plan, with not a single hitch. Lottie managed to meet Ben twice, once in Harrogate and the second time in Leeds. In an antique shop in Harrogate Ben bought her an engagement ring – sapphires and diamonds in a pretty Victorian setting. Back in their own homes they spoke to each other every evening on the telephone. Lottie's exhibitions went well but she didn't enjoy them as much as usual. She wanted time to pass quickly to the end of September, and soon she began to count the days, marking them off in her diary. She and Dulcie had managed to get a half-day off and since they were working in Croydon they had gone up to London and had bought their wedding outfits in Oxford Street. She chose a cream linen suit, far more expensive than she could have afforded if she hadn't been working. It was not bridal white but it looked festive enough. And in Bond Street she pushed the boat out and bought *the* most expensive shoes she had ever had in her life, far more than she could afford. They were court shoes of the softest cream leather, with really high heels. 'And look, there's a matching handbag!' Dulcie said. 'Oh, Lottie, you've got to have it.' So she did.

'Though the suit's not really suitable for Yorkshire in late September,' Lottie said. 'I'll probably freeze. And when will I wear these gorgeous shoes in the country?'

'You won't freeze,' Dulcie said. 'Like that song my mother used to sing, you'll have your love to keep you warm.' She herself had chosen a pale-blue coat with a cream fur collar. They had both opted to go hatless, but to have a special hairdo in Shepton on the morning of the wedding.

The days passed. When the last of the exhibitions ended Dulcie travelled back to Luton with Lottie, having promised to return there the day after the wedding to see to the closing of the flat and the sending of Lottie's bits and pieces – of which there were not many – on to Beck Farm.

192

Privately, Lottie hoped never to have to take part in an exhibition again. She had had her fill. The work had been interesting enough in the beginning but for the last year she'd been bored by it. Handing out leaflets, talking to total strangers about things she didn't understand, spending nights in third-rate hotels, all this had palled on her. Naturally, she would say nothing of this to Dulcie. It wouldn't be fair. Poor Dulcie, though no doubt she too would escape one day. As a bride-to-be herself, Lottie felt quite sorry for her friend.

They arrived in Shepton, where Ben had booked a room for them at the Heifer, in the evening of the day before the wedding. At Lottie's request, he himself was not there, though on the phone the night before he had objected to that. 'Why not?' he demanded. 'I'm dying to see you. It's been far too long.'

'I don't think I should see you until the wedding,' Lottie said. 'It might be unlucky.'

'I thought that was only on the day itself,' Ben complained, 'not the night before.'

'Well, let's not rush it,' Lottie said. 'And just think, Ben, after the wedding we'll be together for good!'

Ben gave in. He had no alternative. 'All right, then,' he said. 'I'll try to be patient.'

Everything went like a dream. From the Heifer, since it was only a matter of two hundred yards, Lottie and Dulcie walked to the Register Office. Lottie's high heels were not compatible with the cobbled street, but at the moment she would have walked through fire and hail without complaining.

Ben, in his best navy suit, was waiting for them. His face lit up when he saw Lottie. 'You look absolutely wonderful!' he cried. 'Oh, Lottie! And you look very nice, too,' he added kindly to Dulcie.

The room was pleasant, nicely decorated with flowers. The registrar had, as arranged, provided a second witness. Lottie remained calm throughout the short ceremony, though Ben was nervous and almost had trouble with his responses. But in a matter of minutes it was over, they were man and wife. There were congratulations all round, and then they left to make way for a waiting couple who had arrived with a large crowd of noisy relatives.

Ben held Lottie's hand on the way back to the Heifer. 'I can't believe it,' he said. 'I can't believe it's really happened. I'm the luckiest man in the world!'

After lunch, of which Ben ate little but which the women thoroughly enjoyed, Ben said to Lottie, 'Well, we must make a start, Mrs Thornton! We must be on our way.'

'Mrs Thornton!' Lottie giggled. It sounded strange. In fact she had wanted to wait until it was time for Dulcie to catch her train, so that they could see her to the station, but Ben was not happy about that. It wasn't due to leave for almost two hours and he wanted to be on his way.

'Don't worry,' Dulcie said. 'I'll be quite happy to look round Shepton for a while.'

She went with them to the car and saw them off. 'Have a lovely honeymoon – as if you wouldn't!'

'And don't forget,' Lottie said, 'you're coming to stay at Christmas.'

'I won't!' Dulcie promised.

The weather in the Lake District was surprisingly good; Lottie, going on what she had heard, had expected it to rain every day. They walked a lot – she reluctantly put away her beautiful high heels and settled for flat ones – had dinner in the hotel each night and, it was Ben's impatient wish, went to bed early. She was surprised by the passion of his lovemaking, which was totally unexpected. She hadn't thought he had it in him.

On the last morning they shopped in Keswick, where he bought her a beautiful silver bracelet.

'Oh Ben,' she protested, 'you spoil me.'

'Why not?' he said. 'You're mine to spoil, now.'

They drove home in the late afternoon. When they reached Kilby it was dropping dark. 'We're going down to the Shorn Lamb this evening,' Ben said. 'I can't wait to show you off!' He felt infinitely braver now than he had before they were married. Two nights of lovemaking had filled him with confidence. Of course he would never forget Moira, how could he, but Moira

194

would want him to be happy – and he was. He was blissfully happy. Every man in the Shorn Lamb this evening would envy him.

The bar was full when they went in. He was pleased to see Joseph and Harry, with their wives, seated at a table. Bernard and Jim Kettle were both behind the bar. There was no sign of Joyce, but she would be in the kitchen – not that it mattered. His arm through Lottie's, he drew her closer still as they walked towards the bar, then stopped.

'Let me introduce my new wife,' he said in a clear, loud voice. 'Not that you don't know Lottie: you've all met her. But now she's Lottie Thornton! We were married two days ago, in Shepton.' He took hold of her arm and raised it in the air, showing the broad band of gold on her third finger.

There was a brief moment of silence and then the congratulations came. Lottie noticed that they came loudly and most clearly from the men.

'You old dog!' Harry said. 'You kept this dark, didn't you?'

'Good for you,' Joseph said, raising his glass. 'All the best to both of you!'

'Hang on a minute,' Bernard said. 'This calls for drinks on the house. Jim, jump to it! There's a couple of bottles of sparkling wine in the fridge. Get them out.' He assembled the glasses, including one for Joyce. She would have to know, no matter what. In any case, when Jim went into the kitchen to take the bottles out of the fridge she'd be in the bar in a jiffy to see what it was about.

Bernard opened the bottles and poured the wine. It was lively, and ran over onto the bar counter. Ben and Lottie moved closer to the bar, hand in hand now. People clustered round them and Jim handed out drinks. 'Raise your glasses!' Bernard was saying as Joyce came in. He thrust a glass into her hand. 'Here's to the happy couple,' he said. 'Every happiness, Ben and Lottie! Cheers!'

'Cheers!' everyone said.

'*What* . . . ?' Joyce began. She was standing close to the bar, Ben and Lottie facing towards her. Then without a pause she

195

threw the contents of her glass in Lottie's face. 'Whore!' she shouted. 'Whore!' And then she turned round and rushed back to the kitchen.

There was no need for Bernard to quieten everyone down. There was complete hush, until he broke it. 'I'm sorry, Lottie, Ben,' he said, then he too turned, and went into the kitchen after his wife.

Jim Kettle handed Lottie a cloth from behind the bar to dry her face. 'Now let's drink the rest of the wine,' he said. 'No point in wasting it. And I'm sure we all wish all the best for the happy couple!'

'How *could* you?' Joyce demanded. 'How could Ben? I won't say how could she – she's capable of anything! I saw it coming. Less than a year since Moira died, her grave hardly settled.'

'Joyce . . .' Bernard began.

'She's not coming in here,' Joyce said. 'Not in this pub. I won't have it. I'll not serve her and nor will anyone else. It's disgusting!' She banged her clenched fist on the table. 'I don't . . .'

Bernard took her arm in a firm grip and forced her to sit down. 'Now, listen to me,' he said. 'I'm not going into the ins and outs of who's wrong, because you won't listen, but you'd better listen to this next bit. There is no way, no way at all, that either Lottie or Ben won't be served here. Ever! This is a public house and they've done nothing to warrant that. The fact that you don't like it is beside the point when it comes to customers. And let me remind you that *I* am the landlord, *I* hold the licence – not you. Whenever they wish to come into my pub, they'll be served, and with civility. I'll not ask you to do it, nor will *you* try to stop anyone else. Is that understood?'

SIXTEEN

Ben was white with rage. Without speaking, he gripped Lottie by the elbow and would have turned her round in the direction of the door, but she resisted him.

'No!' she said. 'No!'

In contrast to Ben's pallor her face was flushed, her eyes bright with anger, but her fury was defiant: she was ready, indeed determined, to stand her ground. 'I'm not going,' she said. Her voice was strong but it was not quite steady. 'I won't submit to being turned out. I've done nothing to deserve that. On the contrary, I want an apology.'

Ben shook his head. 'We'd best go home, love,' he said sharply. 'I'll not stay here and let you be insulted.'

'I've already been insulted,' Lottie said. 'I refuse to run away.'

'Good for you.' Joseph Clark broke the silence of the rest of the company. 'That's the spirit! Come and sit down, love. Finish your drink. You too, Ben.' He moved his chair further round the table to make room for them both. 'Harry,' he said to his friend, 'get some more drinks in. It's your round.'

Lottie took the chair she was offered. A reluctant Ben, looking acutely uncomfortable, saying nothing, took the chair next to hers, then grasped her hand and held it tightly in his. Harry signalled to Jim Kettle to bring more drinks. 'You mustn't leave,'

Joseph said. 'Never give in to injustice. I'm sure we all feel the same.'

They might believe they did, Lottie thought, but no way could they feel as she was feeling at this moment. Several people nodded in agreement with Joseph, though not, she noticed, his wife or indeed Harry's wife. They said nothing; their faces were frozen. It didn't surprise her that that was probably how it was going to be: the men for her, the women against. Well, she'd cope with that. It wouldn't be true to say she didn't care, because she did, but she wouldn't show it. She wouldn't give anyone that satisfaction. She felt most sorry for Ben. He'd been so proud bringing her in, showing her off, and he, if the look on his face was anything to go by, was mortified.

'Joyce isn't herself when it comes to Moira Thornton,' Harry said. 'She's always been the same. Everyone knows that. She puts flowers on the grave every week. They were great friends, you see.'

Lottie said nothing. Nor did Ben.

'Bernard will be very upset if you leave without a word from him,' Joseph said.

It was at that moment that Bernard returned to the bar, though not with Joyce. He had left her in angry tears in the kitchen, and for once he had no sympathy for her.

'I'm sorry,' he said. 'Lottie, Ben, I can't say how sorry I am. It was unpardonable.'

There was a short silence – everyone listening – broken in the end by Lottie. 'It certainly was,' she said. 'I think the least I deserve is an apology. And in front of everyone.'

There were nods of agreement.

'You certainly do, Lottie,' Bernard agreed. 'And I apologize without reserve.'

Lottie shook her head. 'Oh no! It's not you I want an apology from,' she said. 'It's your wife.'

Bernard looked stricken. He saw no hope of her getting one. 'And you're right, of course you are,' he said. 'Joyce is my wife, and I love her, but she's at a funny time of life, you understand. Full of moods – you wouldn't believe. And I have to say she can be as obstinate as a mule, especially when it comes to Moira. It's not you, of course. It would be the same whoever it was.'

Oh no, it wouldn't, Lottie thought. She's reserved this one especially for me! But she guessed Bernard was right about one thing: she wouldn't get an apology from Joyce, not in front of all these people. She'd have to deal with that. And if she let it stop her coming into the Shorn Lamb, what would that do to her and Ben? What would they do in the long winter evenings, which would be here all too soon? There wasn't another pub in the village. She would be taking Ben away from his friends and she'd be denying herself also. All that rushed through her head in a matter of seconds.

'She won't be rude to you again,' Bernard said. 'I can promise you that.' But nor would Joyce ever speak to Lottie again, he thought, and probably vice versa. It would be awful. And not good for business, either. Well, they'd both have to cope with that – and so would he and Ben. Women!

Lottie and Ben refused the offer of another drink from Bernard but they let Harry buy a round. They finished theirs quickly – Ben had still hardly spoken a word – and then left, Lottie with her head held high, Ben subdued but, she could tell, still angry. I dare say they'll all have plenty to say when we're out of sight, she thought. Especially the wives.

She was right about that. Before Ben and Lottie, walking arm in arm, he holding her tightly against him, had gone more than twenty yards along the road Peggy Clark was saying, 'Well, you have to admit it was a bit of a shock. I mean, the pair of them walking in here like that! All lovey-dovey and as bold as brass! You could have knocked me down with a feather!'

'Absolutely,' Beryl Foster agreed. 'Me too. It took my breath away!' Accusingly, she turned to her husband. 'I sincerely hope you wouldn't think of replacing me less than a year after you'd buried me.'

'You're irreplaceable, Beryl love,' Harry said smoothly. 'You know that.' All the same, he thought, Lottie was a very attractive young woman. You could see there was passion there. He'd like to bet she was a ball of fire in bed. He wondered, not for the first time – it had occurred to him when they'd been in Manchester – what she saw in Ben. Well, she'd stood her ground all right this evening, but he'd bet Ben would have something to deal with when they got home.

Close and long-time friends though he and Ben were, Harry would have been surprised to know that Ben – shy, retiring, almost monosyllabic Ben – knew exactly how to comfort his new wife, and soon after they reached Beck Farm he took her upstairs to the bedroom and did so.

Next morning – Ben and Lottie had risen late, she was in her dressing gown and the breakfast dishes were still on the table – there was a knock at the door and, when Ben went to answer it, there on the doorstep stood Bernard Grayson.

'Am I too early?' Bernard said hesitantly, noticing Ben's half-dressed, unshaven state.

'No, no,' Ben said, though Bernard was not the person he most wished to see on this particular morning. After he had made love to Lottie last night she had immediately fallen asleep but he had lain awake for a long time, worrying. What was it going to be like if the village turned against her, as they well might? Joyce Grayson was rooted in the village, partly because of Bernard's position as landlord of the Shorn Lamb but also because she was a respected member of anything of which she could be a member: the Women's Institute, the church, the Bridge club, the Horticultural Society, and she was also a Governor of the Primary School. Her influence was widespread, not only in Kilby but also in the rest of Cordale. She could be friendly to people, but as far as Lottie was concerned Ben couldn't see her ever being so. The circumstances were all wrong.

'You'd better come in,' he said.

Bernard followed him through to the kitchen.

'Would you like a cup of tea?' Lottie offered. 'There's still some in the pot.'

'I would indeed,' Bernard said gratefully – more grateful for the gesture than for the tea.

She handed him a mug. He sweetened it liberally, and took a sip. 'I had to come,' he said. 'I couldn't leave things as they were. I wanted Joyce to come with me but she was a bit busy.'

No-one answered that. It was a weak excuse and patently untrue.

'I wanted her to apologize . . .' Bernard began.

'But she wouldn't!' Ben finished off the sentence for him. 'Well, let me tell you, Bernard – and you can pass it on to Joyce – no-one insults my wife and gets away with it. Not while I'm around.'

'Quite right too.' Bernard nodded. 'And I can promise you it won't happen again.'

'Once was once too often,' Ben said. He was far more angry than Lottie, or than Lottie appeared to be this morning. It hadn't been mentioned between them since last night.

'Don't let it come between you and me, Ben,' Bernard pleaded. 'We've been friends a very long time. I'm sure it was said in the heat of the moment. Moira was such a close friend, as you know. They were more like sisters really and she misses her deeply.'

'I dare say,' Ben said. 'But that's not my wife's fault.'

Lottie spoke up. 'Bernard is right, Ben love,' she said. 'You shouldn't let it cause a rift between the two of you. I wouldn't like that to happen. For that matter, I wouldn't want it to come between me and Bernard. I would like an apology, and I mean from Joyce, but I don't think I'm going to get one.'

Bernard sighed deeply. 'To be realistic, Lottie, I reckon you're right.' Privately he thought that this would be an ongoing enmity, never to be resolved. 'But as I said, she'll not behave like that again. That much I've sorted out.' He hoped he had. He was not totally sure.

It was a slender and brittle olive branch, but Lottie took it. A breach like this one could reverberate through the whole village. People would take sides and there was no way she could win. She was, after all, the stranger in their midst. It would be difficult to walk into the Shorn Lamb but she would do it – and the sooner, the better. Let them get used to her: she was here to stay. She came back to the thoughts she had had the night before. If she and Ben cut themselves off, what would they do, where would they go?

'I shall ignore it,' she said. She wouldn't say she'd forget. She never could.

Bernard's smile was a mile wide. 'That's very good of you,

Lottie. That's wonderful. And promise me you'll neither of you boycott the Lamb.'

'I can promise that,' Lottie said before Ben could speak. 'In fact, we'll be there this evening.'

'I don't know about that,' Ben said sharply. 'That's easier said than done.'

'But we'll do it,' Lottie assured Bernard.

Bernard jumped to his feet, gave Lottie a big hug and shook Ben by the hand. 'Then, I'd best get back,' he said. 'See you this evening.'

'What made you say that, love?' Ben asked Lottie when Bernard had left. 'It's too soon.'

'No, it's not,' Lottie contradicted. 'The sooner, the better. The longer we wait, the harder it will be.' And apart from anything else, she thought, it would put her in the right in front of everybody.

'You're a very nice person,' Ben said.

They went down to the Shorn Lamb rather later than they had on the previous evening. It was more crowded. Lottie thought she detected a slight stir as she went in, a smile on her face, Ben by her side. Joseph and Harry were sitting at a table close by the bar, but their wives were not with them. Joseph called out to Ben and Lottie to join them. No mention at all was made of the previous night's fracas. It might never have happened.

'The ladies are at the evening meeting of the WI,' Harry said. 'They have it in the evening once in a while for the sake of those who can't get there during the day. What will you both have to drink?'

'On the house,' Bernard called out. 'All four of you.'

In bed that night Lottie allowed herself to cry. The strain of walking into the Shorn Lamb, of acting as if nothing of the least importance had happened on the previous evening, had been considerable, and now that she was back in her own home she could at last let go. She didn't cry for long. Ben at once took her in his arms and comforted her. 'You were wonderful, love,' he said. 'I'm sure everybody thought so. And you were right about going and I was wrong.'

As the weeks went by, Lottie realized just how much she had done the right thing. Since neither of them were inclined to go to church, evenings at the Shorn Lamb had become their chief social occasions. There was little else. Fortunately, they saw next to nothing of Joyce. She was mostly in the kitchen, making meals, and Lottie guessed that Bernard warned his wife when the Thorntons were in. Of course in the daytime there were visits to be made to the shops in the village – that passed an hour or two – but there was nothing, in Lottie's eyes – which were used to bigger and brighter places with more interesting things to spend money on than bread and groceries – to make shopping in Kilby much of an event. Not that she had all that much money to spend. Ben gave her an adequate allowance for housekeeping and would willingly have bought her anything else she desired, but spare cash in her purse she did not have.

The days passed. There was little to do in the house because Alice did it all. Even if Lottie had wanted him to – which she didn't because she had no craving for housework – she was sure Ben wouldn't have got rid of Alice. She had worked at Beck Farm for years; she was a widow and she needed the money, he said. Lottie would have liked, perhaps, to make changes in the house – new curtains, some modern pieces of furniture, cushions – but everything was there already, and in good condition; the furniture had been in Ben's family for generations. She was not brave enough to join the Women's Institute. That was Joyce Land. Besides, she didn't fancy it. She saw it as domestic and she wasn't into domesticity. Her mother had seen to that. What she did do was visit the library van that came to Kilby every Thursday. She was allowed to take out four books at a time and these she had always read, cover to cover, before the next Thursday came round. The librarian, Mrs Moss, was a friendly woman who, once she had learnt Lottie's tastes, would save suitable books for her. Lottie liked romances; stories that took her into another world, tales in which, in spite of every possible setback, the beautiful heroine won through happily in the end.

Monday was a better day than most because, it being market day, Ben took her to Shepton. She enjoyed that, especially when Ben disappeared for a while to see a friend or do a bit of business and she was free to wander round on her own. She would visit the stalls, buy small items, then sit in a café in the High Street, watching the world go by – or what in Shepton passed for the world – waiting for Ben to join her.

'I wish we could go to Shepton more often,' she said to Ben one Monday as they sped back home through the narrow roads to Kilby. 'I get a bit bored.'

Ben could not conceive of anyone being bored in Cordale. There was so much to do, so much to see; places to walk to, fells to be climbed, wild life everywhere. Moira had never been bored. For her there were always jobs to be done in the house or something happening in the village. In September, for instance, the apples on the tree had been ripe for picking, but that was something Lottie wasn't interested in. She didn't care much for apples anyway. She had picked a few, and made apple sauce to go with a joint of pork. Ben had picked a few. Mostly, however, they had fallen to the ground and those that had not been eaten by the birds had rotted where they fell.

But Lottie was not Moira, Ben reminded himself. Lottie was herself; she wasn't used to the country, she was a townswoman, but give her time and she'd get used to it. He loved her dearly. He would never wish to change her; all he wanted was for her to be happy.

'If I could drive, I could take myself into Shepton,' Lottie said now (or anywhere else, she thought). 'Couldn't I have driving lessons, Ben?' No way would she suggest that he should teach her, she thought as he whizzed round a corner almost, but not quite, on the wrong side of the road.

'I don't know about that,' Ben replied. 'But you could go to Shepton more often if you wanted to. The bus goes three times a week.'

He had no desire to do so. Mondays were enough for him. He was not one for wandering round shops or sitting in cafés. When he had spare time, of which actually he had quite a lot, he liked to spend it carving his animals, the animals and birds of the Dales, and there were more of those than most people realized. He had seen a kingfisher down by the river the other day. He would make careful drawings, given the chance, or take photographs, but he was patient in watching – he could sit still as long as need be – and able to store a lot in his mind. 'But you enjoy going to Shepton,' he said to Lottie, 'so why don't you do so from time to time? We'll think about driving lessons later.'

'Perhaps I will,' Lottie said.

Three mornings later she awoke with the idea in her mind. Why not go to Shepton today? The previous night's weather forecast had promised a cool day, but with sunshine, and indeed when she went downstairs the sun, filtering through the gap between the curtains, was already making a path across the kitchen floor. She drew back the curtains and looked up at the clear blue sky. She had nothing else in mind to occupy her today. Thursday was one of Alice's days, so she would be around to give Ben his lunch – not that he wasn't capable of getting it for himself. So why not?

Ben came in from feeding the chickens.

'I thought I might take up your suggestion,' she said, filling the kettle. 'Go into Shepton. What do you think?'

'If that's what you'd like, love,' he said. 'Make the most of the fine days while we still have them.'

'Are you sure you don't want to come with me?' she asked. Guiltily, she hoped he might not. She looked forward to a day of dawdling window shopping, taking as long as she wanted over everything.

'Not really, if you don't mind,' Ben said. 'I've a few things to do – the bottom fence, for a start. You'll be all right, won't you?'

'Of course I will,' Lottie said. 'And Alice will get your lunch for you. There's some cold beef, and a salad. Perhaps I'll bring back something from Shepton for supper.'

Ben smiled. 'Don't worry about me. I'm used to getting my own meals.'

The bus, which set off from villages further up the dale, was due to leave Kilby at ten-thirty and would stop several times on the route to Shepton to pick up and set down other passengers. It would leave Shepton for the return journey at four-thirty in the afternoon, which would allow her a nice long day. At twenty-past ten she was outside the village post office as the bus drew up.

There were half a dozen women already on board and two others waiting at the bus stop, neither of whom she had ever seen in the Shorn Lamb. They were talking to each other and didn't speak to her.

Lottie enjoyed her day, at least for the most part. She wandered around the market stalls – there were always some stalls in the High Street even when it was not market day – and went into the shops. She bought a few things: a neck scarf, a new shampoo she'd seen advertised on television, a woman's magazine, mascara. She knew she needed none of them but what was the point of a shopping trip if one went home empty-handed? She had an early lunch – shepherd's pie – in a small restaurant, reckoning that the Heifer might be too expensive. By half-past three she had seen everything and there was an hour to wait before the bus left. She went into the café where Ben had taken her on an earlier occasion and ordered a pot of tea and a toasted teacake. She ate and drank slowly, looking around, spinning out the time. She flipped through her magazine, read her stars – nothing much there. It was still only four o'clock and the stop for the bus back to Kilby was no more than three yards away from the café.

She looked around again. Nothing had changed. Two men of about her own age still sat at a nearby table, clearly talking business, and, in between, throwing glances in her direction. Several of the other tables were occupied, mostly by women, all of them chatting as they ate and drank. In fact she was the only person sitting alone at a table. She felt out of place, almost as if she had no right to be there. She wished so much that she had someone with her – it didn't matter who: anyone who would talk, who'd say what they'd bought, what they'd paid for it, what they might be doing tomorrow, arrange when they'd meet again. To be realistic, she didn't see anything like that happening.

She went back to her magazine, trying to look occupied, immersing herself in the readers' letters on the back page and in the replies of the agony aunt. Could she ever spill out her troubles to a magazine? It was doubtful. She closed the magazine and sent off her thoughts in another direction.

Dulcie would be coming for Christmas, but that was still

several weeks away. There was November to get through, with the anniversary of her mother's death and also her own birthday. Her mother had always planned something special for her birthday. Sometimes they would go up to London to do a show.

Lottie looked at her watch again. A quarter past four. She could leave, she wasn't tied down, and this she finally chose to do. It was impossible to spin out this small meal any longer, not while sitting on her own. Perhaps the bus would come early? If not, she could look in one or two nearby shop windows. As she passed the table where the two men were sitting, one of them looked up and smiled at her. She paid her bill at the cash desk, and left.

'Did you have a nice time, love?' Ben asked her when she was back at Beck Farm.

'Lovely,' Lottie said.

'Good.' Ben sounded happy about that. 'You must do it again.'

'Oh, I will,' Lottie promised.

The days passed. It was November. She got through the anniversary of her mother's death, not mentioning it to anyone. Her own birthday fell on a Monday but Ben was unable to go to Shepton since it was tupping time in Cordale and he had promised to help Joseph through that, as he always did.

'I'm sorry, love,' he said to Lottie. 'It's going to be all go for the next two weeks. It always is at tupping time.' He had already helped Joseph to bring the ewes down from the high fells, and searched for the strays. 'Sheep farmers know all about lost sheep,' he said. 'They don't have to read it in the Bible. You'd be amazed the places sheep get into, and the trouble you take to get them out.'

'Why do you have to do it at this particular time?' Lottie asked. 'Why not just let nature take its course?'

Ben laughed out loud at that. 'What tupping time is is fixing when the new lambs will be born. The farmer needs the lambs to be born when the new grass is coming up in the meadows or else what would they feed on? And in Cordale that's in April. Nature, left to itself, can be very disorganized. Farmers have to give it a helping hand as well as working with it. Anyway, love, I'm going to be very busy over the next week or two. There's the whole business, when we've got the ewes together, of getting the rams to them. That takes organizing, let me tell you. So we all give one another a hand at this time of the year, and I'm a spare pair of hands so I help where I'm needed.'

'I thought you didn't like farming,' Lottie said.

'I don't,' Ben said. 'But I'll not stand back when I'm needed. We all help one another. So you'll have to amuse yourself for a bit. But you'll be all right, won't you?'

'Of course I will,' Lottie agreed. 'As long as you don't ask me to help with the sheep. I'd hardly know one end of a ewe from the other.'

'You can leave that to the rams,' Ben said.

Ben had bought her for her birthday a very pretty new watch, which he'd sent away for by mail order. It was a bit like the custom of giving someone a clock for a retirement present, she thought. She would have all the time in the world to check the passing of the hours and days, though now on a mother-of-pearl dial. Dulcie sent her a birthday card, posted in Exeter. 'Looking forward to seeing you,' it said.

Lottie continued to take the bus to Shepton, usually on a Thursday. She ate shepherd's pie or, as a change, plaice and chips in the same café, made a few purchases and had tea in the same teashop, which seemed to have the same customers, or at least very similar ones. She marked the passing of the hours and days on her new watch. Because Ben was tired in the evenings they went less often to the Shorn Lamb, and seldom for a meal. 'Better not risk it,' Lottie said, feigning humour. 'I expect Joyce would lace my food with poison.'

And then at last it was the week before Christmas and Dulcie was due in two days' time. Lottie thought she had seldom looked forward to anything as much in her life, not even Santa Claus's visit when she'd been a little girl.

SEVENTEEN

Three days before Christmas Ben and Lottie went, in the late afternoon, to Shepton station to meet Dulcie from the train. As long as he lived, Ben thought, he would have happy memories of Shepton station as the place where he had made his last-minute, hasty proposal to Lottie and she had just as quickly accepted him. To the outward eye it was the reverse of a romantic setting. By this time of day the platform was abundantly littered with discarded sweet wrappings, empty cigarette packets and screwed-up tissues for which it had been too much trouble to find a waste bin. Abandoned newspapers lay on the benches. The inadequate lighting was no match for the darkening December day, which could be glimpsed down the line. But Ben saw none of that; it was a special place to him. Nor, for that matter, did Lottie. She was too excited at the prospect of seeing Dulcie again to let her surroundings distract her. Which was a bit strange, she thought, because although she had quite liked Dulcie when they had been registered with the same agency and therefore found themselves working together at sundry exhibitions she had felt no particular attachment to her. That had come from choosing her as her bridesmaid, which she had done partly because Dulcie had been in Manchester and had met Ben, and also because she could think of no-one else. And here she was on the platform, waiting with the same

209

anticipation she might have had for a bosom friend of her early childhood.

They didn't have to wait long. The train was on time and the moment it came to a halt Dulcie, struggling with a large suitcase, stepped down from the first coach. Ben strode forward at once to take it from her. All smiles, she shook him warmly by the hand and then turned to embrace Lottie. 'It's so good to see you!' she cried. 'It seems ages.'

So it did, Lottie thought, though it had been no more than three months. Dulcie looked wonderful; a visitor from another world. She was smartly dressed in what was surely a new coat, of beige wool, with a pale-blonde fur collar, a matching fur hat worn tipped forward – meeting, but not quite covering, one eyebrow – and knee-high tan boots.

'We thought we'd go straight back to Kilby,' Ben said as they left the station. 'Unless, of course, you want to stop in Shepton for anything? It's very cold. I reckon it might snow.'

'Oh, how wonderful,' Dulcie said. 'Snow at Christmas! That would be perfect.'

A townswoman's idea of perfection, Ben thought. It was not his. But he liked Dulcie, what little he had seen of her. She was bright and friendly. She would be good for his Lottie.

'And don't forget, I've not yet seen Beck Farm,' Dulcie said. 'I'm dying to set eyes on it.'

It was totally dark by the time they left Shepton, but this did not deter Ben from driving at his usual speed along the unlit country lanes. Dulcie, who had been all talk ever since she had stepped off the train, subsided into silence except for the occasional gasp, heard by Lottie in the front seat but apparently not by Ben. Speech only came back to her when he pulled up in front of Beck Farm. Caught in the headlights, it did look attractive.

'Oh!' Dulcie squealed. 'Oh, is this it? Oh, isn't it just *lovely*!'

'Which would you like first,' Lottie asked as they went into the house: 'a cup of tea, or a look round the house and to see your room?'

'I'd like to see the house first,' Dulcie said. 'I've never been inside a really old house before. It's so different, isn't it?'

'Certainly different from my flat,' Lottie agreed.

'And mine,' Dulcie said.

She followed Lottie from room to room, giving little cries of delight. 'I'd no idea it was so *big*,' she said. She was more than pleased with her own room, which was at the back of the house. Instinctively she walked across to the window and looked out. It was as black as pitch, the only gleams of light from a house in the distance. 'That's Joseph Clark's house,' Lottie said. 'He had the next farm and then he bought Ben's land from him, so it's all his.'

'I've never seen anywhere as *dark* as this,' Dulcie said. 'It's awesome!'

'You'll like it even better tomorrow, when you see it in daylight,' Lottie told her, drawing the curtains across the window. 'It faces up the dale. A lovely view. Anyway, I'll go down and make some tea while you unpack, or whatever you want to do. Come down when you're ready. We'll be in the kitchen.'

'I'll be down in a jiffy. I won't unpack yet, I'll just freshen up,' Dulcie said. 'Oh, Lottie, you've really landed on your feet, haven't you?'

Lottie didn't answer. It wasn't the first time Dulcie had used that expression and she really didn't like it. It made her uncomfortable. She would have married Ben whatever the size of his house, she told herself. Or his income, for that matter. Not that she was going to say any of that to Dulcie. Her friend would soon realize she'd got it wrong.

When Lottie had gone downstairs Dulcie washed her hands, combed her hair – it had come up quite well this time – and reapplied her make-up. Lottie looked different, she thought. She was thinner, quieter. She had lost her sparkle. And whereas the old Lottie would have giggled at the remark about landing on her feet, she had clearly taken offence. She hadn't said anything, but Dulcie could tell. Anyway, she would do something about her friend. She would find out what, if anything, was wrong. Ben was nice enough. She took one last look at herself in the mirror, adjusted a stray lock of hair, and went downstairs. She wasn't here for long but while she was she would be the perfect guest.

'We thought we'd go down to the local pub for supper,' Lottie said as they cleared away the tea things. ('I will risk being poisoned,' she'd said to Ben when they'd discussed it. 'I don't see why Dulcie should be deprived just because Joyce is stupid.')

'That would be lovely,' Dulcie said. 'Village life! They say everything happens in the pub.'

'You've been watching too much television,' Lottie said. 'But yes, quite a lot does.' Good and bad, she thought.

Bernard had been pleasantly surprised when Ben had phoned to book a table. Joyce had been surprised, though not pleasantly. She had managed to see very little of Lottie in the last few months, and that suited her. She'd be happy never to see her again, but Bernard had different views. Men were all alike.

'And who might the third one be?' she asked her husband.

'She's a friend of Lottie's . . .' he began.

'Enough said,' Joyce retorted. 'I can guess what she'll be like.'

'No, you can't,' Bernard said. 'And I'm warning you, Joyce, I want no trouble and I won't have any.'

'I couldn't care less,' Joyce said. It was not true. She cared deeply. She missed Moira so much. She couldn't bear to think of anyone taking her place, especially this . . . tart! Bernard said she wasn't at all, but she trusted her own judgement before his.

'And you'll cook them a decent meal,' Bernard said.

'You can count on that,' Joyce said. 'I wouldn't lower my standards even if some people have.'

'You needn't even see them,' he pointed out. 'I'll serve.'

The thing was, she wanted to see them, or, rather, she wanted to see this new one. She wanted to confirm that she'd be as awful as she expected. Which was why, when she knew they'd arrived, because Bernard brought the order for their meal, she made an excuse to go briefly into the bar. They'd not yet moved to the table reserved for them: they were standing by the bar, talking to Joseph Clark and Harry Foster, laughing and joking without a care in the world, as if they'd known them all their lives. It was disgusting. She managed not to meet Lottie's eyes but she took in her friend. She was a tart all right. You only had to look at her. Tight dress, low neck, short skirt. High heels and red hair. Dyed, as like as not. She was laughing at some joke, throwing back her head and showing a mouthful of gleaming white teeth.

212

Joyce went back into the kitchen well satisfied. She would now cook their steaks to perfection, the best she had ever done, just to show them. She was not quite sure what it would show them, but something or other. Her head was buzzing and her insides were churning with rage.

'That was the best fillet steak I have ever tasted,' Dulcie said an hour later, putting down her knife and fork. 'You couldn't beat that at the Ritz.' Not that she had ever eaten at the Ritz. She had walked past it but never stepped inside – though who was to know? She said the same thing to Bernard when he came to ask if everything was all right.

'I'm pleased you enjoyed it,' he said. His wife, he thought, was an enigma! 'Now, will you have the apple pie or the trifle?'

'I hope it sticks in her throat,' Joyce said to Bernard when he came back and ordered apple pie all round. It wouldn't, of course. She made the best apple pie in Cordale; golden flaky pastry, apples exactly the right consistency – not too hard, not too pulpy – and the slightest touch of cinnamon. Only Moira's apple pies could come up to hers. It had been Moira who always gave her the apples. There had been none from Beck Farm this year.

'You're beyond me!' Bernard said. 'Do you really want Ben to go on mourning for the rest of his life?'

'He shows no sign of doing that,' Joyce said, dishing up the apple pie and pushing it in her husband's direction.

'Does it never occur to you', he persisted, 'that it's because he and Moira were so happy together that he was pleased to try marriage again? Don't you ever see it as a compliment to Moira?'

'I do not,' Joyce said. 'And only a man would come up with an excuse like that.'

'That was wonderful,' Dulcie said as they walked home in the bitter cold. 'A superb meal.'

The next day Lottie and Dulcie decided to take the bus to Shepton. 'I have last-minute Christmas shopping to do,' Lottie said. 'You can't get everything in Kilby, not by a long chalk. Anyway, I expect you'd like to look at the shops, wouldn't you?'

'Whatever you say,' Dulcie agreed.

Shepton, dressed up for the Christmas season, looked splendid. Silver tinsel was hung high, side to side across parts of the High Street. Every stall and every shop window vied with every other stall and shop window in the matter of decorations: cotton-wool snow, sprinkled frost, baubles, paper chains. There were fairy lights round the entrance to the Town Hall and, outside Boots, Santa Claus was selling brightly wrapped, lucky-dip Christmas parcels from his sack. It was a dim day, so the lights were switched on everywhere. In the church garden, which gave onto the street, a wooden crib, straw-lined, waited for the Holy Child, which would be placed in it on Christmas Eve.

'Isn't this *wonderful*!' Dulcie enthused. 'It's much nicer than Oxford Street.'

They had decided, as a treat, to have the special Christmas lunch at the Heifer. They would both feel at home there, they agreed. 'We'd better go early,' Lottie said, 'or we might not get a table.' They went in at noon and were told they would have to wait a little while. If they liked to sit in the bar, they would be called when a table was ready. The trouble was, there was nowhere to sit, and the crowd was thick round the bar. The only two vacant seats were at a table for four at which two men were already seated. The women hovered, uncertain what to do, and then one of the men looked up, caught Lottie's eye, and immediately smiled at her. It was a smile of recognition, which for a second puzzled her, and then she realized he was the man who had smiled at her in the café, a month or two ago.

'Good morning,' he said. He had a deep, pleasant voice with only a slight trace of the local accent. 'Are you two ladies looking for a seat? If so, please join us.'

'That's very kind of you,' Dulcie said. The look she gave Lottie said 'Shall we?'

'Very kind,' Lottie agreed. 'We will, if you don't mind. We're waiting for a table in the restaurant.'

'I've seen you before,' the man said. 'In the Bluebell café.'

'Yes, I remember,' Lottie said.

'Let me get both you ladies a drink,' he said. 'There's a terrible crowd at the bar. You'll never be able to push through. What would you like? Sherry, beer, gin-and-tonic?'

214

'Gin-and-tonic for me,' Dulcie said.

'And the same for me, please,' Lottie told him.

He stood up. He was taller than she'd expected, and slender with it. Although it was December his skin was still tanned, as if he might be a man who spent a lot of time out-of-doors. His hair was dark, longish and slightly curly. She guessed he was just a few years older than she was.

'Right! Then I'll leave you in the care of my friend, John Carter, for as long as it takes,' he said. 'My name is Richard Chalmers.'

Dulcie was all smiles. This was better than she had hoped for. 'I'm Dulcie,' she said quickly. 'My friend is Lottie.'

'Pleased to meet you both,' he said – and went off to get the drinks.

'So have you not met Richard before?' John Carter asked Lottie.

'Oh no,' she said. 'I only saw him in the café. I don't think you were with him then, Mr Carter.'

'John, please! No, I wasn't. I would have remembered. But Richard meets a lot of people in the course of his job – talking to them in cafés and bars, and so on.'

'So what is his job?' Dulcie chipped in. She believed in asking if you wanted to know.

'Ah!' John said. 'I'd guess you haven't lived round here long or you'd not need to ask. He's a reporter on the *Dales Chronicle*. He does that feature "Around the Dales" – as well as a lot of other articles, of course.'

'I don't live round here,' Dulcie admitted. 'But Lottie does.'

'I don't get the *Chronicle*,' Lottie said. 'Maybe I should do so.'

Richard returned with the drinks. 'Here we are, then,' he said. 'Sorry to be so long. They're madly busy.'

'You must let me pay,' Lottie said. What a silly girl, Dulcie thought.

'Certainly not. On me,' Richard said. He raised his glass. 'Happy Christmas, everyone.'

'And many of them,' John echoed.

They had a long wait for the restaurant table, but it didn't matter: conversation flowed easily. The women learnt that John was a teacher, but as the schools had broken up for Christmas he was on holiday. The men learnt that Dulcie and Lottie used to work together, that the former was here on a visit, and that Lottie was married to Ben Thornton and lived in Kilby.

'I know Kilby, of course,' Richard said. 'I know all the villages and I know the Shorn Lamb, but I don't think I know your husband, or exactly where Beck Farm is. Do you go in the Shorn Lamb?'

'Yes, we do,' Lottie said. She wondered why she'd never seen him there.

'We had our dinner there last night,' Dulcie said. 'It was super.'

'I haven't eaten there,' Richard said. 'I must give it a try.'

They finished their drinks but there was still no sign of the waiter coming to call Lottie and Dulcie to their table. 'I'll get another round,' John offered. 'No point in sitting here with empty glasses. Same again, everyone?'

'So you'll be going to the Farmers' Ball?' Richard said when they were into their second drinks.

'The Farmers' Ball?' Lottie queried.

'Don't tell me you don't know about it,' Richard said. 'It's the social event of the year, locally. It's held here in Shepton, at the Town Hall, actually. Towards the end of January. That's a quiet time on most farms. Everybody goes to the Farmers' Ball. I would have thought there'd be a party going from the Shorn Lamb. You'd better get on to your old man!'

Dulcie clapped her hands. 'Oh, Lottie! That sounds wonderful!' She wondered, if she wasn't working, whether she might somehow wangle herself an invitation. 'And does everyone dress up?' she enquired. 'I don't mean fancy dress. I mean is it a dressy affair?'

'Absolutely,' Richard said. 'Everyone dresses to the nines! Ladies in their ballgowns!' He turned to Lottie. 'You must tell your husband he has to take you.'

'I will,' Lottie said. 'I really will.'

The waiter came at last. 'Your table is ready now, ladies,' he said.

The two men stood up as Lottie and Dulcie got to their feet.

'It was nice meeting you,' Richard said to Lottie. 'I'm sure we'll meet again.'

Back home, Ben came to the door to meet them. 'Did you enjoy yourselves?' he asked.

'We did,' Lottie said.

'Very much,' Dulcie said. 'Shepton looked lovely.'

'You don't look overburdened with shopping,' Ben remarked. 'I'd have thought you'd have been buying up the town.'

'We didn't seem to have time,' Lottie told him.

'We had lunch at the Heifer,' Dulcie said. 'It was crowded, but two men found us seats at their table, I mean in the bar, not for lunch.'

'One of them was a Richard Chalmers. He's a reporter on the *Dales Chronicle*,' Lottie said. 'He knows Kilby. Do you know him?'

'I don't know him. I've heard of him,' Ben said.

'He told us about the Farmers' Ball,' Dulcie said. 'It sounds wonderful. Do you go?'

'Not now,' Ben said. 'I have been in the past.' It had been a while ago, before Moira was ill. She had enjoyed it. 'I'm not one for balls. For a start, I'm no good as a dancer. Two left feet, I reckon.'

'Richard Chalmers said he thought there'd probably be a party there from the Shorn Lamb,' Dulcie said.

'There might be; I haven't heard it mentioned. It's towards the end of January. A good time because it's not busy on the farms then, but a terrible time weather-wise. There can be snowdrifts as high as a house between here and Shepton. The cars can get well and truly stuck. It's a mad time of year to drive anywhere.'

All the same, Lottie thought, I would really like to go. If a party was going from the Shorn Lamb it might already have been arranged. Presumably she and Ben hadn't heard because they hadn't been in much. Or – it was an uneasy thought – it hadn't been mentioned because very likely Bernard and Joyce would be going and all the regulars knew the situation there. She wouldn't pursue it now, she would bide her time – though not for too long or it would be too late.

A little later, when Ben was out of the room, Dulcie said, 'I'll be green with jealousy, thinking of you going to the Farmers' Ball. I've been wondering whether to be cheeky and ask if I could go with you, but actually I'm almost certain there's an exhibition in Sheffield, and if there is I'll have to be there.' For a few seconds Lottie felt a swift envy of Dulcie. Looking back on it, she had enjoyed the exhibitions, though she hadn't always thought so at the time. Now what she remembered about them was the bustle, meeting people, chatting, making new acquaintances and sometimes almost friends. You tended to meet the same people from time to time, on the stands. And then there was usually something to do in the evenings. Not of course, she told herself, that she wasn't contented with her present lot. A good husband, a lovely house. And they were about to have a wonderful Christmas. What more could anyone ask for?

Christmas *was* wonderful, except that it was quieter, less exciting than Dulcie had somehow expected it to be. The threatened snow didn't come. The weather was, for the most part, dim and drizzly. There were no groups of red-cheeked people in woolly hats and scarves going round the village, carrying lanterns and singing carols. It was not the kind of Christmas Dulcie, and for that matter Lottie – for it was her first Christmas in the country – had expected, largely from what they had seen in films. They did go to the Shorn Lamb and joined in the carol singing. When it wasn't raining Lottie and Dulcie went for walks; also, at Dulcie's request – it seemed to her it was the thing to do on Christmas morning – they went to church and sang the same Christmas carols. Ben opted out of that. Moira had been a churchgoer but he never had and he wasn't going to start now just because it was Christmas.

In the Shorn Lamb it was Dulcie, perhaps wanting to do something for her friend, perhaps because she had had too many gin-and-tonics, who brought up the subject of the Farmers' Ball. They were all sitting or standing close to the bar – the Clarks, the Fosters, Dora and Henry Laycock from the village shop, Bernard behind the bar, though Joyce was in the kitchen, one or two others whom she didn't know – when she said, 'So are you making up a party to go to the Farmers' Ball in Shepton, you lucky people?'

There was a slight hesitation – unnoticed by Dulcie but not by Lottie – before Joseph said, 'As a matter of fact, we are. All of us here, plus Bernard and Joyce. What about joining us?'

The atmosphere was decidedly uncomfortable. It was Ben who broke it. 'I don't think so. I'm not one for such things. I never did enjoy it.'

Afterwards, Lottie didn't know what had come over her at that moment except that she had felt a surge of defiance which had to come out. It was not only against Ben; indeed, hardly any of it was. She knew he had replied as he had partly because of the situation between her and Joyce Grayson; he was protecting her. But at that moment she didn't want to be protected.

'But I would absolutely love to go,' she said firmly. 'Is it too late to get tickets?'

'I can get them,' Joseph said. He was well aware what this was all about but he was ignoring it.

'Wonderful,' Lottie said. 'Thank you, Joseph.'

Ben said nothing, not then, not in public. He would wait until they were back at home.

'As a matter of fact,' Bernard said hesitantly, 'it's not certain that me and Joyce will be able to come.'

'Not come?' Harry Foster said. 'But you've always gone to the Farmers' Ball.'

'I know,' Bernard said, 'but Jim Kettle might not be here to take over. He probably has to go into hospital. It's on a Friday night and there's no chance I could be away if Jim wasn't here.'

I don't believe him, Lottie thought. She didn't believe a word of it. He was smoothing things over because of that stupid wife of his. She didn't know what to say, and nor did anyone else, so the subject was dropped.

Joseph turned to Dulcie. 'When do you go home, love?' he enquired.

'In three days' time,' Dulcie said. 'I have to go back to work.'

'Well, we shall miss you,' Joseph said. 'It's been nice meeting you.'

'I shall miss you all,' Dulcie said. It was true.

As they walked home – it was quite late, the Shorn Lamb had had an extension – Dulcie said to Lottie, 'Shall I go to Shepton with you to help you choose your dress for the ball? You'll surely be having a new one?'

'I would have to, but I don't yet know that we're going, do I?'

'Oh, I'm sure you will,' Dulcie said. 'Isn't that so, Ben?'

'I suppose so,' Ben said. He couldn't find it in his heart to refuse Lottie anything but nor could he be enthusiastic about this.

'We'll go to Shepton the day after tomorrow,' Dulcie said. 'Will the sales have started? You might find a bargain.'

They found a dress that Dulcie assured Lottie was exactly right for her. 'Perfection,' she pronounced it. It was a rich red, darker than scarlet but glowing. The heart-shaped neck was cut low and the back even lower. The bodice was close-fitting until, halfway down her thighs, it flared out into the floor-length skirt. It was severely plain, with no trimmings, no glitter. The beauty was all in the cut. 'It's wonderful,' Dulcie enthused. 'You look as if you've been poured into it.'

'You don't think it's too flashy?' Lottie queried. 'I mean the colour. I hadn't thought of red.'

'The colour is perfect for you,' Dulcie assured her. 'You're not the type to wear pastels.'

It was not in the sale, and it was expensive. 'I'm not sure what Ben's going to think about the price,' Lottie said.

'You know perfectly well he'll not quibble about that,' Dulcie said. 'You know he'd give you the earth. He loves you to bits. Just you wait until he sees it!'

When Lottie had paid for the dress Dulcie said, 'And now we'll go to the Heifer for a drink, to celebrate. Lunch as well, if you like. My treat, to say thank you for a lovely Christmas.'

Lottie was slightly disappointed that Richard Chalmers was not in the bar – not that she had actually expected him to be, but she wanted to tell him that, thanks to his putting the idea into her head, she was, after all, going to the ball.

EIGHTEEN

At last the day of the Farmers' Ball arrived. At times Lottie had thought it would never come. The days had crawled by since Dulcie had left, just before New Year. She had had a letter from her, bright and chatty as Dulcie always was, saying thank you for a wonderful visit. She'd described the exhibition where she'd been working, an extra one, coming out of the blue, which she hadn't bargained for. Something to do with medical supplies, it seemed, though what Dulcie could possibly know about medical supplies Lottie couldn't imagine. But of course she wouldn't have needed to, she reminded herself. All she had to do was use her charm to point the punter in the direction of someone who did know. And charm she had in plenty – even Ben had acknowledged that.

'Also,' Dulcie wrote, 'you'll be interested to hear that I met a rather nice man here – but more of that anon.'

Lottie was a little envious, not so much because of the man as on account of the exhibition. She had never done medical supplies. It would, she thought, have been awash with doctors and the like.

She and Ben had been to the Shorn Lamb on New Year's Eve along with, it seemed, most of Kilby, but since then life had been especially dull. The weather was atrocious: rain, snow, then cutting winds blowing straight down Cordale from the north.

For the first two weeks of January Lottie didn't even get as far as Shepton. In the end she had to go, come rain, come shine, because she needed evening shoes to go with her new dress. She possessed nothing remotely suitable.

'You needn't come with me,' she told a relieved Ben. He hated shopping. 'I'll get the bus.'

In Shepton she found the exact shoes she wanted – silver, which would look good with the dress, with slender, very high heels, she hoped not too high for dancing in. Not that she had great hopes of much dancing. Ben had said he disliked it, was no good at it, and she couldn't imagine that Joseph and Harry would ask her, even if their wives allowed them off the lead. About Henry Laycock – he and his wife were going – she didn't know. Bernard Grayson wouldn't be there. He and Joyce, as he'd forecast, couldn't come. Jim Kettle was recovering well from his hernia operation but was not yet back at work. Lottie was a little relieved that the Graysons couldn't be at the ball, but in any case Bernard certainly wouldn't have been permitted to ask her for a dance. All the same, it would be a night out, something to break the darkness and monotony of the winter.

When she had bought her shoes she thought about lunch. The café seemed a dull idea for the mood she was in. The Heifer would undoubtedly be livelier and she could get a sandwich with her drink in the bar. She bought a magazine to read while she was eating. If there was a faint hope in her heart that she might just possibly meet up with Richard Chalmers there she didn't allow it to grow. On the other hand . . . Since meeting him she had bought the *Dales Chronicle* and had found his articles about the happenings in the different dales quite interesting. It therefore seemed appropriate that it was while she was thinking about him that he walked into the bar, spotted her at once, and made straight for her.

'My lucky day!' he said. 'I had a feeling when I got up this morning that it might be.' Without asking, he sat down beside her. 'What are you drinking? Are you going to eat?'

'I've ordered sausage and chips,' she said. 'I've only just started my drink.'

'Sausage and chips sounds fine,' Richard said. 'Excuse me

while I order it.' He went to the bar and came back with a Scotch-and-soda for himself and a gin for Lottie.

'I shouldn't be having two drinks in the middle of the day,' she said. 'I don't ever have a drink at lunchtime at home.'

'Live dangerously,' he said, smiling at her. 'How's everything in Kilby? It's time I paid another visit. I haven't written anything about Kilby for a while.'

'Kilby is, I suppose, as ever,' Lottie said. 'And at the moment cold and miserable into the bargain. I don't know what you'd find to write about in Kilby.'

'Oh, I can always find something,' he said. 'But you've got the winter blues. I shall come and cheer you up. How's your husband?'

'Ben is Ben,' she said. 'The weather doesn't seem to bother him. I suppose he's used to it. Is it always as cold as this?'

'In the winter, yes,' Richard said. 'And it can get much worse than this. February is usually worse than January. February is when the snow comes.'

'Heaven forbid!' she said, shuddering.

The sausage and chips were brought. 'This looks good,' Richard said.

'Do you often come here for lunch?' Lottie asked.

'Quite often,' he said. He didn't tell her that, remembering Thursday was the day she came in on the bus, he had also poked his head round the door of the café to see if she was there. 'Have you been shopping?'

'Yes,' she said. 'I've bought some evening shoes. I've actually persuaded Ben to take me to the Farmers' Ball. I think it was really Dulcie who talked him into it. The day before she left she came with me to buy my new dress.'

'That's great news,' Richard said. 'I shall look forward to seeing you in it. Promise you'll save a dance or two for me.'

'I promise,' Lottie said. Suddenly the prospect of the ball seemed brighter. Aside from anything else, and with no reason at all, she was sure Richard would be a good dancer. 'I didn't know you were going.'

'I am now,' he said. 'Try keeping me away!' He looked at her intently, not attempting to hide his admiration.

She knew he was flirting with her. She didn't mind in the least. There was nothing wrong with flirting.

They finished the meal. Richard fetched himself another drink but Lottie refused one. 'What are you going to do now, I mean until the bus comes?' he asked.

'I haven't thought,' Lottie said. 'Look round a few more shops, I suppose.' There was a pause, then she said, 'Do you live in Shepton?'

'Yes,' he said. 'I have a flat, quite near to the canal. Have you walked by the canal?'

'Not yet,' she said.

'You should,' Richard said. 'It's very pleasant.'

'Perhaps another time,' Lottie said.

'Can I come shopping with you?' he asked. 'Until it's time for the bus. There are some very good small shops round the back of the High Street you probably haven't discovered yet.'

'That would be great,' Lottie said.

The time passed agreeably, in and out of shops. He obviously knew every twist and turn of each small alley. In a gift shop he bought her a small black china cat. 'For luck,' he said.

In the end she said, 'I'll have to go. I mustn't miss the bus.'

He saw her to the bus stop and waited with her until the bus came.

'Thank you,' she said as she left him. 'It's been lovely.'

'We must do it again some time,' he said.

'You look better for your shopping trip,' Ben had said when she'd reached home. 'You look brighter.'

'I feel brighter,' she'd admitted. 'It's surprising what a bit of shopping does. So what have you been doing with yourself?'

His answer was exactly as she'd expected. Give or take the odd item, she could have recited it for him. He'd rebuilt some of the top stones on a bit of wall at the front of the house. Once again he'd repaired the fence in the garden; he'd done something necessary that she didn't quite understand to the chicken coop and, over his lunch (which had been a can of tomato soup and some bread and cheese), he'd read the newspaper. After that he'd had his usual forty winks in the armchair in front of the kitchen fire. Totally predictable, she thought. But he always seemed contented with his routine.

And now the evening to which she had looked forward so long was actually here. The evening of the ball. The weather was cold, with a high dark sky studded with stars. It was not actually snowing but in Ben's opinion it was likely that it would do so well before midnight. Lottie didn't mind that. As long as the weather allowed them to set off, the rest didn't matter. In fact if they *were* to be snowed in at Shepton Town Hall and had to stay there all night it might quite be fun.

They had arranged to travel to Shepton with Joseph and Peggy Clark, in Joseph's car, and they were due to be picked up in twenty minutes from now. Lottie took a last look at herself, full length, in the cheval mirror in the bedroom. She had had her hair done at Miranda's in the village and it had come up much better than she'd expected. She was pleased with it, as she was with her dress, her shoes, the silver neck chain with a single pearl drop, which had been her mother's, and her small silver handbag. 'You look all right,' she said to her reflection in the mirror. Ben had gone downstairs fifteen minutes ago. It had taken him no time at all to get ready, though he had still moaned about having to wear a dinner jacket.

She went down to join him. He was sitting in his chair, by the fire, and didn't hear her enter. 'Well,' she said, standing in the doorway, framed by it, 'will I do?'

He stood up, and turned round to face her. For a second or two he didn't say a word, just stood there, staring at her. Then, 'You look . . . you look *wonderful*,' he gasped. 'You look – oh, you look so beautiful.'

Lottie had never heard him sound so enthusiastic, not about anything. He hadn't seen the dress when she'd first brought it back from Shepton, she had put it away in her wardrobe, not quite sure why except that it was probably a style he wouldn't approve of: it was too *décolleté*, and such a vibrant red. In her head was the idea that the women would wear black, or perhaps a nice, safe pastel colour, which is what she herself might well have chosen if Dulcie hadn't been there to egg her on.

225

'You look stunning,' Ben said. 'You'll be the belle of the ball!'

'Oh, I don't think so,' she said. 'Anyway, you look quite smart yourself.' It was true. He did. She had never seen him dressed up for the evening. And he had obviously been to the village barber. His dark hair, streaked with white at the front, and the sideboards white, had been nicely cut. His dinner jacket was a bit on the old-fashioned side and if she'd seen him in it beforehand she might have tried to persuade him to splash out on a new one. Nevertheless, he looked more than presentable. He took a step forward, put his arms round her and drew her towards him. 'Oh, Ben, mind my hair!' she said, stepping aside. Two minutes later there was a ring at the door. It was Joseph, come to collect them.

In Shepton Town Hall the huge room in which the ball was already taking place when they arrived had been tastefully transformed, presumably by the Parks Department, with exotic-looking ferns, flowers and fairy lights. The band, grouped behind even more foliage on the platform, was in full swing as the party from Kilby came in and were shown to their table. It was a good band, playing a quickstep. Scores of couples were already on the floor and Lottie itched to join them.

As they settled themselves in, waves and nods were exchanged, though not by Ben and Lottie, with friends and acquaintances at other tables. The atmosphere was really good, Lottie thought.

'This seems jolly,' she said.

'Oh, we know how to have a good time,' Harry said. 'We work hard and we play hard.'

'When you get time to play,' his wife Beryl said. 'And that's not often.'

'But tonight we have,' Joseph said. 'Now, what would everyone like to drink? What's your choice, ladies?'

'A sparkling wine would be nice,' Peggy Clark said. 'I don't necessarily mean champagne, but a nice sparkling white wine.'

'If you ladies would like a glass of champagne, then you shall have it,' Harry said. 'We don't do this every night of the week.' He smiled at Lottie. 'You'll find we know how to let our hair down, we Yorkshire tykes.'

While the men ordered the champagne Lottie looked round the room. She had been wrong about the women. Almost all of them were smartly and colourfully dressed and it was clear that Miranda, and her counterparts in the other Dales villages, had been at work cutting, perming, tinting, blow-drying. The men too were transformed from their everyday corduroy and tweeds by their dinner jackets, stiff white shirts, bow-ties. And not only sartorially changed: they seemed brighter, in higher spirits.

The champagne came and glasses were filled. Lottie, sipping hers, watched the dancers on the floor. She knew what she was looking for. She wanted to see Richard Chalmers. Not for anything special, of course, but he would be a familiar face and he had said he'd ask her for a dance.

'Drink up, Lottie love,' Harry's voice broke in on her. 'You're falling behind. And there's more where that came from.'

She smiled, did as she was bid, and Harry refilled her glass.

And then she saw him, Richard Chalmers, dancing his way towards where she was sitting. His partner was petite, elegantly dressed in black, with straight blonde hair falling to her shoulders. I hadn't realized he was married, Lottie thought. But that was stupid of me. Of course he would be; he was far too attractive not to be. And then he steered his partner close to their table and slowed down without quite stopping.

'Good evening,' he called out. 'Nice to see you.' And the two of them were away again without losing a beat of the music, and almost before all at the table had responded to his greeting. All except Ben, who said, 'Who's he?'

'He's Richard Chalmers,' Peggy said. 'You know, the journalist from the *Dales Chronicle*. Have you not met him? We've seen him in the Shorn Lamb from time to time. He did a nice piece about Kilby, it'll be nearly a year ago now.'

'No, I don't recall him,' Ben said. He turned to Lottie. 'But didn't you say you'd come across him around Christmastime?'

The others looked at her.

'It was Dulcie really,' she said, shifting the emphasis. 'We were shopping in Shepton and she wanted to go to the Heifer for lunch. We were waiting in the bar until there was a table free for lunch, but it was really crowded there so we sat with him and his friend.'

'He obviously remembered you,' Beryl said.

'It would be Dulcie he remembered,' Lottie said smoothly. She saw no point in telling them that she'd met him since then, let alone that they'd discussed the Farmers' Ball. 'Would that be his wife he was with?' she asked.

'Oh, I don't think so,' Peggy said. 'I think he's divorced – at least, that's what we heard when he first came to these parts.'

Their attention was diverted when another couple danced past, nodding them a greeting.

'Mary looks nice in that dress,' Peggy said to Beryl as the couple passed out of sight. 'Doesn't the colour suit her.'

'Yes,' Beryl agreed. 'I thought so when she wore it last year. Of course she was a year younger then and she hadn't gone grey. I don't think off-white goes with grey hair, do you?'

Richard Chalmers had dropped out of the conversation as if he had never been. Lottie didn't know whether she was pleased or sorry.

'Isn't it time we got to our feet?' Joseph suggested. 'Tripped the light fantastic?'

Lottie knew they would dance with their wives, certainly the first dance, and so they did. Ben rose to his feet reluctantly and led her onto the floor. He had claimed that he wasn't much of a dancer and Lottie now found this to be painfully true. The problem was that he had no sense of rhythm. It was as if he was moving to a totally different beat from that of the music. He also at one point came down heavily on her silver-shod feet. 'It's no good, love,' he said as they reached their table after one circuit of the room. 'I never could get the hang of it. Shall we sit this one out? I'm sorry.'

'That's all right,' Lottie said. 'We can sit and watch.' It was not at all what she wanted to do. Her whole body, inside and out, was responding to the rhythm.

'I expect Joseph and Harry will ask you,' Ben said. 'They're both decent dancers.'

'Don't worry about it,' she said. 'I expect they will.' She was pinning her hopes on Richard Chalmers doing so if he could tear himself away from the blonde. If he hadn't intended to do so, why had he slowed down and spoken to them? The table he had gone back to was at the far side of the room; there'd been no need to come near them if he hadn't wanted to.

He did ask her, for the very next dance, which was a waltz. As the first chords struck up he came across, and she was glad he did so or she'd probably have been taken by Joseph or Harry.

He was, as she'd recognized while watching him circle the floor with the blonde, a very good dancer. His whole body moved to the rhythm of the music, and her body to his. He could make her glide, turn or bend whichever way he wanted her to. That was what the best dancing was about: two people moving in absolute harmony, as if they were one. They hardly spoke at all. It wasn't necessary. It was all there in the music and the dancing. Because it was a waltz the lights had been dimmed, which added to the feeling that there was no-one else in the room. Lottie wanted it never to end, though clearly it would soon. Any minute now the music would stop.

His voice, close to her ear, broke their silence. 'When are you next coming to Shepton?' he said.

'I'll come in on the bus on Thursday. As usual,' Lottie said.

'Do you usually go to the Heifer now?' he wanted to know.

'No,' she said. 'I often go to the café.'

'Right,' he said. 'Can I dance with you again this evening?'

'I'm not sure about that,' Lottie said. She knew what she wanted. She would have liked to dance with him all night, as long as the music played, but now she didn't know what to say.

'You can't blame me for wanting to,' he said. 'You look so utterly beautiful.'

Everyone was moving away from the floor.

'You'd better go back to your wife,' Lottie said, though she more or less knew it wasn't his wife.

'I don't have a wife,' he said. 'Not any longer. We parted company. I've been dancing with the editor's wife and I'll have to again. He doesn't dance.'

'She seemed a good dancer,' Lottie said. She was fishing around for things to say, finding nothing she wanted to say, that she *could* say.

'Yes, she's good,' Richard said. 'But there's good and there's better – and then there's very, very special.'

They were back at the table. 'Thank you for lending me your wife,' Richard said pleasantly to Ben.

'Did you enjoy that, love?' Ben asked Lottie when Richard had gone.

'Yes,' she said. 'He's an accomplished dancer.'

The snow had not, after all, fallen on the night of the ball. Ben had been wrong about that. They had left Shepton for home a little after two o'clock on Saturday morning under a high sky, bright with stars, and the sharp frostiness of the air piercing through to the bone. Their raised spirits, aided no doubt by liberal quantities of alcohol over the course of the evening, were their buffer against the cold. Peggy drove. She had drunk much less than Joseph. Lottie was thankful that Ben hadn't offered to drive. His driving was scary enough even when a drop hadn't passed his lips. As for the other car – with Beryl driving – Lottie was thankful that Peggy had allowed them to get well ahead. Fortunately, once out of the town, there was almost no traffic on the road.

Ben had fallen asleep within minutes of leaving Shepton. Lottie, sitting beside him in the back of the car, was grateful for that. She wanted to be alone with her thoughts, to wallow in them, give herself up to them. They were all of Richard Chalmers. He had, briefly, danced with her again. She had started out on an 'excuse me' quickstep with Joseph Clark, which Richard had quickly interrupted, but then, no more than half-way round the room – they had hardly spoken to each other, just danced – another man, a stranger to her though she had observed him earlier looking at her from the next table, had claimed her.

She knew, she felt certain of it – sitting there beside her husband, who, around the sharp bends in the road, kept lurching towards her in his sleep – that she would see Richard next Thursday. She was as sure of it as she was that the sun would rise tomorrow. She didn't know exactly where or at what point she would see him. She just knew she would. Nothing was more important. Nor did she give any thought to what made it so important, why it had happened, whether it was right or wrong, wise or foolish. She felt like someone who had walked in the desert for days, with no water, and had suddenly come to a well. It didn't matter whether it was good water or contaminated. She had to drink. She had never felt like this in all her life.

The car came to a jerky halt and they were at Beck Farm. As the car stopped, Ben wakened.

'There you are,' Peggy said. 'Safe and sound, all in one piece.'

'That passed quickly,' Ben said. 'I must have fallen asleep. Well, thank you very much, both of you. It's been a lovely evening.'

'So it has,' Peggy said. 'Perhaps we'll see you tomorrow – or I should say today since it's already Saturday.'

Saturday, Lottie thought as she walked up to the front door with Ben. Five days to go. It seemed a lifetime.

'You looked gorgeous,' Ben said later when they went to bed. 'I told you you'd be the belle of the ball, and you were. I'm a very lucky man!'

He was not as lucky as he'd hoped to be that night. 'Oh, Ben, I'm far too tired,' Lottie said. 'All I want is to sleep.' And dream, she thought, as she turned her back on him.

The threatened snow held off for several days. 'It's too cold to snow,' Ben said. 'It'll have to warm up a degree or two before it comes down.'

It came down during Wednesday night. When Lottie drew back the bedroom curtains on Thursday morning it was to a world that had transformed itself in the hours of darkness. Only the tops of the walls – and not all of those – showed up as broken grey-and-white lines, like a pattern of embroidery on a white counterpane. There were no animals in the fields; they had all been brought inside because of the continuing cold. The trees that marked out the beck were weighted down by snow along their branches. A crow, fitting into the black-and-white land-scape, landed on a gatepost, looking for food.

'My word!' Ben said, sitting up in bed, looking out of

231

the window. 'It's come with a vengeance, hasn't it? Well, that's the way it does in Cordale. But beautiful with it.'

It is *not* beautiful, Lottie thought. It is hateful and horrid. But no way would she let it stop her getting to Shepton. Surely an inch or two of snow couldn't stop the bus?

'There must be nearly a foot of it,' Ben said. He sounded almost happy and for a moment she hated him for it.

The bus did not run. No hope of it. It was several days before Kilby was cleared of snow enough to get things moving. The snow plough, the only vehicle on the road until then, had done a good job but there was no possibility of it clearing the way as far as Shepton. Some people, used to the ways of the weather in the northern dales, came out on skis, with sleds attached to take the shopping. The school was closed. A diminished congregation made it to church on Sunday morning and rather more managed to get to the Shorn Lamb one or two evenings. No-one went short of food, because everyone knew about keeping a supply against such conditions. The worst thing for Lottie was that the telephone lines to Shepton were down.

If only she could have spoken to Richard on the phone, Lottie fretted. But if the line had been free, where would she have rung? She didn't even know where he lived, except that it was near the canal. She was irritated by the calm way Ben accepted it all. 'It's nothing extraordinary,' he said when she complained. 'It's all happened before.'

By the following Thursday the snow had been cleared and the bus ran again.

'I don't know why you're so bothered,' Ben said. 'What's so special about Shepton?'

'I just want a change of scene,' Lottie said. 'A bit of civiliza- tion; a few shops.'

It did not surprise her in the least when she stepped down from the bus in Shepton to find Richard waiting there for her.

NINETEEN

When, alighting from the bus, Lottie saw Richard standing only a few yards away, what she wanted at that moment was to run into his arms, to touch him, confirm that he was there, solid and real. She couldn't do this. For one thing, he made no move to hold out his arms. They were held rigidly by his side. For another, there were too many people around. Too many people, she thought, who might know him, even some who might recognize her from the bus, though she hadn't known anyone who'd boarded in Kilby. But when she walked towards him and he stepped forward to meet her it was all there in his look, as she knew it must be in hers.

'I missed you,' he said.

She nodded. 'I missed you. This was the first bus out of Kilby for more than a week.'

'I know,' he said. 'I also knew you'd be on it.'

Almost nothing had been said between them at the ball. There had been no need. It had all been in the looking and in the dancing, but now words would be needed. They could hardly waltz across the bus park.

'I thought we'd go to the café,' Richard said. 'The Heifer will only just have opened.'

She knew what he meant by that. As a local journalist he was well known in the Heifer and if there were not yet many people

233

there she and he would be conspicuous. The café would be busy: they would melt into the crowd.

'That will be fine,' Lottie said.

He touched her arm briefly as they walked across the car park towards the High Street. The slight contact shot through her. She felt the colour rise in her face. As they had hoped, the café was buzzing; they were lucky to find a table for two, and even luckier that it was in a corner at the back of the room.

'I was desperate to get to you,' Richard said when the waitress had taken their order. 'If the road hadn't been closed nothing would have kept me away. When I found I couldn't even get through on the phone I could have killed someone.'

'I know,' Lottie said. 'I kept trying it to see if the line was back, but even if it had been I didn't know where to contact you. I felt totally cut off.'

'You must have known I would call you if I possibly could,' Richard said.

They were talking as if they had known each other for ever, nothing held back, and to Lottie that felt right and natural. And yet it was strange, because their meetings so far had been few and their conversations both brief and general. At the ball they had exchanged very few words indeed. In fact, they knew little about each other. But it didn't matter. They would learn.

The waitress brought their coffee, and a plate of biscuits. Though they would never know it, she recognized Richard, she knew who he was. The woman, she didn't remember ever having seen her before.

As if he could read Lottie's thoughts Richard said, 'Tell me about yourself. What brought you to this part of the world? How did you come to meet Ben Thornton?'

She told him the whole story: about her mother, about her flat in Luton, about the exhibitions, especially the one in Manchester where she had met Ben, and how they had married, so soon afterwards, in Shepton. Richard hid his surprise about that part of the story. From what little he had seen of Ben Thornton he couldn't imagine him picking up this lovely woman, let alone actually wooing and marrying her. How had he done it? Why had she agreed? They were so different from each other and she

234

couldn't be totally happy or she wouldn't be sitting opposite him now, they wouldn't be having this conversation.

'And are you happy in Cordale?' he asked.

Lottie paused. 'Well,' she said, 'it's very beautiful, of course. I don't think I've ever been anywhere more beautiful, but what I didn't expect was that it would be so quiet. But then, I've hardly ever been in the country before, not right in the country like Cordale. I can't get used to the quiet. And another thing . . .' She hesitated again.

'What?' Richard prompted her.

'I don't think they actually like me. I mean the people in Kilby. A few of them might but some of them certainly don't. If they expected Ben to take up with anyone – and I doubt that they did, because, you see, it's not that long since his wife died – then it certainly wouldn't have been me. I don't fit in.'

He could well believe that. She was like an exotic tropical flower growing by some caprice of nature in a meadow of daisies. Would she ever thrive there? He didn't say that. 'I don't see how they could possibly *not* like you,' he said.

'Well, they don't,' Lottie said emphatically. 'His wife – I mean his *first* wife – was apparently wonderful.'

They had finished their coffee. 'Would you like another cup?' Richard asked.

'Yes, please, I would,' Lottie said. She would like anything that would prolong the moment.

He signalled to the waitress.

'What about you?' Lottie said. 'You haven't told me anything about yourself.'

He shrugged his shoulders. 'There's not much to tell,' he said. 'I was married once. We divorced. She lives in London now. Fortunately we hadn't got round to having children.'

They lingered over their second cups of coffee. There was no rush now to talk, and what they did say was mostly generalities, trivialities. It was enough for Lottie that they were together. She had never felt like this before. She had had crushes, she had been in love, or had thought she was; she had had one or two relationships that had quite quickly turned out to be not serious, let alone permanent. But this, she knew, was different. This was

235

real. And yet when at one point Richard stretched across the table and covered her hand with his, she quickly drew hers away.

'Not here,' she said.

'Very well,' Richard said. 'Then, what do you want to do next?'

'Anything,' Lottie said. Anything with you was what she meant.

It was obvious that they couldn't just stay in the café. The coffee drinkers had almost all left and the tables were being laid for lunch. The waitress had given Richard the bill some time ago, and was hovering, clearly impatient for them to move. In the end she came and spoke to Richard. 'Will you be taking lunch, sir?' she asked.

'No. No. We're just going,' he answered.

He helped Lottie on with her coat. She fastened the collar up round her neck, pulled on her woolly hat and her gloves, and they left. Outside in the street it was even colder than when they'd met in the bus park and, in addition, a cutting north wind was blowing fine flakes of snow down the High Street.

'We could take refuge in the Heifer, have some lunch,' Richard said.

'It would be warmer,' Lottie said. 'But I've no appetite.'

'The sensible thing', he said, 'would be for you to come back with me to my place. It'll be warm there. I could heat some soup if we wanted it. There's three hours or more before your bus leaves.'

'That would be nice,' Lottie said. 'I'd like to see where you live.'

They crossed the High Street. He took her through an alley that opened out into a small square with more shops, and led to a narrow snicket that went down almost to the canal bank. There he stopped outside a shop which sold fishing tackle. 'This is it,' he said. 'I have the floor over the shop. My entrance is down the side.' He unlocked the door. 'I'll go up first,' he said. 'The stairs are a bit awkward.' Nothing was said as they climbed the stairs and went into his flat. He closed the door behind them and then at once he took her in his arms and kissed her, long and deeply. Then he broke off and, clasping her hands, he pulled her across the room and almost roughly took her into the bedroom.

Later, still lying on the bed, he said, 'You knew this had to happen, didn't you?'

'I did,' Lottie said. She could hardly find her voice.

'From the very beginning,' he said.

'Yes.' It was all she could say, all she needed to say. She turned towards him and ran her fingers through his thick dark hair. He traced the contours of her face, her neck, her shoulders with one finger as if he was committing the shape of her to his memory. She shuddered with pleasure.

From that day, for Lottie, Thursdays were never the same again. After that first time it was agreed between them that Richard would no longer meet her from the bus and nor would they go to the café. She would go at once to his flat by the canal and there they would make love, wonderful, unhurried, satisfying love, safe in the assurance that there was no risk of discovery. Afterwards, Richard would make a simple lunch – soup, an omelette, toasted cheese, a salad, it didn't matter what – and soon Lottie would leave on her own to do her shopping in the town, evidence for Ben should he need it, which he didn't, of the reason for her trip to Shepton. Sometimes she would take home something she knew Ben would enjoy for his supper: a nice piece of fish, a fruit pie. She was possibly nicer to Ben on a Thursday than on any other day of the week. 'You're like all your sex,' he sometimes said. 'Shopping puts new life into you.' Nevertheless Thursday was a night when she would never let him make love to her. No matter how much he wanted it, she would find an excuse.

Also, whenever Ben went to Shepton on a Monday she still went with him, though never with any plan to meet Richard then. If they did meet it was by accident, and then the three of them might, or might not – more often the latter – go for a drink in the Heifer. Richard never telephoned her and she seldom rang him, in fact not at all since the evening when she'd been deep in conversation with him and Ben had unexpectedly walked in at the door.

'Well, lovely to talk to you, Dulcie. We must get together,' she'd said quickly before ringing off.

'How was Dulcie?' Ben had asked later.

'She's fine,' Lottie had said. 'She's got a new boyfriend. Things seem to be going well.'

They continued to go well with Lottie for a little while, and then the bad weather, which she had thought was over for good, returned. There were days and nights of gales, when the wind howled round the house; hours of driving rain that found places to get in, through the roof, under the kitchen door. Then there were a couple of hard frosts that seemed to penetrate everywhere and afterwards, when the temperature rose by a couple of points, the snow came again.

Lottie stood at the back window, looking out to the north over Cordale. Everything was blanketed white, except the tops of the walls, which, though they were not black, looked so against the snow. She knew it was beautiful but that made her all the more angry.

'I hate it! I hate it!' she cried out one evening as Ben came in from the henhouse.

He laughed, and that angered her more than ever.

'I don't see what's to laugh at,' she said sharply.

'Well, love,' he said mildly – she hated the way almost nothing provoked him – 'it's only snow, and it *is* still only March. I've known it snow here as late as May.'

'I don't think there's anything funny about that,' she stormed. 'It's . . . it's . . . *uncivilized*!'

He took off his boots, opened the door again and knocked them against the door frame to shake the snow off. 'Well, at least we're tucked into our own house,' he said. 'Beck Farm has stood up to a lot worse weather than this, and will do so again. And so will we.'

'You are so . . .' She hesitated, searching for the word. 'You are so *complacent*!'

Ben said nothing. He put on his slippers, mended the fire, filled the kettle. There was no point in arguing. For one disloyal moment he found himself thinking that Moira would never have fussed about the weather, and then he quickly dismissed the thought. Lottie was not Moira, not like her at all. Lottie needed affection, appreciation, lively company – though these days she

238

didn't seem to need the affection she had once welcomed. He put it down to the weather.

'I'll make a cup of tea,' he said.

He doesn't understand, Lottie thought. He didn't understand – how could he? – that she felt trapped. How could he know that she wanted to be up and away? She wanted – the truth hit her like a tidal wave – she wanted to be with Richard. She'd had all she could take of Cordale, and especially of Kilby. She didn't like Kilby and it didn't like her. And there was nothing she could do about it. She was trapped, trapped, trapped!

Ben made the tea, poured it, cut two slices of cake from the tin, set it all on the table.

'Come on, love. You'll feel better when you've had a cup of tea,' he said.

She wanted to hit him. Also – and this made things worse because she could say nothing – it was now Tuesday and they could be snowed in again by Thursday. What would she do if the bus didn't run? For two pins, she thought – but it was a wild thought – if the bus runs tomorrow I'll get it, and if I get snowed up in Shepton so much the better. I'll stay at the Heifer. No-one will be able to get at me. No-one except Richard.

In fact, though the weather was still awful, and the snow had turned to nasty sleeting rain, blown about first one way and then the other by the wind, the Thursday morning bus did run.

'I can't think why anyone would want to go to Shepton in weather like this,' Ben said. 'Not unless they absolutely had to. Certainly not for a bit of shopping.'

'To quote you,' Lottie said, 'a bit of bad weather never killed anyone.'

'Well, do be careful, love,' Ben said. 'It could get worse.'

What he didn't understand, she thought as she set off down the lane, was that she did absolutely *have* to go. She couldn't bear not to. She had more or less made a pact with God, or Fate, or whoever was in charge – let me have Thursdays and I'll be good the rest of the week. Only, let me have Thursdays!

In Shepton she made straight for the flat. The weather was very little better, just not quite as wild. Richard had given her a key so that, should he be called out on a job, she could let herself in, and indeed on this occasion he was not there. Lottie looked round for a note explaining his absence, but there was nothing. She took off her wet raincoat, stood her umbrella in the sink to drain, made herself a cup of coffee and settled down to wait.

Looking about her she thought how little there was to show what sort of a man lived there. A dozen or so paperbacks on a shelf, all thrillers; a rack with a few newspapers and a couple of motoring magazines. No ornaments, no pictures, no photographs, no clutter whatsoever. It was the room of a man who didn't need possessions. She had never noticed this before, but then she wouldn't have. Richard himself had filled the room, just by being there – and would again when he returned. She took a newspaper from the rack and tried to get interested in it.

Almost an hour passed before she heard his key in the lock. She went into the tiny hall to greet him and was surprised by his surprise when he opened the door and saw her standing there.

'Good heavens!' he said. 'I didn't think you'd come. It's such appalling weather.'

'As if weather would keep me away!' Lottie said. 'You know it wouldn't.'

'Of course I do,' he said. Then he took her in his arms and kissed her and everything in the world was all right again.

'I made myself a cup of coffee,' Lottie said presently. 'Shall I make one for you?'

'I had one while I was out,' he said.

She waited for him to tell her where he had been. 'I looked around for a note,' she said. 'I thought you must be out on a job.'

'I had a meeting with the editor,' he said. 'It went on longer than I expected, but I really and truly thought you wouldn't come today.'

'Nothing would keep me away,' Lottie said. 'You know that.'

He smiled at her. 'Well, you've had your coffee and I've had mine, so what are we waiting for?' He took her hand and they went into the bedroom.

An hour later – a blissful hour, Lottie thought – they sat up in bed. 'I'll make some lunch,' Richard said. 'Making love to you gives me an appetite.' He got out of bed and dressed quickly.

'I'll have a shower,' Lottie said, 'while you're making lunch.'

He was so romantic one minute, she thought, such a wonderful lover – and the next minute so practical, making something to eat. If only, if only she hadn't married Ben! But if she hadn't come to Shepton to marry Ben, then she would never have met Richard, and because that was unthinkable she put the thought away from her. She would live for the moment.

And so she did, throughout the rest of that long, dreary, cold winter, brightened only by one day a week, though on three Thursdays life was not brightened because when she reached Richard's flat it was to find that he wasn't there, he had left her a note telling her that his editor had sent him off on a job and he'd likely be away all day. It was reasonable, she supposed, that he hadn't let her know. They never broke the rule that he wouldn't telephone her at Beck Farm. So on those three dead days she had wandered aimlessly round Shepton, looking at shops in which she had no interest, drinking coffee, killing time until the hour when the bus would take her back to Kilby. Once, she had nipped back to the flat to see if by some chance Richard had returned, but he hadn't.

Eventually spring came – a cold one, but at least it was bright. Before Easter the new lambs were born; the meadows were full of them, bleating, and the ewes baa-ing after them, which for most people in Kilby was music to the ears, but not for Lottie. It drove her mad. She had no affinity with sheep, or with any farm animals, for that matter. Cows frightened her. Ben spent most of the daylight hours helping Joseph, and sometimes Harry, with their flocks. It was something he usually did, he told her. For her part she was glad to escape every Thursday to Shepton.

'Make the most of it, love,' Ben said one day. 'Only a few weeks now and we shall have the visitors back. You won't have as much time to go to Shepton then.'

Nothing will stop me, Lottie promised herself. Ben – or Ben and Alice between them – must see to the visitors on Thursdays. But she would not say so now. She would wait until the time came and then she would just do it.

A week later she took the bus to Shepton and made for Richard's flat. There was no answer to her ring on the doorbell so, vastly disappointed, she let herself in. Her disappointment was mitigated when she saw the note on the table. 'Back soon!' it said. She took off her coat, and then thought, Why not? It will surprise him! So she undressed, and when he came in twenty minutes later she was sitting up in bed waiting for him.

It was not that he wasn't pleased to see her. He made love to her with all his usual skill and pleasure, but there was, she thought, something missing. On these occasions he was always – she searched in her mind for the right word, and found it – joyful. On top of the world. But today, somehow, he was not. He was everything else a lover should be, but the joy was missing. Afterwards, he seemed preoccupied.

'Are you all right?' she asked him as they dressed.

'Of course,' he said.

They went into the kitchen. Lottie laid the table while Richard made omelettes. When the meal was over – it had been mostly silent – Lottie said, 'Are you sure you're all right? You seem a bit quiet.'

'As a matter of fact,' he said, 'I've got something to tell you.'

She went cold. It was the tone of his voice. 'If it isn't nice,' she said, trying to speak lightly, 'don't bother to tell me.'

'I must,' he said. 'Come and sit down.'

There was a pause that seemed to go on for ever.

'Well,' Lottie said, 'what is it?'

'I'm leaving.' He blurted it out.

'Leaving? What do you mean, leaving?'

'Just that,' he said. 'I'm leaving my job, leaving Shepton. I've been offered a new job. In Surrey. A good job. Assistant editor on a weekly. And my own page. Nearly double the money and a chance I'll step into the editor's shoes when he retires.' The last bit was an exaggeration, but he would make it happen.

Lottie was horrified. It was impossible. It couldn't be happening. 'You can't,' she said. 'You can't! What about us? What about me?'

'I have to,' he said. 'I'll never get any further in Shepton. It's a one-horse town. It's the road to nowhere.'

'But what about me?' Lottie repeated. 'I thought you loved me. You said you did. How can you do this?'

'I do love you,' Richard said. 'Believe me, I do. Don't think this is easy for me, because it isn't. But I have to take this chance. Surely you see that?'

'Then take me with you,' Lottie cried. 'Take me with you. I'll make you happy. We'll both be happy. A new life!'

'What about Ben?' Richard said.

'What *about* him?' Lottie said. It was as if, suddenly, Ben didn't exist. There was only Richard, and she couldn't let him go. She couldn't live without him. 'Ben won't miss me,' she said. 'At least not for long. Ben has all he needs in Cordale. There's nothing there for me, not without you. *Please*, Richard, take me with you. I beg you!' She grabbed hold of the lapels of his jacket, pulling at him frantically.

He put his hands over hers, took hold of them and forcibly loosened her grip. 'Hey!' he said. 'It's not the end of the world.'

'Oh yes, it is,' she retorted. 'It's the end of the world for me. I live for Thursdays when I see you. The rest means nothing. You can't leave me, Richard. Not if you love me. I couldn't bear it.'

Tears ran down her face. He was astonished at the intensity of her feelings. Of course he loved her, he had no doubt about that. She was beautiful. She was a wonderful lover – between them they made the world sing. And she was funny, and quite clever.

'I shall miss you too,' he said gently. 'Don't think I won't. Believe me, I don't want to leave you. It's not easy.'

'Then don't,' she said. 'Take me with you. Oh, Richard, we could be so happy, you and I together.'

It was true, he thought. They could be. She was not the woman for Ben Thornton and nor was Ben the man for her. That marriage would never work; it would end in unhappiness for everyone, no matter what.

He held her at arm's length and looked at her intently. Her face was wet with tears, and she had never seemed more desirable. He took out his handkerchief and wiped them away.

'*Please*,' she begged.

There was a long pause.

'Very well, then,' he said at last. 'I'm not sure it will work, but if you are willing to take the risk, then I will.'

'Oh, Richard! Oh, Richard,' she cried. 'I'll make you the happiest man in the world. Truly I will.' And then she broke into fresh tears.

'We'll go together,' he said.

When she had calmed down he talked to her seriously. 'We must plan it properly,' he said. 'I have to start on the first of June, so we must go south towards the end of May, find somewhere to live. You must tell no-one in Kilby, no-one at all. We're in Yorkshire one day, and the next day we've gone – no-one knows where. Can you keep that secret? If not, it just won't work.'

'Of course I can,' Lottie assured him. Keeping mum made it all the more exciting. 'In any case,' she added, 'no-one will care.' Except Ben, of course. He would, but he would get over her. He had friends everywhere. They would rally round. She would never be right for Ben, never had been, and he would soon come to realize that. And in time, she decided, he would find someone more suitable.

'You can rely on me, my darling,' she said to Richard.

TWENTY

Outwardly, life went on as usual at Beck Farm. Inwardly, at least for Lottie, everything was changed. Each night in her diary, which she kept hidden away, she marked off the day that was ending and counted the ones that remained before she would be free. Except for her first few weeks in Kilby, when she was newly married, these were the happiest days she had known. Every day was bearable because, even though sometimes the hours crawled by, she could look forward to the future when she would be with Richard for good. In the midst of her own happiness she even spared a little time to be sorry for Ben, and was therefore kinder to him, though not for a single moment did she waver in her intention to leave him. She convinced herself that it was better for both of them.

The lambs in the meadows grew, and continued to bleat, but the sound no longer annoyed her. She took her turn at feeding the hens, at gathering the eggs, and at various other chores, without complaining, which surprised and pleased Ben. She would make a country wife yet, he told himself. If Alice noticed the change in Lottie she said nothing.

At Easter the visitors came, including the Davises and the Weatherfields. They were pleased, though not entirely surprised, to find Lottie and Ben married. 'I think we saw it coming,' Bruce Weatherfield teased. They stayed for the best part of a week and after that there were no more visitors due until the Whitsun weekend. But I shall be gone by then, Lottie thought.

Every Thursday she continued to go as usual to Shepton. There was no way she would give that up. It was like a weekly blood transfusion, putting new life into her. And Ben didn't question it; he was only too pleased she was happy. It was on these Thursdays that she and Richard made their plans. On the last of them, in the second half of May, she said to Richard, 'After today I won't need to come to Shepton to see you. By next Thursday, my darling, we shall be together for good.'

And so it happened. She took almost nothing with her from Beck Farm, even leaving most of her clothes hanging in the wardrobe. A new life, new clothes, she thought. She neither wanted nor needed any reminders of Cordale. On the final evening in Kilby, on a whim of Ben's with which she was pleased to go along – what did it matter? – they went to the Shorn Lamb, met up with the Clarks and the Fosters and had a pleasant time. Bernard Grayson was his usual affable self but, it being a busy evening, Joyce remained in the kitchen. Everything was absolutely normal, which suited Lottie. If she had any regrets whatever about leaving these, for the most part, nice people they were completely overshadowed by her knowledge that tomorrow she would shake the dust of Kilby from her feet.

The six of them stayed in the pub until closing time and then left together. They walked up the lane until Lottie and Ben turned off for Beck Farm. 'It was a lovely evening,' Peggy said to Lottie. 'See you soon.'

The next morning Lottie, carrying a modest-sized suitcase, and feeling as a prisoner might on the morning of his release, took the bus to Shepton. Ben had left the house before her, having promised to lend a helping hand to Harry. She had left him a note, propped up on the hall table, which he would see as soon as he came in. Walking down the path to the lane, she did not even look back at the house. There was no-one in the bus queue who knew her, no-one who might have given a thought to the suitcase, but if there had been she wouldn't have cared. She would never see any of them again.

She had debated over the last week or two whether she should tell Dulcie about her intentions and her future whereabouts, but in the end she decided that that could wait until the deed was done, until she and Richard were settled in their new home. It was better that way, in case Ben should get in touch with Dulcie – and this he might well do, since her number was in the telephone pad in the hall and possibly there was even a letter or two from Dulcie lying around. But she would certainly contact her before too long. She was fond of Dulcie. She didn't want to lose touch with her entirely.

It was teatime when Ben returned home. When he went into the house – the door was unlocked, they never locked doors in Kilby – he called out Lottie's name, as he always did, and was surprised to get no reply. The bus should have been back from Shepton more than an hour ago. Oh well, perhaps she had slipped down to the village for something or other – not that she often did that. She went less and less to the village. And then he saw the note, with his name on it. The fact that it was in an envelope, not scrawled on a piece of paper, surprised him. He opened it at once and read the contents.

> Dear Ben,
> I am leaving to be with Richard. It's everything I want in the world. Don't try to find us. We shall be hundreds of miles away and I wouldn't come back anyway. I'm sorry and I thank you for everything you've done for me.
> Lottie

He stared at the words until they blurred in front of his eyes. His head spun. He put his hand out and felt for the hall chair. He was going to faint – but he had never fainted in his life. Men didn't faint, not even when their entire life had fallen apart in the space of ten seconds. The words cleared and he read the note again, then closed his eyes as if that might make it disappear, but when he opened them it was still there, a small piece of white paper that seemed to float in the air, the words in Lottie's childish handwriting standing out. 'I am leaving to be with Richard.'

'How could it be?' he asked himself. It was not possible. It was not true. It couldn't be! Everything had been going so well between them, better than ever in the last few weeks.

What he knew at once was that he would tell no-one. She would come back; he knew she would. He would get her back. It was no more than a silly impulse on her part; something, he didn't know what, had upset her. He read the note yet again. 'Don't try to find us. We shall be hundreds of miles away and I wouldn't come back anyway.' Silly girl – but she would come to her senses. She must. He couldn't bear it otherwise. *He could not bear it!*

He didn't leave the house for the rest of the day. He sat near the telephone in case she should ring. When night came he stayed up, waiting for her return. In the end, when it was almost dawn, he went upstairs to bed, but lay there, not undressing. From exhaustion, towards dawn, he finally slept for a couple of hours.

His first encounter the next morning was with Alice, who came in as usual at nine o'clock. He had his story ready; he had worked it out during the night.

'Lottie's been called away,' he said. 'Her friend Dulcie – she's ill.' No need to go into details. Lottie could give those when she returned, and when she *did*, he told himself, there would be no recriminations on his part. She would be totally welcome. 'Only let her come back, God,' he said out loud. He was not a man given to praying; he left that to the women.

Of course she didn't come back. After a few days, he couldn't wait any longer. He found Dulcie's telephone number and rang her. He hadn't wanted to do this too soon: he wanted to give Lottie time to return and then no more would be said about it, no-one would know.

Dulcie was astonished. 'I can't believe it! It never occurred to me! I had no idea. Oh Ben, it's terrible! What can I do?'

There was nothing she *could* do, he told her. He would just hang on and wait. Later, he told everyone the same story he had told Alice, neither more nor less. In the end – it took time, during which kind enquiries were made about Dulcie's welfare – he realized that no-one believed his story any longer. They stopped asking questions. He lost the last vestige of hope that had been in his heart and he faced the fact that Lottie was not coming back. Not ever. He stopped making excuses for her absence and eventually, at least in his presence, the subject was dropped, though he had no idea what they said behind his back. All his friends were kind to him when he did meet up with them, which was not often, since for the most part he avoided places where he might encounter them.

To pass the endless time he now seemed to have on his hands he went back to his woodcarving: small animals, birds. Stoats, weasels, foxes, hares, mice, lambs. Blackbirds, lapwings, snipe, robins, grouse. Some he did at first hand, observing them; some he did from memory, for he had watched them from childhood and knew them by heart. But when he had completed each one he put it away in a cupboard and didn't look at it again.

It was when he had carved every small animal and bird he could think of that he started to carve Lottie's name on a piece of oak. He did it with great care and precision, sometimes with love, at other times stabbing the wood with fierce anger. When that was finished he did not put it in a drawer, he hid it away in the garden.

The time passed. He ran out of things to carve, jobs to do in and around the house. There seemed to be nothing left to fill his time. Summer changed to autumn and then the winter came. On a bitter day in February, Cordale deep in snow, the roads out of the dale all but impassable, and a bitter wind blowing, he recalled how Lottie had hated the winter – and having allowed the thought of her to stray, yet again, into his mind, from which he had tried, unsuccessfully, to banish her, he wondered where she might be, what she might be doing.

For a time after she had left he had not allowed himself to do this. He had been too deeply shocked, and then too angry to make any attempt to find her. He would wait for her return, even though her note had been so final. He had contacted Dulcie once or twice, the last time just before Christmas, but to no avail. Either she knew nothing more of Lottie, or she knew but wouldn't tell him. Also, although she was sorry for him, she was immersed in her own life; on the brink, it seemed, of marriage.

But now, he decided, the moment the road cleared and he could get through he would go to Shepton, to the offices of the *Dales Chronicle*, and find out where Richard Chalmers had gone to. He should have done that in the first place. He knew that now and had probably known it then, but he had been too humiliated, and also he had wanted to make it easier for her when she came to her senses and returned to him.

The editor was away, but the assistant editor saw him. It was of little use. All he could tell him was the name of the publication Richard had gone to. It was in Surrey. He didn't know the address but he obligingly looked it up in a trade journal. 'Chalmers didn't say much before he left and no-one here has heard a word from him since,' he said. 'I reckon he's shaken the dust of Shepton off his feet.' There was no mention of anyone he might have gone with, and Ben did not enquire into that. Even now he felt protective towards Lottie. He was left with the feeling, though nothing was stated in so many words, that Richard Chalmers's departure had not been a matter for great regret.

Ben left the newspaper office and went straight to the Heifer, with some half-formed thought of drowning his sorrows, but the place held too many memories for him – not least of his wedding day – and he abandoned his half of bitter after a few sips and set off home.

In the first few months after they left Shepton, Lottie had been blissfully happy with Richard in West Pengate, the small Surrey town to which his new job had taken him, though she would, she thought, have been happy with him anywhere – in the Sahara Desert or on the far side of the moon. She missed him dreadfully when he actually had to go out to earn his living in the daytime, but the evenings, and more particularly the nights, made up for that. It was like another honeymoon, and though she had no complaints about her previous one, this was on a different level altogether. The fact that it was not legitimate, in that she was not married to Richard, mattered not at all. He was the world's best

250

lover and she felt more truly married than she had ever done with Ben.

They had found a small, ground-floor furnished flat close to the town centre, which suited them well enough for the present. In any case it seemed impossible to find an unfurnished flat and, for another thing, though there were houses for sale in the area they were far more expensive than similar ones in the north and no way could Richard afford the deposit. Nor, he said, did he wish to have a mortgage hanging round his neck. Lottie would have felt more secure in a house of their own, but she shrugged that off. It didn't matter. As long as she could share it with Richard she would have settled for a tent in the garden.

She was happy enough. It was no more than a short walk into the centre of the town, and there she could wander round the shops to her heart's content. In fact, it was mostly a question of window shopping. She had very little money to spend after buying the bare necessities. No more, actually, than she had had with Ben. Not that she made the comparison. In her new-found happiness she gave very little thought to Ben.

It was different for Richard. As the weeks, and then the first few months, passed Richard could tell that his new job wasn't going to amount to much. He had imagined – although he had not given a great deal of thought to it, because everything had been done in a hurry – that in the south everything was different. Things moved faster; events were more dramatic; even the weather was superior. This was how it appeared on television. In fact, West Pengate – after a few months he admitted it, though only to himself – was less lively than Shepton. His job was no more exciting. Nothing much happened, and what did was small, country-town stuff. Funerals, fairs, council meetings; arguments about road widening, ongoing correspondence in the press about the proposed new bypass. Even the crime was small-scale; no juicy murders. It was difficult to fill his page with anything worth reading. And worse, his salary didn't stretch as far as it had in the north. Everything cost more.

'Then why don't I go out to work?' Lottie suggested one evening. 'Part-time, at any rate. There must be something I can do.' She would scrub floors for Richard.

So when he readily agreed she took a job as a waitress in a pub, the Oak Tree, which did a steady trade in lunches. She worked five lunchtimes a week and sometimes, when the landlord was short-staffed, she helped behind the bar in the evenings. She quickly grew to prefer the evening shifts to the midday ones. They were more convivial. Male customers flirted with her and bought her drinks, both of which she enjoyed, though the flirting meant nothing. Her passion was Richard and her real time was when she went home at the end of the day to be with him.

Several weeks later the other evening barmaid, Muriel, for whom Lottie had been substituting more and more often, gave in her notice to leave. The landlord, Dan Firth, immediately offered the job to Lottie and Richard was happy for her to take it, which she did in addition to keeping on the lunchtime work. 'God knows, we could do with the money,' Richard grumbled. 'For one thing, I'll have to get a new car soon, before this one falls to pieces.' It was taking up more money in repairs than they could afford, and the MOT was due. So, after Lottie's second full week's wages and tips, he changed the car for a less elderly Audi. Not a new car, but a good second-hand one. It would not make his job any more interesting but at least he would feel better driving it around. 'If I have to report one more council meeting,' he said bitterly to Lottie, 'I will shoot that bloody, long-winded chairman!'

It was hard, Lottie soon realized, working a double shift in the pub. Sundays were her only day off. She would have liked to have gone somewhere nice on a Sunday – a run in the new car perhaps – but it was the only day she had to catch up with he housework and, in any case, they got up late and Richard spent much of the day reading the great pile of Sunday papers he had ordered to be delivered. She didn't dislike her job – quite the contrary: the customers were friendly and she got to know some of them quite well – but she was always tired.

When she had first started in the bar in the evenings Muriel had shown her how to accept the offer of a drink and take the money without actually drinking more than a very little of it. 'It's what you have to do,' Muriel said, 'or you'd end up flat on the floor. And always choose a short. It costs more, and the punters never mind paying, especially when they've had a few. In fact they'd be insulted if you didn't accept a drink.' So Lottie had taken the money for vodka-and-tonics but drunk only the occasional one – perhaps two in an evening, and then, as the weeks went by, perhaps three or even four. She had started out not really liking it – she would have preferred lemonade or cola – but it grew on her. It also, she told herself, perked her up, made her feel less tired towards the end of a busy evening. Of course, the more drinks she actually downed, the less money went into her pocket. But there it was, she told herself, she'd earned it.

Sometimes Richard came into the pub towards the end of the evening, and would be there to take her home. Sometimes he didn't. 'Work to do,' he said. 'Another bloody meeting. Why did I ever take this sodding job?' On these occasions, sometimes a mite unsteadily, she walked home alone. It wasn't far, she felt safe, and she always knew that Richard would be there, waiting for her.

And then one evening – she'd been working at the Oak Tree several weeks by then and Richard didn't come to see her home as often as he used to – she left the pub at a quarter past midnight to walk home. It had been a busy evening and the clearing up had taken ages. It was dark, and drizzling with rain. She hadn't had the foresight to bring an umbrella and she turned up the collar of her jacket to keep the raindrops from going down her neck. She would be glad to be home.

As soon as she drew near the house she realized that the flat was in darkness; there was no light coming from any of the windows or from the coloured-glass panel in the front door. Oh dear, she thought, Richard has gone to bed. But it wasn't like him: he was a night-bird, much more than she was. What drew him to bed, he said, was the thought of her in it. She fished in her handbag for the key, opened up, walked in and switched on the hall light. It was only as she did this that she realized the car hadn't been parked in its usual place a few yards along the road. Richard must have been called out on a job, which was unusual because, as he often complained, nothing ever happened in this one-horse town.

And then she saw the note, propped on the hall table. It would explain everything. Without waiting to take off her jacket she unfolded it.

The words jumped out at her.

> Sorry, love. I can't take any more. I'm off! I hate this
> bloody country and I'm getting out of it altogether.
> Don't look for me because you won't find me. It was
> lovely while it lasted. Take care of yourself. All the
> best.

And his name, in his usual bold handwriting, scrawled at the bottom.

She felt . . . she didn't know how she felt. Sick? Spinning in the head? Her legs giving way. All that and more besides. And there was something familiar about the note. As if she had dreamt about it before. And then suddenly she knew what it was. In essence it was exactly what she herself had written to Ben in what now seemed like another world – but wasn't. It was this world, in which she had been deserted, flung aside, exactly as she had flung Ben Thornton aside.

TWENTY-ONE

To Lottie, the realization that she had been done to as she had done to Ben did not help at all. Only for a fleeting moment did she think of Ben before her own grief overwhelmingly took over again. What she had done to Ben was, to her, as irrelevant as it had been inevitable. The two of them had been totally unsuited and would never have been happy together. At the same time as she had freed herself, she had freed him. He too would be able to make a new start. Thus went her tangled, irrational thoughts.

For Richard's action, on the contrary, she could see no possible reason, no justification. They had been happy; blissfully so. Of course he hadn't liked his job, but he would have learnt to deal with it; things would have improved in time. And if they hadn't, then he could have turned to something else. She had told him so many times. If necessary she would have found another job, worked longer hours and earned more money. She would do anything for Richard. She would give her life for him.

But he didn't want her life, did he? He didn't want anything she could give him. She had been living in cloud-cuckoo-land – and for how long?

She didn't believe that Richard would come back. She had none of the false hope that had been Ben's. The note left her no room for hope. It was lying on the floor now, where it had dropped from her fingers. She didn't pick it up; she needed no

255

reminder of what it said. She knew every word and she would never forget any one of them.

The next day – she had cried every bit of the night, not gone to bed at all – she phoned the Oak Tree. 'I have flu,' she said. 'I'm afraid I can't come in.'

'You sound terrible,' the landlord's wife said. 'Go to bed and keep warm. Is there anything you need?'

'I *feel* terrible,' Lottie said. 'No, there isn't.'

Richard was all she needed. 'Oh, Richard!' she cried out. 'Where are you? Why have you done this to me?'

The week that followed was horrendous. She spoke to no-one, no-one telephoned. She never left the flat for a moment, except when on the second day she dragged herself to the off-licence and bought two bottles of vodka. As she had hoped, they gave her some hours of oblivion. They also made her sick.

At the end of that week, for which she knew she would not get paid, she went back to work. She had to, she needed the money and the vodka was finished. Its purchase had eaten into her purse and she had very few savings; she had never thought of herself as needing savings. No money had gone on food: she wasn't hungry, she doubted she would ever be hungry again.

In the following weeks, at work and at home, she drank steadily. All her tips went on vodka and when there were not enough tips to pay for it she found ways of stealing the odd measure. It wasn't all that difficult; she simply had to choose the right moment, and be careful. Also, a certain craftiness, born of need, had got into her. There was always a jug of water behind the bar and what vodka went down her throat could be replaced in the bottle from that. And if any of the customers thought their vodka-and-tonic or bloody Mary was on the weak side, none of them actually said so.

At night she stayed up late; she couldn't bear the double bed, in which she still lay on her own side, hugging Richard's pillow close in her arms, telling herself that it smelt of him. And when she did go to bed it was morning before she fell asleep, so that she overslept and was then late for work, which after the first time or two didn't go down well. 'You'll have to do better than this,' the landlord said. 'A waitress half asleep so that she can't take the orders isn't much use to me. What's the matter with you these days?'

So she went to the chemist's and bought some painkillers, the strongest there were to be had without a prescription, in the hope that they would make her sleep. Not that anything on the chemist's shelves would ever kill her real pain. She was also running very short of money; vodka did not come cheap and she needed it in the hours she spent at home, alone. Thus it was one evening, at the lowest point she had yet touched, everywhere she turned in the flat reminding her of Richard – the chair he always sat on, his toothbrush, which he had left behind on the bathroom shelf – little things, but they were driving her mad and she couldn't bear it – that she made the decision to ring Dulcie. She had to tell someone or she would die of the pain.

Dulcie was appalled, and deeply saddened by Lottie's news. She hadn't approved in the least of the way Ben had been treated, but Lottie was her friend, and clearly in trouble. It was also clear that she had been drinking, but who could blame her?

'I'm so sorry, love,' she said. 'Why didn't you ring me earlier? I couldn't ring you: I didn't have a number.'

'I'm sorry,' Lottie said.

'Well, never mind now,' Dulcie said. 'I'll come down and see you, try to cheer you up. Perhaps we'll go out somewhere.'

'When will you come?' Lottie demanded. 'When? Can you come soon?'

'Well, not for the next ten days or so,' Dulcie said. 'I have an exhibition in Reading. But when I get back from that I'll drive over to West Pengate. It's only an hour away and we can have a long chat. How will that be?' She had news for Lottie, too. Not only that she was due to be married in a few weeks' time but that she was newly pregnant. But that news could wait. They were not exactly the kind of happy circumstances to throw at Lottie at the moment.

'Have you told Ben about this?' she asked.

'Of course I haven't,' Lottie said. 'Why would I tell Ben?'

'He might be able to help you,' Dulcie suggested tentatively.

'I couldn't possibly speak to Ben,' Lottie said. 'You haven't told him where I am, have you? You haven't given him my number or something? Because if you have—'

'Of course I haven't,' Dulcie broke in. 'I didn't know where you were myself. In any case, I haven't spoken to Ben for months.'

'Good,' Lottie said. 'Because I could never go back. It's not only that I couldn't go back to Ben, it's also that I could never go back to Cordale.' She should never have gone there in the first place. She'd been looking for security, but security had turned out to be captivity. And who could expect her to go back to Ben after experiencing Richard? A fresh wave of longing swept over her and her whole body ached at the thought of him.

'As you wish,' Dulcie said. 'And I'll see you as soon as ever I can. Keep your chin up, and don't hesitate to phone me if you want to.'

'All right, I will,' Lottie said. But for Lottie, almost from the moment when the phone call ended, everything went from bad to worse. To make enough money to buy the vodka and a minimum amount of food, she sold a few things Richard had not taken with him. The television, his collection of CDs and videos, a few books. Then she sold her own bits of jewellery. Her engagement ring, and the silver bracelet Ben had bought her. An opal ring, which had been her mother's, and also the silver neck chain with the pearl drop. She hated parting with that. She had worn it on the night of the Farmers' Ball. Richard had run his finger around it, against her neck.

The days and nights began to merge and in her fuddled state she seldom knew what time of the day it was. She could no longer go into work. She attempted to speak with the landlord and he advised her to see a doctor. What good would a doctor do? she asked herself as she slammed down the phone. He couldn't bring back Richard, and that was the only thing she wanted, the only thing to make her better.

Little more than a week later, at ten o'clock in the evening, Dulcie had been home only an hour when her phone rang. It was Lottie, incoherent and clearly drunk. 'I can't go on,' she slurred. 'I tell you, I can't go on. It's no use.'

Dulcie listened to her patiently. She could make very little sense of her. 'Go to bed, love,' she advised. 'Get some sleep. I'll be there tomorrow. I'll leave home in the morning. It's a promise.'

True to her promise, Dulcie drove to West Pengate the next morning. She left home at ten and, having been held up by roadworks, arrived there at half-past eleven. Lottie's instructions about how to get to her flat had been incomprehensible but, once in the town centre, Dulcie stopped at a post office and asked for directions. 'It's quite easy,' the postmistress said, and so it proved.

The curtains were still drawn. Sleeping it off, Dulcie thought – and just as well, poor lamb. She knocked at the door but there was no reply; then, for no reason at all because it didn't make sense, she tried the door and to her surprise found it unlocked, the key on the inside. She went in, drew back the curtains, found the kettle and filled it. She washed and dried two mugs from a pile of dirty crockery in the sink. She would waken Lottie with a pot of tea. When it had brewed she walked through to what she presumed would be the bedroom, and indeed it was.

Lottie was lying back against the pillows, her head lolling to one side as if it couldn't take its own weight. Dulcie, though she had never seen death before, knew at once that this was it. She thought she would scream with horror, or drop the tray, but she did neither. Possessed immediately by an icy calm she put the tray down on a small table, then touched Lottie's cheek with her finger. It was, as she had known it would be, as cold as ice. On the bedside table was an empty vodka bottle, and on the bed itself an opened packet of what Dulcie guessed were painkillers, though she didn't recognize the brand name.

Her instinct was to telephone the doctor – but which doctor and where? Or to run to the nearest neighbour. But no doctor could do anything for Lottie now. She was beyond help. I was too late, Dulcie thought. I should have dropped everything and come last night.

She went back into the living room, located the telephone and rang the police. Within ten minutes a constable, young, fresh-faced, everything about him at the opposite end of the spectrum

259

from death, was at the door. She let him in and took him into the bedroom. He stood there and looked at Lottie, lying on the bed. Gently, he felt for her non-existent pulse, then he shook his head and turned to Dulcie.

'What happened?' he asked.

'I don't know,' Dulcie said. 'I arrived only a few minutes ago. This is how I found her. She is dead, isn't she?'

'Oh yes,' the constable said. 'So how did you come to be here?'

She told him everything she knew, which was pitifully little. 'If only I'd come down straight away, last night,' she said.

He tried to console her. 'You weren't to know,' he said. 'I take it she didn't say anything that made you think . . .'

'Not this,' Dulcie said. 'She was unhappy, but that wasn't unlike Lottie. She was either up or down; it was her way.'

He had already seen the vodka bottle and the pack of pain-killers. Taken in enough quantity – and the vodka bottle was empty – they were a lethal combination. It wasn't the first time he had come across it.

He looked round the room. It was untidy, with things left where they had dropped. Not dirty, but messy. In his experience – it was a strange thing and it wasn't only his experience, it was well known in the Force – if women were going to take their own lives they tidied up first, they didn't leave the house in a mess. It was as if they were going to be judged, or have to account to someone for the way they'd left things. Men didn't do that. Men didn't bother about tidy deaths. Only women.

'I'll call my sergeant,' he said. 'While we're waiting, perhaps you can tell me a bit more. For a start, is the room much as it always was?'

'I don't know,' Dulcie said. 'This is the first time I've been to the flat. Lottie's been here less than a year. I didn't hear from her much, but when I did she sounded happy. Until the last two calls, after Richard left her.'

'Was Richard her husband?' He was wandering round the room as he talked.

'No,' Dulcie said. 'Her husband lives in Yorkshire. In the Dales. Ben Thornton.'

'So they're not divorced?'

'No,' Dulcie said. 'She left him. There was no talk of divorce.'

'Then he's her next of kin.'

'Her only kin, I'm fairly sure of that,' Dulcie said.

'And do you know how we can get in touch with him?'

She nodded. 'Oh yes. I know where he lives, I've been there. And I have his telephone number.'

The sergeant arrived. The constable went to the door to let him in. Dulcie followed.

The sergeant was a middle-aged man, kind, fatherly. Reassuring. He heard Dulcie's story, listened to the constable's observations and checked that nothing had been overlooked. It seemed to him, and he and the constable were in agreement, that this was no scene of crime: nothing pointed to the involvement of anyone other than Lottie.

From that moment everything moved with what seemed to Dulcie incredible speed. Wheels were set in motion and spun swiftly and efficiently. Neighbours were contacted, but knew nothing. Lottie had kept to herself, had not been seen about much. No, they had never noticed any visitors coming or going.

Ben was contacted. The Surrey police informed the relevant authorities in North Yorkshire, who sent a police constable to Beck Farm to break the news to Ben. The constable was a stranger to Kilby and to Cordale. Normally it would have been Fred Spears, who was Kilby's local constable and knew Ben – and everyone in the village and the dale. It was a great relief to Ben that Constable Spears was away on leave, having gone with his wife to attend their daughter's wedding, which was taking place in New York. If it had been otherwise the whole of the dale would have known. He wanted no-one to know anything. He had kept Lottie's secret so far and he would do so to the end.

In West Pengate the police had found Dulcie a hotel to stay in. She would be required later, but in any case she wanted to stay at least until Ben arrived. She liked Ben, he had been kindness itself to her and she hated the thought of him facing this alone and in a strange place. She doubted he had ever been far away from Kilby except on the occasion when he had met up with Lottie in Manchester. An ill-fated meeting, as it had turned out. Where would they all have been now if it had never taken place? Not here. Not seeing policemen, coroners, courtrooms, pathologists, funeral directors, kind and sympathetic though they might all be.

At the inquest, unsurprisingly, a verdict of Accidental Death was returned – and sympathy expressed to the bereaved husband. Not a word was heard about Richard; he had vanished from the scene. It was unlikely he would ever know, Dulcie thought. No-one had the least idea where he was. His existence was not a subject Ben wished to hear about.

The cremation took place in West Pengate. Dulcie and Ben were the only mourners. 'Keep in touch,' Dulcie said to Ben as they parted, she to go back to her fiancé and the prospect of her new baby, he to Beck Farm.

Back in Cordale, Ben again told no-one anything. He had been away for a short holiday and now he was back. There was nothing more to be said.

Within days he went to see his solicitor in Shepton, to whom he gave the bare facts of his wife's death, and then made a new will. Except for a moderate legacy to Alice, he left all he had, including what would arise from the sale of Beck Farm, to animal charities. Animals gave you everything and never let you down.

A stormy autumn followed his return from Surrey, followed by a bitter winter, one of the worst on record. Flu was everywhere and he, who never caught anything, this time did so. It quickly turned to pneumonia, and on a day in February he died. His swift death surprised everyone. He had been such a strong, healthy man. 'But he seemed to have no resistance,' the doctor said. 'There was no fight in him.'

He was buried in the same grave as Moira. 'A fitting end,' his friends said. 'Poor Ben.'

FRANCES

TWENTY-TWO

On that night, as Frances and her mother had walked back to Beck Farm, Frances had been almost silent. She had been moved and saddened by the story and somehow felt a little guilty that, unknowingly, she had sparked it off. Her mother was less silent.

'Fancy all that happening in a small place like this,' she'd said. 'It's like something in a book.'

Frances hadn't answered. She didn't want to encourage her mother to talk. When they'd reached home she'd made her a cup of Ovaltine and then they'd both gone to bed. But, on Frances's part, not to sleep. In her mind she'd gone over the evening's conversation. If I'd heard all this beforehand, she asked herself, would I have bought Beck Farm? It had not been a happy house.

She'd tossed and turned in the darkness – the nights here were darker than any she had ever known – and then in the end she'd taken herself to task. It had probably been happy for much of the time for Ben and Moira, she'd told herself, and surely some of the time for Ben and Lottie? Almost certainly in the long years the house had stood there many people had lived in it happily. Bricks and mortar, or in this case stone and wood, weren't what counted; what mattered was what one brought to it and made of it, and whatever Beck Farm had gone through in recent years she would make it a happy house again. When the visitors started it would spring to life, with people coming and going. When friends came – and already she was making friends in the village – they would contribute. But poor Ben, she thought. Her heart ached for him. And perhaps poor Lottie? Who knew? Neither of them were around to give their own side of the story. It had all come from others, some of them clearly prejudiced, and few of them, because of Ben's silence, knowing many of the facts. All she could add to the story was what her own imagination supplied. Eventually, she fell asleep.

The next morning, the morning after the scene in the Shorn Lamb, she went into the garden, straight after breakfast, and picked up the block of wood with the name carved on it, the name that was no longer that of a dog, albeit a well-loved one, but now a memorial to a woman, a woman who, no matter what she had done, had been loved and mourned. The skilled carving of the name was proof of that. It had been done with care, no sign of anger.

She felt strange, holding it – as if it was all that remained of Lottie and it was now in her charge. No-one had expressed a wish to do anything about it, or even to see it. Without anyone actually saying so, it had been left to her. She fetched a small, stiff brush from the kitchen and set about cleaning it, brushing away every trace of dirt and soil, front and back, until it was as near pristine as such weathered oak would ever be. Then she looked about, searching for a suitable site to move it to, a place of its own, a permanent place.

The garden was so messy and untidy, so overgrown and neglected, that there seemed to be nowhere fitting. In the end she decided on the ground beneath the apple tree. The tree was perhaps one permanent thing in the garden that would not, as she tried to put things to rights, be chopped down, uprooted, thrown away. Lottie would have known the tree, perhaps sat in its shade. Here the memorial could be left in peace.

She put it down – carefully, it was no longer just a block of wood – and went to one of the outhouses, where the gardening tools were kept. When she came back she marked out a small circle round the base of the tree trunk, dug it out, cleared the weeds, trimmed the edges until everything about it was tidy, and then she propped the slab of oak against the trunk and firmed the bottom edge of it into the soil so that it was as permanent as she could make it. When it was done she leaned back on her heels and looked at it. Yes, it was in a good place now. She felt happier. The apple tree would look after it, though the apple tree itself, she thought, was in need of care. Its branches were too intertwined to allow enough light to get to them. On the grass beneath, a few fallen apples still lay rotting. It was only a small circle she had dug out, not much more than a foot in radius, nothing ostentatious. She would, she thought, plant in it some small spring bulbs: crocuses, perhaps snowdrops; nothing that would grow tall enough to hide the inscription.

She was still on her knees when she heard footsteps on the path, and turned her head to see Alec walking towards her.

'Hi,' he said. 'Your mother said I'd find you here. I have a query on one of the showers. I thought I'd sort it out with you right away.'

'Fine,' Frances said. 'I'll come into the house.'

He held out a hand and helped her to her feet. She brushed traces of soil and blades of grass from her jeans.

'You look busy,' he said. 'Have I come at a bad time?'

'Not at all,' she said. 'I've finished what I came out to do.' She pointed to the block of wood, in its new place. 'I felt I had to do something about it. I couldn't just leave it lying around. Am I being silly? I mean, considering I didn't know either Lottie or Ben?'

'Not a bit,' Alec said, smiling. 'It was a good thing to do. They lived in your house. You could say they have a claim to being in your garden – as long as it doesn't upset you.'

'It doesn't,' Frances said. 'In fact, I feel better for it.'

'The apple tree doesn't look in good shape,' Alec said. 'I reckon you've done that a favour at the same time, digging out the soil round the trunk. Grass is greedy for moisture. It will have been soaking up the rain before the tree had a chance.'

'Well, I didn't know that,' Frances said. 'I'm an ignoramus when it comes to gardening. I just wanted to make this bit look nice. But what you say makes sense.'

'So do most things in gardening,' Alec said. 'I reckon the tree needs a bit of loving care. Pruning and so on.'

'I'm sure you're right,' Frances said. 'I don't know how to set about that but I'll get someone in to advise me. Shall we go into the house?'

Over a month had passed since that awful evening in the pub and Frances and her mother had been to the Shorn Lamb many times since then. No-one had mentioned Lottie and Ben again: it was as if they had never existed. Things had been moving quickly in her own life too. The B&B advertisements, which included a small line drawing of the house she herself had done, and the details about it, had gone in the relevant news-papers and magazines. She was pleased with the ads. They looked well on the page. She had taken space in publications far from Yorkshire, as well as locally, especially in county magazines. It had cost a pretty penny – she'd had no idea advertising was so expensive – but she hoped it was an investment in the future. And, of course, she had advertised the house under its new name, Beckside House, though the sign had not yet been fixed. Malachi had taken his time – he was not one to be rushed, Alec had said – but now it was ready and they would collect it the following weekend.

The alterations to the house were going well, too. There was no doubt that everything would be ready for the visitors by Easter, or perhaps sooner. Of course she would have to refurnish some of the rooms; new beds, curtains, a few new rugs on the wood floors. Towels, pillows, bed linen, etcetera. She hoped to buy some of these in Shepton in the January sales. It would all take money, but then she had budgeted for that. Possibly she could make the curtains, she thought. Her mother had brought her sewing machine with her.

On the appointed Sunday, Alec took her over to Kirkholme to see Malachi and collect the sign. Her mother had taken to churchgoing with enthusiasm and wouldn't consider missing the Sunday service, so she was left behind. 'I'll be back in time to see to lunch,' she said. 'And you can bring Alec back with you if you want to.'

Malachi was pleased to see them, and very proud of the sign. With good reason, Frances thought. It was beautifully crafted.

He flatly refused to take any payment for it. 'I had the wood. It gave me summat to do wi' my time,' he said. 'It were a pleasure! And now you must stop long enough to have a glass of cider wi' me.'

While they drank, he talked mainly to Alec.

'So how are the childer?' he asked.

'Quite well,' Alec told him.

'They'll be growing.'

'All the time,' Alec said.

'So how old are they now?'

'Peter's seven, Mark is five. He's at school now.'

There was a short silence then Malachi said, 'It's not right for a man not to be wi' his childer.'

'It happens,' Alec said.

Malachi shook his head. 'Not in my day, it didn't. Not till they were full grown and left to make a living of their own.'

Nothing more was said on that subject until Alec was driving back through Tendale. Then he said, 'My boys are coming to spend next weekend with me. They do that from time to time.'

Back at the house Frances passed on Madge's invitation to stay for Sunday lunch. When he hesitated she said, 'My mother will be disappointed if you don't.'

'In that case,' he said, 'I will.'

They all enjoyed the meal together. He was a nice man, Madge thought: easy to talk to and not the least bit condescending, as young people sometimes were to the old; flattering them, buttering them up. He talked to her as an equal.

It was he who brought his children into the conversation, telling her, with evident pleasure, that they were coming to visit him next weekend.

'Then you must bring them to see us,' Madge said without hesitation. 'We'd like that, wouldn't we?' she said, turning to Frances.

'Of course,' Frances agreed. All the same, she didn't think her mother should have said it: Alec might not want others to be involved. Probably he'd rather go off somewhere on his own with the children.

'That would be very pleasant,' he said quickly. 'There's not a lot for them to do when they come to Kilby. It's a far cry from living in a city. Perhaps we'll go for a walk up the path by the beck, to the top of the hill, then if it suited you we could drop in here on the way back.'

'Fine,' Madge said. 'We'll have a real Yorkshire tea.' She looked to Frances for confirmation.

'Lovely,' Frances agreed.

When they had finished lunch Alec fixed the new sign on the wall to the left of the door. 'It looks really good,' Frances said. 'I'm pleased with it.'

He grinned at her. 'You do realize no-one will call it Beckside House. At least, no-one locally. It will still be Beck Farm. Except to strangers.'

'*I* will,' Frances said firmly. But then, she reminded herself, she *was* a stranger. For how long would she be?

It was December now and the days were short; the darkness came down before the afternoon was over so, on the occasions when the two women decided to go down to the Shorn Lamb, unless there was a full moon and everything was bathed in its light, they had to carry pocket torches. There were street lamps in the village, but none close to Beckside House. Madge didn't always go to the pub. She tired early these days and found the cold trying. There were evenings when she preferred to sit close to the fire and to go to bed early; if not to sleep, then to watch television from the comfort of her own bed. A TV of her own had been Frances's present to her on her last birthday. It suited both of them; their choices of programmes were quite different.

This was one of those evenings. 'Shall we go down to the Lamb?' Frances asked her mother.

Madge sighed. 'I won't, if you don't mind, love,' she said. 'I'd like an early night and there's *Inspector Morse* on television. I'll be all right.'

'Are you sure—' Frances began.

'Quite sure,' Madge interrupted.

It was a chilly walk down to the Shorn Lamb. There was a sneaky wind, which, Frances thought, her mother wouldn't have enjoyed. She herself didn't like it all that much and she wondered why she had chosen to come. Because – she answered her own question – she looked forward from time to time to being with other people, somewhere where there was light and warmth and the buzz of conversation. There was almost always someone in the Lamb with whom she could chat. She had grown to like the people in Kilby – well, most of them. They were frank, plain-speaking, even blunt. It was not what she had been used to, living most of her life in the south, but she had quickly grown used to it, had almost come to like it.

The warmth greeted her like a blanket as she went into the bar. Heads were raised as the cold air gusted in.

'Put the wood in the hole, love,' someone called out.

'Shut the door,' Joseph Clark translated.

She knew what it meant. It was a phrase her father had used.

Joseph's friend Harry Foster was there, too, though neither of their wives were with them. It was Jim Kettle's night off so Bernard was behind the bar, but there was no sign of Joyce. Since it was well out of season now, evening meals were not being regularly served. Frances was not particularly disappointed by Joyce's absence. Although they were back on reasonable terms she and Joyce were unlikely ever to be close friends. Joyce, she thought, still viewed her with some suspicion. Glancing quickly around the room, she was a bit disappointed not to see Alec there, though of course he wasn't what one would call a *frequent* regular in the Lamb any more than she was. He was not of the same ilk as Joseph Clark and Harry Foster.

She had got to know Alec better at the weekend when he had come to tea with his children. She had seen another side of him. There had been little of the successful businessman then, only the father. His love for his sons, his ease and comfort in their presence, was palpable – and they were totally comfortable with him. It was all very civilized, she thought, but not in her mother's eyes. Madge would have agreed with Malachi Flint on that score. It was not the way things should be done. In spite of, or perhaps because of that, she had got on well with the boys, and they with her. The generation gap between them was of no consequence at all.

'Come and join us, Frances,' Joseph Clark called out. They moved the chairs along so that there was room for her to do so. 'What will you have?' someone asked.

'A glass of red wine, please,' Frances said.

'Where's your mother?' Joseph asked. 'It's not often you come without her. Is she all right?'

'She is and she isn't,' Frances said. 'She *says* she's all right but I reckon she's not quite herself – hasn't been for a day or two. She's very tired, so she's gone to bed.'

'Oh well,' Harry said, 'an early night and a good sleep never did anyone any harm.'

Frances nodded. 'You're right.'

She was halfway through her glass of wine when Alec came in. As he pushed open the door a slight flurry of snow came with him and there were a few flakes on his shoulders.

'I told Joyce it was cold enough for snow,' Bernard Grayson said. 'Even though it is a bit early. I don't like it when it comes early. It means a long winter.'

Alec fetched a chair and joined them at the table, sitting next to Frances.

'I'm pleased to see you here,' he said. 'But where's Madge?'

She told him.

'I'm sorry to hear that,' he said. 'But she's done the wise thing. It's turning really cold out there. Anyway, tell her I asked after her.'

'I will,' Frances promised. 'That will please her.'

'The boys really enjoyed being with her,' Alec said. 'I reckon all children should have a grandmother, if only to spoil them. My lads have no grandparents on either side of the family.'

'My mother would agree with your sentiments entirely,' Frances said. 'It's one of her biggest disappointments in life that I never had a child she could spoil.'

'Is it to you?' he asked.

'Not really,' Frances said. 'Perhaps when I'm older it might be, but not now.'

The talk at the table had turned to Christmas and what might take place then.

'Next week,' Bernard said, 'we'll start putting the decorations up. The last vicar didn't like that much – the timing, I mean. He said no Christmas decorations should go up until Christmas Eve. I don't know what Clive will say. What I know is that the customers like it to start early. It brightens things up, which is all to the good at this time of the year.'

'You mean it brings the money in,' Joseph said.

'That as well,' Bernard agreed mildly. 'Anyway, Clive might quite like that. When the church folks come to sing carols here at Christmas they get a nice collection for church funds. That's not to be sneezed at. The Reverend Saul Denham was always pleased to have it, despite his objections.'

Frances turned to Alec. 'What do you do at Christmas?' she asked.

He shrugged. 'It's not easy,' he said. 'The week before, as soon as school breaks up, I take the boys into Shepton and buy them the presents of their choice. I'm a bit extravagant about that. And we have a slap-up meal somewhere. They enjoy all that, and so do I. But when it comes to Christmas itself it's a bit more tricky. Naturally they like to spend it with their mother, and she wants them there. I'm always invited but there's the fact that her second husband is there. I feel a bit of a spare part.'

'I can understand that,' Frances said.

'Anyway,' Alec said, 'it's going to be a bit different this year. The boys will spend Christmas Day with their mother and stepfather but first thing on Boxing Day morning my ex and her husband are taking off for France on a week's skiing holiday. It's apparently something they've always wanted to do and the chance came up, but there are no children included in the party. So the boys will come to me early on Boxing Day, and stay. I shall take a few days off.'

'In that case,' Frances said, 'perhaps the three of you will join me and my mother on Boxing Day, or at any other time. We don't have any plans at all. But only if you've nothing better to do. My mother would love it.'

'So would the boys,' Alec said. 'But what about you? Are you sure?'

'Of course I am,' Frances said. 'I'd like it very much. We'll fix something up.'

When it came time to leave the Lamb, Alec said to Frances, 'I'll see you home.'

But Joseph chipped in. 'No need, old boy,' he said. 'I've got the car and I pass the gate. I'll give Frances a lift.'

Joseph was as good as his word. However, because the road now had a covering of snow he left the car close by, and walked up with Frances to her door and waited there until she let herself in.

'I hope your mother will be better tomorrow,' he said. 'Give her my best.'

Standing in the hall, Frances could see the light from her mother's bedroom spilling out onto the upstairs landing. She called out, 'Mother, I'm back.' There was no reply; her mother must be asleep. Stopping only to shed her coat and gloves – she had left home without a hat and, glancing in the hall mirror, she saw there were flakes of snow in her hair – she went quietly upstairs.

She tiptoed across the bedroom. Her mother was asleep, but she was not sleeping peacefully, that much was clear. She looked another person, as if, during the short time she had been alone – which was not more than a couple of hours – what had seemed no more than ordinary fatigue had changed to illness. Usually she was pale of face, but now she was flushed and her breathing was short. Frances looked down at her, worried. This was not like her mother at all. She was seldom ill – Frances couldn't remember when the last time had been – and now she looked as though she really was.

She had pushed away the bedclothes, as if the heat from them had been too much for her, and her shoulders and arms were bare. Very gently, so as not to waken her, Frances pulled up the sheet to cover her and as she did so her fingers inadvertently touched her mother's cheek. It was burning.

Madge opened her eyes. They were uncommonly bright.

'Are you all right, Mother?' Frances asked. 'I'm sorry I wakened you.'

'Not too good. Very hot,' Madge said. She tried to fling off the bedclothes. Frances covered her up again.

274

'I'll get you a nice cool drink,' she said. 'You'll feel better for that. I won't be a minute, love.'

She filled a glass with water and found a thermometer in the bathroom cabinet. She should never have left her mother alone; she shouldn't have gone out, but she'd seemed no more than very tired when she'd done so.

Back in the bedroom she said, 'I'm just going to take your temperature before you have a drink of water. You look a bit flushed to me. Why didn't you tell me you weren't feeling too good? You know I wouldn't have left you.'

She put the thermometer under her mother's tongue and sat down beside her, holding her hand, which was also burning hot, and dry. When she took the thermometer out again and looked at it she said, 'You've got a bit of a temperature.'

'I could have told you that without the thermometer,' Madge said with some of her usual spirit.

'Do you have a headache?' Frances asked.

'A corker,' Madge said.

'Then I'll give you a couple of aspirin and you can drink this water and as much more as you can. And in the morning I'll give Dr Fortune a ring.'

'Oh, I don't need a doctor,' Madge said. 'A good night's sleep and I'll be better in the morning.'

But when Frances went into her, early next morning while it was still dark, she was not any better. Nor had she had a good night's sleep. And she was still burning hot, and uncomfortable. Without arguing the point, Frances rang for the doctor.

TWENTY-THREE

The church clock was striking eleven as Dr Fortune rang the doorbell. Frances was there almost before he had taken his finger from the bell push.

'Good morning, Mrs Hamilton,' he said cheerfully. 'I'm sorry to hear your mother's not well. I'd have been here earlier but I had a full surgery today. Time of the year, I suppose.'

He followed Frances through the hall and up the stairs, chatting amiably all the while. She had met him before, soon after they came to Kilby when she and her mother went to register with him. They had both liked him on sight, which was just as well since he and his partner in the practice were the only two doctors in this part of Cordale, and his partner was a woman, Dr Jean Pearson, which would not have suited Madge at all. 'It's not that I'm prejudiced,' she said whenever the subject came up, 'but women aren't the same, are they? All right for the kiddies, of course.'

They'd heard all about Dr Fortune from the clientele of the Shorn Lamb, who had recommended him highly. His father, they were told, had been a doctor before him, in the dale, though he was now retired and lived in Harrogate. It was because his father had been here and for a short time they had practised together that the son was known to most people as 'Dr Bob'. He was in his forties, they said, with a nice wife and two daughters,

276

the younger one away at school and the elder one at Leeds University. 'Learning to be a doctor,' Harry Foster had said. 'She'll follow in her father's footsteps, that one.' You'll like Dr Bob, they'd said – and so far they'd been right.

When he followed Frances into the bedroom Madge was sitting upright, as if at attention. It would not have occurred to her to remain lying down when the doctor came into the room, not even if she had felt herself at death's door. She was not of that school.

Dr Fortune pulled up a chair and sat beside the bed. 'Well, Mrs Fraser, so how are you?' he asked.

'Not too bad,' she answered in a quiet, stoical voice.

'She was not at all well when I phoned you this morning,' Frances interrupted. 'And really quite poorly last night.'

The doctor smiled. 'But she's not going to admit it,' he said. 'Well, some ladies are like that, and some are quite the opposite.' He spoke with the confidence of a man who could easily sort out one from the other. 'So let me have a look at you, Mrs Fraser.'

He took her temperature – but didn't say what it was – felt her pulse, tapped her chest, put the stethoscope to her back and listened intently, invited her to cough; then he sat back and looked at her.

'Well, yes,' he said, 'flu. There's a lot of it about.'

'But I never get flu,' Madge protested. 'Never. Nothing more than a cold in the head.'

'Well, Mrs Fraser,' he said, 'I'm afraid what you have now is a classic case of flu, or I'm not a doctor! And you must stay right where you are, keep warm, drink lots of fluid – water, tea, soup, whatever. Do you have a headache?'

She admitted that she did.

'Then a couple of paracetamol, as and when.' He turned to Frances. 'I expect you have some?'

She nodded.

'I'll give your daughter a prescription, which she can get filled for you,' he said to Madge. 'It might make you feel easier, though flu tends to take its own time.' He paused, and then looked at her again. 'Remind me how old you are,' he said.

'I'm seventy-three,' Madge said.

'These days we don't consider the seventies all that old,' he said. 'Nevertheless, you won't mind my saying, you're no spring chicken. When you get something like flu – and it is *not* the same as a cold in the head – you have to take it seriously. If you neglect it at your age it can settle on your chest and turn to pneumonia and you wouldn't want that, would you? So take it easy, give yourself time to recover. Drink plenty of fluids, as I said, do as your daughter tells you, and rest up while you have the chance. I know what your generation is like. My mother is the same. Always on the go. I think it's partly having gone through World War Two. You had so much responsibility then, you ladies. You can't seem to shake it off.' He got up to go. 'Do you enjoy reading?' he asked.

'When I have the time,' Madge said.

'Well, now you have,' he pointed out. 'Get a pile of books from the library van and lie back and read them all. And if you fall asleep reading, so much the better.'

When he reached the bedroom door he turned back. ''Bye for now, Mrs Fraser. I'll stop by tomorrow to check that you're doing as you're told!'

He trotted down the stairs, Frances hurrying after him. On the doorstep he paused. 'Look after her,' he said. 'Of course I'm sure you will, but I doubt she's quite as tough as she thinks she is. Neither her chest nor her heart are what I'd call first-class. But don't worry, when she's got over this we'll look at the rest. And get the prescription filled this morning. It's half-day closing today. In fact, I'm going down to the village now: I'll drop it in for you if you like. Mr Slater might have someone free to bring it up to you.'

'That would be a great help,' Frances said. 'Thank you very much.'

'No trouble,' he said.

A dozen of his long strides and he was back in his car. As he turned the corner into the road he put his hand out of the window and gave her a wave.

Going back up the stairs Frances thought, Have I been neglecting my mother? Have I been so full of my own affairs that I haven't noticed her? If it was so, it had never been intentional;

she had just allowed herself to be too busy. But from now on she would keep a watch on her. Not let her know it, of course. That would never do.

Madge was lying down again. 'How do you feel?' Frances asked.

'The funny thing is,' Madge said, 'the minute the doctor tells you what's the matter with you, you feel a bit better. You stop wondering if you were making a fuss about nothing and you're pleased to know you weren't. Confirmed by the expert. Do you know what I mean?'

'Of course I do,' Frances assured her. 'And it also means you can let go. You're not guilty. Anyway, I'm going to make you a hot drink and then perhaps you can go back to sleep. What would you like?'

'Bovril,' Madge said without hesitation. 'I always like a cup of Bovril if I don't feel well. In fact,' she said thoughtfully, 'it's one of the ways I *know* when I'm not well. I get this longing for Bovril and cream crackers.'

'I never knew that before,' Frances said. 'I shall certainly watch out for it.' She looked at her watch. 'Violet's late,' she said. 'I hope there's nothing wrong with Daisy.'

'So do I,' Madge said. 'Or the other children. Anyway, when she does come she mustn't bring Daisy up here. I wouldn't like her to catch anything from me, the little love.'

'I'll make quite certain she doesn't,' Frances said. 'In any case, when you've had your Bovril you are to go back to sleep and I'll see that you're not disturbed. There are plenty of jobs for Violet to do downstairs.'

She returned within minutes with the Bovril, and with a small, brass bell in the shape of a crinolined lady. 'I remembered this,' she said. 'It's been around for ever. I always wondered what possible use it could be to anyone.'

'And now you know,' Madge said. 'It belonged to my mother, your grandma.'

'And now I know,' Frances said. 'I'll leave it on your bedside table and if there's anything you want you only have to ring. Otherwise I'll leave you in peace.'

Violet, bringing Daisy, now came in only two mornings a week since much of the house had been cleared and cleaned. Most of what was left was routine, or things only Frances herself could do, amongst which the sorting out of what she thought of as the 'little room' was now top of the list for things to be done on a wet day, which this was; chilly and drizzling. As yet she had hardly put her head inside the door. It was something she had been putting off, though aware at the back of her mind that it would have to be done. Who knew what the room held beyond what a cursory glance had revealed?

'I'm afraid my mother's not well,' she informed Violet. 'Quite poorly, in fact. The doctor says it's flu, so it would be as well if you didn't take Daisy near her. We both know how much she looks forward to seeing Daisy but we shouldn't take any chances, should we? I mean for Daisy's sake.'

Violet agreed. 'In any case,' she said, 'Daisy isn't herself. She's a bit grizzly. I reckon she's teething, though it's a bit soon for it. Still, the others were forward with their teeth.' As if on cue, Daisy emitted a fractious cry from her pram which, as usual, was parked in the hall. 'There she goes,' Violet said. 'I'm never sure what to do with her, though you'd think I would be, seeing that she's my third. But the other two were no trouble. One day they had no teeth and then in no time at all they had a full set.'

'You were lucky,' Frances said. 'And so were they.'

'You're right, Mrs Hamilton,' Violet said, jigging the pram with no effect at all. 'Do you know any remedies for teething babies?'

Frances laughed. 'You're asking the wrong person there,' she admitted. 'I don't know a thing about babies. Now my mother, though she's only had the one, certainly would, but I'm not going to ask her at the moment because with any luck she'll have dropped off to sleep.'

Madge had not dropped off to sleep. Even if she had wanted to, Daisy's cries, which had grown louder and continuous, would have prevented it. She picked up the bell and rang it. It was a satisfying sound and brought Frances running up the stairs.

'Whatever is the matter with the little mite?' Madge said. 'It's not like her.'

'Apparently she's teething,' Frances said. 'That's Violet's verdict. I'm sorry if she wakened you.'

'I wasn't asleep,' Madge said. 'So what's anybody doing for her, poor little lamb?'

'Violet,' Frances said, 'in spite of Daisy being her third, seems to have no more idea of what to do than I have. What would you do, Mother?'

'Well, for a start I wouldn't leave her in her pram, crying her heart out,' Madge said firmly. 'I'd pick her up, give her a cuddle, rock her to sleep.'

'And what else?'

'Oil of cloves. Or a little neat whisky, massaged into the gums. It worked with you.'

'Neat whisky! Mother, you didn't give me neat whisky at that age? I don't believe it.'

'I didn't give you a *drink* of whisky,' Madge said. 'I wet my finger with it and rubbed it on your gums, as I just said. And it seemed to do the trick. It numbs the pain. Anyway as far as I can see it hasn't had a lasting bad effect on you. You're hardly an alcoholic, are you? But failing that, I suggest you tell Violet she can go home right now and call in at the chemist's on the way: ask him to give her something. I expect he'll have remedies on his shelves for teething babies, poor little things.'

She started to cough, largely, Frances thought, from indignation. 'If only I could just hold her for a few minutes I dare say—'

'Well, you can't,' Frances interrupted. 'But I'll do as you say. I'll send Violet home.'

She was halfway down the stairs when Daisy, with a final small sob, fell asleep. Nevertheless, Frances suggested to Violet that if she started to cry again she might like to take her home. 'For her sake,' she said. 'It does sound painful.'

But Daisy had decided to sleep. Violet went back to her work and after a while, when she had done a few jobs, Frances went upstairs and looked in on her mother. She was sleeping; not entirely quietly – there was a little rasping sound in her breathing as if it didn't come easily – and her face was flushed, but at least she *was* asleep. Her arms and hands were outside the bedcovers. Frances took them gently, one at a time, in her own, and put them under the sheet, and then she crept away, leaving the door slightly ajar so that if the bell were to be rung she would hear it.

She had not been in the little room since that first day when she had given it a quick glance. There had been too many other things to do – more important things, like getting the place ready for next season's visitors – but now those things were at a stage where she couldn't take much part. They were in the hands of Alec's workmen, though progress had come to a temporary halt. They were not here today because Alec, with many apologies to her, had had to call them off to attend to an emergency in Shepton. 'But it will only be a couple of days,' he'd promised. 'They'll be back with you the day after tomorrow.'

She didn't mind for a day or two – and as things had turned out with her mother it was a blessing. At least she would be free from the noise. But she would be truly thankful when they had finished their part and she could bring the decorators in, though she doubted if that would be before the New Year. Her turn would come when the very last workman had moved out and she could put everything into place and add all the finishing touches. She looked forward to that.

The little room – which when she came to look at it was not all that little, it was simply crowded – looked as daunting as ever. She hardly knew where to make a start. Probably, she thought, she would have to throw a great deal away. There wasn't much good furniture there, it was mostly odds and ends, but the six-drawer chest was mahogany and would look well in one of the refurbished bedrooms. There was also, in the far corner, a single wardrobe, which she hadn't noticed on her first cursory inspection. That might come in useful.

She crossed the room to the window. It was what she did in any room on first going into it. She had to know what view lay outside. There were no curtains. She looked out to the east, across the narrow road that ran north to Joseph Clark's property and beyond. At the other side of the road, beyond the low wall bordering it, there were large green meadows. A line of trees in the middle distance marked where the river ran, and beyond that the land climbed steeply to the top of the fell, on the other side of which, she knew, was Tendale. A good view, or it would be on a fine day. At the moment it was blurred in a mist of fine rain, and the sky was grey. All the views from the house were pleasant, but she preferred the vista from the windows on the north side, which looked up the length of the dale.

She was still looking out of the window – a man and a woman on horseback were riding up the road, at a trot; it looked so appealing in spite of the rain, and she wondered if she might take up riding as soon as she could spare the time – when Daisy's voice broke in on the scene, loud, insistent, complaining; rending the air. And less than a minute later, even more demanding, came the sound of her mother's bell. She left the room at once. It was probably not a good idea to combine putting this room to rights with looking after her mother, and her mother was more important.

The sound of the bell went on without ceasing, as did Daisy's cries. It was difficult to say which was more clamorous. As she went towards her mother's room, so Violet appeared downstairs and homed in on Daisy in the hall.

'I'm sorry, Mrs Hamilton,' she called out. 'And I'm afraid she's woken up your mother.'

The bell stopped as Frances went into her mother's room, though not Daisy's piercing cry.

'Whatever is the matter with the child?' Madge demanded. 'I can't bear to hear her in pain. It goes right through me.'

'Violet has gone to her,' Frances said. 'Did she waken you? Had you gone to sleep?'

'I was just nodding off,' Madge said. 'Just losing myself.' She seldom admitted to having actually slept.

'I'm sorry,' Frances said. 'She does sound in trouble, doesn't she?' Daisy was still screaming away, though at a different pitch, which told Frances that Violet had taken her out of the pram and was holding her. 'I'll go down and see if there's anything I can do. But I really think it's best for all concerned if Violet wheels her down to the chemist's. I'm sure he'll know what to do.' She felt inadequate that she didn't and she knew that if this went on she was going to find it difficult to prevent her mother getting out of bed and going downstairs to take charge. 'Anyway,' she said, 'perhaps being pushed down the road in the pram will soothe her.'

By the time Frances was downstairs Daisy's loud yells had become pathetic little cries, like those of a mewing kitten. 'I think you'd better take her home,' Frances said – with which Violet was only too ready to comply. 'Give me a ring later,' Frances added. 'My mother will be anxious to know.'

Dr Fortune came the next morning, just before lunch. 'And how is your mother?' he asked Frances when she answered the door. 'Better?'

'Not really,' Frances said. 'She had a restless night; she was quite hot. Of course, she'll tell you she's much better.'

'Of course she will,' he agreed. 'I think I have the measure of your mother. But we'll see.'

Frances took him upstairs. Madge was sitting up, waiting for him. She had heard his voice in the hall and would like to have known what he'd said, but though she had strained to catch the words they had been indistinct.

'So how are you today, Mrs Fraser?' he enquired.

'I'm all right,' she said. 'A bit headachy, a bit tired.'

'You look a bit tired,' he said. 'Have you been doing as you were told?'

'Absolutely,' she assured him. 'Frances wouldn't let me do anything else.'

'Good,' he said. 'Well, keep on behaving yourself – keep on with the paracetamol if your headache's bad, but not too often. And while I'm here I'll take your blood pressure.'

'Why do you want to do that?' Madge asked.

'Oh, it's just one of those things,' he said. 'People your age, if they get near a doctor, have their blood pressure taken. It's par for the course. Do you mean you've never had it done before?'

'No,' Madge said. 'But then, I've not seen a doctor for – oh, I don't remember how long. As I told you yesterday I'm a very healthy woman.'

'I'm sure you are,' he agreed. 'Just roll up your sleeve.'

'Not too bad,' he said when it was over. 'I'll keep an eye on it from time to time. Now, I shan't see you tomorrow but I'll look in in a day or two and I'll expect to find you quite a bit better. Just continue to do as you're told.'

Frances saw him to the front door. 'Is she really all right?' she asked. 'You see, she's not one for telling.'

'She will be,' he said. 'Her blood pressure's a bit high and also I think when she's well again it wouldn't be a bad idea if she were to see a cardiologist, but we won't bother about that for the moment. If she hasn't seen a doctor for a long time she'd be no worse for an MOT, so to speak. But for now we'll concentrate on getting her over the flu. Don't worry.' He changed the subject. 'Are you settling in here?'

'Oh yes,' Frances said. 'I like I very much. We both do.'

He'd told her not to worry, Frances thought, and she expected he knew what he was talking about, but it was difficult not to do so. She was not used to her mother being unwell; she hardly remembered her having a day in bed. But no-one could say Madge had had an easy time in the last few months. Frances resolved, as she went into the kitchen to make a pot of tea for the two of them, that if it was the only way she could get her mother to do so, then she herself would try to slow down. True, there were some jobs that couldn't wait for long, but there were others that could. For instance, the little room, which she'd been so determined to deal with this very day, could wait. It could wait indefinitely. She had as yet no concrete plans to use it and as far as she could see there was nothing in it that mattered.

Frances made the tea, put some shortbread biscuits on a plate, and went upstairs. She would stay with her mother for a while, talk to her, give her some time. She wanted her to be well enough to enjoy Christmas, which by now was not far off. It would be their first Christmas in Cordale, and it would be awful if her mother was not well enough to appreciate it.

Later in the evening the telephone rang. She answered it quickly. Her mother had gone to sleep and she didn't want her to be disturbed. It was Alec.

'I just wanted to reassure you that the men will be back

285

tomorrow. I'm ringing from the Lamb. I thought I might see you here. Are you coming down?'

'No,' Frances said. 'I can't. My mother's ill.' She told him all about it. 'So it might be a little while before I'm in the Lamb. I'm not going to leave my mother.'

'Of course not,' Alec agreed. 'I'm sorry she's ill. But the doctor's right, there *is* a lot of flu about, certainly in Shepton. Shall I come up and see you?'

'Not this evening,' Frances said. 'I hope that doesn't sound rude, but it's not been the best of days. My mother has gone to sleep now and I'm going to have an early night.'

'Tomorrow, then,' Alec said.

'That would be lovely,' she said. 'I look forward to it.'

TWENTY-FOUR

At half-past eight the next morning, on the dot, the men were back at work. It was possibly a bonus that the sounds of their hammering, drilling and sawing were partly muffled by the incessant stream of pop music issuing from the small portable radio that accompanied them everywhere. Or possibly not? Madge, lying in her bed two rooms away, was not sure. On the whole, she thought, she slightly preferred the noise of the tools. Not that she had any choice.

'I'm sorry, Mother,' Frances said. 'There's not a lot I can do, other than asking them to turn the radio down – which I've done. We really need them to get on with the job.'

Madge sighed. 'I know, love. But I wish I had some earplugs. I don't suppose you can buy earplugs in Kilby?'

'I wouldn't think so,' Frances said. 'But I have to go down to the shop later. I'll ask Dora Laycock. It's surprising what she does stock.'

Her mother was looking better today, and admitted that she felt better. The fever seemed to have died down. When asked if she had slept well she said, 'On and off!'

'That can't be bad,' Frances said. 'Actually, when I came in to take a look at you in the early hours you were well away.'

'Oh, I'm sure I'm on the mend,' Madge said defensively. 'And

287

I don't enjoy just lying here, you know. It's not me. I'd far rather be up and doing.'

'I'm sure you would,' Frances agreed. 'But not for another day or two. Wait until the doctor's been again. Now, will you be all right if I nip down to the village in about half an hour? There are a few things I must get. The men are here and if you need them for anything you only have to ring your bell and they'll come right away.'

'If they hear it over the sound of the music,' Madge said.

'They could hear that bell over the top of a brass band playing the "Ride of the Valkyries",' Frances said. 'Is there anything you want from the village?'

'Only earplugs,' Madge said.

Frances left the bedroom and went downstairs. Thank goodness Violet and the teething Daisy weren't in today, she thought – though of course she did hope Daisy was better. If pre-toothache was anything like toothache, then it was hell.

She was at the bottom of the stairs when the telephone rang. On the line was Alec, wanting to speak to one of his men.

'Sure,' Frances said. 'I'll get him.'

'Wait a minute,' Alec said. 'How's your mum?'

'She's a mite better, thanks.' Frances told him. 'She's complaining a bit today, which I suppose is a good sign. She wouldn't have said boo to a goose yesterday.'

'If it's OK with you,' Alec said, 'I'll call in on my way home today. See how the job's going and say hello to your mum at the same time.'

'She'd like that,' Frances said.

'OK, then. Six-ish?'

'Fine,' Frances said. 'I'll get John for you now.'

'That will be something to look forward to,' Madge said when Frances gave her the news. 'Not that I kid myself he's coming to see *me*, but I'm always pleased to see him.'

'I'll be off, then,' Frances said. 'Is there anything else you want, then?'

'Nothing,' Madge said. 'I wish I was going myself.'

'In a few days, perhaps,' Frances said. 'In the meantime, try to have a little nap.'

288

'With all this going on?' Madge queried. 'You must be joking!'

Walking down the lane to the village, Frances breathed in deeply. The air felt fresh and clean, though it was chilly, even for December. There was frost still on the grass. It was good to be out of the house. She found everything she wanted at the shop with the exception, of course, of the earplugs.

'We don't get much call for them,' Dora Laycock said. 'I could offer you a packet of cotton wool. I'd heard your mother wasn't well. I'm sorry about that. She's a nice lady, your mum.'

'You'd heard?' Frances queried.

'I can't think who told me,' Dora said. 'Word gets around.'

Alec arrived on the dot of six. The men had already left and all was peaceful. He came into the house carrying a poinsettia in a pot. 'For your mother,' he said. 'I didn't bring cut flowers because they need more looking after. And I apologize that it's a poinsettia but the shops seem to be full of them, and not much else. It's the time of the year, I suppose. Coming up to Christmas.'

'Please don't apologize,' Frances said. 'My mother will love it, and it will certainly brighten up her room. Would you like to go up and see her? I know she'd enjoy that. She's getting a bit bored.' She broke off, laughing. 'Oh dear, that sounds rude,' she said. 'Of course she'd like to see you, whether she was bored or not.'

'OK,' Alec said. 'And at the same time I'll look at how the work's getting on.'

He stayed with Madge for a while – she was delighted with the plant and no less by his visit – and then with Frances he inspected the rooms his men had been working on. 'It all looks fine to me,' he said. 'Are you happy with it?'

'Absolutely,' Frances said. 'And I can't wait to see it finished.'

'It won't take much longer now,' Alec said. 'They'll be through before Christmas. How's the rest of it going?'

'Quite well,' Frances told him. 'But I'm taking a little break while my mother's not well. I was about to start sorting out the little room – that's what I call it; it's really something of a junk room right now.'

'What's in it?' Alec enquired.

'I hardly know. It seems to me that everything was shoved in there when the rest of the house was cleared, though of course I don't know that. I'd say there'll be a lot of stuff to get rid of – give away or whatever. I'll probably ask your advice on how to set about that. But not until after Christmas. I want to concentrate on getting my mother better. Our first Christmas here. She'd be so disappointed if she wasn't well enough to take part in the festivities, whatever they are.'

'Well, bear in mind that if it's not convenient you can scrub having me and the boys here on Boxing Day,' Alec said. 'I don't want to give you any trouble.'

'Oh, but we *want* you to come,' Frances said. 'My mother would be very disappointed if you didn't, and so would I. In fact, I've decided that I do actually like children when they're like yours, at the age when I can talk to them – and they'll talk to me. I've never experienced that before, you see, having no brothers and sisters and therefore no nieces and nephews.'

'Good,' Alec said. 'And they're certainly looking forward to coming here.'

'I must think about Christmas presents,' Frances said. 'I don't have a clue. And I reckon I'll have to go into Shepton to get them. Anyway, do you have time to stay for a drink?'

'Why not?' he said. 'Thank you.'

'Would you mind if we sat in the kitchen?' she asked. 'It's warmer than anywhere else.'

'I'd prefer the kitchen,' he said.

They found a lot to talk about, and for once, she thought, it was nice to have him to herself. Mostly she seemed to have shared him with her mother. And then she reproved herself for the thought, though without quite relinquishing it.

'I've done quite a bit in the garden these last few weeks,' she said. 'But not this week because it's been too cold. And I don't suppose there'll be much more I can do with the winter coming on.'

'I could give you a hand when you start up again,' Alec

offered. 'My garden's about the size of a handkerchief. It takes up no time at all. Oh, and by the way, I came across someone who knows what to do about apple trees. He says that they're best pruned when they're dormant – that's to say in the winter or the very early spring. If you want to get the best fruit, that is.'

'Well, mine certainly needs pruning,' Frances said. 'Even I can tell that. And yes, I would like to have good fruit. Does he do it for other people?'

'Not that I know of,' Alec said. 'But I'm sure he'd come and advise you. And I'd help you to do it.'

'Wonderful,' Frances said. 'In the New Year, then?'

They continued to talk about this and that, nothing of world-wide importance, but it was relaxing and enjoyable. In the end he looked at his watch and said, 'I must go. I'm keeping you from whatever you had in mind to do, or whatever you wanted to do for your mother.'

Frances laughed. 'I think Mother must have fallen asleep,' she said. She was sure if she hadn't she'd have been ringing the bell, curious to know what was going on.

She saw Alec to the door. It was a perfect winter's evening; the sky a dark navy-blue, but starlit; the air still frosty. 'Don't stand here,' Alec said. 'It's far too cold.'

Nevertheless she watched until he got into his car and drove away.

A day or two later Dr Fortune said that Madge could get up. 'But not for long; not for a whole day at a time,' he counselled. 'An hour or two at first and then, if it goes well, a little longer each day. It's not thought a good idea, these days, to stay in bed too long.'

'I'll be mighty pleased to be up and doing,' Madge assured him. 'I'm not one for lying in bed – and I do feel a lot better.'

'Up,' he said, 'but not so much of the doing. You must take it easy. You're not a young woman, Mrs Fraser, and I don't doubt you've worked hard all your life.'

Madge nodded. 'Indeed I have,' she said.

But when Frances was seeing him to the door he said, 'Keep an eye on her. She *is* much better, her chest is OK, but I'm not totally happy about her heart. As I told you before, I think early in the New Year she should go and have a second opinion.'

'Oh dear,' Frances said. 'Ought she really to go right away?'

'No,' he said. 'I think she should get over the flu first.'

Madge continued to improve, though slowly, until in the end she seemed almost herself again. Even so, Frances kept a careful eye on her, watching that she didn't go beyond her strength. Christmas was almost upon them, so they discussed what they would do.

'I'd like to go down to the Shorn Lamb fairly soon,' Madge said. 'I haven't been for ages. I miss seeing people.'

'If you feel like it, and if you're well enough, we'll go down tomorrow evening,' Frances promised. 'But I won't let you walk. I'll take you in the car.'

They discussed what they would do on Boxing Day when Alec came with the boys; what they would have to eat, what they would do to entertain them. 'My opinion is that we should buy as much of the food as we can, not spend ages cooking it,' Frances said. 'Children usually like mass-produced stuff better than homemade. I know I did when I was little.'

Madge looked shocked. 'You never said so!'

'Oh, I don't mean you didn't make nice things,' Frances said. 'But when they came from one of the big shops . . .'

'Which they seldom did,' Madge said defensively.

'I know. That's why shop things seemed more exotic. They were fancier. Pink icing, little silver balls. Anyway, I don't want you standing on your feet making cakes and trifles and the like. As for the entertainment, I'll buy one or two games we can all play – whatever's the rage – and a couple of videos. That should be quite enough. It's only one day!'

'Whatever you say,' Madge agreed. She gave in very easily.

'The thing is, I shall need to go to Shepton,' Frances said. 'Will you be all right if I leave you? I don't think you should attempt to come with me. It will be very busy and tiring, and the weather's cold.'

'I'd rather not go with you,' Madge admitted. 'And I'll be perfectly all right here. What are you going to buy for the boys?'

'I haven't a clue,' Frances said. 'And I don't suppose you have any ideas, do you?'

'I'm afraid I don't,' Madge admitted. 'There's so much choice, isn't there? I wouldn't know where to begin. And worse still, you have to know what's in fashion.'

'You're right,' Frances agreed. 'It's so difficult.'

'In my opinion, and for what it's worth,' Madge continued, 'children of that age almost always prefer to have money. Then they can go shopping in the school holidays and have a spending spree.'

'I don't want to seem as though I haven't given it any thought,' Frances said. She didn't want Alec to think that either.

'You won't,' Madge told her. 'I'm not suggesting you just push a fiver each into their hands. Give them something else – a box of sweets or something – with the money attached. And you must let me join in as well. That way they should get a nice present each.'

'I expect you're right,' Frances said.

'And what about Alec?' Madge asked. 'Should we give him something?'

'Oh, I don't think so,' Frances said, though doubtfully. 'I wouldn't want to embarrass him.'

The weather was kinder the following evening, not quite as cold as it had been. Frances was pleased to find a parking space immediately outside the Shorn Lamb. When the two of them walked into the pub they were given a surprisingly warm welcome and, although the bar was busy, a place was immediately found for them to sit, well away from the door. The room was awash with decorations: paper chains, the mirrors framed in tinsel, and a tall Christmas tree, hung with baubles.

'We heard you weren't well, Mrs Fraser,' Bernard Grayson said. 'It's nice to see you up and about again. What would you like to drink?'

'Thank you,' Madge said. 'I'd like a sherry. It's nice to be here, I must say, though Frances says we mustn't stay long. She makes me go to bed early.'

It was an altogether pleasant evening. Both women, as they

relaxed in the company, realized how much they had missed it. Alec came in soon after Frances and her mother had arrived, and he joined them.

'Mother and I were talking about Christmas earlier,' Frances said to him, 'among other things. And about what the boys might like for presents. I'm ashamed to say I just don't know, and it's so easy to give the wrong thing, but my mother thought money would be acceptable.'

'Your mother is quite right,' Alec said. 'Not that they'll be expecting presents, but there's nothing they'd appreciate more than money. They always have something in mind they want to do with it and since they don't get a lot of pocket money saving up isn't easy.'

'I'll find something small to go with it,' Frances said, 'when I get to Shepton – which I must do very soon. I don't like to leave my mother for too long but she swears she'll be all right.'

'If you can go tomorrow – ' Alec said, 'I mean, if your mother can spare you – perhaps we could have a quick lunch when you've finished shopping? The men will be at your place, so they'd keep an eye open for her.'

'That would be lovely,' Frances agreed. 'And of course Violet will be in tomorrow.' Daisy seemed to have got over, at least for the time being, her teething troubles. They had resulted in one small pearly white tooth, her first, on the bottom row. 'But I will have to see how my mother is in the morning.'

'Give me a ring,' Alec said. 'And don't worry about parking. It's hellish busy in Shepton at this time of the year so I'll save you a space in my yard.'

'Thank you,' Frances said. 'That would help. And now I think I should take my mother home. She won't want to go but I think she should.'

'I certainly don't want to go,' Madge protested. 'I'm enjoying myself. But I'll go quietly if you'll promise we can come in again on Christmas Eve.'

'Oh, you *must* come then,' Joseph Clark said. 'That's when we have the carol singers in.'

'We will,' Frances promised. 'As long as my mother behaves herself between now and then.'

She *was* able to go to Shepton the next morning. She gave her mother breakfast in bed, left a cold lunch on a tray, and extracted a promise from her that if she needed any help in getting up she would call on Violet.

'Of course I won't need any help,' Madge protested. 'Don't fuss! And don't hurry back.'

With only three days to go before Christmas Shepton was, as Alec had warned her it would be, ferociously busy, but the shopping went well. She bought the kind of food – and quite likely too much of it – that would keep over the holiday, or go in the freezer, and need very little preparation or cooking. The man in the toyshop, which was like an Aladdin's cave, advised her on the games that were suitable for five people with an age range from five years to seventy-three, and at the same time were in fashion, must-haves. For her mother, in Shepton's best department store she bought a lambswool cardigan and a bottle of perfume, and on a last-minute impulse she bought a small pocket diary to give to Alec. It was nice, but not too personal. Her last call was at the bank to draw out cash, where she persuaded the clerk to give her brand-new bank notes. Much nicer for the boys, she thought, than something soiled and crumpled.

After that she went back to Alec's showrooms, off-loaded her shopping into her car, and he took her to lunch in the Heifer. 'I booked a table,' he said. 'I thought you wouldn't want to be hanging around too long – I mean because of your mother.'

'I don't,' Frances agreed. 'Though I'm pretty sure she'll be all right. In fact, she might like to have me out of the way for a bit. We have been under each other's feet for a while.'

He looked at the menu. 'They're serving Christmas lunches,' he said. 'I expect they'll be doing that all this week. Is that the kind of thing you'd like?'

'I'd sooner have something lighter,' Frances admitted. 'I do like the Christmas stuff, but not too long beforehand.'

He agreed. They both chose fish pie. Tucking into it, they didn't talk much, but the silence was a comfortable one. When lunch was over – they didn't linger: she was anxious to get home and he had appointments with customers – he took her back to her car.

'Thank you very much,' Frances said. 'I really enjoyed that.'

'So did I,' Alec said. 'Shall I see you in the Lamb on Christmas Eve?'

'Oh, I really do hope so,' Frances said. 'It depends on my mother, of course.'

They arrived at the Shorn Lamb in good time on Christmas Eve, knowing it would be busy – as indeed it was. Half the village seemed to be there; certainly people she'd not seen before. Delicious mince pies and sausage rolls, courtesy of Joyce, were served with the first drinks.

'Make a wish,' Madge said. 'Always make a wish with the first mince pie.'

The carol singers arrived an hour later, together with the vicar and the church organist, the latter to accompany them on the piano.

'Laura couldn't come,' the vicar apologized. 'You know how it is. Christmas Eve, and the children all excited. But she sends you all her best wishes.'

They sang all the old, familiar carols, everyone joining in. A collection was taken. 'Not for the church, for once,' Clive said. 'On Christmas Eve, as most of you know, we collect for the homeless. So please give generously.'

Bernard served drinks and mince pies to all the singers and then they left. 'We have several visits to make,' Clive said. Then, straight-faced, he said, 'I do hope I'll see you all in church tomorrow!'

'Well, he will me,' Madge said when he had left. 'That is, if I can get there.'

'I'll take you,' Frances said. 'In fact, as it's Christmas I might even go with you.'

They stayed until almost ten o'clock, by which time Madge was flagging. 'We must go,' Frances said.

Alec saw them out to the car. 'We'll see you on Boxing Day,' he said. 'What time shall we come?'

296

'We'll eat about one,' Frances said. 'But come as early as you like.'

Much to the pleasure of her mother, Frances not only took her to church next morning, but went in with her. There was a good congregation, though not so many as had crowded into the Shorn Lamb on the previous evening. Afterwards, on the way out, people gathered in small knots and it was obvious from the number who called out greetings to Madge that she had already made friends with several, one or two of whom Frances also recognized.

Walking back through the churchyard her eye was caught by a grave, close to the path, on which a wreath of holly and Christmas roses had been laid. On an impulse – she wasn't sure what inspired it but perhaps the white flowers against the green leaves and red berries made it stand out – she paused, and looked closer. There was a card on the wreath. 'To darling Moira,' it said, 'With all love from Joyce. Never forgotten.'

'That will be Joyce Grayson,' Madge said. 'They say she puts fresh flowers on this grave every week – all the year round.'

'Ben Thornton, husband of the above,' the headstone said beneath Moira's name, but there were no flowers to him.

Boxing Day went exceptionally well. The boys were delighted with their presents – ten pounds each – as was Alec with his more modest one. 'I get trade diaries often enough from suppliers,' he said, 'but never anything small enough, or personal enough, to carry round with me.' He gave Madge a box of expensive soaps, and to Frances, to her great surprise and delight, he gave a leather-bound copy of Shakespeare's sonnets.

'This is wonderful,' she said. 'How could you possibly know it was exactly what I would like?'

They stayed late, playing the games and then watching the video. The boys were half asleep, but complained when Alec insisted that they must leave. Madge, though she had thoroughly enjoyed her day and had refused to go to bed early, was by this time looking worn out.

'We've stayed too long,' Alec said.

'Not at all,' Frances told him. 'We've all enjoyed it.'

'Then I hope you have a nice, quiet day tomorrow,' he said.

'Tomorrow,' Frances told him firmly, 'I shall brave the sales. And after that I shall tackle the little room!'

TWENTY-FIVE

'Do you have to do it today?' Madge asked. 'Can't you give yourself another day's holiday?'

'I can, but I won't,' Frances said. 'I made up my mind I'd start on the little room the minute Christmas was over and I'm going to stick to that. I don't want to do it at all, but the longer I leave it, the less I'll want to do it.'

'You'll be cold,' Madge warned.

'There's a portable radiator in one of the rooms. I'll plug that in,' Frances said. 'And I'll wear warm clothes.'

'Well, I'll give you a hand,' Madge offered.

'You will do no such thing,' Frances said firmly. 'It's not fit for you. And in any case it's a job I'd rather do on my own.'

'You're very obstinate when you make up your mind,' Madge complained.

'And I wonder who I get that from?' Frances answered.

Where do I start? Frances asked herself. Where in the world do I start? The room had clearly served as a substitute for an attic: everything had been piled in there until some later, indefinite date when it might (or might not) come in useful.

From a glance, the six-drawer mahogany chest struck Frances as being the only decent piece of furniture in the room. She had marked it out as something she could use, but it couldn't be

299

moved until one of the guest bedrooms was ready to take it, and in any case she would need to go through the drawers. There was a shabby oak, two-door cupboard, about four feet high, and a single wardrobe and a bureau. Goodness knew what they contained. And bang in the middle of the room there was a square, deal table, which might once have lived in the kitchen before that had been fitted with matching units. There were also two, non-matching, upright wooden chairs that had seen better days.

The surface of the table was covered – there was hardly an inch to spare – with all manner of odds and ends: a matching jug and basin set with a floral design, two willow-pattern ginger jars, a tureen without a lid, a small table lamp, various boxes . . . She stopped counting. A shelf against the right-hand wall held a dozen or so shabby-looking books, a couple of which looked like ledgers. They might be interesting when she got around to them.

Frances began by clearing the top of the table, putting everything in three piles on the floor in the furthest corner – the only space available. The first, a heap of things to be thrown out; the second, a heap of things that could be used elsewhere – the table lamp, for instance, could go in one of the guest bedrooms; and the third group was of items about which, as yet, she couldn't make up her mind. A few of them might be saleable on the second-hand stall in Shepton market. This third group was by far the largest.

She had just about cleared the table top when her mother brought her a mug of coffee. Madge stood in the doorway, her eyes alight with curiosity. 'Are you sure you don't need a hand, love?' she asked.

'Quite sure,' Frances said. 'And you mustn't stay here. It *is* cold, and by the time I've moved a few more things it's going to be dusty. It will do your chest no good at all.'

Madge left reluctantly. 'I'll come up and tell you when your lunch is ready,' she said.

'Don't do any such thing,' Frances ordered. 'Just give me a shout or ring your bell if you prefer to. This is forbidden territory at the moment.'

She drank the coffee, then looked round again. What next?

She decided on the two-door cupboard. It was a shabby old thing. Once she had sorted out the contents it could probably go into one of the outhouses to await its fate – which she judged might well be a bonfire.

The cupboard was locked but the key was still in the keyhole. When she opened it, it was at once clear that it had been kept locked to prevent the contents bursting open the doors and falling out, which two drawing pads immediately did, tumbling to the floor at her feet. The upper half of the cupboard – it was divided by one shelf across the middle – was crammed, mostly with papers, pads, artists' materials of every kind. She stooped to pick up the two pads that had fallen to the floor, and at the same time glanced at the bottom half of the cupboard. She could hardly believe her eyes. There were no papers, books and drawing pads there. The space was completely filled, crammed, with woodcarvings, heaped high, one on top of the other, higgledy-piggledy. Looking at the crude disorder she had the feeling that as soon as each piece had been completed it had been added to the pile, as if, once carved, there was no further use for it. The act of carving had served its purpose.

She stretched out her hand and indiscriminately picked up the nearest one. It was a life-size model of a very small bird. At least, she assumed it was life-sized; she knew very little about birds, but she thought it might be a wren. Its perky tail stood up almost vertically to its round body; its head was held at a jaunty angle. In spite of the fact that it was carved from a dullish brown wood it looked totally alive, as if at any moment it might burst into song, or even fly away. It was perfection; it was exquisite. She cupped it in one hand and stroked it gently with the other as if it was indeed alive, as if to hold it too tightly might do it harm; and then she took it to the table and deposited it there before going back to the cupboard.

There were animals as well as birds, mostly small, many of which she did not recognize. There was a mouse, three inches long, so lifelike that as she put it down on the table she almost expected it to scamper away. There was a kitten, much smaller than life size, that looked at her as though begging for a saucer of milk. There was a hedgehog, not curled into a ball but showing its feet, and its small nose held near the ground. There was a squirrel, sitting on its haunches, cracking a hazelnut.

One by one she took the carvings out of the cupboard and laid them carefully on the table, until the bottom part of the cupboard was empty and the table top full. She was still contemplating them, wondering what she would do, when her mother's voice floated up the staircase.

'It's lunchtime! Don't let it get cold!'

Frances went to the top of the stairs and shouted down, 'I'm coming right away.' She had no clear idea why, but she knew that she didn't want her mother to come upstairs and see the carvings. Not yet. She would have to see them in the end, but at the moment they seemed too intimate. It was as if Ben Thornton was still in the room and she couldn't bear anyone to disturb him. She left, closing the door behind her, and went downstairs.

When she went back to the room after lunch, leaving her mother to have an afternoon nap in the armchair by the fire, Frances still had no idea what to do about the carvings. She couldn't just do nothing – that would be terrible: they were works of art. Nor could she hang on to them, secure in the theory that finders were keepers and that she had, after all, bought the house and such few contents as had been left in it. She had an overwhelming desire to know when Ben Thornton had done these carvings and, even more, why he had put them out of sight, piled in an old cupboard. There was not a single example of his work on display anywhere in the house.

She turned away from the carvings and went back to the cupboard. The top shelf was still packed with exercise books, papers, drawing pads large and small and – when she looked further – with pencils, sticks of charcoal, tubes of water colour paints, and an assortment of knives of different sizes and shapes, which she took to be woodcarving tools.

She picked up the two pads that had fallen to the floor when she'd first opened the cupboard, chose another large one and a couple of smaller ones, and sat down on one of the two chairs to examine them. Every page was filled with drawings of birds – lapwing, snipe, pheasant, black grouse, song thrush, more than she could ever have seen or would have recognized – and mammals, probably, she thought, all native to the Dales. So finely drawn, everything seemed to have been done from close observation. They were mostly in pen or in charcoal, and almost all of them were annotated. 'A vixen with cubs'; 'An otter by the river Cor'; 'Dog fox – not easy to draw, wouldn't keep still'; 'A badger – I sat up all night to get this!'; 'A foal – its mother kept a sharp eye on me'; 'A barn owl at dusk'; 'Red squirrel. Not so many of them about these days. The greys have taken over'. And then, amid the almost crowded black-and-white drawings, a painting on a page to itself. It was a watercolour of a kingfisher, its brightness singing out from the page: brilliant blue-green plumage, orange breast, white throat. 'Seen on the river Skirfare in Littondale', was written underneath it. And, further down the page and clearly added later in a different coloured ink, 'She was like a kingfisher. All beauty, all colour. Darting swiftly. Here one minute and flown the next. But what would a kingfisher want with a house sparrow?'

There were many others; a weasel, a stoat, a cat with a mouse in its paws. The dates written against them showed that Ben had made the drawings in the larger pads over several years. In the smaller book, the one that contained the kingfisher, all the dates were in the year he had died. With the exception of the kingfisher, everything in that book was black or grey. There was no colour. She recognized from the drawings, and comparing them with the carvings, that many of the latter had also been made in that year. It was the period soon after Moira died and the time when Lottie came suddenly into his life, and as quickly left it. It required very little imagination to think of him, sitting in this room, carving, carving, carving, whittling away the terrible time, and then discarding, burying the results in the cupboard.

Frances knew she would have to do something about her find, but she didn't know whom to ask for advice. Would Joseph Clark have any idea? Would Malachi Flint? He seemed to know about Ben Thornton's woodcarving. It was while she was thinking, but not reaching any conclusion, that the phone rang. It was Alec, wishing to speak to one of his workmen.

'I'll get him for you,' she said, 'but before I do, can I ask you about something?' She told him about her discoveries. 'I'm not the best judge,' she said, 'but I think they're rather special. When you have a moment, would you come and look at them?'

'I'd be glad to,' Alec said. 'Though I don't know that I'm qualified to judge them either. I could drop in on my way home.'

In the middle of the afternoon Madge came upstairs, bringing a cup of tea and a buttered scone. There was no question of her not seeing the carvings: they were there in front of her, on the table, as she came into the room. There was also no reason why she should not see them. It had just been that in the first hour of her discovery, and especially as she looked at the drawings and read the comments in the book, Frances had felt too much emotion to show them to anyone.

'Goodness gracious me!' Madge said. 'Wherever did you find these?'

'In that cupboard,' Frances said, pointing. 'They're rather fine, aren't they? I'll have to decide what to do with them, and I don't know. Alec is going to call in on his way home and take a look at them. But until I work out what's to be done I think we'll keep quiet, don't you?'

'Oh, I shan't say a word,' Madge said. 'You can rely on me. Do you think they might be worth a bit of money?'

'I hadn't got as far as thinking about that,' Frances said. 'But I certainly don't think they should be hidden away in a cupboard.'

'They could do with dusting,' Madge observed. 'Shall I make a start?'

'No,' Frances said. 'Let's just leave them where they are for the time being.' Some of them were so delicate, so finely carved, that anything other than the most careful handling might damage them. For instance, the long, thin beak of what she now knew from the drawings to be a snipe looked as though it might snap off as easily as breaking a matchstick. It was a miracle that some of them had survived so long in the crowded cupboard.

On the point of leaving the room Madge turned round. 'Don't you think you've done enough for one day, love?' she asked.

'No,' Frances said. 'There are just one or two more things

before I'll call it a day.' She could happily have spent the rest of the afternoon examining the carvings, and the drawings, more closely, but she mustn't allow herself to do that. She looked round the room. There was still the six-drawer chest, and in one corner the narrow, single wardrobe which she hadn't given much thought to. The chest would be a marathon job – every drawer to sort and clean – and where would she put anything until the table was cleared of the carvings? Best wait until tomorrow. On the other hand, the wardrobe was too small to contain much.

It was locked. She searched around and in the top drawer of the chest she found a key that fitted. She turned the key and opened the door.

There were only two garments in the wardrobe, two garments and a pair of shoes. On the first hanger was a cream linen suit. It looked brand-new, she thought. Behind it on the second hanger was an evening dress. It was a glowing, rich red, with a heart-shaped neckline, cut low. The skirt, narrow to a point halfway down its length, then flared out and fell in folds to the floor. It, too, looked completely new. Whose were they? Why had they been left here?

The answer to the first question was quickly obvious. They could only have been Lottie's. From what she had heard of Moira, neither of these would have been her style. But Lottie's – yes! Frances was immediately reminded of what Ben had written about Lottie in relation to the kingfisher. Not that he had used Lottie's name, but Frances was left in no doubt.

She picked up one of the cream leather shoes. So beautiful, so delicate and flimsy. The slender heels must have been four inches high. How could anyone walk in them, especially in the Dales? Common sense told her they must have been bought for a special occasion in which walking was not involved. But who could she ask? She had found very little empathy with Lottie in Kilby, especially amongst the women. And why, when she'd left Beck Farm, had Lottie also left these particular garments behind? Why had Ben kept them in the wardrobe, not given them away?

Alice, she thought, might have known the answer, but Alice was in Australia and, judging by the brief message pinned up in the Shorn Lamb, was not thinking of returning. It seemed an insoluble puzzle. There was something so intimate about the clothes – and by now she felt she had developed some kind of intimacy with both Lottie and Ben – that she could not possibly drag her discoveries into an area where they would be subject to conjecture or gossip. For the moment, though her mother had already seen the carvings, Frances knew she couldn't tell her about the clothes.

She closed the wardrobe door, locked it, and put the key in her pocket. She would do nothing more. Lottie must have made a deliberate choice to leave the garments there and Ben would almost certainly have found them, but, whatever the explanation, she would keep the secret.

She turned her attention to the bureau. Again, it was locked, but among the bundle of keys she was beginning to accumulate from different places in the house she found one that fitted. The pigeonholes held a conglomeration of paid bills, business correspondence and letters that appeared to have come from past visitors to Beck Farm. Among them, not particularly tucked away, was an envelope addressed to Ben. It had already been opened and, though not without a sense of guilt, Frances took out the contents. It was a letter, signed with the name 'Dulcie'. Feeling even more guilty, she read it. It was clearly in answer to one received by the writer from Ben Thornton.

Dear Ben,
Thank you for sending me the lovely carved bird. It did remind me of Lottie. So graceful – and somehow like Lottie in that it was poised for flight.

Don't be too hard on her. I know she was selfish but she had been totally spoilt by her mother, who gave her everything she wanted, and after her mother died she never seemed to be able to settle down in one place.

I know you loved her, too well perhaps, and I know she was fond of you in the beginning. She didn't marry you for what she could get, so please believe that.

It's sad that she left behind her wedding outfit –
that was such a happy day, wasn't it?

And the lovely red dress she wore to the Farmers'
Ball. I remember going with her to choose it. You
must get rid of them, like you've done with the rest. If
I were there I'd do it for you.

I don't know what else to say, Ben. I'm no good at
letter-writing. This is the longest I've ever written.

Please don't think too badly of her. Whatever she
did wrong she paid for it in the end.

Yours truly,
Dulcie

Frances folded the letter, put it back in the envelope and
returned it to the desk. What she would do with it she didn't
know, but she hadn't changed her mind about keeping the
clothes where Lottie had left them.

Frances was in the kitchen with her mother when Alec arrived.
Without asking, Madge poured him a cup of tea, which he
accepted.

'Bring it upstairs with you and I'll show you the carvings,'
Frances said.

He gasped when he saw them. 'These are absolutely beautiful!'
he said. 'Wonderful! I had no idea . . . Of course, I'd heard
that Ben Thornton was good at woodcarving. I reckon my
mother must have told me. She knew him – though I didn't –
very well. But I had no idea . . .' He repeated himself, shaking
his head in wonder as his eyes ranged over the display on the
table.

Frances nodded in agreement. 'They *are* quite something,
aren't they? And it wasn't only the carving he was good at. These
pads and notebooks have detailed drawings of almost all the
carvings, and notes about the animals and birds. And there is this
beautiful watercolour.' She showed him the painting of the
kingfisher.

'That is superb,' Alec said.

'I thought so. But what am I to do with them? As far as I can make out there's no-one left in Ben Thornton's family. And I can't just keep them, can I?'

'I suppose legally you could,' Alec said. 'Though I'm not sure. You'd have to find out about that.'

'In any case I don't think that would be right,' Frances said doubtfully. 'OK, I could give a few to his friends, people who knew him, but I do actually think they should be seen by a wider public.'

'Oh, I agree,' Alec said. 'And I wonder . . .' He hesitated.

'What?' Frances prompted him.

'Well, there is a Dales museum. They have terrific displays, temporary and permanent, of all kinds of things to do with Dales life – and especially with Cordale. They might like to have them, including the drawings, of course.'

'Yes,' Frances agreed. 'That would seem to be exactly right.'

'Then, suppose I were to take you there with a selection of the carvings and all the drawings? We could see what they thought.'

'That would be wonderful,' Frances said.

'Shall we say next Monday?' Alec suggested. 'I'm busy the rest of this week but Monday would be fine.'

'It's very good of you,' Frances said.

Alec shook his head. 'No, it's not. It'll be a pleasure. Perhaps we could make a day of it?'

'I'd like that,' Frances said.

When they went back downstairs Madge said, 'Will you stay for supper? There's a beef casserole in the oven. You'd be very welcome.'

'I'd like to,' Alec said, 'but I can't. I've brought a load of work home with me.'

Frances went out with him to his car.

'Your mother looks tired,' he said. 'Is she all right?'

'I hope so,' Frances said. 'The flu took a lot out of her. She's to see a cardiologist in Shepton next week, so let's hope that will be good news.'

After Alec left, before supper was quite ready Frances went back to the little room. She looked again at the carvings. It would not be easy to let them go but if the museum would accept them, that would be a good solution. One thing she knew, though: she would not part with the painting of the kingfisher. That she would keep to herself. It spoke to her with a particular poignancy. She would have it framed and would hang it in the house. Ben, she felt sure, would not begrudge her that.

She had not been able to bring herself to tell Alec about the garments in the wardrobe. One day she would, though not yet. She doubted if she would ever bring herself to get rid of them.

Her mother's voice floated up the stairs. 'Supper's ready, love.'

'I'll be right down,' Frances said.

TWENTY-SIX

In the second week of January the weather turned colder. The temperature dropped suddenly. There had been three or four particularly pleasant days; sunny, and with very little wind. It was on one of those days that Alec had taken a day off work to drive Frances to the Dales Museum. She had packed a large box with a selection of carvings, all carefully wrapped in newspaper, and the notes and drawings in a carrier bag. Almost at the last minute Alec surprised her by saying, 'Why don't we take your mother? It would be an outing for her. She hasn't been out much lately, has she?'

'No further than church,' Frances said. 'It's a very kind thought, but are you sure?' Inwardly she was a little disappointed at the idea. She had looked forward to spending the whole day with him. Then she chided herself that Alec, and not she, had been the thoughtful one.

'Of course I'm sure,' he said. 'It might do her good to get out. And the museum's an interesting place.'

Madge was delighted to be asked, but to Frances's surprise – and almost to her shame – her mother declined the invitation. 'Another time,' she said. 'I've got a few little jobs to do. And to tell you the truth, I'm a wee bit tired. You don't mind, do you?'

'Of course not,' Frances said. 'But I don't want you rushing around doing things.'

'Oh, I won't,' Madge promised. 'Just a few odds and ends. I'll make myself a bit of lunch, and this afternoon I'll sit by the fire and read. I'm in the middle of a very interesting book.' She had never really been a reader, or only of magazines and the more gossipy bits of the newspapers, but since her illness she'd really taken to it, and discovered that what she liked best were crime novels. Ruth Rendell, P. D. James, Elizabeth George. 'And all written by women,' she said to Frances. 'Women are so clever these days.' It was a funny taste to discover at her time of life, she thought, but better late than never, and now she couldn't get enough of them.

'All right then, if that's what you want,' Frances said. 'And we shan't be all that long. We'll be back before it drops dark.'

The staff of the museum were delighted, and very impressed, by the carvings and the drawings. 'I like this little water vole,' the curator said. 'And the wood mouse. Just look at those pointy ears standing up! So lifelike – you would think he was listening to us. We had no idea that Mr Thornton did anything like this. Of course we knew him. He came in and looked round from time to time, but he was a quiet man, he didn't say much.' He broke off, smiling at Frances. 'But you knew that, of course.'

'Not really,' Frances said. 'He died before I came to the Dales.' But she felt that she did know him. She felt that she knew him more intimately than she did some people she'd been acquainted with all her life.

'I'm afraid we couldn't afford to buy them from you,' the curator said. 'We've spent all our budget for this year – which isn't a great deal anyway.'

'Oh, there's no question of that,' Frances said at once. 'In fact I don't know whether they're rightly mine to sell. What I thought was that you might have them on permanent loan. That way, if anyone turns up with a claim to them they'll be available. Not that I think that's likely.'

Before they left the museum, arrangements were made for the curator to come with his small van to pick up the rest of the carvings from the house. 'There are quite a few more,' Frances said. 'But I would like to give one each to the friends who knew him.' Joseph Clark, she thought, and Harry Foster. The Laycocks. Bernard Grayson – but not Joyce, of course. That wouldn't do at all! Perhaps Jim Kettle. She would ask around for advice. And Malachi Flint. He had spoken with so much admiration of Ben's work.

They went for lunch at a pub within walking distance of the museum. 'A job well done,' Alec said as they sat at the table. 'Are you pleased?'

'Very well pleased,' Frances said. 'And thank you for bringing me. I'm truly grateful.'

'It was a pleasure for me,' Alec said. 'But you must know that.'

She smiled at him. 'And for me too. And I expect *you* know that.' She was always so happy with him. She saw no reason to hide it.

Dusk was dropping as they arrived back at Beckside House. True to her promise, Madge was deep in her book and the fire was blazing. 'I've had a nice little sleep,' she said. 'Shall I make a pot of tea?'

'No,' Frances said. 'Stay where you are. I'll do it.'

Alec followed her into the kitchen. 'I wondered', he said, 'if your mother might like to go down to the Shorn Lamb this evening? We can go early. If she wraps up well she won't come to any harm, will she?'

'I don't think so,' Frances said. 'And she'd love it.'

'Right, so I'll have a cup of tea with you, shoot back home, then see you in the Lamb – shall we say half-past seven?'

'Fine,' Frances said. 'But you needn't go home first. You could stay and eat with us. My mother always cooks enough for at least one extra. She can't seem to get out of the habit.'

'Thanks, but I won't,' Alec said. 'I have a few things to do.'

'I know you're a busy man,' Frances said. 'It was good of you to give up the whole of today.'

'Don't be silly!' Alec said.

There was no doubt that Madge enjoyed her evening, but by half-past eight she was flagging, tired, ready to go home.

'I'm sorry, love,' she said. 'It's not like me. I used to be able to stay up half the night and not feel it. Your dad found that annoying. He was an early-to-bed man.'

'That's all right,' Frances said. 'I'm a bit tired myself. An early night will do us both good.' It was not true that she was tired. She could happily have stayed where she was until closing time or beyond.

Alec saw them to the car and Frances drove home. 'I'll ring you in the morning,' he said.

'I'll fill a hot-water bottle for you and bring you a cup of Bovril to bed,' Frances said to her mother.

Madge was undressed and in bed when Frances brought the Bovril, and two cream crackers. She shook up her mother's pillows and sat with her while she sipped at her drink.

'This will do the trick,' Madge said between sips. 'You know, love, I do like being here. I'll admit now, I wasn't sure about coming. It seemed such a long way – even though Yorkshire is where I come from. But I haven't regretted a minute of it. It's been lovely. I'll just be glad when winter's over and spring comes.'

'We all will,' Frances said. 'And it won't be very long, now that we've turned the year.'

She waited until her mother had finished the Bovril – she didn't want the biscuits. 'Now have a good night's sleep,' she said, 'and don't try to get up early in the morning. There's no need to. So goodnight, love.' She gave her mother a hug and a kiss, and left her.

Twice during the night she looked in on Madge, and each time she was sleeping. She looked rested, Frances thought.

But there was to be no getting up in the morning for Madge. There was to be no spring for her to look forward to, at least not in Kilby. 'She died in her sleep,' Dr Fortune said when he came. 'She would have had no pain. It was a wonderful way for her to go.'

'I know! I know!' Frances cried. The tears poured down her cheeks. 'But I wasn't ready for her to go. I wasn't ready.'

'*She* was ready,' Dr Fortune said. 'If she had gone to see the consultant next week he would have warned her of this. She

313

might have been told that she must live a quiet life, constrained – which wouldn't have suited her, from what I've seen of your mother. As it has happened, she's been spared the pain and discomfort that goes with the condition.'

'Would it have been different if she'd seen the consultant sooner?' Frances asked.

'I doubt it,' Dr Fortune said. 'I know it's hard for you, but you couldn't have wished for anything better for your mother. And now I must do something for you,' he added. 'I shall pour you a drink, and if you'll give me a number I'll phone a friend. Who will it be?'

Alec, she thought. Who else but Alec?

Madge was buried in the churchyard. Clive conducted the funeral and gave the short eulogy. 'Madge wasn't in our community long,' he concluded, 'but she quickly became one of us.'

'There is nothing', Frances said to Alec as they left, 'that my mother would've more liked to have been said.'

It was no more than coincidence – simply a case of where there was room – that Madge's grave was very close to Moira's and Ben's. She would have liked that also. After all, they had lived in the same house.

In the days that followed after Frances had returned to a Beckside House which would never seem exactly the same again – though she faced it honestly: her mother had sometimes been an irritant – she felt almost as though she had lost a limb. At times, especially when she lay awake in the early hours of the morning, she questioned whether she should be there at all. Should she have stuck it out in Brighton? But she always came back to the same answer: her mother had loved it here in Kilby. She had said so explicitly on that last night of her life. And if we had not come here, Frances thought, I would never have met Alec. So I shall stay here.

The resolve to do so was strengthened a hundredfold in the week after the funeral. In the post were letters from two families requesting bookings to stay in the summer. Both, in their own way, said the same thing. 'We have not been to the Yorkshire

Dales before, but we have heard about them. So we look forward to coming.'

She had shown the letters to Alec and he had been positive she should agree to accept them – and any other requests that came. 'As I'm sure they will,' he'd said. 'In any case,' he added sensibly, 'you've done so much in the house, almost all of it with the idea of visitors in mind. You can't just drop the B&B plans.'

'You're right,' Frances said. 'And what would I do, rattling around in this large house?'

He was right, too, about other bookings following. Before long all the rooms were let from the spring bank holiday until almost the end of summer.

Frances had given a woodcarving each to Joseph, Harry, Henry, Bernard and Jim Kettle, and one to the vicar for his kindness to her mother. Then one day she and Alec had gone over to Kirkholme to take one to Malachi Flint. For him she had chosen the black grouse, to her mind one of the finest of the carvings. 'My word,' he'd said, 'what a good likeness! It's that alive you'd swear you could see it breathing. We don't see black grouse often now, but we used to when I were a lad. And Ben must have seen them wi' them sharp eyes of his.'

At the beginning of March Alec brought over Mr Mason, the man who knew all about apple trees. He looked at the one in Beckside House garden for a minute or two, shaking his head and tut-tutting. Surely, Frances thought, he's not going to say it should come down? Then he spoke.

'Well,' he said, 'there's no doubt it's been very much neglected in the last few years, but I'm sure we can do something about it.'

'I'm hoping you'll tell me exactly what,' Frances said. 'I'm ashamed of my ignorance.'

'I can see you've made a good start,' Mr Mason conceded. 'You've dug out the area around the base of the trunk, and that you should always do. Keep it moist, keep down the weeds, don't let anything, including the grass, take away the goodness of the soil that should be going into the tree. In fact, I wouldn't encourage anything much to grow within the drip line.'

'Drip line?' Frances queried.

315

'The circumference around where the branches end,' Mr Mason explained.

'Oh dear, I've already planted a few bulbs,' Frances admitted.

'Well, if they're small ones that'll be all right. They won't take from the soil. And always keep weeds out – and mice and suchlike. You don't want them little beggars nibbling at the bottom of the trunk.'

'There's a lot to learn,' Frances said,

'Oh, it's nobbut common sense,' Mr Mason said. 'Now, as for pruning, there's summer pruning and there's dormant pruning, and if you want a good crop of fruit this year the dormant pruning needs to be started straight away.'

'Will you do that for me?' Frances asked.

'I will, love,' he promised. 'I'll come tomorrow.'

He turned up as promised. He talked about 'uprights', 'scaffold branches', 'leaders', 'limbs', 'horizontals', all of which was a foreign language to Frances, but as he put the words into action she saw the new shape of the tree emerging and she began to understand.

The whole undertaking, she thought, was not unlike her own life. The tree before he had taken it in hand was as her own life had been before she came to Cordale: a mess. And now she was reshaping that, cutting out the old wood, making space for growth, adding nourishment, as she would to the soil around the apple tree. And not only to the apple tree, but to the rest of the garden.

'Gardening', Mr Mason said as if he could read her thoughts, 'teaches you a lot about living.'

And now it was May. In a rare spell free from looking after the visitors – at the moment they were all out striding the fells – Frances lay back in her garden chair under the apple tree, looking at the pink and white blossom against the bright blue of the sky glimpsed between the branches. Were the branches laterals, or scaffolds, or what? She didn't know. But the results were exquisite, and if they all set fruit, and she thinned out the apples when they were the size of nuts, as Mr Mason had advised her to, then she would have a prodigious crop later on.

Did Lottie ever lie under the apple tree? she wondered. She didn't suppose Moira ever had the time, but Lottie might well have done so on an afternoon like this.

Frances knew what she would do with the apples. In one of the ledgers in the little room – and that by now had been transformed almost beyond recognition – she had come across recipes for all kinds of dishes. Stews, breads, cakes; pickles and other things bottled or dry-preserved; medicinal cures for boils, stomach aches, whooping cough. On the flyleaf was the name of someone – she felt sure it was Moira's mother – at an address in York, but halfway through the ledger Moira's own recipes took over. Her writing was quite different from her mother's. Among them was the recipe for apple chutney, which must be the one people in the village had so often mentioned. 'Moira used to have it on her stall in the markets,' they'd said. 'It went like wildfire!'

This is what I shall do when the apples come, Frances thought. I shall make the chutney and I shall sell it in the shops up and down Cordale, wherever I can. I shall keep some jars in the house and sell them to the visitors. And I shall label them 'Moira's Apple Chutney. Original recipe'.

She was lying there, planning the project, when she heard Alec's footsteps. She could tell his footsteps without looking round.

He bent over and kissed her lightly. 'Slacking?' he said, smiling.

'I wasn't slacking,' she said. 'I was planning.'

'Oh,' he said. 'Well, we should be able to make a start on the outhouses the minute the last visitor's gone.' Since her mother had left her a moderate sum of money it had now become possible to do this – and her mother would have loved it.

'I wasn't planning buildings,' Frances said.

Alec lay down in an adjoining chair. 'What, then?' he asked hopefully.

'Apple chutney,' she said.

'Oh!' he said. 'How disappointing.'

'Why?' Frances enquired. 'It could make good money. And it's something I'd rather like to do for Moira.'

'Sure,' Alec said. 'That sounds OK. But I had hoped you were planning when I could move in with you. We've discussed it. You said you'd think about it. You know I'd be happy to marry you – not that marriage has done much for either of us – or to live in sin. Either way. But I would like you to make up your mind. I do love you.'

She stretched out her hand and took his, held it in hers. 'I love you too,' she said. 'And I have thought about it.'

'So?'

'Like you, I'd be happy either way,' she said. 'But I think Kilby would be happier if we married. So why don't we go for that? And if we do it before this heavy blossom turns into fruit you'll be able to help me with the apples!'